D1367025

LEONARD NIMOY'S
PRIMORTALS™

LEONARD NIMOY'S
PRIMORTALS™
TARGET EARTH

STEVE PERRY

ASPECT®

WARNER BOOKS

A Time Warner Company

Aspect® name and logo are registered trademarks of Warner Books, Inc.

Warner Books, Inc., 1271 Avenue of the Americas, New York, NY 10020

 A Time Warner Company

Printed in the United States of America
First Printing: April 1997
10 9 8 7 6 5 4 3 2 1

Library of Congress Cataloging-in-Publication Data

Perry, Steve.
    Leonard Nimoy's primortals : target earth / Steve Perry.
        p.   cm.
    ISBN 0-446-52011-X
    I. Title.
PS3566.E7168L46   1997
813'.54—dc20   96-34453
                                                   CIP

Book design by H. Roberts

This book is for Dianne;
and for
Danelle and Mÿk
and
Dal and Rachel.

ACKNOWLEDGMENTS

This book would not have been written without the assistance of a number of people. Mistakes herein are due to my imperfect translation of their perfectly good input. My thanks go to the Tekno-Books folks and BIG; Marty Greenberg, Larry Segriff, Mitchell Rubenstein, Laurie Silvers, and Jim Chambers; to the Warner Books people, Betsy Mitchell and Wayne Chang; for help in research, artist and writer Chris Warner, and editor Tim Walsh of *SETIQuest* magazine. Put in Mike Byers for some military hardware that flies. And, of course, thanks to Isaac Asimov, whom I knew too little, and to Leonard Nimoy, for shepherding the idea into the light and allowing it to frolic (and who is one of the nicest people I've met in a long time). And, as long as I am here, gracias to my agent, Jean Naggar, for helping keep the wolf from the door. Hard to write with lobo howling and clawing to get in.

Thanks, gang. Couldn't have done it without you.

"There are more things in heaven and earth, Horatio,
than are dreamt of in your philosophy."

William Shakespeare
Hamlet, act 1, scene 5

FOREWORD
by
Leonard Nimoy

This book contains the opening chapters of a story that first sparked my imagination several years ago. During my work on *Star Trek IV: The Voyage Home*, I visited a SETI (Search for Extraterrestrial Intelligence) listening post, where a group of dedicated scientists and students used giant radio telescopes to ardently scan the heavens for any recognizable sign of life on other worlds. I was struck by the possibilities, and the genesis of the work you now hold in your hands sprang to mind in the form of a very simple question: What if? What if these men and women, seeking so hopefully for the smallest sign of extraterrestrial life, received a signal?

I went a step farther. What if the originators of the signal were on their way to Earth?

The legendary writer Isaac Asimov brought new elements to the mix, with some terrific ideas that greatly enhanced the story.

And at that point, we were on our way.

I've always felt science fiction offers a "broad canvas" to work on, but what fascinates me most about this story is the human element— the reactions of ordinary people to an extraordinary event. I'm an optimist who believes we're always moving forward one step at a time on the "Human Adventure," so the kind of science fiction stories that interest me most are character driven—stories about people whose lives are changed by science and how they deal with it.

Few events would change human lives as much as the first contact with intelligent life from another world. Business. Communications. Politics. Religion. Social issues. Everything would be different, shaded by the compelling knowledge that we are not alone in the universe. Yet, at the same time, life would go on. People would still need to eat, to sleep, to make a living, to survive. And that, man's desire to solve problems, to get past difficulties and learn, is at the heart of *Primortals*.

If any message can be taken from this tale, it is let's be prepared to problem solve, to look forward to a positive, expanded, intelligent future.

Originally, this story was intended to become part of an anthology of short science fiction stories, but instead it made its way to BIG Entertainment and into the pages of a monthly comic book series. I had read comics when I was young, but *Primortals* was my first exposure to them from the creative side. I couldn't have enjoyed it more.

And that led to writer Steve Perry and this book, a format that offers even greater opportunities than comics. New story lines. New characters. New events. But still my original question: What would life be like if extraterrestrials came to earth? How would people react to the discovery? And how would life change once the aliens actually arrived?

It's been over two years since *Primortals* first posed these questions. In that time we've told some good stories, stories of wonder and adventure. Come with us now as we explore new stories, new characters, and new adventures in *Target Earth*.

PART ONE

CQ, CQ

1

Stewart's charged-particle cannon sputtered. The bright emerald beam paled, blinked a couple of times, faded through the colors of dying pond scum and putrid olive, then winked out altogether.

Just like that, he was unarmed. And in big danger.

Damn.

The purple slime monster charged. Leaped on Stewart. Bones crunched, red spewed, Stewart yodeled like Goofy going over a cliff in an old Disney cartoon: *Waaaah*hoohoohoo-hoo! The scream got quieter as he disappeared down the monster's morphing-ever-bigger gullet.

"Crap," Stewart Davies said. He tapped commands into his computer keyboard and the half-constructed video game stopped. He brought up the code and scanned it. Ah. There it was. That line was the problem. That's why the CP cannon failed, there was an error in that sequence, right there . . .

He erased a line, rebuilt it.

Debugging code was the least interesting part. Had to be done, of course, otherwise he wasn't ever going to get rich and famous. The game was called OmniQue, and if it turned out the way he hoped, it would have all the best features of Mortal Kombat, Tetris, Myst, and Shadows of the Empire, with maybe a little Darkseed thrown in.

Stewart smiled at the thought. Sure, if it came out like he hoped, he'd be CEO of a major games company in a year, with several million in the bank, a personal Cray or two to play with, and a house on Maui. Then he could concentrate on his serious computer work. The Nobel Prize–winning stuff, the pure research and science.

Right . . .

He was plugging in more code to sustain the particle spitter when the SETI monitor cheeped at him.

He blinked, and for a moment had no idea what the sound meant. He shook the game-trance and refocused. The equipment on which he was being *paid* to work had just logged in an incoming call.

Stewart saved the game and switched programs. He glanced at the onscreen clock. *Lord, look at that—two-thirty* A.M. *How'd it get to be so late?* It was only a few minutes ago he got here at nine, seemed like.

The computer would log the signal in automatically, of course; he was pretty much the equivalent of a night watchman, as far as radio astronomy went. The cubicle in which he sat was small, windowless, and smelled like hot circuit boards and stale pizza. Unlike Harvard, where they thought such research worthy, SETI—the Search for Extraterrestrial Intelligence—was a barely tolerated stepchild here at the U, which is why a grad student in computer science could pick up a few bucks and credits working here instead of having a "real" astronomer doing it.

Stewart leaned back in his seat, a rickety, armless typing chair somebody had swiped from somewhere, and stretched his back and shoulders as the signal was processed. He'd been sitting here for hours without moving, he was stiff and cramped. He needed to get up and move; better, he needed to work out, to pump a little iron or swim a few laps or something. Yeah, he was a computer guy, but he knew the importance of a sound body in which to house a sound mind. Too many computer students became nothing more than extensions of their systems, deteriorating organic hardware who never did anything physical. Bad idea in the long run. If there was going to *be* a long run.

The SETI program used a bouncing-bar graphic to show the signal, and it did look promising. Of course, he'd logged in a couple of those before. First time, he'd gotten all excited, called Professor Karagigian at three in the morning and woke him up for what turned out to be a stray beam from a leaky weathersat. That had been bad. And while this one *seemed* as if it could be coming from deep space, according to the ascension and declination, and it *seemed* to be purposeful, he wasn't going to be waking up full-tenured professors unless it got repeated. Piss off the doc a couple more times and he'd be flipping burgers at Mickey D's to earn money, and they didn't offer a lot of grad-student credits on the theory and practice of Big Mac-ery. Hey, dood, you want fries with that? A nice apple pie?

Plus there was always the chance that a couple of bored MIT students were deliberately bouncing stuff off the ionosphere again, trying to give SETI folks heart attacks. Guy at Harvard got caught in one of those hoaxes last year, and it pretty much killed any credibility he'd ever have when he started contacting everybody and her kid sister claiming he had an alien incoming call for sure.

The signal graphic stopped building and began to flash onscreen, indicating it was done. *Mm. Big pulse, lotta binary info in it, maybe.* He'd play with it some, but first, he did need to drop an e-mail note into Karagigian's box. That wouldn't wake him up, and the prof did want to know if anything good showed up. Of course, somebody else would get the signal first, META, BETA, or SERENDIP, where they had real money to spend and hard- and software that made this setup look like a tin can wired to a flashlight battery.

He opened his mail program, copied Karagigian's e-mail address into the send-to box, typed in a quick note. Because he had a fairly serious encryption program installed and he liked playing with such things, he ran the message through it. If you had the key, the mail would open so fast you'd never notice the encryption. If you didn't have the key, you could spend six months with a decent workstation trying to break the vault and not manage it. It was about as secure as you could get on the Net. Of course, if you had the professor's password, you could open the message from *his* end easier than opening your wallet, but that wasn't Stewart's problem. And the password was so simple somebody with a two-digit IQ could figure it out if he knew anything about Karagigian at all.

He logged on to the U's system, shipped the e-mail, logged off.

Presto. Faster than a speeding bullet, especially since the note didn't have to go out-of-house.

Now, let's see how that promising message looks. Maybe there is something there and I can decode it . . .

The cheap and worn hinges on the SETI shack's door squealed behind him and a cool fall breeze blew in, bearing upon it the smell of fresh pizza. Stewart turned in the creaky chair.

Jess.

"Good morning, boy wonder. Even geniuses need to eat." She had a Pizz-o-matic box balanced on one hand, a six-pack of Cokes in the other hand.

Jess Rossini had long brown hair worn down past her shoulders, deep brown eyes, and a bright smile that showcased some fairly expensive orthodontia. She filled out a green sweater nicely, wore faded and tight Levi's 501s, also stretched in all the right places. At twenty-one, she was gorgeous, bright, and beautiful. Homecoming queen in high school, voted Most Popular, Friendliest, Most Likely to Succeed. Valedictorian, too. She was a senior, majoring in history. That she was here at this hour of the morning might seem unusual to some people, but with Jess, you never knew. She had her own internal clock and it ran on some schedule Stewart could never predict.

He smiled nervously. He was glad to see her, of course. He still wasn't sure what she saw in *him*. He wasn't in her league. Yeah, sure, he wasn't exactly a dullard, and yeah, he'd picked up a few pounds of muscle since he'd been a shrimpy science club dork in high school, but still . . .

"So, has ET called home?"

"Maybe. I just got a signal that looks promising."

"That's nice. How's the game going?"

"Slow. The purple slime monster keeps eating me."

She flashed her bright smile. "Isn't that always how it goes? You get up, the sun is shining, and *blap!* the purple slime monster gets you."

That brought another nervous smile from him. "Smells good."

"Zen pizza," she said.

He looked puzzled.

"One with everything."

He nodded, kept the smile fixed in position.

"You need to get out more, Stew; that's a real old joke."

"Yeah, yeah. So, are we going to eat it or just talk about it?"

She moved closer. Even through the wondrous pizza smell, he could detect the faint scent of her perfume. He didn't know what it was, it had a spicy, kind of musky odor to it. He liked it, though. He pulled a wedge of pizza out, slopped it onto a napkin, reached for a Coke can. Too bad he couldn't sort Jess out like he did a line of code. Life would be a lot easier if he could.

Sherwood, Oregon—11:45 P.M., Sunday

Jake Holcroft looked at the clock and realized he had to hurry.

He tapped furiously at the split keyboard of his Mac, hacking his way into a university e-mail system more than two thousand miles away. It was easy enough, even if he was only eleven; you could find all kinds of stuff on the Net if you were patient. And if you had an open-ended account on your server.

Jake leaned back and let the break-in program run. He glanced to his left, smiled at the Darth Vader lamp on the bookshelf next to the models of the starship *Enterprise* and the *Apollo 11* capsule. He had his computer rigged so that when it started up, old Darth asked, "What is thy bidding, my master?" Clipped right out of the movie, complete with breathing effects. And when the system shut down, Arnold said, "Ah'll be back." He had installed Aaron, with its 3D icons, long before that release of the Copeland OS, and he had a 28.8 modem, a laser printer, a scanner, and a Connectix grayscale cam all hooked into his Power Mac. Pretty good system for a kid his age in Middle of Nowhere, Oregon. He'd earned it, though.

The computer chimed and an info crawl ran up the screen: "Welcome to Long Island State University's server, you devious hacker, you." Jake grinned. He had a few places he liked to play when he was online here. He brought the name and code book file up, watched the window twirl open. That was a cool effect; he wished he'd thought of it. He went down the list. Ah, there was Dr. Karagigian. He hadn't checked on his mail tonight.

He logged in the professor's secret code, waited for the mail program to show him the inbox. The guy who'd sent the letter, old Stewball Stewart, had stuck it into an encrypted vault, but that didn't help if the doof you sent it to didn't bother to use a decent code. You could run a dictionary strainer that would eventually find most codes. The one he had started with the most common words before it jumped to the unabridged, which would give him most one-worders. But there wasn't any point in using the strainer if you could do it easier and faster. Jake had learned pretty quickly from walking the Web that most people picked simple passwords, something they wouldn't forget. Lotta people used their birthdays, some used their middle name, or maybe their spouse's or kid's name, or some easy word connected to their job. If you wanted to break into somebody's system or mail, first thing you did was try to find out stuff about them. Like the professor; he had a biography on file at the university, and Jake had gotten a bunch of information from that. It had only taken him six tries to open Karagigian's e-mail 'cause the prof used the name of his project for a password: SETIscope.

Well, *duh!*

The professor was pretty sharp at what he did but not too bright when it came to computer security.

Jake clicked on the letter. His screen blossomed with the contents. It was a quick read.

Man, man, look at that! Old Stewball has picked up an ET signal!

Jake pumped his fist up and down like he was pulling an old Mack truck horn. "Yes! The bug-eyed monster sends in his dinner reservations!"

There came two sharp raps on the bedroom door. From outside, a deep voice said, "Lights out. Shut it down and hit the rack, boy."

Aw, shit!

"Okay, Dad. Just finishing up my homework, almost done."

He heard his father lumber down the hall toward his own bedroom. He was a big man, his father, six-two, two hundred and thirty pounds, all of it muscle. Including inside his head. He could run ten miles wearing a heavy backpack, kill you with a gun or either hand or foot, and climb a rope as fast as a monkey, all without breathing too hard. Master Sergeant Seth Holcroft, U.S. Army, retired, now chief firearms instructor for a right-wing paramilitary organization, the Northwest Freedom Fighters.

And the mean bastard who had driven Jake's mother away.

The flash of anger surged, then receded a little. His teeth were still set as he scrolled through Karagigian's other messages: How could he have been cursed with a father like that? A man who would pull him away from his computer every day and make him do push-ups and sit-ups and run the obstacle course he'd built in their half-acre backyard? A man who would have been a whole lot happier if Jake would become a—a—*football* jock who liked to hurt people rather than a "damned little computer geek."

It wasn't fair.

But she was coming back for him, his mom. She'd said so. As soon as she got a place where Jake's father couldn't find them, she'd said, she'd sneak back when Seth wasn't around and get him. They'd leave together and never have to see the old man again. She'd promised. It had been six months, but it took time, he knew. He could wait. Somehow.

His fingers danced expertly across the keyboard. Good thing he could touch-type, because it was hard to see with the way his eyes were watering. They did that whenever he thought about his mother.

National Security Internet Monitoring Station, Washington, D.C.—0300 hours, Monday

Major Steve Hayes watched surreptitiously as Army Staff Sergeant Emile Pinkus pulled the sheet from the laser printer's outbay and walked the three steps to where Corporal Leon Faulk sat with his feet propped up on his metal desk, reading the current issue of *Playboy*. Hayes was in his office, Pinkus and Faulk in the outer office, such that it was. The monitoring unit was in a Pentagon sub-basement where the light of day never came—small, cramped, and smelled like old sweat socks even when the air conditioner worked, which it usually did not.

Hayes watched from behind the glass, bored. He flipped on the audio feed from the bug he'd stuck up near Pinkus's desk.

"Man, you wouldn't think a woman that old could look that good," Faulk said. He turned the magazine so Pinkus could see the pictures.

"Very nice. How old is she?"

"Forty. Can you believe that?"

Hayes laughed to himself. Given that Pinkus was himself a year past that age, he was maybe not quite so astonished. Maybe a little irritated at Faulk's youth and ignorance.

"Old enough to be my *mother* and look at those boobs!"

"I see a big boob right here, though he isn't so good looking and probably not half as smart as that pair. Do you think you can tear yourself away from your adolescent fantasies long enough to deliver this to Major Hayes?"

"Sure thing, Sarge." Faulk dropped the magazine and took the hard copy. He glanced at it, shook his head. "Government sure has a lot of ways to waste its money, don't it?"

"Spare me the economic criticism and just deliver the material, Corporal."

In his office, Hayes switched off the bug. He wadded another sheet of scrap paper into a tight ball and launched it at the wastebasket he'd set up next to the door. The improvised ball hit the rim, bounced up, and fell into the can.

"Incredible! Hayes fires one from three-point range as the final buzzer goes off and wins it for Washington! And the crowd goes wild!"

Corporal Faulk tapped on the frame of the open door, twice, clunk, clunk.

"Yes, Corporal?"

"Sir. Incoming intelligence." He passed the sheet to Hayes, who glanced at it. It was on official NSIMS stationery, with the eyes-only underprint and noncopy watermark and official codes headstamped on it. An e-mail message from some SETI watcher to his boss. Oh, joy.

Hayes dropped the sheet onto a six-inch pile of like papers on his desk. They got a dozen of this kind of thing every week or two, along with thousands of other bits of useless information the upstairs brass thought worthy of their multimillion-dollar top-secret monitoring gear. Christ.

Faulk came to a kind of attention. "Will that be all, sir?"

Hayes gave the boy a half smirk and a salute more like a wave-off. Faulk turned and marched out. Nobody was big on parade-ground soldiering down here.

Hayes found another piece of scrap paper and wadded it up. He wondered if it was possible to be bored to death. Sure, this was a career track he needed if he was going to make the jump to light colonel, but God, he hated it. That was the trouble with a peace-time army; there weren't the same kind of opportunities to prove yourself in battle and get promoted for it. He'd much rather be an adviser tromping around in the jungle down in some banana republic or the sandy Middle East or even in the Bosnian mess than a lousy intel op in D.C., spying on dipshit scientists—and his own staff. The big domes got all excited and thought they were talking to little green men when they picked up a Mets game on their radio gear. But it was the paper pushers who got the rank in times of peace, and a colonel with a solid intelligence background had more options than a major. Well. His next assignment would be more exciting. It would have to be.

He launched the paper toward the wastebasket, a nice, high arc . . .

Airball.

He shook his head. God.

2

With Jess on his lap and the kiss going hot and heavy, Stewart almost missed the second incoming SETI message. The little cheep repeated a couple of times.

Well, maybe more than a couple.

He broke the kiss. It was a little past three A.M.

"What?" Jess said, her breathing pretty heavy.

"I—uh, the—the—computer," he said.

"What about it?"

"It—I—there is another message."

"So? It's all automatic, isn't it? You keep saying the only reason you're really here is in case the place catches on fire and you have to save the backup tapes."

"Uh, yeah, but—"

She slid off his lap, blew out a deep breath. "Go ahead. I don't want to distract you from your job."

Stewart swallowed and hunched over a little, so that how excited he was wasn't so . . . apparent. Here was another one of those dilemmas. She *said* she didn't want to distract him from his job, but the tone of her voice indicated something else.

"Never mind," he tried. "It can wait."

"No, go ahead."

There was a definite coolness in her tone.

Coolness? said that little voice he sometimes heard inside his own head. *You maroon, you could freeze oxygen on that. A couple more degrees, it'd be at absolute zero!*

Shut up, he told his inner voice.

"Jess . . ."

"No, go on. Log in the message. I really don't mind."

He didn't know what to do. Why were people so—so complicated?

Then he looked at the screen, just glanced at it, really, and what he saw made him forget that Jess was angry with him.

The signal was back. The same signal. The array had shifted, panned to other locations, but when it came back to where it had been for the first sig, there it was again. Same quadrant, same strength, same duration.

A repeated signal!

He watched the graphic.

"So, is this a big deal?" She straightened her sweater, stretched her neck this way and that.

"Oh, well, depends on how you look at it. If it's from another intelligent race, it would be right up there with fire and the wheel."

"Really?"

"Really."

Then he was absorbed in watching the screen, so much so that Jess just seemed to fade into the background.

It was after midnight and Jake had shut off all the lights in the bedroom except for the computer screen. He'd also killed all system sounds; his paranoid old man sometimes woke up if a floorboard creaked wrong. Once, when Jake had gone into the kitchen late one night for a snack, he'd turned around to see his father standing there in his skivvies with a .45 in one hand, ready to blast an intruder.

If the old man realized Jake was still online, there'd be another fifty push-ups added on to morning calisthenics. And wake-up call was at six, so maybe he'd better shut it down and get some sleep—

The screen flashed: *Mail!*

Well, actually, *he* didn't have any mail, it was one of the accounts he had tagged. Pretty late for somebody to be sending a note. He tapped it up.

Professor Karagigian again. Hmm.

"Second signal, same quadrant, identical to previous." There was a list of coordinates, then it said, "Should we ask for protocol confirmations?"

Oh, *man!*

Jake couldn't believe it. It had to be another hoax, more of those college dudes with nothing better to do than futzing signals.

But what if it wasn't? What if it really *was* an ET signal? A long-distance call from another civilization?

Jake blinked and found that the idea of going to sleep was completely beyond him.

What if, on some planet a hundred light-years away, there was an alien version of himself, sitting in front of whatever passed for a computer on its world, sliding tentacles across an input device?

Man! That would really be *some*thing!

Steve Hayes counted the paper wads next to the wastebasket. Not so good, he was shooting about sixty percent. Yeah, there were guys in the NBA who got paid millions and did worse, but still . . .

The corporal came in grinning, waving another hard-copy sheet.

"What now? Somebody discover a new nematode in a Mexican cave? A new form of quartz in some mile-deep stratum?"

"No, sir. We got a repeated signal on that SETI post in New York."

Hayes affected a yawn. "Oh, my."

"Sir, Sarge says a repeatable signal means this coded transmission could be legit."

"Really? An extraterrestrial signal?"

"Possible, sir."

Hayes pulled his feet off the desk and reached for the paper. He scanned it, shook his head. "Put in a call to General Hightower."

"Sir? May I remind the major that it is just past oh-three-hundred hours?"

"I know how to tell time, Corporal. Call him. It's a standing order for Priority Alpha Intelligence. The general puts ET signals in that category."

"Begging your pardon, sir, but the sarge said this is a 'possible,' not a for sure."

"Don't want to wake the old man up, do you?"

"I hear that if you step outside of the Alaska Ring Station and spit, it freezes before it hits the ground. I would rather not be posted there, sir."

Hayes grinned. "Just make the call. I'll talk to him."

"Sir."

Hayes glanced at the hard copy again. Hightower had a bug up his butt about space monsters, had for a long time, according to the rumors.

He looked up, saw the enlisted man still standing there.

"Something else?"

"Sir. Sarge says somebody has read this guy's mail. Some hacker."

"How does he know that?"

The corporal shrugged.

Hayes said, "If this thing turns out to be legit, you can book it Hightower will want to put a muzzle on it. Can Pinkus find out who the peeper is?"

"Sarge can find out what the guy had for breakfast last Tuesday, Major."

"Fine. Run it down. Stupid hacker is probably going to find himself scooped up in a National Security net if this is real." He tapped a finger against the hard copy on his desk. "Teach him to stick his nose where it doesn't belong."

"Sir."

The corporal turned and left.

Larry Hightower sat on the edge of his bed, looked at the crisp hospital corners where the blanket was tucked in. He punched in the phone number from memory, glanced at the bedside clock. Almost four in the morning. A little early, but he'd have been up on his own in another hour anyway.

Her voice was clear and she sounded perfectly awake, though he knew she'd have been sound asleep a few seconds before. A neat trick, that.

"Miz Sherman. Scramble, please. Sequence one-three."

Four-star General Lawrence Hightower, chairman of the Joint Chiefs, touched a control on his own phone. The military-grade scrambler built into the unit went on. Laurie Sherman, the president's chief of staff, had a like electronic protector on her private line. These were state-of-the-art devices, top-of-the-line gear. Anybody tapping into the conversation would hear gibberish. Supposedly. Hightower didn't altogether trust the scrambler—he knew how easily *his* intelligence people eavesdropped on supposedly secure conversations. Still, he had to call her. Besides, he was a widower and she was single, it wasn't as if they were hurting anybody else.

"Scrambler's on," she said.

"Guess what I'm wearing," he said.

She laughed. "Blue-and-white striped cotton pajamas, with military creases ironed in. Leather no-back slippers."

"Lucky guess. And you'd be in the . . . pink nightgown?"

"The black one. What's up, Larry?"

He smiled at the idea of the black nightgown. He was sixty-two, she was not quite forty. She was also drop-dead gorgeous, sharp as a whip, and the only woman he'd been with since Sasha died six years ago.

"Larry? You fall asleep?"

He chuckled, got back to serious business. "One of my lesser-known intel ops units has a university SETI report of a repeating extraterrestrial radio signal. I just had it verified by the navy's VLA and the old DEW Line observatory north of Hudson Bay. The transmission is encoded and we don't know what it says yet, but it's there."

"What does it mean?"

"If it is a legitimate signal, it means we aren't alone in the universe."

"Congratulations. That's something you've always wanted, isn't it?"

"Yeah, since I was a kid in Minnesota, reading those old pulp science fiction magazines. Back then, I would have given my left arm to be able to shake hands with the first Martian humans ran into."

"But . . . ?"

"But I wasn't in charge of protecting my country then. I am now."

"Why is a radio signal from, what? billions and billions of miles away—to coin a phrase—a problem?"

He took a deep breath. "Well. The thing is, our gear is a little better than the SETI station that picked up the signal. I don't know how we know for sure, some kind of Doppler shift, wave compression, something like that, but the signal isn't light-years away. It's coming from within the solar system. And it is moving in our direction."

"Holy shit!"

"Exactly. I don't know that you need to wake the president up at this hour because it's not like whoever—or whatever—is responsible for the signal is going to be knocking on the White House door tomorrow morning. It could be something like a probe, a robot ship. Could be a lot of things."

"Could be an alien from another world coming to call?"

"That too," he said. "And if we can hear it, it can hear us."

"Holy shit." There was a brief pause and he could almost see her mind working. "So what now?"

"I'll get all the pertinent data and set up a meeting with the president ASAP. Meantime, I'm going to invoke National Security and try to keep a lid on this for as long as possible."

"Which won't be long once more than three people know about it," she said.

"I know. But this is a big deal. The more lead time we can get before it becomes public, the better. I'll have NSA and MI ops paying a visit to the SETI people who heard the call, and to anybody else who might pick it up. In this country, at least."

"Tricky business," she said.

"Yes, indeed. But there is nothing to be done for it. The media would have a field day. You remember the panic around the Orson Welles radio broadcast of *War of the Worlds*? People thought it was the end of the world."

"That was a little before my time," she said, her voice dry. "In the late thirties, wasn't it? My father would have been about six."

Hightower felt a slight twinge in his bowel. Her father was only two years older than he was. And while he didn't remember much about it, he did remember the stir caused in his house by the radio show. His grandmother had fainted and collapsed on the woodstove, and she wore the burn scar from that on her arm until she died.

"Besides," she continued, "we're a little more sophisticated than that now. I doubt people will run screaming into the streets because somebody heard something on a radio."

"I hope you're right," he said.

* * *

Zeerus the Avitaur, former governor of Achernar Three and leader of the failed revolution against the Paxus Majae on that planet, was angry.

Really angry. Teetering on the edge of a black rage.

He glared at his reflection in the opaqued viewplate of the stolen ship. The dark red of his scaly skin gleamed dully back at him. He shook his head, and the double rows of needle-sharp teeth lining his elongated jaws flashed brighter in the mirrorlike surface of the plate.

They hadn't taken that away from his people. The teeth of a carnivore.

He had much to be angry about. The failure of his fight against the Majae. His capture by Primaster. The inadequacy of this blasted ship he had stolen.

And most of all, what was taking those thin-skinned *fools* on Earth so long to translate and answer his hail? How stupid were they?

That was a bad sign.

For the tenth time that day, he gave the same order to the ship. "Computer, scan visual channels."

"Scanning." The computer's voice was low, quiet, almost fuzzy, probably programmed by some idiot who liked mammalian tones. Bah.

The holoproj console in front of Zeerus blossomed and three-dimensional images of the humans played in the air, tiny reproductions. The scan mode shifted. Here came a set of one of their wars, with the oddly uniformed humans firing projectile weapons and chemical bombs and rockets at each other, slaughtering each other by the hundreds.

Ah.

"Hold on this channel," Zeerus said.

He watched the images. This, at least, was good—he needed a species familiar with war if he was going to shape them into proper tools to use against the Majae.

Against Primaster.

But how could he begin his manipulations if they wouldn't respond to his call? Oh, how low the planet of his species' birth had sunk!

True, it had been many millions of years since the Majae had harvested his ancestors from this insignificant world, but even then, surely his unevolved precursors must have been brighter than this mammalian *ape*-spawn! How could they not?

He tried to imagine what it must have been like back then. How joyful it must have been, to be a winged reptile soaring the skies of a young world, no civilization, atmosphere thick and heady with gases from active volcanoes, the ground rumbling with tectonic growing pains. Life rampant below as his kind soared and glided down to kill prey, to slash and eat hot and bloody flesh . . .

He growled. It wasn't as if he didn't have plenty of time to consider such fantasies. He was still months away from arrival, moving at sublight speeds necessary inside stellar systems. But it was a waste of time, these . . . flights of fancy. He needed to be working on his plan, a plan that would, of necessity, have to be altered and refined as it went along. Because Primaster would be coming for him. Oh, of that, there was no doubt. Zeerus's henchmen would delay that inevitability, perhaps, but not for long. He had chosen big and fierce beings as his lieutenants, but they had not a prayer against the forces Primaster and his lieutenants could muster. And despite the Paxus Majae's aversion to taking life, Primaster would not be feeling benevolent toward Zeerus after that bloody escape from the Majae's flagship. Not hardly.

Zeerus knew his own limits. Primaster and his peacekeepers had squashed the rebellion like Zeerus might squash a bug. Had captured the ringleaders easily, bound them, taken them into the flagship. It was a miracle Zeerus had managed to escape.

No, when Primaster came, Zeerus could not stand alone against him. Primaster could wield forces against which no ordinary being could hope to overcome. It had been Primaster's species who had collected Zeerus's kind, along with the thousands of other species from Earth all those millions of years ago. Primaster's species who had installed the collected specimens on worlds with appropriate biospheres, then guided their evolutions until many of those species achieved intelligence. A very slow sculpture, that, requiring a great deal of patience and—as much as he hated to admit it—a lot of wisdom.

Leaf eaters—the term was a curse to Zeerus—leaf eaters were the instigators of the Paxus Majae, with their own history so ancient that even they didn't know from where they had come. They had no passion, no desire to dominate, no heart for the hunt—and they had mostly bred such feelings out of those they guided.

But not all of us.

Zeerus slammed a hard fist down onto the console. The thick muscles behind his shoulders flexed and his wings flared, then refolded against his back. His great-many-times-grandfather would not have recognized Zeerus as one of his kind, save from the shape of the head and the wings, perhaps. Evolution had been kind. The Avitaurs had gained weight, strength, the bipedal abilities of apes on the ground while retaining their mastery of the air. The perfect species.

The holoprojic images danced as the console absorbed the hammer of his fist, but resettled. The ship was built to take more than an angry Avitaur's bare hand.

"Respond, damn you!"

But the earthlings did not answer.

3

I t was nearly six A.M. and Stewart still had an hour to go before his shift was over. Jess had already left; she had to get some sleep before her first class, which, fortunately, wasn't until noon. He didn't have anything until seven P.M.

The phone rang. Odd, because nobody ever called him here.

"Hello?"

"Stewart?"

He recognized the voice. "Dr. Karagigian?"

"Yes. Listen, do *not* send out queries regarding the signal. I, uh, have reason to believe the, uh, signal is a hoax."

Stewart felt a wave of disappointment wash over him. Damn! He was afraid of that. Hoping it wasn't, but worried that it was. Of course. Somebody else gets to make history, not him. Too bad.

"Continue to monitor as normal," Karagigian said. "I, uh, have spoken to some . . . government investigators, FCC, who want to run the signal down. They are going to make an example of the perpetrators when they catch them."

Good, Stewart thought. But even as this occurred to him, so did something else: It was a little early in the morning for the FCC to be calling Professor Karagigian, wasn't it?

Well. That wasn't his problem, was it? He had enough on his plate. Jess had said she was fine, but he wasn't at all convinced she was. How was he supposed to deal with stuff like that? He replayed their conversation in his mind.

"Um, oh, sorry, Jess, I got caught up."

"No problem."

"You okay?"

"I'm fine."

"Really?"

"I just said so, didn't I? I'm *fine*. I have to go."

And that was the end of that.

Oh, Lord. When a woman said something like that, how were you supposed to respond? She said she was fine but he knew she wasn't and she didn't want to talk about it. A reasonable man had to take somebody at their word, didn't he? Wasn't that the logical thing to do? Ask a question, get an answer, assume that was that, right?

Not when it comes to women, buddy boy, his little voice said.

"Shut up," Stewart said. He shook his head.

Jake was still wide awake, even though he was tired, when he heard his dad flush the toilet. He didn't need to look at the clock, it would be 0535 hours, on the nose. You could literally set your watch by his dad's morning ritual. 0530 arise, 0535 finish his morning BM, 0536 brush teeth, 0540 begin precooking breakfast, 0600 reveille, up and at 'em, soldier . . .

He lay in bed in the dark, listening to his father running water in the kitchen. There would be coffee, eggs, bacon, hot cereal—but only after the morning's run and then at least one pass through the obstacle course. The run was two miles through the neighborhood, and too bad for anybody's dog stupid enough to chase them—his old man carried pepper spray in his pouch, next to the .38 snubnose. Then the course. If he was having a good day, Jake could hold his time under three minutes, and if he did, he only had to run it once. If he blew three, then his old man made him run it twice more, even if he came in under time the first rerun. Either way, they'd be back in the house by 0630 and eating ten minutes later. It was the same every morning except Sunday, when they went to church.

Not that the old man was anything more than a Sunday Christian. Jake suspected that the only reason they went at all was to show the wingnuts his father worked for that they were God-fearing. They were big on that.

Jake thought all religions were fairy tales and he didn't believe any of it.

On Saturdays after morning drill, they went to the gun club and spent two hours practicing. Jake was pretty good with a rifle, okay with a handgun, as long as both were small bore. The big guns still made him flinch. This was the same place where his father taught the militia, mostly in the evenings.

After breakfast, his father would usually go to meetings of one kind or another, leaving Jake alone to catch the bus for school. Which Jake would do, except that he got off and walked a few blocks to the EZ Mail place first. His dad didn't know about it.

Jake had his own box at EZ Mail, and this is where he collected his shareware money.

A year ago, Jake had uploaded a font he had created on to a couple of the major online services, America Online and CompuServe. It was a sans serif typeface, kind of like Helvetica, but if you centered it, it had a perspective and vanishing point so it looked like the credit crawl on the *Star Wars* movies. Anybody could do something similar with Fontographer™ or a couple of other programs, even a half-assed thing in Photoshop™, but a lot of people couldn't afford those and he only asked for five dollars. With shareware, people could download a program and try it out, and if they liked it, they'd mail you the money. It was the honor system.

He didn't make a lot of money, but it still amazed him how honest most people were. Every week or so, he'd get thirty or forty dollars from people who liked that font. He'd named it "The Dreaded Emperor."

Since then, he'd uploaded three more fonts and people seemed to like them, too. In a good month, Jake got checks totaling as much as three hundred dollars. He'd opened a bank account, gotten an ATM card, and had almost eighteen hundred stashed in the bank, plus another three hundred in cash taped behind his sock drawer.

In the last six months, he had added a bunch of stuff to his computer, had pretty much replaced or enhanced everything. His father didn't care for computers, couldn't tell that the system was any different than the basic one Jake's grandfather had given him originally. He also had a secondhand laptop, an old Duo 210. It was a black-and-white, didn't have much memory, and the batteries didn't last too long before they had to be recharged, but it was about the same size as a thick magazine. He could put it in his book bag, and even with the charger it didn't take up much space. He also had an external floppy drive and a modem for it. In a really boring class, which was most of them except computer sci, he could work on a new font or game. It needed a new hard drive because the one it had was kind of noisy. Maybe he'd get one soon.

No. He was saving his money. When he got three thousand, he was going to find his mother.

He heard the kettle start to boil. His old man would make one cup of coffee for each of them before the run. He'd be coming down the hall soon.

Jake blew out a sigh and got out of the bed. It was November and getting colder out there. Not freezing yet, but close, and gray and foggy. His old man hadn't stoked the woodstove yet—no point in that since they were going to be gone, why bother to heat an empty house?—and the room was chilly. He dressed in a hurry, sweatpants and shirt over a T-shirt and his jockey shorts, white socks and his running shoes. He even had a little can of pepper spray his father had given him, with a clip to hook it to his waistband. He didn't really need it, the dogs in the neighborhood had gotten the message real quick. They barked, especially the little flea-trap terrier in the house behind the obstacle course and those two German shepherds down in the turnaround, but none of them got too close anymore. A snout full of burning pepper wasn't something they forgot real soon.

But his father would notice if he didn't take the spray, so Jake clipped it onto his drawstring over his right hip.

He picked up his glasses, breathed on them to fog the lenses, wiped them off with the bottom of his sweatshirt.

He heard his father padding down the hall when the doorbell rang.

Jake blinked. Who could it be at this hour of the morning? They didn't get many visitors and nobody ever before reveille.

He moved to the window, peeped through the slatted blinds. His bedroom was closest to the road.

For just a second, he hoped it was his mom. But then he saw the car, a big gray American model, a Ford or maybe a Chevrolet. It had U.S. government plates, and a man in a dark suit and sunglasses leaned against the hood, watching the house. The guy had what looked like a Walkman or a hearing aid plugged into one ear, and as Jake watched, he reached up to press the earphone, as if listening to something. The guy reminded Jake of something, and it only took a second for him to remember what it was: He looked like one of those Secret Service dudes who followed the president around.

Couldn't be. Why would he be here? Maybe the president was coming for a visit, maybe they wanted to talk to Jake's old man, to warn him to stay out of town or whatever. His old man had written a few stupid letters to the White House.

The little flea-trap terrier out back went off, yap-yap-yap-yap! What was he barking at now?

Jake heard his father get to the door. He'd be holding his .45 behind his butt with one hand while he opened the door a crack with the other hand.

"What?"

"Mr. Holcroft? I'm Special Agent Howard Brandon, with the FBI."

Jake opened his bedroom door and stepped out into the hall. The front door was around the corner, he couldn't see it from here. He padded toward the kitchen, where he could get a look at the door through the front room.

"What do you want?"

"Can I come in?"

"State your business right there—or show me a warrant."

Before Jake could get to where he could see the door, however, he saw another man in a suit outside the kitchen door in the back.

This man had a gun in his hand. The pistol was pointed at the ground. Jake thought it was a 10mm Smith & Wesson, but it scared him. He turned around and headed back to his bedroom. As he got there, he heard the fed at the front say, "—understand you have an Internet account with Teleport, in Portland, is this correct?"

Oh, *shit*! They weren't here to see his dad, they were here for him!

What had he done? Sure, he poked around where he wasn't supposed to go, but he hadn't stolen anything or damaged anybody's files,
he was very careful about that.

The kitchen door squeaked. The old man, paranoid as he was, had
deliberately fixed the hinges so they'd do that. Even when the alarm
system wasn't on, the hinges were loud enough to be heard at night
when things were quiet.

Jake felt a moment of panic. If an FBI agent came into the house
and saw his father standing at the front door with a loaded and cocked
.45 behind his back, what would happen? Would the fed shoot his
father?

As much as he didn't like his old man, he didn't want to see him
get killed, especially not for something *he* had done. But if his father
saw somebody coming at him with a gun, Jake knew exactly what the
old man would do. Jake had heard too much about Ruby Ridge, about
Waco, about the Freedom Boys in Montana. About how a man's home
was his castle. And if he started blasting, the FBI was in trouble: Jake's
father could shoot marbles off a tabletop from ten feet away without
scratching the finish.

What could he do?

Jake took a deep breath. "Dad! There's one coming in the back
door with a gun!"

With that, Jake leaped into his bedroom. He heard two dull
booms from the front, recognized the reports as those of a .45 Colt
automatic.

The fed in the front must have pulled his gun or tried to get in.

Jake hoped the man was wearing a vest.

The president of the United States sat at his desk in the Oval
Office. General Lawrence Hightower stood on the thick rug in front of
the desk. He liked to move when he gave a presentation. To the president's right, Laurie Sherman sat in a white dress whose hem stopped a
few inches short of her knees, her ankles crossed. She had great legs. To
the president's left—and appropriately so—was the secretary of
defense, William O'Connell, a man Hightower figured would walk
three miles out of his way in a pouring rain to avoid stepping on an ant.
How on earth O'Connell had ever gotten this job was beyond

Hightower. The man had the backbone of a plate of overcooked spaghetti.

"How sure are we about this, General Hightower?" the president asked.

"Very sure, sir. Our people at MILCOM and Bethesda have vetted the results of the DEW Line and the Very Large Array. It's an artificial radio signal being beamed toward Earth from a region beyond the orbit of Neptune."

"And we don't know what it says?"

"No, sir, not yet. We've got our cryptographers working on it."

"Bill? What do you think?"

"Well, sir, I don't see that we have to get our shorts all bunched up over it. So far, all we've got is an unidentified signal. Even if it is coming from some kind of . . . alien vessel instead of something maybe the Russians sent up that got turned around, I don't see that we should start unlimbering the nukes just yet. Or stomping all over the populace in the name of National Security."

Hightower kept his face as carefully neutral as he could, even though he wanted to do a little stomping of his own over to O'Connell and slap that smirk off the man's face, along with a few of his bleached teeth.

The president looked back at Hightower, waiting for what he knew was going to be a contrary response. The chairman of the Joint Chiefs of Staff got along with the secretary of defense about as well as two bighorn rams did with each other during rut. Had it been up to him, the general would have gladly butted heads instead of chatting politely, smiled as he knocked the secretary onto his corpulent, liberal ass.

Hightower took the conversation where he knew the president would most likely follow his lead. He said, "The secretary's concern is certainly valid, Mr. President. I am not suggesting we act in haste. I don't want to declare martial law or fill the shuttle with H-bombs and launch it. But wouldn't it be prudent to err on the side of caution?"

He knew that would hit one of the president's buttons. The man was not one to make any decision without due consideration as to how it would affect his image. Hell, he couldn't go to the bathroom to take a leak without commissioning a poll to see if that was all right with the electorate. He very much wanted a second term, and next year was the election.

"Larry has a point, Bill. What do you think, Laurie?"

The president's chief of staff smiled. "Well. While I can understand General Hightower's caution—it is, after all, his job to keep a sharp eye out for any threat to our country—I can also understand Secretary O'Connell's reluctance to leap to hasty conclusions. We do have to allow for the possibility that this . . . signal could be generated by some terrestrial craft, an old Soviet rocket, or maybe Japanese or even one of the Euro Alliance satellites."

Hightower fought down a grin. They did not want their personal relationship to become public. Especially since the commander in chief seemed to have a moralistic streak that frowned mightily on unmarried adults living in sin. She would not rubber-stamp everything he said, certainly not in front of a twit like O'Connell. He said, "We keep fairly good track of anything that goes up, Ms. Sherman. It does not appear to be a human craft about which we know."

"I didn't mean to imply you were derelict in your duties, General. But isn't it possible one might have gotten by—before your watch, of course?"

"I suppose, Ms. Sherman, it is *possible* there is a fire-breathing dragon flying circles around the Capitol dome at this very moment, but I for one do not believe it is so."

O'Connell jumped in: "Ah, but a little green man from outer space in a ship heading our way, that's different?"

The president smiled. Hightower knew the man liked to watch his people nyah-nyah amongst themselves. He would have been at home in some medieval castle, tossing a bone to the hounds to see which one outfought the others to claim it. But he wasn't stupid and he did want to keep the job. The chairman of the Joint Chiefs had a little more clout to offer than the secretary of defense and the president didn't need to be a weatherman to know which way the wind blew.

"All right, Larry. You do what you have to do to keep things quiet until your people figure out about this thing."

"Even if that includes violating somebody's civil rights?" O'Connell said.

"If I'm wrong, we can apologize and offer a settlement," Hightower said. "Might as well get some use out of all those lawyers

DOJ has on its payroll. But if this is a little green man come to call, his technology will be ipso facto superior to ours—or it would be us paying his people a visit instead. We can't assume another race will have the same goals and desires that we do."

"Worried that it's a cookbook?" O'Connell said.

Hightower felt himself flush with anger, despite his resolve to keep a lid on it.

The president didn't get the reference. Hightower explained. "There was a science fiction story some years back," he said. "Got made into an episode of an old TV show, *The Twilight Zone*. The aliens landed and said they were benevolent, offered to give humans their technology, take passengers to visit their home world, like that. The aliens had a book with them. The humans got a copy of the book and managed to translate the title: *To Serve Man*. They went along with the alien plans. Then, after thousands of people had left to visit the alien planet, somebody discovered that the title had a different meaning because when they translated the text, they found out it was a cookbook."

The president smiled. "Ah."

Hightower looked at O'Connell. "They pay me to be suspicious, Mr. Secretary."

O'Connell was, despite his twitiness, not a fool. He knew he'd lost this argument and his parting shot had been pro forma, nothing more. "Well, if that's how you see it, Mr. President."

"It is subject to change," the president said. "That's just how it is right now." He looked at Hightower.

"We'll let you know as soon as we know, Mr. President."

As he headed for the door, Hightower allowed himself a tight grin. This was not the kind of battle he enjoyed most, verbal swords with politicians, but he knew how to riposte and parry and go for the touch when he fought with words instead of armor.

And it was better to win any kind of battle than to lose.

4

Laurie Sherman watched Bill O'Connell and Larry Hightower leave the president's office. She wasn't worried that she'd pushed it too much—Larry had more ammunition than he needed to beat O'Connell and by pretending to be dubious, she kept the fiction going that she and the chairman of the Joint Chiefs didn't much like each other. Which was a long, long way from the truth. Her boss believed in the old definition of adultery: anybody who wasn't married sleeping with somebody else. He might let it slide if the fornicators were officially engaged to be be wed, but otherwise it was a sin and he was against it. Amazing he could still have that attitude in today's world, but that was part of what got him elected.

"Laurie?"

She turned and smiled at her boss. "Sir?"

"How's the schedule look for the rest of the day?"

"Busy. You've got the Israeli ambassador coming for breakfast, the Russian delegation at ten, the Boy Scouts at eleven-thirty. Lunch with your daughter and grandchildren, then we've got the labor speech at three. Plus the usual nine hundred things to be signed or vetoed or otherwise move from the in- to the outbox."

"Joy."

"Hey, you knew the job was dangerous when you took it."

"Dangerous, yes. Boring, no. Well. Best get to it. I'll see you . . . when?"

"In the limo for the labor thing."

"Right."

She left the Oval Office and headed down the hall. Larry wouldn't be far away. They were going to try to get together for a visit at lunch, at the little condo he'd rented under his sister's name. This was a risky game, politically, anyway. If it got out the two of them were together, in the biblical sense, it would probably get her fired. Maybe him, too. Her boss wasn't a particularly vindictive man, but he looked after his own professional hide first, last, and always. There couldn't be any hint of scandal or even a suspicion of undue influence in his administration, he'd pull the rug out so fast you'd do a triple somersault before you landed on your backside far away. And he had a thing for adultery—he couldn't abide it.

Even so, it was worth the risk. For a man old enough to be her father, Larry still had a lot of life left in him. He was a considerate, caring lover and he didn't have any ulterior motives for being with her, at least not any she had been able to see.

She smiled as she passed one of the Secret Service agents, who nodded at her. Her smile wasn't for the guard, though.

Over the years, Zeerus had been forced to learn a certain amount of patience. Had he learned it a little better, he might have held off on his coup a bit longer, consolidated his forces better, and perhaps avoided this predicament. At the speed he currently enjoyed, he'd be on Earth in six months or less. He might be able to cut that some by coming in at a higher velocity then doing a tricky loop around the system's primary, using the sun's gravity as a brake.

While this ship was not capable of translating most of the terran languages carried by the radio waves painting it—when he had stolen this vessel, he had not been afforded the luxury of much choice—he knew a little about the world toward which he traveled. Six months to get there. Not so bad. Their pitiful space probes had taken twenty times as long to arrive at that big gas giant whose orbit he had yet to reach. What was it called? Joperus? Jupitah? Something like that. The earthlings were all proud of themselves that their little unmanned vessel had swung into orbit around the giant world, had dropped a robotic probe into the atmosphere that lasted a little more than an hour of their time before the dense gases and gravity had crushed it like a bubble.

Ah, they were an arrogant people, but better with words than deeds.

Of course, that might be said of Zeerus in some quarters. His attempts to throw off the admittedly loving hands of Primaster's people and forge a new destiny had been less than triumphant, had they not? In fact, the term "failure" was much more appropriate.

He remembered how it felt to be dragged before Primaster on the flagship, bound in glowing bands of encum-energies like a common criminal, a thrum rifle jammed into his spine.

Primaster, green and muscular, puffed up in his righteous indignation, had pointed a finger at him and said, "I will determine your fate later, Zeerus."

Bah.

And that gray-skinned abomination Prisar, fat horn jutting from between his beady eyes, with his winged lackey Quickwing fluttering pinkly around his shoulders, all but begging Primaster to kill Zeerus there on the spot. Smarter than he looked, Prisar. Of course, he would have to be.

But Zeerus was not without supporters, even in the heart of Primaster's flagship. Krude and Krate and Krutch, with perhaps one brain's worth of intelligence shared among them but loyal to a fault, had overcome his guards.

"Shoot, fool!" one of the guards yelled.

The guard's neurobeam splashed against the organic bulkhead next to Zeerus's head, missing by a handspan, and then Krude smashed the guard's head with his fist, stretched him out on the deck like a fallen tree.

Zeerus claimed the thrum gun, spun and fired it thrice, took down three of the remaining five guards. A lack of marksmanship had never been one of his problems.

His troops thumped or blasted the other two and of a moment, Zeerus was free.

"Go—that way!" Zeerus yelled.

He knew the layout of the ship as well as he did his own home. Of course, he had not planned to be arriving here a captive but as an ambassador dealing from a position of power when he'd memorized the giant craft's interior. Ah, well.

"But—but most of the big star leapers are docked the other way," Krude said.

"And that's exactly why they'll expect us to go there," Zeerus said.

They hurried down a wide corridor. Somebody poked a scaly orange head out of a side passage and gaped at the fleeing quartet. Krutch fired a power bolt at the startled being, missed, but caused him to vanish nonetheless.

"We'll pick up some hostages," Zeerus continued. "Go to the left."

Well, actually, his rescuers would do that, collect some hostages. Zeerus had other plans. Primaster's reluctance to use violence would work against him if they had a few live bodies in thrall. Primaster would try to figure out a way to keep from killing hostages *or* terrorists, and that would buy Zeerus some time. True, all of the ships he had in mind stealing were small; but then, whichever one he took had only to transport a single passenger—his troops would not be going with him. They were expendable. They believed Zeerus had a plan to allow them to break free once he had gotten clear.

They believed wrong.

"There should be a contingent of Shree that way and two turnings to the right," Zeerus said. "Go there and take them. Primaster will want to negotiate for their release. Stall him as long as possible. Tell him you'll exchange them for a ship, for a pardon, whatever. Keep him occupied. Once I've gotten clear, I'll contact the secret armada and have them attack. They'll be so busy, you'll be able to escape easily."

"I didn't know you *had* a secret armada," Krude said.

"If you did, then it wouldn't be a secret, now would it?" Krate responded. That brought a grin from Zeerus. Fools.

"I'll see you later," he said to the trio.

Yes. On the other side of the Bridge to the Afterlife.

The Capra tech Zeerus forced to power a ship up had lied about it being a full-range Class One leaper. Zeerus shook his head, frowned at the memory. The Capra was dead, but he would have had the little bi-horned creature suffer had he known it was going to *lie* to him.

So now Zeerus, formerly one of the most powerful beings outside the Paxus Majae, was alone in a tiny second-rate ship with a third-rate biomech brain that had almost no translation capabilities.

Still, Zeerus supposed it was better than the option. Primaster might not have killed him, but he could have easily stuck him into stasis and loosed the robo-psychiatric programmers on him as he lay sleeping. Zeerus liked to believe he was too strong-willed for the mind-benders to change his ways of thinking, but he had seen the results of a decade or two of their relentless probings and input. Beings who had been flaming psychotics once willing to try to take down a durasteel wall barehanded now wore tepid, beatific smiles as they made baskets or watered flowers. Even a powerful mind such as Zeerus's might have problems resisting a thousand years of such mental butchery. And no doubt Primaster would have been willing to keep him static that long, if he thought he could make Zeerus change his evil ways.

Well, at least his troops had kept Primaster busy long enough for Zeerus to drop the ship clear and kick it into hyper. A risky proposition, that, lighting the drive so close to a mother ship and inside the bounds of a planetary system as well, but one he'd had to take. It paid off. He was free, on his way to a new power base, plenty of time on his hands to reflect on the mistakes he'd made.

Mistakes he would avoid next time.

Jake didn't have much time, he knew. When his father's gun went off, he leaped for his desk. He scooped up his book bag, jerked open the drawer where his cash was stashed and tore the taped bills loose, shoved them into the bag. He grabbed his wallet and stuck it into his waistband, so that half of it went inside his pants and the other half hung out like a leather hinge.

There were two more shots. Didn't sound like a .45, they were sharper. Probably one of the feds.

Another shot. His father's .45?

Go, go, go!

Jake leaped for the window, jerked the blinds up, shoved the window as wide as he could. He glanced back over his shoulder for a second. All his stuff—his books, his games, his computer—he would miss it. But he couldn't stay here, and better to be going on his own than dragged away under arrest by the feds.

There was a commotion at the back door. The guy who'd been standing by the government car was gone, probably to the front door.

There weren't any more shots from the front. Either his dad or the fed, maybe both, were down. Otherwise, they'd still be shooting.

Jake shouldered his bag, bailed out of the window, hit the damp ground, and cut to his left toward the obstacle course. He had his long-range escape plan all figured out. He'd been working on it for months, though he'd figured on using it against his father.

He was close to the house when he darted past the back porch. He made it almost all the way to the low plywood wall when somebody behind him started yelling.

"Hey! Kid! Stop!"

Jake sped up.

"Stop right there! FBI!"

Jake leaped, caught the thick rope draped over the wall, hauled himself up, and rolled sideways over the wall. He ran for the mudpit, caught the first of the dangling rings, and swung. He almost missed the second ring, but managed to snag it. It was the backpack weighing him down, he realized, throwing his timing off. He swung, caught the third ring, adjusted his grip, and lunged for the fourth and last ring.

"Stop, you little bastard!"

He heard the FBI man hit the low wall and scrabble up it. Jake hoped the man wouldn't get so mad he'd shoot. He sounded pretty pissed off.

Jake dropped to the ground, ran a few meters to the nest of razor wire, fell onto his belly, and crawled into the central tunnel. It looked bad from outside but there was actually plenty of room if you kept your face pushed into the dirt.

His pack snagged.

Oh, no!

Jake struggled, frantic. He was caught!

But the nylon tore free. He elbowed and kneed faster. By the time he was clear of the wire, the fed chasing him had gotten to the mudpit. There was a chain-link fence funneling in on both sides, three meters tall and topped with more razor wire, so he wasn't going to be able to go around without having to swing way wide.

"Stop right there, dammit!"

Jake cut right. He could circle and avoid the tires, the rope bridge, and the high wall, and he'd be almost on the next street. He glanced back, saw the FBI agent jump up and catch the first of the rings, still moving from Jake's passage. The man swung, reached for the second ring—

Missed it and fell facedown into the mudpit. A big sheet of reddish brown splattered to both sides. The mudpit was almost five feet deep. That would slow the man down some.

If it had been his father, Jake would have smiled, but he didn't have time for that. He ran.

Rusty Burroughs, a year ahead of Jake, lived on the corner, and his bike was parked and unlocked under the carport right where he always left it. Jake grabbed the bike, swung into the saddle, and pedaled like crazy. The idea was to get to the bus stop and catch a TriMet into Tualatin, then another bus to Hillsboro or Salem. Once there, he could hit a money machine for the maximum—three hundred dollars—then catch a Greyhound headed north. When he got to a bigger city, Olympia or Seattle, he'd grab a cab and transfer to another carrier, probably an airline, get a ticket and head to the Midwest. He was thinking maybe Kansas City or St. Louis. Wait a day or two, download some more money from his account—nobody should even know about it— then take another plane ride east. He had set this whole idea up a long time ago, figuring that he'd have a whole day's head start on his father if he left on a school day. He didn't know if the FBI would start pulling buses over or like that, but probably not. It wasn't like he was on the ten-most-wanted list or anything. They couldn't have that many agents looking for him, could they?

Like his EZ Mail box, the bank account was under his pseudo-nym, Leonard Jones, from Leonard Nimoy and James Earl Jones— actors in two of his favorite movies, *Star Trek IV* and *The Empire Strikes Back*, so he should be able to keep taking out three hundred dollars a day until he had all his money. He'd made a fake library card and stu-dent ID using his scanner and laser printer, and the ATM card matched those. Less whatever it took for transportation and food and all, he ought to have enough money left so he could get to Secaucus, New Jersey.

That was where his mother had gone when she'd left. Secaucus.

His father never knew that; she'd told him and made him promise not to tell, and Jake had kept it to himself. His mother had a friend there, from college, and she'd told Jake the woman's name. Jake didn't have the name written down anywhere his father might find it, but he remembered it. He'd find the woman and then his mother.

Assuming they didn't catch him before he ditched this bicycle and got on a bus out of town.

He pedaled. He sweated, despite the cool morning around him. His father had been right about one thing. All that running and obstacle course stuff was worth something after all. He was free.

5

Steve Hayes was drinking a frosty mai-tai and sunning on a nude beach in Florida next to a beautiful naked brunette when a harsh ringing jerked him from the warm vision. The sun's heat faded, the gentle surf's sounds were drowned out by the loud noise. The beautiful brunette waved good-bye. . . .

What—?

He woke up in his own bedroom in Washington. He had the blackout curtains drawn against the day, so his apartment's bedroom was dark. He looked at the glow-in-the-dark clock on the bedside table. Not yet ten-thirty in the morning. Crap, he had just gotten to sleep. And it had been such a great dream, too.

He grabbed the phone, more than a little irritated. "What?"

"Sorry to disturb you, Major," the voice said. But it didn't sound sorry, it sounded spiteful in a way only a career noncom's voice can when he knows you can't touch him for causing you grief. "This is Master Sergeant Pressridge, daywatch at ops. Please hold for Colonel Barker, sir."

Hayes rubbed his eyes as he was put on hold. Barker was a pain-in-the-butt regular army desk jockey who got bent out of shape if somebody forgot to dot an *i* or cross a *t* on a report. But he was also a full-bird colonel, and if he wanted to call and rout Hayes from his hard-earned beauty sleep, well, rank had its privileges.

"Hayes. Barker."

"Sir?"

"We have a security situation. You recall an operations report you logged in at 0300 hours?"

For a second, Hayes drew a blank. Then he remembered. The UFO thing? "Yes, sir."

"This concerns that. It's a WEO, no telecom. Get down here ASAP."

Hayes cradled the already-dead phone. Oh, Jesus, now what? Did the little green men land during the night? WEO—warm ears only—was another of those stupid top-secret acronyms that usually didn't mean squat. But if they were ready to pull him in when he was off-shift, maybe it did mean something this time.

He slid out of bed and padded toward the shower. He had some leave time coming.

Maybe a trip to Florida wasn't such a bad idea.

Hayes, feeling only a little better after a needle shower and two cups of coffee hurriedly gulped in the car on the way in, stared at Colonel Barker. "Sir?"

"I realize it is early for you, Major, but which part of it didn't you understand?"

"Begging the colonel's pardon, sir, but the part I don't understand is why this concerns us at all. I mean, the FBI agent was bruised some under his protective vest. The shooter sustained an arm wound and is safely in custody for assaulting a federal officer, plus a number of unregistered weapons' charges. Why is it our business?"

"Because General Hightower *says* it is," the colonel said. He leaned back in his chair and stared at Hayes. "The computer hacker, this eleven-year-old boy, is still at large. The general wishes for us to have a . . . presence in this matter."

"Again, sir, meaning no disrespect, but isn't the FBI a lot better qualified to undertake this matter?"

"Major, if the FBI were qualified, they would have the boy in custody."

"So, who is he going to tell? The Russians? The Iraqis? His junior high school chess club?"

"That's your problem, Major. Best you find him and collect him before he tells anybody anything."

"Sir—"

"Major, your dissatisfaction being stuck here as a pencil pusher is well known. Well, now you've got your wish—you've got a field job. Your orders are being cut and will be waiting at the master sergeant's desk on your way out. Dismissed."

Well. That was that.

As they were both in uniform and Barker was such a stickler for it, Hayes saluted, a snappy up and down that would have done a West Pointer proud. But as he pivoted and marched out, he was mentally shaking his head. Yeah, sure, he wanted to be out in the field—but tracking down a preteen computer geek? Come on. He must have stepped on somebody's toes somewhere along the line to get saddled with this piece of work. Damn Hightower and his mania about space monsters.

The master sergeant, a red-faced, balding porker pushing forty-five, grinned like an old tom after a night on the rooftops. "Sir. Your orders."

Hayes took the sheaf of papers and scanned them. "Where the hell is Sherwood, Oregon?"

"About twenty-five hundred miles that way, sir." He pointed. "More or less."

"Thank you, Sergeant."

"Yes, sir, happy to be of service, sir."

Disgusted, Hayes headed for the door.

It was almost noon when Stewart Davies woke up. It was a nagging in the back of his mind that did it, a little stab of paranoia he couldn't quite put his finger on, something about those messages from last night—well, early this morning.

He sat up on the edge of his bed, rubbed sleep from his eyes. He shouldn't be awake yet, he'd only had a few hours' rest. He had hours before his evening class, time enough to get cleaned up, get something to eat, and maybe find Jess and see how she was doing. Maybe do a little work on the game. Get in a few laps at the pool, or maybe a workout in the gym.

Right, and why not finish your thesis in your copious spare time, too? How much you think you can fit into one afternoon, hmm?

Stewart sighed. That had been an ongoing problem, using time
wisely. He always had twenty-four more things to do than he had hours
in which to do them. He could usually winnow them so he did what
absolutely had to be done—or at least partially done—but he always
had leftover stuff he couldn't get to.

So, here it was again. He had all these things he ought to be
attending to, but what was bugging him were those messages he'd gotten at the lab. The ones Karagigian said were frauds.

He went into the bathroom, hit the on switch for the TV on the
way, used the facilities, considered going back to bed. No. He was up.
Might as well make the best of it. He reached for his toothbrush,
squeezed a blob of white-and-blue toothpaste onto it, ran a little water
over the blob.

The noon news came on, the sound of it muted over the running
water.

As he brushed his teeth, it came to him what was wrong: *How
could Karagigian have possibly known those signals were a hoax?*

He'd sent e-mail to the professor telling him about the signals.
That electronic letter got there in the middle of the night when the professor should have been asleep. He'd known the man for almost five
years and Karagigian was an early-to-bed-late-to-rise person, probably
slept ten or eleven hours every night, at least. Come ten P.M. and he
nodded off, no matter where he was, and Stewart had never seen the
prof awake before nine in the morning. And long before the man
should have been up and about, he had called and told Stewart to hold
off on SETI-protocol queries.

He thought about that for a minute. Either Karagigian got up in
the middle of his night, read the e-mail and went straight to the phone
to call Stewart, in which case, how could he have possibly known the
signals were faked without seeing what they looked like? Or, he called
the FCC and they told him to hold off, which also didn't make any
sense, since, why on Earth would he *make* such a call? And if *he* didn't
call *them*, then *they* must have called Karagigian to warn him off. In
which case—how had *they* known about the signals?

Unless they read Karagigian's e-mail before the professor got to it.

Stewart spat a mouthful of toothpaste foam into the sink and
looked at himself in the mirror.

And did the FCC normally read a college professor's e-mail? He didn't think so. And even if they *did*, why had they been all hot to jump all over this with both feet before dawn? Unless these hoaxers had been bleeding all over every SETI system in the country—which they hadn't or Stewart would certainly have heard about it—why bring out the big guns?

Something smelled rotten here.

So. Maybe it was another of those agencies with initials, one more concerned with this kind of thing than the Federal Communications Commission would be.

Careful, boy. You might not want to go down this road.

But Stewart had one of those logical minds that, once it started along a trail, kept choosing the most reasonable fork it could figure out until it got where it was going. And right now, all those choices kept heading in a bad direction.

So, let's assume as a working hypothesis that it *was* some federal agency who snooped open Karagigian's e-mail and found Stewart's note. If the message were fake, then what was the point? Stewart or one of the other grad students or Karagigian would figure that out fast enough. They'd decode the sucker, get a horse laugh from the MIT or Harvard technoheads who put it together, and that would be that. Why would the feds even bother?

Ipso facto, Stew, old son. They wouldn't. Unless . . .

Unless they knew the messages *weren't* fake!

Bingo. Give the man a prize. No, wait, don't. Look how long it took him to plod here to figure it out.

Oh, man!

He wiped his face, stared at his reflection. His whiskers would have to wait.

He had to get back to the SETI lab.

He walked into the bedroom, opened his dresser drawer, pulled out a clean shirt and socks.

"—and in other news, the FBI reports that the terrorists responsible for the explosion on the Golden Gate Bridge last Sunday were taken into custody in Dallas, Texas, early this morning. Details when we return."

Stewart glanced at the tube. The news channel's logo flashed on screen, along with the deep voice of the movie-star announcer: "This is MNN, the McMahon News Network."

Stewart shook his head. First it was Ted Turner, now it was Tyler McMahon helping blow the old networks off the air. News-wise, at least. If something broke anywhere in the world and you wanted the story, you flipped on CNN or MNN to get it. ABC, NBC, CBS, they'd gutted their news departments over the years, at least that's what Jess maintained. Tyler McMahon, a very rich man, had decided to give Ted Turner a run for his money, and so far seemed to be doing pretty well at it.

He pulled his shirt on.

Lawrence Hightower kissed Laurie Sherman's slim and delightful neck, just above her equally delightful collarbone.

"Oh, yes, I do believe I like that."

He leaned back, slipped his jacket off and tossed it at the couch. "How long do you have?"

She glanced at her watch. "I have to meet the presidential limo for an AFL-CIO gathering at one-thirty. That gives us, let's see, sixty-seven minutes, allowing ten for a shower and dressing. You up for it?"

He laughed. "Now there's a turn of phrase. Why, yes, Miz Sherman, I do believe I am up for it."

She leaned over and kissed him on the chin. Her lips were soft, warm, wet.

"You want me to open some champagne?" he asked her.

"Nope. This will do just fine, General Sir, sir." She grabbed his shirt lapels and pulled him toward her. She slid her hands around his back and raised her face for his kiss. He obliged.

It was amazing that she could stir so much passion in him. He was not, after all, a young man. He had been fairly interested in sex most of his life. His wife, bless her, had been pretty fiery throughout their marriage. Because of his job, he had been gone a lot and when he had come home for however many weeks or days or sometimes only hours the army allowed him, he and Sasha had made the most of the time. They'd had dozens of honeymoons. When the kids were still at home, that had been harder, but once they were off to college and out on their own, there had been a resurgence of play. Sometimes they made love in the living room in front of the fireplace, sometimes even in the kitchen while supper burned merrily away. But in the six years since Sasha had died, he hadn't had much interest in it. He was fit, he exercised, ran, ate well, but he'd figured that part of him was buried with his wife.

Not so, once he'd met Laurie. That part of him wasn't dead, merely sleeping, and Laurie had awakened it easily.

He bent to kiss her again and a part of him deeper than language arose. His brain faded and his body took over.

Jake bypassed the Greyhound station and went to the Royal Coach place. He found a cash machine there and took out three hundred dollars. Then, just for fun, he put his card back in and tried it again. The machine gave him three hundred more. Hmm. It wasn't supposed to do that, must be a glitch in the system. That apparently happened a lot. He'd seen a thing on the news about some guy who swiped an ATM card from some old lady a couple of months ago and somehow had gotten like ten thousand dollars a day for five or six days out of the cash machines because of a glitch, and she hadn't even had that much in her account.

In ten minutes, he had all of his money out in cash. It was all in twenties and it took a lot of room. Part of it he put into his pack, part of it into his pockets.

This was great! He was set, now.

Since there were more buses heading south and the next one he could catch was only ten minutes away, Jake got a ticket for it. He bought a round-trip to Eugene, though he planned to get off in Salem. He had seen enough cop shows to know that a one-way ticket was a red flag. Plus he told the clerk he was thirteen and paid an adult fare. If a fed got here and showed this clerk a picture, they'd know he was headed to Salem, but it was only an hour and something away, so unless they were fast, he'd be ahead of them. They couldn't check every bus on every line, they didn't have enough agents for that. Of course, they could call in the local police, but now that he was a little calmer, Jake really didn't think they would. For a hacker? It wasn't like he was Mickey and Maude or somebody.

"Royal Coach Lines bus number six, leaving for Salem, Eugene, Weed, and Sacramento, is now boarding in bay one," said a bored voice over the intercom.

About twenty people in the small waiting room shuffled toward bay one. There were only two bays, and they were side by side. You had to go through the same door for both, so Jake thought the announcement was fairly stupid.

He gave the driver his ticket and climbed onto the bus. There were a few people ahead of him and he moved past them and found a pair of empty seats. He put his bag on the aisle seat and sat by the window. He took his laptop out, logged in his password, and waited for the hard drive to spin up. He shut the sounds off so nobody would hear and remember them. He could work on his new font. The battery was good for maybe an hour and he had two spares in his pack. After that, he'd have to find a plug and recharge.

People passed by the empty seat. A few minutes later the driver got on, made an announcement about where the bus was going, and shut the doors.

After they got rolling, Jake felt a lot better.

Once he got to Salem, he decided, he'd find a phone and hook up his modem. He could order a plane ticket via the travel service on AOL, take a cab or a bus to the airport, and get on a plane. Maybe instead of heading east, he'd go south, to San Francisco or Los Angeles. Get a plane east there. He didn't think anybody was really after him, but he didn't want to screw up now.

He wondered if his father was dead, or if the FBI agent was. It would be too bad if the agent was, but as to his father, maybe that would be the best thing. That way, he wouldn't be coming to look for Jake and his mother.

If his old man was dead, well, okay, that wouldn't be *good*, but he would have brought it on himself.

Jake found he didn't want to think too much about that. He bent over his computer and called up the font program. He'd think about his father later. After he was sure he had gotten away.

After he found his mother.

6

Laurie stood in the shower and allowed the hot water to rinse away the lather on her body. She wished she had time to wash and dry her hair but she and Larry had cut it pretty fine timewise, so she wore a plastic cap. She held her face under the spray. It was very relaxing. She smiled into the pulsing water. Much more relaxed and she'd be unconscious. After the lovemaking, she could easily have dropped off for a nice long nap. She very much liked falling asleep cuddled next to Larry, his arm around her. They didn't get to do that very often. Ah, well. Another time. You didn't get to be the president of the United States' chief of staff by dozing away the afternoons.

She turned around, let the water flow down her back. She'd certainly earned the job. She'd been working for the president since he'd been a newly minted congressman twenty years past. She had started as a volunteer while still in college, addressing letters, stuffing envelopes, making calls to voters. It wasn't as if she'd thought he was the greatest politician ever, but she agreed with many of his stances on issues and saw that he had a certain charisma with people. He was basically a decent businessman who wanted to make a difference. A bit too self-centered and worried about his image, maybe, but it could have been a lot worse.

Two years later, during his reelection, college graduate Laurie Sherman had gotten a job as paid staff on the campaign, an assistant fund-raiser. Two years after that, she was elevated to campaign manager when the man who'd held the job before had a stroke. She got the job mostly because everybody thought the race was a walkover. There hadn't been any opposition in the primary and the other party's choice was as likable as poison ivy. Unfortunately, the congressman's opponent somehow managed to dig up some old and questionable business deals and the election became a neck-and-neck horse race. Had it not been for some fancy footwork and spin control, they might have lost, but they didn't and Laurie got—and deserved—the credit. So the next year, when the incumbent senator was forced to retire due to a scandal of his own, Laurie was a natural to manage the congressman's first run for the Senate. Quite a coup for a woman just turned twenty-six. She had been paid with the chief of staff job for the newly elected senator, and eight years later when he gave the presidency a shot, Laurie had been right there, pulling in favors, twisting arms, putting the bite on pocketbooks. The primaries had been hell. The convention and nomination worse. The general election had been close, but a narrow margin was all that mattered, a win was a win.

She shut the water off, stepped out of the shower onto the bathmat, reached for one of the beach-sized fluffy towels Larry liked.

He was gone, back to the Pentagon for a round of high-level meetings that concerned the fates of nations and the details and deployment of the most powerful military force in the world. Boring stuff, he told her, but probably a lot more interesting than a meeting with a bunch of teamsters who had to be courted for their vote and who probably would vote for anybody but the president when it got right down to it.

She dried herself with the giant towel, lowered it, and looked with a critical eye at her somewhat foggy reflection in the mirror. Not too bad for a woman on the downside of forty. She was still tight, her breasts small enough so they didn't sag all that much but not so small she had to use an A cup. She had two pieces of gym equipment in her condo and she alternated her workouts, thirty minutes a session on the stair stepper Mondays, Wednesdays, and Fridays, thirty minutes on the CardioGlide on Tuesdays and Thursdays. She took the weekends off.

She half turned, looked at her rear end. Not too bad there, either. In the soft focus of the fogged glass, she could have passed for twenty-five, so all that exercise paid for itself. Never having had children helped. Her sister had four, three boys and a girl, and being the old maid aunt was quite enough for Laurie. A few nights of babysitting pediatric earaches and changing dirty diapers had convinced Laurie she wouldn't enjoy the role of mommie. Even though Jenny's kids were all teenagers now and not so messy, that age had its own set of problems. She enjoyed having the kids for a little while, but giving them and the responsibility back to someone else had to be part of the process for her.

Not every woman was cut out to be a mother.

Larry's oldest son was not much younger than Laurie, and Larry had told her that at his age, the idea of grandchildren was nice—he had three—but new babies of his own at home were not okay. Start a new one and he'd be pushing eighty when the kid graduated from high school. That wouldn't be fair to the child or to him.

Larry laughed at her when she rode the CardioGlide, though. It looked like a bicycle without wheels, and he said she looked like a cowgirl riding a bucking bronco when she used it, pulling with her arms and pushing with her legs. Yehaw! Or a woman on top making love, he sometimes said. She liked that image better.

She shook her head. Better get dressed and stop this postcoital woolgathering. While the teamsters would probably like to see her naked and she'd almost consider letting them if they'd vote her way, she wasn't going to get anything done admiring her girlish figure in the mirror. She had nine minutes to get dressed and five minutes to get to the White House and she would barely make it if she were the Flash.

She finished drying herself, drew a heart in the condensation on the mirror so Larry would see it when his next shower fogged the glass, and hurried to get dressed.

From the air, Portland, Oregon, looked clean and wet. Mountains surrounded it, some of them big and snow-covered, there was a lot of forest greenery, and a cloud cover the jet broke through a few thousand feet up. Hayes, now in civilian clothes, had hitched a ride on the first-available military craft heading west, an Oregon-based National Guard C-130 cargo hauler. The crew happened to be big basketball fans. In fact, while they hadn't said so, Hayes figured they had arranged their flight to the D.C. area in order to watch the Portland Trail Blazers play the Bullets. There had been a couple of Guard units busted for doing that kind of thing, joyriding in the company planes, but it still went on. They were feeling good and happy to have a Washington fan to lord it over, since the Blazers had stomped the injury-plagued Bullets by sixteen points.

"Free throws killed your guys," the navigator said. "Portland used to be that bad, shooting fifty, sixty percent, now they're averaging almost seventy-four percent from the line."

"How'd they get turned around?" Hayes asked.

"Easy. Coach keeps each man at practice until he makes ten in a row or midnight, whichever comes first. Sometimes he has a couple of guys who don't get to go home until real late."

They smiled at each other.

"We'll be on the ground in ten," the navigator said. "You're not bad for a Bullet fan, Major."

"Thanks, Lieutenant."

Hayes flashed his orders at the OD's desk and got a ride to the government motor pool, where he was issued a car. It was a basic four-door plain-vanilla Chrysler, automatic transmission with a small engine. Not going to win any road races, but it should get him where he was going and back.

He got a map, drove through the city and west on something called the Sunset Highway to 217 heading north, then exited at a place called Tigard. Name reminded him of Winnie-the-Pooh. It was cold and gray outside the warmth of the car's heater. A light drizzle began to fall, just enough to use the wipers on pause.

He drove west again, passing through what was probably a bedroom community for Portland, suburban sprawl, shopping centers, McDonald's. There was a patch of country past that, the speed limit went up to fifty-five, and he passed a huge pile of bark dust and what smelled like a cattle yard before he neared the town of Sherwood. Not more than twenty-five or thirty miles from downtown, if that. He left the state highway and turned into the town.

The main road going in had a twenty-five-mph speed limit and it looked almost like a movie town the farther he got from the state highway, small, quaint, slow. He cruised around for a few minutes to get a feel for the place. If the cold drizzle bothered anybody, he couldn't tell. People walked around in windbreakers, a few had hats, but he didn't see any umbrellas. And teenagers, of course, wearing shorts and T-shirts, some of them. At that age, looking cool was much more important than being comfortable. Hayes had known he was getting older when he realized he would look out his window before deciding what to wear these days.

There was an old downtown area, somewhat renewed, a theater, railroad tracks, small stores and office buildings. The houses were neat, yards well-kept, the energy that of small-town middle America.

Welcome to the village of the happy nice people. Would you like some milk and cookies?

Well, except that the people in *that* mythical town probably didn't shoot it out with FBI agents who'd come to talk to their kids about hacking into private computer systems. Hard to imagine Ward Cleaver with an Uzi mowing down a G-man. Well. It had been a long time since *Leave It to Beaver*, even here.

Hayes located the address on the map and drove to the house where the feebs had been outfoxed by a preteen boy and his gun-nut father. He parked the car and got out. The mist wasn't so bad, once you got out in it. He buttoned his windbreaker, left the bottom one unsnapped so he could get at the Smith & Wesson revolver holstered on his belt behind his right hip. NSA military liaison field agents weren't required to carry a weapon and it wasn't likely he'd need one to find a kid in grammar school. Still, he'd gotten used to carrying it in D.C. whenever he wore civilian clothes. The crime rate there was probably a little higher than it was here. Issue was either a Glock or a Beretta 9mm or .40, but he didn't much like automatics. The Smith was a .357, a model 66, same one he had carried in Desert Storm, and he was happy with it, despite its lack of firepower. He figured if he couldn't get it done with six bullets in a sidearm, more wouldn't help. And a revolver seldom jammed, nor did it throw the empties into your face like the Glock did.

He walked around the house, looked at it, tried to get some hit on the people who lived here.

He had the FBI's report and background information on the man they'd arrested, an ex-military, right-wing survivalist militia type. And as soon as he got done with his own look around, and assuming his cell phone worked like it was supposed to on roam, he'd put in a call to the local FBI for a more official tour.

He saw the obstacle course in the backyard and grinned. The feeb's report had mentioned a failed pursuit of the "youthful suspect," but had failed to point out that the pursuing agent had fallen into a mud hole and nearly drowned trying to get out. That had come secondhand word-of-mouth from the special agent in charge in Seattle, a man who owed Hayes a couple of favors and who also didn't much care for the man who'd lost his grip on the swinging rings and done a belly flop into the mud. It was hard not to rejoice at your enemy's misfortune.

Hayes walked to the nearest window and peered into the house. Not much to see. He could go in, and if anybody called the local law, he could wave his National Security Agency ID at them, but he'd rather wait for the feebs. He walked back toward his car, pulled his cell phone as he did so. Chilly out here.

He made the call.

Zeerus had underestimated Primaster when he had started the revolution too early. And Primaster had in turn underestimated Zeerus when he'd been brought to the mother ship. Still, it had hardly balanced out, had it? Zeerus had lost a war, hundreds if not thousands of loyal troops, a planet's governorship, and a chance at immortality. Ah, but Primaster had lost Zeerus, and thus much more. For Zeerus alive was and would always be a threat to the Paxus Majae. Always. Alone in the stolen ship, Zeerus went over the mistakes he had made for the thousandth time. Failure to adequately secure the shipping lines. Failure to maintain control of subspace communications. Inadequate troop strength in reserve. And, the most damning of all, his overeagerness. Had he but waited another month, perhaps two, he could have held power long enough to establish control, to seed the planet with protonics, enough to shatter the world. There would have been a threat Primaster could not have ignored: Hear me or watch a planet die. A planet full of beings, most of whom were total innocents.

But, no. He'd leaped too fast. Because he was very much a hands-on leader. When that idiot Loid Shimol had started issuing threats, well, what could Zeerus do but strangle the fool right then and there?

A mistake, that. No two ways about it. He'd had little choice but to continue, and he wasn't ready.

It wouldn't happen again. If these humans were not the proper tools to accomplish all that he wished, well, he would use them to delay Primaster until he could *find* the proper tools. If a few billion of them had to be spent toward his goal, well, so be it. A good general had to be willing to make such sacrifices, and if that willingness alone could be translated into military adeptness, why, then, Zeerus was the greatest general who had ever lived.

Why didn't they *answer* him! The coded message was simple enough! If they couldn't figure it out, they would be useless save as cannon fodder—and it would take time to get them to that state.

Ah, well. Those who would be great must be willing to suffer the small to achieve their goals. Not gladly, perhaps, but willing nonetheless.

"Send it again," he told the computer. "And record their incoming signals and build a dictionary and grammatical construct. You can do that, can't you?"

The computer indicated that it could.

"Fine. When you get the dictionary and grammar finished, put it into a tutorial."

The computer acknowledged and obeyed.

He'd have to learn how to speak their language. While this ship's stupid computer couldn't do much, it could put together a program to teach that. It wasn't as if he had a lot of other things to occupy his time. If they hadn't translated his signal by the time he learned their language, he would resend it in their own speech.

"General Hightower?"

Hightower looked up from the foot-thick pile of documents on his desk. Colonel Gray, his aide, stood there.

"Yes, Earl?" Hightower had long ago learned to tune out the smile that wanted to arise every time he spoke to his aide. The spelling was slightly different, but to be named Earl Gray must have dogged him all his life.

What, like the tea?

You had to admire a man who held on to his name under that kind of pressure.

"MILCOM stats are incoming on the overseas deployment. Casualty lists show six dead so far."

Hightower shook his head. "Six? They aren't even in-country yet."

"Three sailors from the crane accident in Italy. One marine fell off a troop carrier en route and is presumed drowned, though they are still looking. Maybe he's floating around on his pants like that other one did a while back. One reservist had a heart attack. One GI truck driver put his vehicle into the drink at the staging docks. One second lieutenant got drunk, depressed, and ate his Beretta."

"God."

That was the problem with the logistics of moving troops and materiel. Civilians tended to forget that people died in car wrecks or got mugged or slipped and fell in bathtubs every day in any good-size town. When you moved eighty or a hundred thousand men and women from one country to another, you were moving the equivalent of an entire town. No battle plan survives first contact with the enemy, and sometimes the enemy is weather or terrain. Accidents were bound to happen.

"Your briefing with Admiral Vasquez is at 1630. We've allowed an hour, but it won't take that long. You've got Generals Stoddard and Bean for drinks at the Hamilton at 1800; Stoddard has a new granddaughter you should ask about and Bean just broke a hundred for the first time golfing at his club. You have dinner with Senator Dupuis at 2100 at the Club Louisiane. He wants the base in his home state taken off the closure list and he is in a position to be very helpful if we do him this favor. Ambassador Puska's soiree runs until midnight, officially, though the party won't die until well into the wee hours. Black tie or dress uniform."

Hightower allowed himself a small sigh. "Anything else?"

"Not much, the usual. Oh, except that we've detached one of our NSA liaisons on that SETI hacker thing."

"That officer would be . . . ?"

"Major Steven Hayes."

Hightower smiled. Ah. Young Hayes. "I bet he loved that."

"Colonel Barker at the listening post indicated that the major was quite happy to get a field assignment."

"Oh, I'm sure. Keep me posted on this, would you?"

"Of course."

After Gray left, Hightower rocked slightly back and forth in his leather and wood chair, listened to the squeak of the big springs, and stared at nothing. The cryptographers hadn't broken the message codes yet.

It could be a robotic probe. But if there was anything alive on that vessel, if there was an alien piloting it, then his childhood dream of shaking hands with a creature from outer space might come true.

If the thing didn't have a blaster in its hand when it landed.

7

When Stewart got to the shack, Tommy Dixon was working the SETI board. Dixon was a short man with a lopsided smile and a strong southern accent. He was a senior in astronomy from Mississippi, and while his speech had speeded up some, the rhythms and constructions were unmistakably Deep South.

"Yo, Stew, 'sup, hoss?"

"Hey, Tommy Dee. I, uh, left a piece of my game here. Okay if I download it?"

"Don't matter none to me. You just have on at it, Mister Nin-ten-do."

Tommy rolled his chair to the side and went back to reading the magazine he held.

Stewart brushed past him and took the spare chair. "What are you reading, Johnny Reb? *Soldier of Fortune*? Or you just looking at the pictures?"

"You know what a cliche is, hoss?"

"A redneck reading *Guns and Ammo*?"

Dixon smiled. "No, a cliche is a Yankee fool who thinks anybody born outside of New England is an illiterate moron." He waved the magazine. It was the current month's issue of *Scientific American*.

"An illiterate moron as opposed to a *literate* moron?" Stewart could talk and work the keyboard at the same time. "What kind of morons you run with, Dixie?"

"Look in the mirror, hoss, look in the mirror."

Tommy went back to his reading and Stewart called up the messages from last night. Well, early this morning.

They were gone.

"You haven't been dicking around in here, have you, Tommy?"

"Me? Shoot, no. Ain't touched that booger all day. Whut's a'matter, you lose your file?"

"Nope, I must have stored it under another name. I'll find it."

Stewart didn't like this, not at all.

He tapped at the keyboard, called up the retrieval utilities. Maybe whoever had wiped the file—had to be Karagigian—had just done a simple delete.

He waited a few seconds for the utility program to load.

Okay, let's see here. . . .

Yes! There it was. Stewart did a retrieval. The file wasn't that big, a few megabytes. He sent it to the zip drive and saved it under the name "OmniQue-revisions." Now he could take it to his apartment and work on it. He popped the zip disk out and waved it at Tommy. "Got it, Bubba Joe Jim Bob. I'm outta here."

Tommy glanced up at the ceiling. "Praise Jesus."

"See you later, Cracker boy."

"Not if I see you first, son."

As he left the SETI shack, Stewart tucked the zip disk into his notebook pocket. Whatever was going on around here, they'd have to get up a lot earlier in the morning to get past him. He was still mentally patting himself on the back when he saw the two men get out of the plain tan Ford parked in the circle in back of the astronomy building.

Two men in dark suits, wearing sunglasses.

Ordinarily he didn't pay much attention to the people wandering around on campus, but since he was feeling paranoid, he noticed these two. They were headed toward the SETI shack, and Stewart paused behind the cover of a ragged cedar tree long enough to see that the pair went inside.

Uh oh.

Maybe he ought not to put the message he had just copied onto his system at home just yet. And maybe he ought to put the disk somewhere safe for a day or two until he figured out what was what.

Jake got a nasty surprise when he started trying to find a flight from Salem to Los Angeles.

First problem was, Eaasy Sabre didn't even *show* any flights from Salem to anywhere. Either nothing landed in the capital of Oregon—which didn't seem real likely—or the reservation system couldn't access the feeder connections. So he tried Eugene, only an hour or so past Salem.

When he saw how much a full-price one-way airline ticket would cost for a same-day flight from there to Los Angeles, he almost choked on the Coke he was drinking.

He was at a phone in the bus station, his modem connected to the transceiver. He stared at the computer screen. Man! The top end was more than a *thousand* dollars and the cheapest was a couple of hundred! Well, there were cheaper ones than that, eighty or ninety dollars, but they required a three-day advance booking. He didn't want to stay in Oregon that long.

He had to do better than that. He was going to have to figure out how to crack into a reservation computer somewhere and backdate himself a ticket or something. That might be a little tricky. He'd never done that before, though he'd read a pretty good piece in a Net newsgroup that explained how you could do it. Thing was, you had to have access to something like a travel agency's computers or log-on numbers to do it like the thread had explained it.

Well. He could find a travel agency, could look one up in the phone book, that wouldn't be hard. Get there and somehow figure out how to access their system.

Either that or blow a whole bunch of his money to get to Los Angeles by air.

He didn't think so.

Buses were a lot cheaper, but it would take a day or two on the ground, only a couple of hours in the air.

Hmm. He'd better figure this out pretty quick.

* * *

After he had exhausted the ship's pitiful store of knowledge about this system he found himself in—a task that occupied precious little time—Zeerus decided to do a bit of survey work on his own. It was always wise to know the territory in which one traveled, if for no other reason than to be able to find the fastest way out should the need arise.

And, when facing the eventual arrival of an irritated Primaster, knowing the fastest way out was not a luxury, but a necessity.

The stolen vessel had rudimentary telescopic and particle/wave viewing equipment. Hardly state-of-the-art gear, but it was sufficient to allow any user with half a working brain to resolve images of solid objects a few hundred meters across at the short distances found in a typical stellar system. Anything more than a few light-weeks away would be beyond this idiot ship's ken.

He could scan in the visible, infrared, and ultraviolet spectrums, though the magnetic imaging equipment was only just able to pick up the largest fields, those of the primary where most of the system's mass existed, and maybe a couple of the gas giant planets. Pitiful.

Well. One had to make do, always the way of it when using hastily borrowed material.

He was not an astronomer but the equipment was easy enough to use. A quick scan revealed that he was coming in slightly above the plane of the ecliptic, the planetary orbits. Or below it, given that up and down were all meaningless in space without a gravity well.

A few minutes' work with the ship's machineries showed him that there were a number of heavy-metal inner and gaseous outer worlds orbiting the primary—seven, eight, nine, a couple of which appeared to be double worlds. The outermost planet had a moon that was large relative to it, perhaps eight or ten percent as big, as did the third planet, Earth, his destination. Most of the larger outer worlds had several moons, some a dozen or more, most of these rocky and gasless. There was a belt of worldlets between the fourth planet and the fifth, probably a shattered world, plus the usual array of comets, meteoroids, dust, and other debris flying around. Three of the larger planets had captured some of this debris into rings that encircled them. Very . . . picturesque.

The largest of the gas giants, the one whose name he could almost remember, acted as a kind of shield for the inner planets, its bulk and gravity blocking many of the comets or runaway worldlets that might have otherwise smashed into the inner worlds to destroy the fragile ecology. This was common in systems where life had originated naturally; planets exposed to large chunks of cosmic detritus seldom produced life very far up the evolutionary scale without being bashed by an asteroid or some such. The result of such an impact was often explosive and climate-altering enough to wipe out most of the higher life-forms.

In fact, according to certain little-known histories he had read, it was one of the oldest methods of attack by one planet on another, to stand off a few light-minutes and hurl large rocks at the enemy. Made life quite uncomfortable for the inhabitants without the means to block such attacks.

Pity he had never had a chance to try that tactic.

The rumor was that it had been such a cosmic collision that had originally prompted the Paxus Majae to collect specimens from the third planet, the only world in this system with an intelligent species.

Rumors usually had some grain of truth in them, but with the Paxus Majae, one never knew what the truth was. They only allowed their client races to know what they thought was good for them.

The only other carbon-based life in this area at all was on one of the larger moons circling the largest gas giant. And the most complex form there was a jellylike blob that drifted in a salty water sea under a thick sheet of ice, doing nothing but eating a kind of algae, excreting, and reproducing asexually when it got large enough. Why even bother?

Jupiter—ah, that was the local designation for the big gas planet.

Zeerus turned his attention to the primary. The single yellow sun was a dwarf-size, medium-temperature main-sequence star, about midway or a little less on the Autok Scale, and the most common type around which planets with intelligent life were apt to be found. Common as biters on a bingtu. The star was about ninety-five percent hydrogen, the rest helium and a few trace elements, also the usual pattern. Chronometric readings showed it to be in the neighborhood of ten decannums old. What would that be in local time on the planet Earth? He surely had enough of a dictionary to translate standard measurements by now? He asked the computer and was rewarded with the answer. The star—called Sol or the Sun—was about five billion *years* old. Probably had about that much more time before it was reduced to burning helium and blew up into a nova and ate the inner planets. He wouldn't want to be here then.

No, by then, even his extended life span would have run out. Before that happened, where he wanted to be was far away and in charge of a mighty armada of ships, chasing down and exterminating the last of the Majae.

He had a lot to do before then.

He turned his attention back to the scanners.

Laurie Sherman smiled at the ambassador from some small and newly renamed African country. From his demeanor, he was much more interested in seeing her in positions other than as the president's adviser. According to a friend of hers in the diplomatic corps, the man was known as the Octopus, and if you were female and under the age of eighty, you shouldn't get into an elevator with him alone.

Laurie smiled. She had learned how to avoid that kind of man a long time ago. She could do it with words most of the time, and when words failed, a high heel on the top of the foot or a knee to the groin usually worked wonders.

"Perhaps I could show you my vacation home some time?" the ambassador said. "It has a spectacular view of the mountains and sometimes you can see leopards mating from the second-story bedroom window." His English held only a trace of an accent. Probably South African, since she understood he'd been educated there.

"And would your wife be there?"

"Alas, no, we travel in different circles. She hates the country life, prefers the big city. She stays mostly in the capital."

Laurie smiled again. Since the capital and biggest city in the ambassador's reshuffled country had a population totaling all of twenty-five thousand, most of them living in tiny houses without running water or electricity, she found his characterization of it rather amusing.

Time to cut this would-be Casanova loose. "Excuse me, please, Mr. Ambassador, but I need to speak to the secretary of defense; I see him just over there. Delighted to have had this chance to visit with you."

She hurried away to where William O'Connell stood nursing a glass of scotch on the rocks. He liked good single malt, as she recalled.

"Bill."

"Laurie, how are you? Ambassador Octopus giving you a hard time?"

"He wishes. I told him I had to talk to you."

"By all means. Party is pretty much a dud, and you are the best-looking and brightest woman here."

Laurie smiled. She had a good working relationship with Bill. He was an old-fashioned liberal, a nice enough man, and his personal flattery was no more than that: He'd been married for thirty-six years, had four children and six grandchildren, and didn't play around—if the FBI reports could be believed. He was also politically adept enough to know that getting on her bad side would cut down on his access to her boss, so he made an effort to be cordial. She appreciated that.

He said, "So what's the latest on the little green men? Hightower's folly?"

She shrugged. "You know what I know. No new developments."

He sipped at his scotch. "Much as I hate to admit it, Larry might have a point. If there's anything to it, it would do more than drop the Dow a couple of points."

"So I understand."

"Ah, I see the Octopus has zeroed in on other prey."

Laurie glanced at the ambassador. He was talking rather animatedly to a blonde Laurie thought was staff for the junior senator from Florida. "You can sometimes watch leopards mating from the upstairs bedroom of his vacation home, did you know that?"

O'Connell grinned into his drink. "Really? Maybe he'll invite me to see that."

"I wouldn't hold my breath if I were you."

She looked around. "I guess I can make the rounds one more time and then leave," she said.

"Kind of takes the fun out of a party when you have to work it, doesn't it?" he said.

"Yeah. See you later, Bill."

He raised his nearly empty glass in a silent toast to her.

Laurie glanced at her watch as she moved away from O'Connell. Almost midnight. If she stroked a few more dignitaries and laughed at a couple of bad jokes, she could go home. Larry would be asleep by

now, and while it was tempting to drop by and wake him, she
wouldn't. Since this was more or less an official function, she had a car
and driver waiting downstairs, and one of the first rules in Washington
was never share anything you wanted kept secret with anybody who
had something to gain by blabbing it around. A limo driver was a prize
job in this town, as was most of the personal service domestic work.
People tended to forget that maids, waiters, drivers, and hair stylists
had ears. The smarter ones knew how to use what they heard, too.

She looked around again, saw Senator Atkinson's obese wife,
Cherie, waddling in her direction. Working parties was a major part of
politics, and usually she enjoyed it, but she was tired. She allowed herself a small sigh, then brought out her smile and shined it at Mrs.
Atkinson. Ah, well. She'd known the job was dangerous when she
took it.

"Cherie! How nice to see you."

8

What he had to do, Steve Hayes realized, was think like an eleven-year-old boy. And not just any preteener, but one who was a computer geek with a father like Jake Holcroft's gung-ho daddy. It might not be all that easy.

It had been a while since Hayes had been that age, and his background had been completely different. He'd been a child of the sixties, parents started out as straights, became hippies, became yuppies, then cycled back into New Age stuff after he'd left home. They still didn't understand how he could have gone into the military. Shoot, they didn't even understand how there could even *be* a military.

Jake Holcroft was an only child; Hayes had two younger sisters and an older brother.

Jake was into computers and Hayes had been into basketball, fishing, and hunting.

Jake's folks had split up, Hayes's parents had more or less been together for almost forty years.

He drove the issue car to the motel room he'd rented, back on the state highway just outside Sherwood. He'd spent most of the day after having the FBI show him around Jake's house snooping, trying to get a feel for the kid. He talked to teachers, classmates, people who ran the local market. Jake didn't have many friends at school, no outside activities to speak of. Somebody had swiped a bicycle the next block over about the time the FBI had busted into the Holcroft house, and the local cops found the bike racked neatly at a bus stop. The FBI theorized that Jake had stolen the vehicle. That's what they called it, a vehicle.

The bus drivers who'd made the morning runs where the bike was found didn't remember Jake, but that meant little; there were a lot of kids on the buses in the mornings. Who paid attention to one more?

The FBI techs had found a drawer lying on the floor in Jake's room. The drawer had a piece of tape on the back of it with traces of ink and paper that matched U.S. currency, so he had some money with him.

The computer techs were going through Jake's home computer but so far they had not been able to do much with it. He had protected his system with some kind of encryption program and the FBI had not been able to break it.

Hayes smiled as he pulled the car into the motel's lot and parked it in front of his room. Funny, a grammar school kid's computer being too tough for the feebs to crack. Oh, they'd get in, he didn't doubt that, if for no other reason than to prove they could, but Hayes didn't think they were going to find any deep military secrets when they did. The way he had it figured was the kid was precocious, bright, and probably bored, and he'd hacked his way into systems that interested him. Given all the *Star Trek* and *Star Wars* and other sci fi toys and posters in Jake's room, that was why he had been peeping into a SETI professor's mailbox. Big deal.

It was kind of hard for Hayes to imagine an eleven-year-old secret agent.

But his was not to reason why, just to get the job done. If the chairman of the Joint Chiefs of Staff wanted a grunt major to go out and chase little geniuses, well, that's how it would be. And on a personal level, Hayes very much wanted to accomplish his orders. A thumb up from Hightower would be a gold star express elevator for his career. A thumb down and he might as well quit now and start looking for a civilian gig. Otherwise, he'd retire the army's oldest major—if they couldn't figure out a way to get rid of him before then, and surely they could.

No, dumb as it was, he had to run this kid down and deliver him. No ifs, ands, or buts.

He got out of the car and walked to the door to his unit. So far, he didn't have much to go on. He'd checked the kid's computer stuff out with what the FBI knew. Jake had accounts at Teleport, America Online, and CompuServe that they knew about, and the FBI already had the names he'd used and copies of correspondence he had there. With the magic words "National Security" waved in their faces, it was amazing what people would give up, and there was a fairly thick file on Jake from these computer services in Hayes's briefcase. He planned to prop himself up on the bed in his room and read the file, see if he could develop a better picture of his quarry. The only way he was going to beat the FBI to this kid, assuming Jake didn't do something weird and get picked up by accident, was to learn something about the boy the feebs would overlook.

When he was a boy, Hayes had spent a lot of time with his father's father, given that his parents were constantly off to a love-in or a weekend psychedelic party. His grandfather had done the usual grandfather things, and among them, Hayes and his brother and sisters learned how to fish and hunt. The old man—he must have been all of what? forty-five?—had taught them that before you picked up a rifle or a shotgun and went out the door, you had to know as much about your quarry as possible. "Can't shoot a rabbit if you don't know what a rabbit looks like, can you? And no, they don't look like Bugs Bunny."

When Hayes bagged his first rabbit with a single-shot .22 that had been an antique when his father had learned to use it, he knew a hell of a lot about the critter's predilections—a word of which his grandfather was very fond.

If he was going to catch Jake Holcroft, he needed to know *his* predilections, too.

In the end, it hadn't been too hard to get the airline ticket thing set up. Jake went into a small travel agency with only one woman there. He told her his mother had bought tickets for a plane trip and when she went to a file drawer to look for the name he'd just made up, Jake read the access and flight codes he needed from a sheet taped to the desk right next to the reservation computer.

It was hard to believe they'd just do that, tape the code right there, but people weren't very smart when it came to stuff like this. They did it all the time.

He wrote the codes on the palm of his left hand with a ballpoint pen.

Now all he had to do was phone his way into the reservation system, find somebody who was going to pick up a ticket at the airport later today or tonight, and change the name to his. He'd get there real early and get the ticket. He would pay for it—he wasn't a crook or anything—and that would be that. Oh, sure, the guy who bought the ticket would have some hassle when he got there and they couldn't find his ticket and all, but the airlines would make good on it. The ticket clerk at the airport wouldn't know the difference, there wouldn't be any way to trace it to Jake unless they knew a lot about computers, and if they did know a lot about computers, why would they be working as a ticket clerk at an airport in the first place?

And once he got to Los Angeles, he could do it again, get himself a ride from there to somewhere else—

"I'm sorry, I can't find your mother's reservation," the woman said. "Maybe I should talk to her?"

"Uh, she's out shopping right now. I'll tell her to call you when she gets back, okay?"

The woman smiled. "Sorry."

"No problem."

Jake glanced down at the numbers and codes on the palm of his hand, smiled, and walked out.

After he'd made the switch to his phony name—it was a little hard getting through, the line was busy—he unhooked his modem and packed his computer away and went to look for a McDonald's or a Burger King. He could splurge a little on a taxi to get to the airport since he'd saved a bunch with the ticket thing. He could get a new computer magazine to read while he waited for the plane.

He'd be in Los Angeles in a few hours. He wasn't doing so terrible for a kid.

He had a bad moment when he looked up and saw a cop standing next to a cop car. He thought for sure the officer was looking right at him, but it turned out he was watching a wino stumbling along the sidewalk behind Jake. When the cop went to get the wino, Jake crossed the street in front of the bus station and headed for a BK he saw a couple of blocks away. Maybe he could get one of those neat toys from that new movie while he was there.

So far, so good.

* * *

General Hightower stared at the stack of hard-copy reports on his desk. It never seemed to get any smaller, that stack. As fast as he would go through and sign off on them, more came in to replenish the pile.

He sighed. He had had enough of desk jockeying for one morning. He was going to take an extra hour for lunch and go over to the range and burn a little powder.

"Log me out, Earl," Hightower said. "I'll be at the range for a while."

"Sir. Take your cell phone."

"Yes, Mother."

He grabbed his cell phone and hooked it onto his belt.

His car and driver were waiting and the enlisted man already knew where they were going, courtesy of Colonel Gray.

The Washington sky was overcast, threatening rain, might even have a few snowflakes mixed in, it was just about cold enough. They left the Pentagon and drove away from the city. It wasn't far.

The new underground firing range was a perk for high-rank officers who liked to prove they could still use a sidearm or shoulder weapon. Hightower returned salutes until he got to the dressing room, where he changed into issue chocolate-chip camo from his personal locker. He pulled his garrison cap down, smiled at himself in the mirror, then went out to speak to the rangemaster, an old master sergeant who'd been teaching soldiers to shoot for forty years.

"General."

"Sarge."

"What'll it be today, sir? Beretta?"

"No, I think I'll try the longarm today."

"Sir. Sign here."

While Hightower filled out the requisition form with the beat-up Bic ballpoint pen chained to the counter, the rangemaster went to unlock the racks and fetch the weapon. The M-16 was the standard army issue now, but Hightower had trained with the old M-1. He didn't think he'd ever forget the litany he'd been taught as a green enlistee: "Sir, my weapon is a nine-point-five-pound-semi-automatic-clip-fed-gas-operated-shoulder-weapon, sir!"

And add another pound for the bayonet.

He smiled. The old piece was clunky, heavy, had more of a kick than the smaller-caliber-but-more-efficient M-16, but it felt like quality when you held it; the weapon was all steel and wood, it had heft, it smelled like boiled linseed oil and issue bore cleaner, an outdoor, manly stink.

When he was training, his drill sergeant had said that if any man jack in the unit could break the forestock when executing order arms from inspection arms, it would be worth a week's liberty. Although everybody had slammed the hell out of those rifles trying, nobody had ever cracked one. Not in his squad, his platoon, his company, or the entire brigade.

And if you were stupid enough to leave your thumb in the action during inspection when you released the bolt, the M-1's spring *would* close the action hard enough to break the bone. You got no sympathy from anybody for that one.

Hightower liked to think of himself as up on the latest regarding today's technological soldier. He was privy to all the state-of-the-art research on computerized SIPE suits with their ceramic armor, personal radar, and communications gear. He knew about the high-tech experimental weaponry, from caseless carbines to plasma rifles. But an expert with a well-tuned M-1 could still knock an enemy over at six hundred meters, more on a good day, and the weapon was cheap, solid, dependable—and it didn't look like some piece of plastic crap made in some third world country.

He smiled again as the sergeant brought the M-1 to him. The rangemaster racked the bolt back to show the weapon was empty. Handed it to Hightower, who automatically inspected it. A fine piece of machinery, rifling polished bright, not a speck of dirt on the action.

He'd still rather drive a manual transmission than an automatic, too, and when he could, he used an ink pen that had to be refilled from a bottle instead of a cartridge. His wristwatch had a dial instead of a readout.

He was basically, he realized, an analog man in a digital world.

The sarge passed him a set of headphone sound suppressors and a box of hardball and clips. "Take lane sixteen, sir."

The underground range was huge compared to most indoor ranges, though small next to an outdoor shooting area. The rifle lanes were only a hundred meters long.

Hightower went to his assigned lane. He would shoot standing, kneeling, and prone. He would take his time, make his shots count.

This was about precision, not about actual combat. In a shooting war, he would be so far away from the front lines it would take half a day to get there in a fast jet. He wouldn't be wading ashore in a photo op with his ivory-handled six-shooter strapped on, smoking a pipe and peering from behind his aviator shades at the camera crews for CNN. No, he'd done his time in the field, at the tail end of Korea and in the jungles of Vietnam. Now, he was a REMF, at the top of the chain of command, lacking one, and this was as close as anybody was going to let him get to combat. Sure, he could go on inspection tours with the secretary of defense, the weasely bastard, but that was it.

Too bad. There was something to be said about slogging across a rice paddy not knowing if you were going to make it to the other side. It made you appreciate every breath you took afterward.

The chairman of the Joint Chiefs put his headphones on. He loaded a weapon that was, like him, an antique. He took a deep breath and let part of it out, brought the rifle up, left elbow under the fore-stock, right elbow out, spot-welded the sights in front of his right eye. Lined up the target.

There wasn't a gunny calling cadence—"Ready onna right! Ready onna left! Ready onna firing line! Lock and load one magazine ball ammunition and commence firing!"—but Hightower could hear the DI mentally. He smiled.

Fired.

The jolt against his shoulder was satisfying, the instant stink of burned gunpowder and vibrations of the explosion more so. He lowered the M-1, leaned over, looked through the built-in spotting scope focused on the distant target. The round had hit a hair high and right, not a bull's-eye, but still in the black. Could be better but at least it wasn't Maggie's drawers—a clean miss. Were that target a man, he'd be dead or well on the way there.

Hightower smiled again. It was always good to know his roots were still close enough that he could get back to them.

He reassumed his firing stance.

9

ess was surprised to see him at her door. But happy anyway—or so
he thought.

"Stewart! Come on in."

Well, she was smiling. That was a good sign.

He ambled into her small apartment. As usual, there were dirty
clothes piled up outside the bathroom, pizza boxes stacked on the
kitchen table, books, magazines, and newspapers scattered everywhere
else. Jess was gorgeous and could make an old pair of jeans and T-shirt
look like high fashion, but she was pretty much a slob when it came to
housekeeping. Her roommate, Linda, was just as bad, one of the reasons
the two women got along so well together. Stewart knew he'd go nuts if
his place looked like this. It greatly disturbed his sense of order. Things
had a place and they ought to be there when they weren't being used.

"What's up, Stew?"

He pulled his thoughts away from the rat's nest in which Jess lived
and back to why he'd come to see her.

"Uh, well, you know those messages we got at the SETI shack?"

"Yes? You want a Coke or something?"

"No, thanks." They moved to the couch and he watched as Jess
shoved a heap of jackets and wadded-up shirts off onto the floor. "Have
a seat."

"Uh, well, anyway, something screwy is going on."

He sat, she sat next to him, leaned over and kissed him. "Go on."

He told her about the call from Karagigian, the theory he'd developed, the two men who'd showed up at the shack.

"So, what are you saying? The messages are real and the feds are trying to cover them up?"

He sighed. "It sounds kind of strange, but I guess that's what I'm saying."

"Maybe not so strange. Our government has a pretty long history of lying to the people who put them in office. Radiation experiments, biowarfare tests—remember that bacteria thing the navy did in San Francisco Bay in the fifties? Not to mention the way-out stuff like UFOs and presidential assassinations. Historically, the government tends to tell us what they think we can handle and they sit on the rest."

That sounded like Jess's history professor talking, but he couldn't argue with the statement.

Plus, Jess was not much of a fan of the federal government. One of her uncles had been an undersecretary of something or other in the sixties and he'd told his family some very interesting stories. There were still secret bases in the desert you couldn't even mention by name officially.

"So, what are you going to do?"

He shook his head. "I'm not sure. I mean, I want to know if the message is real." He patted his coat pocket. "I downloaded a copy of it, I thought I might take a crack at translating it."

"Can you do it?"

"I don't know that for sure, either, but if it is a message from an intelligent race, there ought to be some basis for communication. The code might be a simple binary. It'd be the language difference that would be the main problem, but there are bound to be things both species would be likely to know we could use for translation."

"Such as?"

"Science. Some of our early space probes like *Pioneer* and *Voyager* had gold-plated pictures or copper audio records on them. Greetings in a bunch of languages, stuff like that. One I remember—I think it was *Pioneer 10*—had drawings of a man and woman, a hydrogen atom, a schematic of our solar system showing which planet we live on. Plus a bunch of pulsars and their frequency and a kind of map that showed how far away we were from the center of the galaxy. Had a picture of the craft on it to give the human figures scale. I think Carl Sagan's wife or somebody drew it. Somebody else joked about sending out a record of Bach's work—said if aliens heard that, they'd think we were bragging."

"You know, that doesn't sound too bright. What if some bug-eyed monsters who want to toast us over a fire find a map showing them right where the treats are?"

"You read too much science fiction," he said. "Anybody smart enough to *get* here is not going to need to swipe our water or eat us for lunch, they'll have technology that would take care of all that and a whole bunch more."

"Yeah, maybe. But what if they are *really* alien compared to us?" she asked. "I mean, they can't see what we see, hear what we hear? Don't think like we think?"

"That's possible. But if they use radio and can send messages, there's something we have in common."

"I suppose that makes sense."

"And I guess maybe I should go and talk to Professor Karagigian, too," he said. He smiled at her. "Thanks, Jess."

"For what? I didn't do anything."

"Yeah, you did. You were here. You listened." He paused a second, then said, "Look, can I ask you a favor?"

"Sure."

"Can I dump a copy of the file into your computer? Just in case something happens to mine?"

"Sure."

He had to move a grease-soaked brown paper bag of dried Chinese food containers to get to Jess's zip drive, a piece of hardware he'd insisted she get. He inserted the disk, copied the contents into a folder marked "Misc," and ejected the disk. "You really ought to avoid putting junk like this next to your system," he said. He waved at the garbage.

"Yeah, yeah," she said.

"Okay, look, don't tell anybody I put this here, okay?"

"What, you think the FBI is going to knock on my door?" She laughed.

"They might."

When she saw he wasn't smiling, her own grin faded. "Wow. This has really got you spooked, hasn't it?"

"Well, maybe not 'spooked.' But real curious. I'm going to go see Karagigian and see what he has to say."

"Be careful, boy genius."

"You know it. Thanks again, Jess."

She leaned over and kissed him. Put a little more into it than usual. He was tempted to forget all this paranoid crap and get more serious about Jess, but she broke the embrace. "Gotta run," she said. "I'm supposed to meet Linda in the library in about ten minutes."

"I'll walk you over," he said.

"Thanks."

Dr. Karagigian—he had a first name, it was Bruce, but Stewart had never heard anybody actually call him that—was in his office, looking harried as usual. Karagigian was somewhere west of sixty, of average height, had thinning gray hair and a neatly trimmed Van Dyke beard and mustache under pale blue eyes that always looked a little puzzled about something. He wore a suit that was new thirty years ago and was visibly well-worn at the elbows and probably the seat of the pants.

"Ah, Mr. Davies. Come in."

The windowless office looked as if it was constructed of books. There were shelves on all the walls packed thick with volumes, with more jammed between the overfull cases and more still stacked on the floors, desk, chairs, and pretty much everything but Karagigian himself. Propped on yet more books was the professor's laptop computer, this being connected to a twisted mass of dock, modem, fax, and printer cables. It might be portable in theory, but this computer never went anywhere. Might as well have a full-sized one.

"To what do I owe the honor of this visit?"

"Well, sir, it's about those messages I logged in."

"What? Oh, those. I thought I explained that. A prank, a hoax, the FCC is going to take care of the perpetrators."

The man was a lousy liar. He wouldn't look at Stewart and he waved his hands about as if doing so would make both his student and the question he raised somehow vanish.

"Excuse me, sir, but—bullshit."

Karagigian blinked several times, as if unable to understand the final word in Stewart's statement.

"I beg your pardon?"

"I don't believe you, sir. I can't imagine the FCC would call you in the middle of the night, and even if they would, how they would know to do so. I went to the shack to check and the messages had been deleted. We've never done that before, even when we knew they were hoaxes. What is going on, Dr. Karagigian?"

The professor sighed and shook his head. "You don't want to know, Stewart."

"Yes, sir, I do want to know."

"No, you don't. You want to turn around and go back about your business and pretend you believe what I told you about those messages."

Stewart looked blank.

"You may not be aware of it, but I was once . . . involved in certain governmental projects of a . . . secretive nature. I had a security clearance and a certain measure of trust. Which is why I'm still sitting here and you are still standing there. If I had not achieved this clearance and trust, Stewart, I would not have been able to convince certain people to leave us alone."

"Sir?"

"If those messages you recorded had been real, and if I had not had certain influence, you and I and anybody who knew about them on this campus would be . . . guests of our government at this moment, do you understand what that means?"

Stewart swallowed dryly. He nodded. Yeah, he understood what that meant. He said, "SETI and CETI protocols have been superseded by national security."

"Precisely. It is an unpleasant situation, one about which I am most unhappy, but one about which I also have no choice. Were I simply a musty old professor, I might be railing and prattling on about academic freedoms, but since I once worked for certain agencies, I can tell you that this is the way of the world. These people have a very large hammer, Stewart, and if you irritate them, they will use it on you."

"I understand."

"Good. Now, run along. I have a thesis to finish reading. We'll speak of this later. At a more propitious time."

Stewart swallowed another mouthful of sun- and wind-dried desert sand. "Yes, sir."

As he left the office, he saw the two men in suits coming down the hall.

Jesus. *Now* he was spooked.

10

Laurie Sherman sat in the back seat of the limo on her way to meet Melanie Fawcett, the president's press secretary, at a luncheon for Women in Televised Communications. Traffic was stop and go and she was going to be a few minutes late, so she was already reaching for her purse to call Fawcett when the unlisted cell phone she had in her purse—one of two she carried, both tiny Motorola units that weighed no more than couple of ounces each—cheeped. Sherman knew which one it was by the sound. One cheeped and the other one buzzed. Only three people had the number to the cheeper. She dug the phone out.

"Hello?"

"Hello."

She recognized the voice. Larry.

"Yes?"

"When you get to a land line, please call me."

"I see. Should I hurry?"

"It's not an emergency."

He broke the connection. She stared at the tiny phone for a second before she tapped the code for Melanie. You didn't say anything over a cell phone you weren't prepared to hear blabbed all over the evening news. Anybody with a scanner and an IQ equal to his belt size could listen to such calls, it was like tuning into talk radio. People tended to forget that.

So. Larry wanted to speak to her. Could be business, could be personal, and buried somewhere in her purse was a small device she could hook to a phone to scramble her speech when she was away from home or the office. Larry's phone would be likewise secured and that conversation would be private. Anybody who happened to pick up the cell call they'd just had wouldn't get much from it. No names, no places, no nothing: Hi. Call me.

Let's see Dan Rather make something out of *that*.

What, she wondered, did Larry want?

"Melanie Fawcett," came the bright alto voice from Sherman's phone.

"Hi, Melanie, it's Laurie. I'm stuck in traffic here and crawling. Looks like I'm still ten minutes out."

"'salright," Melanie said, "I'll try to hold 'em at bay until you get here."

"I appreciate it."

"I love this town. A paper bag blows across the street and every car on the road slows down to look at it. It's as bad as L.A."

Laurie laughed. "Ain't it the truth? Almost as bad as L.A. See you in a few minutes, kiddo."

She disconnected and closed the little phone, dropped it into her purse. A few years ago if somebody had told her she'd be carrying a pair of cell phones in her purse and having conversations with the chairman of the Joint Chiefs of Staff and the president's press secretary in the space of a minute, she'd have laughed at them.

Not even to mention *sleeping* with the four-star general.

She smiled. Life certainly was interesting.

On the plane to Los Angeles, Jake read half a dozen comic books.

Once on the ground there, he wandered around a couple of the different terminals while waiting for a Delta flight to New Orleans. They had a pretty neat people mover, a big slidewalk conveyer.

He hadn't intended to go to New Orleans in particular, but when he saw the reservation, he decided what the heck, might as well. Plus it was cheaper than the jet to St. Louis, even though it was farther away. Weird.

The flight to New Orleans was half empty, a big L10-11. They gave him a set of complimentary headphones and he watched the in-flight movie, the one with Arnold and Sly both in it. What a great movie. He'd already seen it in the theater, it was better on the big screen, but it was still pretty good. The computer special effects were really terrific, all kinds of morphing and composite shots. Someday he'd like to maybe do that kind of work.

The flight attendant came by to check on him a couple of times, asked him if he was okay, if he needed anything, and he told her he was twelve and that his uncle was meeting him at the plane. If you were a kid under twelve, they kept track of you, made sure some pervo didn't grab you, and Jake didn't want them keeping that close an eye on him.

When he got to the airport in New Orleans, he ate some dinner, fried shrimp and potatoes, then took a nap for a couple of hours in the United Airlines area. He found a bathroom, cleaned up, bought a new sweatsuit and some more comics in the gift shop. They might be looking for him but probably they weren't looking for a kid wearing a Tulane sweatshirt. The air sure smelled funny here, kind of damp and swampy.

Nobody bothered him. Thing was, nobody paid much attention to a kid in an airport. They all figured he was waiting for a plane, which he actually was. He had to wait until morning to catch a plane to New York, and he slept across three chairs. Woke up kind of stiff, went to the bathroom again, went to his gate for the flight to New York an hour early.

Once he got there, the plan was to get a bus to Secaucus. With any luck, he'd find his mother pretty quick. After that . . . well, he hadn't even bothered to think about after that. His mom would be happy to see him, he'd be happy to see her, and the old man would be in jail.

What could be better?

Hightower leaned back in his chair. "Go ahead, Captain."

The captain, a marine attached to Naval Intelligence, cleared his throat nervously. "Sir. The actual construction of the message appears to be a simple compressed-binary hex code, as far as we can tell. It is fairly dense, so we think there is possibly some visual information as well as written material, unless they are just real long-winded. However, the alphabet—if that's what it is—does not correspond to any known language. It's like somebody sent you a letter in Chinese.

You can decode it enough to see the actual symbols, but not know what they stand for."

The captain nodded at the fat folder on Hightower's desk. It was as thick as the Washington, D.C., phone book. The general opened the folder and looked at the first page. "Looks like some kind of hieroglyphics."

"Yes, sir, we think the language is pictorial, and our translators are working on repeating symbols and such. What we're hoping to find is a key. We think that an intelligent race attempting to communicate would realize the language difference and put some kind of a dictionary into the document."

Hightower looked at the first sheet of symbols. An alien language. Amazing. He said, "You don't believe this is a hoax, do you, Captain?"

"No, sir. Not unless the perpetrator is a stone genius. This is too complex to be a prank. In my opinion, sir."

"Continue. You were speaking about a key."

"Sir. It would make sense to have a key rigged to something we could find fairly easy, and have it based on something that would be the same there as here."

"Which would be . . . ?"

"Numbers, maybe. The value of pi, the periodic table of the elements, a particular frequency in the radio spectrum. They'd know if we could pick up the message, we'd have to know about radio."

"Makes sense."

"We'll break it eventually, even without a key, but that might take longer."

"How long?"

"No way to tell, sir."

Hightower nodded. "All right. Is there anything I can do to make things go faster or easier?"

"Sir, a priority status for use of the super-Cray at Livermore would likely expedite matters."

"Tell Colonel Gray who to call on your way out, Captain. You'll get your time."

After the marine was gone, Hightower flipped through the thick document. Amazing.

What are you trying to tell us?

* * *

The first thing that Stewart realized when he started playing with the message was that it was compressed and therefore a lot bigger than it seemed to be at first glance. It was going to fill up half his two-gig drive when expanded, if it was what he thought it was, a binary code. He barely had enough room.

He backed up everything else on his system, saved it all to zip disks in case this huge file somehow trashed and crashed his computer. Then he started trying to get into it.

When Stewart's father, Brian, had been a kid, Stewart's grand-mother had sent him to the store for something. On the way there, the boy—he was about eight—had seen a yo-yo contest being held next to a 7-Eleven or somesuch. His father had wandered over to watch, and while he'd never played with one of the little stringed toys, somebody loaned him one. The yo-yo man would show him the trick, then Brian would duplicate it.

Without any previous experience, Brian won the contest.

It was, Stewart's father told him, like some kind of magic.

Six years later, Brian Davies and his yo-yo won a trip to Florida, and once there, a ten-thousand-dollar college scholarship in the national yo-yo finals. It had been his gift, his father had told him, the one thing in his life at which he was ever a natural.

Stewart understood the story, for Stewart's trick was playing with computers. Once he put his hands on a keyboard and began tapping his way into cyberspace, he was in his element. He could think with his fingers, delve into the most complex of programs almost as if by instinct. As if it was some kind of magic.

When it came to this, Stewart was a natural.

Thus it was that he wasn't too surprised when he discovered the key to the pictographic language. It practically jumped up and bit him. There was a number sequence, right there—1, 1, 2, 3, 5, 8, 13, 21, 34, 55.

A Fibonacci sequence.

Steward blinked. Could it be that easy? In Fibonacci numbers, each term was the sum of the two terms immediately preceding it. One plus one is two, two plus one is three, three plus two is five . . .

Of course, if you were trying to talk to an alien, you'd want some-thing simple, wouldn't you?

What the hell. It couldn't hurt to try it.

He did. It didn't work.

Damn.

But the Fibonacci progression was there. Maybe it led to something else?

He fiddled with it. Twisted it. Ran it backward. Tried everything he could think of, and still couldn't get it.

Then a thought occurred to him. What if it was a double sequence? One nested inside of another? He built a grid and laid it out.

Nope.

A *triple* sequence?

He began plugging it in . . .

Yes! There it was.

Things started happening. It took a few hours for him to get to the point where he was pretty sure he had something.

A dictionary.

Man.

PART TWO

WE ARE NOT ALONE

11

A lot of people wore their hair short these days, so if you dressed in faded jeans and a T-shirt with an old leather jacket, they didn't automatically peg you as a cop or as being in the military. And if you didn't have a lot of tattoos or piercings, they might not think you were a skinhead Nazi. Whenever he could, Hayes preferred to keep a low profile. He'd bypassed getting a government vehicle this time and rented a standard small car, a Geo, from Alamo. Not a muscle car anybody was apt to remember.

He drove the gutless piece of crap from Kennedy to New Jersey, where he had figured out his quarry was heading. It was a pretty good bet Jake was looking for his mother.

The boy's paternal grandparents were both dead, his mother's mother lived in England, and his grandfather on that side hadn't been part of the family for thirty years. It was natural he'd go looking for the mother who ran away and was hiding from her abusive husband.

It hadn't been that hard to run it down this far, even though the kid had done all right for somebody his age, without any training. He didn't have the advantages Hayes had. That National Security crowbar had been heavy enough to pry loose computer records from the major airline, once Hayes had a name.

That had been the easy part, the name. He'd gotten that lying on the motel bed back in Oregon.

It seemed that the kid did some business online. Put out some shareware. Once Hayes had that name and the EZ Mail address that went with it, it was easy enough to run down.

The owner of the mail and package shop told him that Jake got a fair amount of mail from all over the country. So he probably had money.

A government brick through the banking window locally found out that indeed, Jake had more spending cash than most kids his age. Clever of him to use a made-up name to get a card so he could get his money out without having to face a teller. And to hide it from his father.

Most of the bus lines didn't require a name to buy a ticket, or any ID if they did, but airlines were a different story.

And while it had taken a couple of days to strain all the train and airline records, he'd found the name. Kid was really sharp, he'd swapped his name for already-bought tickets, they'd had to crunch the lists the long way to spot it.

He'd gone to Los Angeles, then to New Orleans, then to New York. It stood to reason he was going to find his mother, and once Hayes had it narrowed down to the area around New York—Jake didn't fly out of Kennedy, so he must have taken a cab or bus from there—then he could plug in the information on the mother.

Since the woman was running from her husband, she'd probably be using a phony name. Hayes went through her history, background, family, schools, everything they could find out about her. Nothing led to this area, save one item: One of Mrs. Mary Long Holcroft's college roommates, a woman named Nelda Baumgardner, lived in Secaucus, New Jersey.

Not much, but at least it was a place to start.

As he drove along the turnpike, Hayes once again reflected on the idiocy of this quest. The problem with the military machine was that while it ground very fine, it ground slowly, not to mention that the chain of command was only as bright as the dumbest link in it. By the time he ran this kid down—assuming he managed it—the reason might be long moot. But you didn't get promoted and assigned some-where sexy if you mentioned that to the wrong people.

A big truck blew past him doing seventy and the wind from its passage nearly knocked the Geo off the highway. Jesus.

So, he'd go to Secaucus, find the roommate, and check her out. See if somebody who looked like the pictures he'd borrowed from Jake's room was around. He was willing to bet that if she was, the boy would show up eventually.

In his apartment, Stewart stared at the computer screen, astounded. It was a message from an alien. He—she—it? was on a spaceship already inside the solar system, and if he-she-it could be believed, would be here inside six months. On Earth.

An alien!

Once the language was laid out, complete with video and still images to demonstrate exactly what the dictionary meant, it had been pretty easy. Stewart built a program to translate, based on the images and words in the message. Foreign language wasn't his greatest strength, but with all the computer translators, it didn't have to be. Plus, whoever had built the message code had thoughtfully provided an alphabet, numbers up to a million, and spaces for equivalent words. Thus when a picture of a ball appeared with the alien word for it, there was a place for the English—or whichever language—right next to it. All you had to do was plug in enough material and the program had something to work with. He'd spent all night and most of the next day matching alien words as best he could. Some of it was probably wrong—a ball might be an orange or something—but enough of it was right so he could understand the basics.

And with those basics, there was a request to answer the message.

Man.

His SETI shack didn't have anything that went the other way like a CETI unit did, but Stewart knew a couple of guys who were deep into radio, two-meter and ham operators. If he wanted to, he could call the alien—seemed to be named Zeerus, if Stewart had gotten the alphabet right—and communicate with him directly.

A pretty big responsibility. And maybe somebody else had already beaten him to it—but was he going to call?

Bet your ass he was.

He was still staring at the screen when there came a knock at his door.

Huh. Wonder who that was?

When he looked through the peephole, Stewart felt the pit of his stomach go cold, as if he'd suddenly swallowed a quart of liquid nitrogen.

It was the two guys in suits.

Oh, crap!

Maybe he was paranoid, but he had a bad feeling about them. He ran back to his computer, popped the zip disk. Went to the window and looked out. His apartment was on the second floor and there didn't seem to be anybody around. He opened the window, dropped the disk into the azalea or whatever-they-were bushes below, then he hurried back to his computer and dragged the message file onto his Crematorium icon.

You sure you want to do this? the screen asked him.

No, but do it anyway. He tapped the command.

The drive started to whir. Crematorium was a nifty little utility program that permanently erased files. Unlike a simple delete, it overwrote the file, including the name. Once you cremated something, it was gone forever. Didn't matter how good you were, there was nothing left to pull up but a big chunk of zeroes.

That started, Stewart went back to the door.

"Yes?"

"Stewart Davies? FBI. I'm Special Agent Boyle, this is Special Agent Zito." The two men held up badge cases with their left hands. "We need to talk to you."

Up close, they looked just like you'd expect FBI agents to look. Clean-cut, kind of military, all hard stares.

"Sure. Come on in. What's it about?" Stewart raised his eyebrows, the picture of innocence. He had nothing to hide. At least nothing they could find *now*.

"You are employed part-time by Professor Bruce Karagigian as a research assistant on the SETIscope program, is that right?" Zito said.

"Yes, sir. I watch the board a few nights a week."

"It is our understanding that you use the computer system there to work on a game." That from Boyle.

Stewart tried to look puzzled. That wasn't very hard to do. "Yeah. So? It's not like anybody else is using the station at two in the morning, and I pay for my own backup disks. That's not a federal crime, is it?"

They ignored his response. "We understand too that you recently downloaded some material from the university computer at the SETI lab. Would you mind if we took a look at that material?" Zito again. Taking turns.

"No, I wouldn't mind. What's going on?"

"We're not at liberty to say at this juncture," Boyle said.

"Okay. In here."

He led the two agents to his computer. Crematorium was done, the file was vaporized. He picked up his box of zip disks, took his game backup out, held it up.

"Would you mind?" Zito said, nodding at the computer.

"No, go ahead."

Zito sat, popped the disk into the drive, waited a beat, and began punching keys. Knew what he was doing. That made sense. If they were going to send feds out to poke around computer systems, it would be smart to send one who could at least point and click.

Boyle drew his attention away, saying, "I understand you are a graduate student."

Stewart nodded. These guys sure "understood" a lot of things. Peripherally, he was able to see that Zito was running through the hard drive, getting a list of everything in the disk.

"That's right."

Stewart let Boyle divert him. There wasn't anything in his system to cause him any grief. Good thing, too. If these guys opened up a file marked "OmniQue" and found a decoded message from an alien in a spaceship heading for Earth, Stewart had an idea he'd be in some very deep shit.

When the last speech was done on the final day of the Women in Televised Communications meeting, a very informative piece on personal grooming, Laurie found a pay phone bank and called Larry. She slipped the little mouthpiece thing over the receiver and looked around to make sure nobody was close enough to eavesdrop on her.

"Yes?"

"Hi. It's me."

"Ah."

"What's up?"

"Our people are making progress on that SETI thing. It definitely is a message."

"Do you know what it says?"

"Not yet. Soon as we do, I'll need to talk to your boss."

"No problem." She looked around. Nobody nearby, except a short and swarthy man in a coverall cleaning the frame on a large painting at the other end of the phone cul-de-sac, and he was far enough away so he couldn't hear her conversation. "So, how's your personal schedule look?"

"Full afternoon. Then I talk to a group of aerospace industry people at an early dinner. Should be through by eight or nine."

"How about I meet you at your place at around ten?" she said.

"Best news I've heard all day," he said. He sighed.

"Something?" she said.

"The usual snafu. Every day it seems my job is less and less like a military officer and more and more like the CEO of a major corporation, crossbred with a career politician. Sometimes you just want to grab some of these people and shake the stupidity out of them."

"That might be a chore."

"Amen to that," he said. "I've got to go. I'll see you tonight."

"I am looking forward to it," she said.

Laurie removed the scrambler and dropped it into her purse. She cradled the receiver. Glanced at the picture cleaner. Let out a little sigh of her own. She understood how Larry felt. There were times when she wished she had a job like that little dark man dusting the painting there. It might be hard work but it was probably cut-and-dried. Clock in, get your gear, clean this and that, clock out, go home. Honest work, useful, nothing complicated about it. Not like the dirty infighting you did every day in national-class politics.

It started to rain before the two FBI men left. They seemed satisfied that the game disk they'd checked was okay. Stewart guessed that if they weren't, they'd be back with a warrant to download his files, but he wasn't worried about that.

After the feds were gone and he could breathe normally again, he looked out of his window. Didn't see them. He eased down the stairs, went outside, under the roof overhang. The rain was coming down pretty good. He slipped along the side of the house to where he'd dropped the zip disk.

There it was. In a deep puddle of runoff water from the broken downspout. Damn!

Stewart picked the disk up. Maybe if he dried it off real good, it would be okay.

But an hour later, when he tried it, his computer told him it couldn't read the zip disk. Damn, damn! Now the only place he could get the message to reconstruct it would be Jess's. And he needed to do that pretty quick—otherwise, somebody was going to figure it out and get a call in to Zeerus before Stewart could. He didn't want that.

He called but there was no answer at Jess's. He got her machine. He didn't leave a message. He'd go and find her.

12

His mother had cut her hair short, changed the color, and lost weight since he'd seen her. She wore a black skirt and a white blouse and no shoes. When she opened the door and saw him there, Jake had a sudden pit-of-the-stomach sensation like something was alive in his belly, trying to get out. His greatest worry surfaced: What if she didn't want to see him?

"Jake!"

His mother grabbed and hugged him and everything was right in the world. She was happy to see him. He thought she would be, but you never could be sure of anything.

She looked around, to see if Jake's father was around, and he quickly said, "He doesn't know where I am. And he's either in jail or dead."

"You don't know how glad I am to see you," she said.

Inside, Jake met her mother's friend, Ms. Baumgardner, a tall, thin woman with black hair and thick eyebrows. She went to get Jake some hot chocolate while he sat on the couch with his mother.

"Tell me what happened," she said.

He told her. He didn't know exactly what had become of his father. He'd looked for a report about it in the paper while he was waiting at the airport in New Orleans but there hadn't been any stories about the FBI in a shootout in Oregon. Either way, Seth Holcroft wouldn't be bothering them here.

Jake's timing, his mother told him, was perfect. She had a job, was about to get her own apartment, and had been trying to think of a way to contact him so Seth wouldn't know about it. Just perfect.

They had a whole day together.

Then, early the next morning, somebody knocked on the door.

Jake felt cold all over, like the time he'd fallen through the ice on the duck pond near his house. He knew, *knew* the knock was trouble.

He still had his can of pepper spray, he carried it everywhere since he'd run away. There was so little metal in the container it never triggered the detectors in the airports. He reached into his pocket, pulled the container out, kept it by his leg. It was only about as big around as a hot dog and maybe half as long. He slid his thumb under the safety spring cover and onto the spray button.

Jake's mother opened the door.

"Yes?"

There was a tall, short-haired man wearing a leather jacket standing there. He saw Jake and grinned. He pulled a thin wallet from his jacket and Jake knew, too, this was some kind of fed.

"Morning, ma'am, I'm Major Steve Hayes, National Security Agency. I wonder if I might have a word with your son, Jake?"

Jake had already started forward. When he was right behind his mother, he smiled at the man, lifted his pepper sprayer slowly, so as not to startle him with a sudden move, just like his father had taught him.

The short-haired man blinked and looked puzzled, but by the time he figured it out, it was too late.

Jake pressed the button and squirted the red stream right into the fed's eyes, waved it back and forth to be sure to get them both.

The man lurched backward, grabbed his eyes, and screamed: "Shit!"

Jake's mother also screamed but Jake was already past her and the blinded guy stumbling into the wall. It had been too good to last.

They'd found him. Now what was he going to do?

By the time Hayes got the swelling in his eyelids down enough to see, with help from Mary Holcroft and a lot of cold water and ice, his quarry was gone.

Damn!

This was not going to look good on a report, a prepube kid hosing a trained military man with pepper Mace and hauling ass. Unless he caught the boy quickly, maybe he wouldn't put that part in at all.

"Do you have any idea of where he might go?" Hayes asked Jake's mother.

She shook her head. "No. I don't know how he managed to get this far on his own. He's very resourceful."

"Yeah, I noticed. It is imperative we talk to him. He's not going to be put in jail or anything, it's just that he overheard something he shouldn't have—I am not at liberty to say exactly what—"

"You mean about the aliens?"

Hayes stared at her. "He told you?"

"Yes. And about his father and the FBI. I hope nobody was hurt."

"The FBI man wore a vest. He took two shots on it. He got bruised, that's all. Mr. Holcroft sustained a minor wound to his arm."

"The agent was lucky," she said. "My husband is an expert with firearms. His third shot would have been to the head."

"Listen, Mrs. Holcroft, here is my card. That cell number is good anywhere. If Jake comes back or contacts you, please have him call me. I just want to talk to him."

That wasn't strictly true about Jake, but it wouldn't be smart to tell her to tell her son they were going to grab him and haul him away until all this spaceman stuff got sorted out. "It is a matter of national security."

"This alien thing is real?"

"I'm not at liberty to talk about it. And you probably ought to keep that talk to yourself. Please, have your son call me when he contacts you."

Hayes left the apartment, considered his next move. He could call the local police and put out a bulletin on Jake, that would be his best bet. Of course, an eleven-year-old federal fugitive might raise a few eyebrows, but to hell with that. The boy couldn't have gotten far yet. And Hayes was willing to bet his pension that Jake wouldn't use the same name if he took to interstate public transportation again. He was a bright kid, he'd figure out how he'd been traced.

When Hayes emerged from the building and started toward his car, his eyes were still blurry. Maybe that's why he was slow reacting when a man with a handgun stepped out of the bushes twenty feet away from him. Hayes had time—seemed like hours went past in that brief moment—to notice that the man wore black and had a bandage wrapped around one arm. He'd seen the face somewhere before, and recently, too.

Hayes reached for his revolver on his right hip and dodged to his left at the same time.

He stepped on a wet patch on the walk and skidded, lost his balance. Fell.

It saved his life, that slip. His vision tunneled. All he could see was Holcroft and that pistol, it was as if the rest of the world went gray and fuzzy. He saw the muzzle flash from Holcroft's .45, felt a slight tug at his right side, though he couldn't remember hearing the shot. He was falling in slow motion, it was as if time had thickened to a crawl. He might have yelled but he wasn't sure. He saw Holcroft turn and sprint away, moving oh so slowly, a man running in a dream.

Hayes hit the ground hard, did a clumsy shoulder roll, over and to his feet into a wide-legged isosceles squat. Time accelerated, resumed its normal pace. He pulled his Smith & Wesson, brought it up . . .

Holcroft—it had to be him, he'd seen the mugshot and the pictures in the house—Holcroft was gone.

Hayes stood and took deep breaths, blew out the carbon dioxide, tried to steady himself. The bullet had creased his side, torn his shirt, and burned a long blister next to his ribs without even breaking the skin. There was a hole in the back of his leather jacket he could put his thumb through.

Jesus. It didn't get any closer than that.

When he could breathe more or less normally again, he holstered his weapon. He saw a few faces at windows looking at him. He reached for his cell phone.

The battery was dead. Shit! Probably somebody would call the cops to report the shooting, it was a good enough neighborhood such things probably didn't happen every day.

He'd better go back and tell Mrs. Holcroft she needed to find another place to stay—unless she wanted to talk to her husband.

Jess said, "Are you sure?"

Stewart answered. "Pretty sure. If it's a hoax, it's one put together by a genius."

He tapped away at her computer, redoing the dictionary he'd had to trash when the FBI showed up at his place. It was a lot easier since he knew what to do this time, but it still took a while.

He knew he'd gotten lost in it when Jess offered him a fresh piece of hot pizza and a Coke and he didn't remember her leaving to go out for it.

"What time is it?" he asked, blinking his way up from the computer trance.

"About two in the morning."

"Man, how'd it get to be so late?"

"You've been working there for eight hours. How's it going?"

"I've got most of it back," he said.

"Take a break. Eat. Drink. Pee."

"Um. Yeah. Though not in that order."

When he came back from the bathroom, Jess was staring at the computer. He picked up a piece of pizza and bit into it.

"So this is the sender, this . . . Zero person?"

"Zeerus. And if person is the right word, yeah."

"What are you going to do?"

"Well, my first thought was to go talk to some guys I know who have access to some pretty sophisticated radio transceivers."

"You were going to call him back?"

"Yeah."

"But not now?"

"Well, maybe. I was thinking I'd go talk to Dr. Karagigian first." He explained about the earlier conversation he and the professor'd had, and the FBI agents snooping around.

"So Karagigian thinks this is real," she said.

"From what he said, that's what I think."

"You aren't worried he might just pick up the phone and turn you in?"

"The thought had crossed my mind, but—no. I think he's too good a scientist to pass this up. I'd also bet big bucks if I had 'em that he's got a copy of the message somewhere and has been working on it. The feds surely do, whether they got it from us or somebody else or from one of their stations. And the code is pretty simple, so if we don't get on it pretty quick, somebody is gonna beat us to it."

"Do you feel qualified to do this, Stew? Be the representative of humanity for first contact with an alien?"

He sighed. "Maybe not. But then again, maybe so. Anybody smart enough to figure out the message can make the return call. Why shouldn't it be me? It's not like I'm gonna sell this Zeerus Manhattan Island for some beads or like that. I don't have to talk policy with him. It can just, you know, be a friendly visit."

She laughed. "Right. Say, alien-from-another-world, how's the weather? Read any good books lately?"

"C'mon, Jess, you know what I mean."

"I think so, Stew, but I don't know if it's a good idea. You could get into a lot of trouble if they find out."

"I'm already in a lot of trouble if they find out. Might as well get the glory before I get busted."

"You're crazy, you know that?"

He grinned at her. "People have told me that, yeah."

"Okay. Let's do it."

" 'Let's'? As in, 'Let *us*'? I dunno, Jess—"

"Excuse me, but isn't this *my* computer with the outer space message from Zorro up there clogging up the hard drive?"

"Yeah, but—"

" 'But' nothing, Stewart Davies."

Uh oh. She'd used his first and last names. A bad sign. "Okay, okay. Let's go talk to Dr. Karagigian."

13

Colonel Calvin from Cryptography on line niner-zero," Colonel Gray said.

General Hightower nodded. "I'll take it." He reached for the phone.

"Colonel Calvin? You have something for me?"

"Sir. We've got a preliminary on that item."

"And . . . ?"

There was a pause.

"This line is as secure as MI can make it, Colonel. Using electronic codes your unit devised, I am given to understand."

"Sir. It seems the item is a multimedia message. It purports to be from an alien being en route to Earth on a starship. Sir."

Hightower felt his pulse all over his body. For a second, he wondered if he might be having a heart attack. Yes! It *was* an alien!

"Purports to be," he said.

Calvin said, "Sir. It includes within it a rather extensive words-to-pictures dictionary which our translators were able to use to decode the text and images of the message proper. This dictionary is not in any known language. It looks something like Egyptian hieroglyphics, Farsi, and Sanskrit, but it is none of these. If it is a hoax, it is a well-developed one. Sir."

"You are understandably cautious, Colonel, and I appreciate that. But give me the bottom line, man to man, no rank. Do *you* think it is legitimate?"

There came another pause, longer than before. "Yes, sir. I believe what we have here is first contact from an alien species."

Yes!

"And what does it say?"

"It says his name is Zeerus and that he is coming to visit. It asks for a reply."

Hightower realized he was holding his breath. He blew it out. "Good work, Colonel. If this turns out to be real, you might want to dust off those brigadier stars you've probably got stashed somewhere. You'll need them soon."

"Yes, *sir!*"

Hightower glanced at his watch. "I want a hard-copy file of everything you've got on my desk by 1530."

"Yes, sir."

Hightower cradled the phone. He needed to go over it, of course, but he might as well set up his appointment with the president now. This wasn't something that could wait.

He reached for the phone, tapped in Laurie's private number. He grinned as he thought about what the expression on the secretary of defense's face might be when he heard the news.

"I've got your cookbook right here, asshole."

"Sir?" Colonel Gray said from the outer office.

"Nothing, Earl. Carry on."

Karagigian looked up from his computer at Stewart and Jess. "This is amazing work, Mr. Davies."

"You think it is real?" Jess said.

"I do," the professor said. "And I think the federal dinosaur believes so, as well. Else why would they be trying so hard to stamp it flat? Incredible. First human contact with an alien species!"

"Well, not quite," Stewart said.

"Excuse me?"

"He–it–whatever, has contacted us, but we haven't called him back. He's asked for a reply."

Karagigian looked at Stewart sharply. "Are you proposing that we do that, Mr. Davies?"

"Yes, sir, I am. Somebody is going to. Wouldn't you like it to be us?"

"Oh, my, yes. But I don't know about this. The government will doubtless take a dim view of such an activity."

"Let them. We won't have broken any laws, will we? There's no rule against answering a radio message, is there?"

"Not as such, no. But there are treason statutes—"

"We won't be giving any military secrets away, not offering comfort to our enemies. Nobody has told us *not* to call him, have they? We'll just say hello. What's the harm in that?"

"You're a devious young man. This isn't one of your computer games, Mr. Davies."

"No, sir, I'm aware of that."

Dr. Karagigian chewed at his lip for a moment, fiddled with his short beard. Grinned.

Aha. Stewart had him.

"I know a post-doc research fellow in the CETI lab at Harvard," Karagigian said. "He's got a transmitter capable of reaching that far. We'll have to take the train up, are you prepared to do that?"

"Yes, sir, I'd walk to get a chance to do this. Jess?"

"Count me in."

The professor looked at his watch. "Hmm. If we hurry, we can be there by late this afternoon. I'll call him and tell him to expect us."

"Can you be sure he'll go for it? Take the risk?" Jess said.

Karagigian grinned. "Oh, he'll risk it. Any CETI man worth his salt would. Besides, he is my sister's son and I'm his favorite uncle."

Laurie could feel the energy in the president's office as if it were some kind of static electricity, crackling up from the carpet through their shoes and into the four people there. Larry, with a big grin on his face and a phone-book-size folder; Bill with his worried frown; the president, with raised eyebrows and a wonder as to how this was going to affect life in his country. He was, after all, the man in charge. This was big.

"So you don't think this is a hoax?" the president asked.

"No, sir," Larry said. "What I think it is, sir, is a visitor from another world coming to call."

"Good Lord," the secretary of defense said.

"We don't have any reason to believe it's going to be like *The Day the Earth Stood Still*," Larry said, "but we need to be prepared for whatever this visitor has in mind."

"How are we going to do that?" the president asked.

"Well, sir, the first thing we should do is answer him. Find out what he's willing to tell us about himself and his mission."

"Can I see that message?"

"I have a printout of the text," Larry said. "The multimedia stuff needs a computer to view."

"The text will do fine."

The chairman of the Joint Chiefs nodded and passed a single sheet of paper to the president. He also handed copies to Bill and Laurie.

She looked at the message. Larry had already shown it to her, but she read it again.

"People of Earth, I am Zeerus of Achernar Three. I am traveling via starship through your stellar system and will arrive in the vicinity of your planet in six months. I come in peace and friendship. Please acknowledge and return my signal on the same radio frequency as soon as possible. We have much to discuss."

"Amazing," the president said. "So, we aren't alone in the universe."

"He says he's on a peaceful mission," Laurie put in.

"I don't believe we can altogether trust that," Larry said.

"For once, I agree with General Hightower," Bill said.

"You concur with his recommendation?" the president said.

"Yes, sir. We should talk to this . . . being. Given this dictionary, we can probably talk to him in English, but if not, we can translate it back into his language. If what he says is true, it could be the greatest thing to happen since fire. He might be willing to share his star-going technology with us. We could change the face of our world."

"If he doesn't change it for us," Larry said. "But I do think we should initiate a dialog as soon as possible, sir. The more he says or maybe doesn't say, the more we can prepare ourselves."

The president nodded, almost to himself. "Right. I think maybe I'm going to call a Cabinet meeting. I want to run this past my advisers, get a consensus. We'll meet first thing in the morning. Eight o'clock. Clear everything else, Laurie."

Laurie nodded.

"But, sir—" Larry began. "Time is of the essence."

"If this alien is still six months away, one more day won't matter, will it, General Hightower?"

Clearly Larry thought it would, but he shook his head. "No, sir, I suppose not. Though we might not be the only people who heard him."

"Leave that report, I'll have copies made for the meeting."

The meeting was over. Larry nodded, and he and Bill got up and left.

After they were gone, the president said, "Laurie get a hold of Scott Wells. Have him run a quickie poll, today. One question. 'How would you feel if you found out a creature from another planet was coming to visit Earth?' Tell him to give it a couple of one-to-five spins—excited to not interested, worried to not worried, like that. I want some numbers on my desk before the meeting tomorrow."

"Yes, sir."

"Get Reverend Jimmy and Father Leon on the phone for me. I want to get a hit as to the churches' position on this. And that shrink, whatshisname, Wilson?, get him, too. We play this right, it could be a landslide for us come November. Shoot, if an ambassadorship to France or England is valuable, what would an embassy posting to wherever this alien is from be worth? There are all kinds of possibilities here."

"Yes, sir. If the alien doesn't come in throwing atomic bombs or shooting death rays."

"He says his mission is peaceful."

"Yes, sir. But people have been know to lie for not much reason. If this is really an alien, we don't have a clue as to how he'll behave. Maybe where he comes from, you lie about everything to see how smart the people you're talking to are."

"You do have a way of raining on a parade, don't you, Laurie?"

"Sir. We have to consider the possibility, like General Hightower says. If the man from outer space drops in and vaporizes Kansas, that could create a problem."

"Hell with Kansas. They voted for my opponent." He smiled.

"What if he vaporizes New York? You got those votes and you need them again. Not to mention what even losing Kansas would do to your credibility as commander in chief."

"Hmm. Okay. You have a point. I'll keep it in mind."

As she was leaving his office to set up the calls he wanted with his secretary, Laurie's cell phone rang. She knew who it was.

She and Larry would have a lot to talk about tonight.

14

Jake's head was thick with panic. He ran, blinded by fear, his mouth dry as dust, his heart pounding. Oh, man, oh, *man!*

The joy he'd felt when he'd found his mother was sure gone. He didn't know what he was going to do now. They had found him, tracked him down, and man, spraying a National Security guy with pepper spray had been a really, really *stupid* thing to do. He should have given himself up. Shoot, he was just a kid, they couldn't put him in real jail, only juvie, and it was a first offense, how long could they have kept him there? But, no, he had to assault a federal officer! Guy was probably so pissed off he would shoot to kill if he saw Jake again.

He'd watched *The X-Files*, one of the few TV shows his father liked. Showed you what these federal agencies were capable of, his father said. Lying, cheating, conspiracy, murder . . .

Oh, man, oh, *shit!*

No, he couldn't just turn himself in now, he'd screwed that up. They'd put him away forever, or worse.

But what was he gonna do?

He wasn't sure exactly how long it had been, but it had been a while since he'd taken off. Hours. It was sometime in the late afternoon. He'd left his watch, too, and hadn't seen a bank sign lately.

Jake stopped moving long enough to look around. He was on a city street in New Jersey, though it could have been anywhere. It wasn't raining but it was gray and chilly. There was a drugstore, a little market, a bakery, a furniture store. People moved up and down the sidewalks, drove past in their cars, waited for buses. People who had lives that probably didn't include being chased by the government.

Think, Jake, think!

He saw a police car cross the intersection just ahead, but it kept going, didn't turn and screech toward him.

Okay, okay, probably the fed, he'd said his name, Steve somebody, would call the local cops in pretty quick. There were a lot of kids his size and age around, but the guy had seen him, had seen what he was wearing, so he had to get away from this area, fast. He needed transportation and he didn't want to risk waiting for a bus or taking a cab, they'd check that right off.

Come on, *think* of something!

He walked, tried to come up with a way to get away without anybody figuring out what he'd done. He got to the corner, turned to the right. Behind the row of shops was an alley. Jake turned into it, walked a little faster. He was heading back in the same direction from which he'd just come, but at least he was more or less out of sight. Though he was pretty sure he was just putting off the inevitable. He was doomed. Any second now a police car would roll into the alley and cops would jump out and point their guns at him, and if he batted an eye they'd blast him. Man. Why had he ever stuck his nose into somebody else's computer system?

There was a guy unloading TV sets or something in big boxes from a big truck behind the furniture store, but he was busy, maybe he wouldn't notice Jake—

Hel-lo?

Jake stopped. Watched the guy roll the loaded dolly onto a hydraulic lift on the back of the truck and lower it. Once the lift was on the ground, he rolled the TV into the store.

And there was this big truck, all enclosed, just sitting there. . . .

Jake moved closer, saw that the delivery guy was out of sight. He looked around, didn't see anybody else.

Well. You didn't have to be a rocket scientist to figure this one out.

He climbed up into the back of the truck. It was full of cardboard boxes: TV sets, kitchen ranges, dishwashers, refrigerators. He looked at the addresses on the boxes. The ones closest to the back were the same, to an address here in Secaucus, probably the store the delivery guy was inside right now. The boxes farther in were to go to Union City, and the next batch to Weehawken. Jake didn't know where those towns were exactly, though he seemed to remember seeing a sign that said "Weehawken" on his way from the airport. Whatever. They weren't *here*, that was the important thing.

They were hard to move, but he managed to lever one of the refrigerator boxes out from the wall of the truck a little, enough to squeeze in behind it and sit down. He hoped the driver didn't hit the brakes too hard and squash him, but it was a risk he had to take.

After a few minutes, the guy came back and off-loaded another box, then another and another and finally, he was done. He pulled the metal door down with a loud ratcheting noise and a big clunk. Jake heard the sound of the lock mechanism snapping into place. It was very dark in the back of the truck now. Like the inside of a cave.

He was afraid. Not of the dark, but of what was going to happen to him. He didn't have his computer, he didn't have anything except his wallet and his money and his can of pepper spray.

Even when he'd been living with his old man, things hadn't looked quite as bleak as they did now. He wanted to cry. He wasn't a baby anymore. He was eleven. And boys his age didn't cry over every little thing.

But maybe this wasn't so little.

Karagigian's nephew Jerry must have favored the other side of the family tree: He was short, rotund, and nearly bald, though he couldn't have been more than a couple of years older than Stewart. Didn't look a thing like his uncle. But he had a big grin and he was definitely interested in being a part of this transaction.

His lab was a beautiful piece of work. It was kind of small, barely room for the four of them to crowd in around the console, but it was all shiny and high-tech, radio gear, Doppler, computers, printers, must have been a couple hundred thousand bucks' worth of stuff in the little space. What you got when you were affiliated with some place like Harvard where they took science seriously.

After the introductions were made, Jerry jumped right in.

"I've got the frequency set. You have a message ready?"

Stewart nodded. "Yeah. I worked on it using my laptop on the train. I'm not sure about some of the letters or pictographs or whatever, but I had my program generate them as best I can. All I need to do is upload it."

He handed Jerry a printout of the message.

"Looks like a bunch of squiggles and stick figures. What does it say?"

"Basically, 'Greetings from Earth. We are four scientists who have received your message and are delighted to respond. Our names are Karagigian, Davies, Rossini, and Cowart and we welcome you on behalf of mankind.'"

"Wow, I'm a scientist now?" Jess said.

"I didn't want to confuse the issue," Stewart said. Yeah. Maybe this alien didn't have two sexes. Or maybe it had more than two. He hadn't gotten around to looking at all the pictures yet. He didn't want to try to explain about girlfriends.

"Hey, thanks for including me," Jerry said. "I look forward to seeing my name in the history books. This is so great!"

"That's assuming you don't see all our names on a post office wall first," Jess said.

"Are we ready?" Dr. Karagigian put in.

"Ready."

"You have the com, Scotty," Jerry said.

Stewart nodded. He sat down in front of the computer and popped the disk into the floppy drive. Opened the foreign language program he'd built and brought up the message file he'd put together on the train. He looked around, saw everybody waiting expectantly. Took a deep breath. "Okay. How do I transmit it?"

"Hit that button right there and then the return key," Jerry said, pointing.

"I wrote the message," Stewart said. "Who wants the honors?"

None of the other three moved.

"It's your board, Jerry," Karagigian said. "Go ahead."

Jerry smiled, nodded. "Sure. Why not? Might as well be hung for a sheep as a goat." He reached out, tapped the controls. "There she goes. Call me sysop to the stars."

A collective sigh escaped from the four.

"What now?" Jess said.

"Now, we go have dinner," Stewart said. "And find a place to spend the night. Even at the speed of light, it's going to take a while to get there."

Jess looked puzzled. "How long?"

"Well," Dr. Karagigian said, "we cannot be certain. The incoming message says the traveler is within the solar system but not how *far* in. If the vessel is, for instance, as far away as Pluto's orbit, it will take more than four hours for the radio wave to arrive. Assuming Mr. Zeerus answers right away, the soonest we can expect an answer will be double that, plus a bit. Eight hours, minimum. Less if he is closer."

"Really? That seems like a long time."

The professor's tone took on the aspect of a lecture: "The most distant planet, Pluto, has an orbit that is somewhat eccentric. Sometimes it is closer to us than Neptune. I confess to not knowing the planet's current position exactly," Karagigian said. "But it could be anywhere from 2.75 billion to over 4.6 billion miles away from the sun. Subtract Earth's rather small 93 million and there you have it. Light travels at a mere 186,000 miles per second, so you must divide that number into the distance to get the total number of seconds, then divide that by sixty to get minutes and *that* by sixty to get hours—"

"Yeah," Stewart said, interrupting what sounded like the beginning of an Astronomy 101 lecture, "we aren't going to having a conversation in real time until he gets a lot closer."

"Perhaps dinner would be in order," Karagigian said.

In bed naked with Hightower, Laurie said, "Wow. You look pretty good for an old guy. Hold that thought while I run to the little girls' room."

"Would you like me to get your stroller?"

"Nah, I'll just use your walker."

They laughed.

While she was gone, he sat up and put a pillow behind his back. Truth was, he didn't look his age, at least not from the neck down. He ate pretty well, hit the Pentagon's new gym two or three times a week, mostly swimming and some on the Nautilus machines.

She came back to the bed, leaped onto it in a belly flop, then propped herself up on one elbow and looked at him. "Okay. So talk to me about the little green man."

He reached over and smoothed her hair with one hand. "Well. In the morning, your boss—our boss—will meet with his top people to try and come up with a politically correct message for us to send back to the alien. That should prove interesting, since the president has at least one of every ethnic group in the country in the Cabinet. Getting them to agree on something that won't be offensive to an unknown alien race could take six months, and I wouldn't bet on that."

"You're awfully cynical for a soldier."

"Am I wrong?"

"No, I just thought I would point it out. Go on."

"I will do my best to try to convince the Rainbow Coalition to hurry things along."

"Why? If the spaceman is six months away, what's the hurry?"

"He's only six months away *physically*—if he can be believed. We're sitting on our scientists, the ones we know or suspect have intercepted the incoming message, but we can't sit on them forever, nor can we control what the Chinese, the Germans, or the Swedes might be doing. If somebody else tuned in to the message, they might decipher the code and decide to make a call on their own. We want to talk to him first. Other countries might not have America's best interests at heart. Imagine what might happen if certain Middle Eastern dictators started telling the alien that we're white devils and should be wiped off the planet."

"Why would he believe them? And even if he did, he might not have any warlike tendencies—or capabilities if he did buy it. It's just one ship."

"The first voice you hear when you've sent a complicated message in code is apt to be more impressive, isn't it? Wouldn't you think it was the smart guys who'd get it first?

"We don't know if it's just one ship, too far away to see, even with the Hubble. Plus, if we sent just one battleship to visit the Stone Age natives of some remote tropical isle, how well do you think they would fare if we opened up on them with the big guns and missiles? We can level a city from so far away the inhabitants can't figure out where the bombs are coming from. This alien's technology might be so superior to ours as to make us look like monkeys scratching our butts in the jungle."

"There's a pleasant thought."

"If he came from another star system—and we're sure he must have—either he is real old, real fast, or real smart. Maybe all three. We haven't put a man on Mars and this alien is hopping light-years. Trust me, his magic is bigger than ours."

"You can sound so paranoid sometimes, you know?"

"They pay me to think about such things. Anyway, you could be right. Maybe this is the space-going version of Albert Schweitzer or Gandhi. If he is, I'll leave him to the politicians and they can dissect him with words. But if he's more along the lines of Genghis Khan, then it's my job to stop him. Hell, we don't know if the ship he's on is the size of a city bus or an aircraft carrier. There might be thousands of them oiling their atomic blasters and just itching to cut loose."

"Boy, you sure know how to talk a girl into the mood for wild hot sex."

"Thanks. Those atomic blasters do it every time. Come here."

They laughed again and hugged. And then they did much more interesting things than talking about aliens . . .

15

Major Steve Hayes had had better days. First he'd gotten pepper sprayed in his face—his eyes still hurt, dammit—then his quarry had gotten away. And, for all the good the local and state police had been able to do him, that quarry, one eleven-year-old boy genius Jake Holcroft, had vanished from the face of the planet. An all-points bulletin had gone out with zip results. The police swore that Jake hadn't taken a bus, a plane, or a train out of the city.

Where he might be, maybe God knew. Nobody else seemed to.

Hayes stood in the line at a local cafeteria. He already had a greasy hamburger steak, greasier rice and gravy, and a green salad on his tray. The cherry pie looked good, too, what the hell. Couldn't run down a prepube kid with all the resources of the federal government behind him, might as well eat and get fat. He put the saucer of pie onto his tray.

He moved to a small table, sat in one of the two chairs. One table over a bearded Indian or maybe a Pakistani man wearing a turban ate what looked like bread sticks, washed down by something that could have been green tea.

One table past the turbaned man a large black woman in a blue-and-red patterned dashiki sat in front of a tray piled high with mashed potatoes and breaded cutlets. She liked the cherry pie, too.

Behind the black woman, a Latino couple held hands, arms, shoulders, and parts south and bathed each other in warm, liquid Spanish. Hayes knew just about enough of that language to order dinner in a Mexican restaurant, but he caught a few words, "hot" and "wet" among them. He'd bet they'd be leaving soon.

Regular melting pot in here, like the bridge of the starship *Enterprise*.

The cafeteria was fairly busy for midnight. Hayes understood that; it was the only place other than a fast-food joint he could find still open. He was hungry, more than a little tired, and a whole lot pissed off. This was a snafu of the worst order. National security wasn't at risk, but Hayes's personal security sure was. One did not undertake a pet mission directly from the chairman of the Joint Chiefs and expect to make colonel if one screwed it up. If he didn't find this kid pretty damn quick, he was going to be standing in a cesspool with the crap up to his chin. Maybe stationed in a place cold enough so that if you peed, it froze before it hit the ground. What a pleasant thought *that* was.

The hamburger steak felt like oily metal going down, and it lay in his stomach like chunks of lead. He pushed the meat away, tried the rice. Not much better. And the pie was made with lard or Crisco, it tasted altogether *too* good, which made him eat it too fast. He hoped he had remembered to pack his Tagamet and Pepcid; he was going to need it. The hunger he'd felt was gone, replaced with depression.

Now what was he going to do? He didn't have a clue.

At the last stop on the driver's route in Weehawken, Jake sneaked out of the truck while the man hauled a kitchen range into the store. He didn't know exactly where he was, it was dark, and he didn't know what he was going to do next. Finding a place to stay for the night would be good, but he didn't think he could just walk into a motel and rent a room or anything, even if he had the money. They probably didn't get a lot of kids renting rooms. Or maybe they did, but Jake didn't want to take that chance.

It wasn't too cold out. The best thing would be to find a sports store, buy a sleeping bag, and camp out somewhere nobody would stumble across him. Maybe the roof of a building. He'd seen an article in the paper last year about street kids in Portland. A group of them had set up a semipermanent camp on some rooftops downtown, moving whenever a watchman or somebody spotted them. A couple of the kids had even staked out a movie theater's roof and figured out a way to get in and out. They'd watch movies, then climb up and into a little tent they had pitched on the roof.

All that forced camping with his father would come in handy. A tent, a sleeping bag, a little one-burner propane stove and some freeze-dried food, he'd be set for a few days. He could sneak up a fire escape and make a camp for a couple of days, long enough so the cops or feds or whoever would probably think he was long gone.

He didn't have any better ideas and maybe it wouldn't do him a lot of good in the long run. Then again, like his friend Mitchell used to say, in the long run, we're all dead.

Jake headed for a nearby phone booth to find the address of a camping supply store.

Zeerus was exultant! Yes! The moronic ape-spawn *did* have enough sense to decode and answer his message!

A small group of scientists. That made sense, those who spent their hours seeking the unknown, yes, they would be the ones to hear him first. Of course, even in a primitive technology such as this one, they wouldn't be the only ones. He had not been broadcasting on tight-beam frequencies, so at any given time, half the planet would be bathed in the beam. If anybody else was listening, they should have heard him. These scientists were simply the first to decode the message.

Eventually, of course, he would have to deal with some kind of governmental overfunctionary, that was always the way of such things. Governments everywhere were much the same. Their primary function seemed to be to make more government—and secondary to that, to regulate every deed, word, or thought its citizens had. But he would not make it simple for them to stick him into a narrow slot. He would spread himself around. Divide and conquer. That, too, was the way of things. The more people who heard his message, the more confusion he could sow. Governments were also adept at managing—suppressing—information they considered any threat to their rule. Just as the Majae did, over and over.

He read the message over again. His teeth gnashed as his jaw muscles spasmed in primal joy. All that would sort itself out. For now, he had established contact.

Time to compose his second message. Not too much, just enough to spark a bit of paranoia in them.

Ape-spawn were easily spooked.

The phone jangled, and Hightower came out of a dead sleep. He reached for the instrument.

"What?"

"Sir, Major Ward, Special Ops. Our monitoring station in Bangor has picked up a coded radio transmission on the frequency band you had us scanning."

It took Hightower a second to focus. What the hell was he talking about? Next to him, Laurie stirred. She rolled over, looked at him with a sleepy frown, but didn't say anything.

"Go ahead, Major."

"Sir, the transmission was initiated at 2030 hours ET from the vicinity of Longitude 71.06 W, Latitude 42.22 N, and lasted for approximately forty seconds."

Hightower looked at his clock. 2030? It was 0340. Why had it taken them more than seven hours to get back to him? And—

Wait a second—the message *originated* on Earth?

He was fully awake now.

"Where exactly does that latitude and longitude cross, Major?"

"We aren't sure of the exact location, sir. Approximately, it is somewhere in Cambridge, Massachusetts, sir."

Cambridge. What was in Cambridge?

Harvard.

Dammit!

He had it in that instant, no doubt in his mind.

Somebody was talking to the damned alien!

Hightower shook his head, angry, worried, a little frightened. He went with the anger.

"Ward, if another such transmission happens, you had better hop on it with both feet so hard it rattles your teeth fillings. I want a precise location—use whatever tech you need to get that—and I want it a whole helluva lot faster than this leisurely piece of business you've just handed me. Is that understood?"

"Y-y-yessir."

"Get that coded message to Colonel Calvin at Cryptography and get it to him *yesterday*, is that part clear as well?"

"Sir!"

"That's all, Major."

He slammed the phone down. "Shit!"

"What?" Laurie said.

"Somebody has beaten us to the goddamned alien. A message went out on that frequency more than seven hours ago. Cambridge, probably Harvard. Somebody is already talking to the sucker and we're still trying to decide on politically correct policy!" He used a few choice words he'd found comforting when under attack in Vietnam. They didn't do much good.

She rolled over and reached for her purse.

"What are you doing?"

"Calling the boss."

"It's a little late for damage control," he said.

"Maybe so. But maybe we can save part of the barn before it all burns down."

He watched while Laurie pushed the autodial button that rang a private line in the bedroom of the president of the United States.

Jake had a pretty good camp set up, he figured. The building was one of the taller ones, kinda off by itself, so nobody would get up in the morning and look out and see his tent. He got one of those little dome hoop jobs that didn't need stakes, just the fiberglass pole frame to erect. He had a foam pad under his sleeping bag, a battery-powered lantern, a little propane stove, and a cook kit. He pitched the tent next to a big air-conditioning unit that would block him on one side from any passing airplanes, and he was feeling pretty good.

He had dozed off, but he woke up around four in the morning when something in the building rumbled, some kind of machinery. He knew the time because he had bought a cheap watch, one of those with the little light that went on when you pushed the button. He turned on his lantern, ate some dried apricots and trail mix, washed it down with water from his new canteen, then started thinking about what he was gonna do next. When morning came, he'd break the camp down, stash the tent and sleeping bag somewhere, and try to keep anybody from seeing him. He didn't think too many people came up on the roof; there wasn't a garden or anything, just pea gravel and tar or something, and from all the undisturbed pigeon crap piled up on the sill of the door going into the building and the little structure the door was in, nobody had been up here lately. He should be okay.

"Not a bad camp," said a man's voice from outside the tent.

Jake sat up, terrified. The voice—it was—oh, no!

The tent flap zipped open. The smiling man bent and climbed inside.

"Hello, Jake," his father said.

16

Stewart was dozing in front of the board when the call came in. A beep brought him out of sleep, and caught the attention of the others sitting or sprawling on chairs around him. After dinner, nobody had wanted to go elsewhere to sleep and maybe miss the call from the alien if it came.

And here it was.

"What, what?" Jess said.

"The phone is ringing," Stewart said.

"You got the translation program working?" Jerry Cowart said.

"Yeah. No point in slowing down this long-distance communication any more than we have to."

The message took only a few seconds, less than a minute, then it was done. Stewart ran it through the decoder to get the binary cleared, then into the translator. It took a few minutes, the program had to make three passes to guess at the parts it wasn't sure about.

He read it aloud:

" 'Fortune smiles upon us, Earth scientists, we have linked. The galaxy is a place of great wonder—but also a place of some danger. It will be to the mutual benefit of our peoples to speak of such things. I regret the time lag of our communications due to distance. To remedy this, I will have my computer beam to you the construction plans for a simple subspace radio unit. Once you have built this device, we can engage in a faster dialog."

" 'Zeerus ending transmission.' "

Stewart turned to look at the others. Karagigian's face held the most wonder, but Jerry's was not far behind.

"Man," Stewart said.

"What?" Jess asked.

"He is just gonna beam us the plans for subspace radio, blap, just like that," Jerry said. "Jesus H. Christ and all the hairy little angels."

"Faster-than-light radio," Dr. Karagigian said. "Amazing."

"Hold on a second," Jess said. "This sounds wonderful and all, but how do you know he isn't going to beam down the plans for a super bomb that will blow the whole planet to smithereens when you switch it on?"

"Jesse—" Stewart began.

"Ms. Rossini has a point," Karagigian said. "Before constructing and activating such a device, we would check it very carefully."

"How?" Jess said. "If this is based on scientific concepts about which you and every other scientist knows diddly-squat, *how* are you going to check it to be sure it isn't going to go *boom!* when you slide the last piece into place?"

"I thought I explained that," Stewart said. "A race advanced enough to have interstellar travel wouldn't need to do such things."

"Pardon me for being stupid," she said. "But how the hell can you know that? You're assuming a being with a totally different physiology and psychology, coming from a different environment, is going to behave like a reasonable human being would. Let me point out that there are people on *this* planet who would just as soon bash your brains out as look at you."

"Crazy people, sure—"

"And how do you know this Zeerus *isn't* crazy? Maybe he escaped from the alien equivalent of a bug ward. Or maybe blowing people up isn't crazy for his species, maybe it is the norm."

Stewart felt a great wave of frustration build in him. How could he make her understand?

"Once again sociology brings up questions we as scientists sometimes fail to consider," Karagigian said.

"What?" Stewart said.

"She's right. We cannot make assumptions about Zeerus's motivations," Karagigian said. "Perhaps his people are conquerors and perhaps they achieve their victories by sending gullible species plans for devices that are other than they are purported to be."

"I don't buy that," Stewart said.

"Because a species might have the intellectual or technological capabilities to build, say, a Dyson sphere, does not mean they are vegetarians or peaceful," the professor said. "Logically that does not follow."

"Yeah," Jerry put in, "could be they don't do Spiderman's Dictum."

Jess frowned.

Stewart said, " 'With great power comes great responsibility.' "

"Which brings us to us," Jess said. "Are we qualified to keep this conversation going? What if he sends us the plans for his super-radio? What do we do with them?"

Well. She had them there. Stewart was pretty good with computers and not completely stupid about basic physics and such, but a device capable of transmitting and receiving signals faster than the speed of light, up until now a pretty solid constant, well, yeah, that was beyond him. They'd have to bring somebody else in on that. And while the government tended to plod along, it did have feds all over this thing. Sooner or later, they might figure out that Stewart Davies and a few of his friends were chatting with a man from another planet, and when they did, they damn sure weren't going to like it.

Food for thought, all right.

Right now, he needed a shower. He was feeling grubby and probably smelling a little rank, too.

Laurie watched and listened as Larry dressed, made calls, and issued orders. She could see how he had gotten to be the ranking general of the United States military. He was crisp, decisive, and brooking no nonsense.

"Charles? Larry Hightower. I have an outgoing radio signal originating in Cambridge, Mass. I'll have the frequency and particulars sent to you. I want a federal agent pounding on the door of every commercial radio or television station capable of generating such a signal. Cross it with the FCC. Check *everything*—cable and phone companies, university research projects, ham radio operators, kids with walkie-talkies. If you can't get enough FBI bodies, you can use military intelligence, all branches, and if that isn't enough, get the Boy Scouts."

He hung up. Before he could call out again, the phone rang.

"Go," he said.

He listened for a minute. Swore. Said, "Get it translated. I'll be at the White House in fifteen minutes, deliver the hard copy there."

He turned to Laurie. "Another transmission, this one coming from space. Looks as if our spaceman is having a regular gabfest with somebody. Somebody who is going to be in deep shit when I catch them." He paused. "You want to ride with me to the White House?"

"Better not," she said. "No point in adding to our problems."

He nodded, preoccupied. She could understand that. The president wasn't real happy about being jerked out of bed at four in the morning, but she was able to make him understand the gravity of the situation. She hoped.

"I'll see you there," he said.

Jake's father wasn't as mad at him as Jake expected. In fact, he seemed almost . . . proud. There wasn't anything Jake could have done when the feds broke in, so running was a good idea.

They were in a black van driven by a man in military camo clothes, a brother in the Movement, his father said.

"How did you find me?"

"I knew you'd head here," his father said.

"You knew where Mom was?"

"Of course. I've known where the bitch was all along. The Militia has friends everywhere. She just wasn't worth my trouble to come and punish."

The driver went through an intersection as the light turned red. Somebody in a car honked and yelled at *him*.

"Sit on *this*, dickweed!" the driver yelled back as he shot the car the finger.

"Easy, Mikey," his father said. "We don't want to get pulled over."

Jake swallowed. The driver had a pistol in his lap. An AK-47 lay on the floor by his father's feet, plus he had a .45 stuck in his waistband. Despite the bandage on his arm, his father didn't look the least bit helpless. If a traffic cop pulled them over, he was probably going to die for his trouble.

Seth turned to look at Jake in the back. "So what I want to know is, why is the FBI after your little ass, son? And that guy who came out of that bitch your mother's apartment, he wasn't a feeb, he moved like military. You got into some big trouble here. Talk to me."

Jake swallowed again. Oh, man. What was he going to do now? His old man would just as soon backhand him as look at him, and if he tried to lie and got caught, he would get the stuffing beat out of him. At the least.

But why lie? What did it matter if his father knew? Jake didn't have a lot going for him right at the moment. His old man was paranoid, he would believe just about anything about the government, as long as it was bad.

"Aliens," Jake said.

"Wetbacks?" Mikey said.

"No, sir. Real aliens. From another planet."

"You had better not be pulling my chain, son."

"I'm not. I found it on my computer. A university program, SETI—that's the Search for Extraterrestrial Intelligence. Guys who listen for radio signals from outer space. They found one. I hacked into a professor's mail and read about it. Somehow the FBI found out I was there. That's why they came to see me."

"Bullshit," Mikey said.

Jake's father turned to stare at the driver. "If my kid said that's what he saw, then that's what he saw. He can't shoot worth a crap but he is damned good with that computer junk." His voice was a stone; you could sharpen a knife on it.

"I didn't mean nothin', Seth. It's just that—aliens? Little green men?"

"Don't you read, Mikey? About Hangar 18, about that alien they cut up back in the fifties, about Roswell? About Area 51? You think the air force is telling what it knows?"

"No, but—"

"But nothing. Something stirred up the feds. You heard the word from the network. They're running around like ants from a stepped-on anthill. Maybe we're gonna have some new immigrant mud people to worry about." He looked at Jake again. "What else?"

Jake shook his head. "I don't know. That's all I got."

Seth Holcroft nodded, looked into the distance. Said, "Can you get more? If we got you to a computer?"

"Maybe. Probably not. They're watching."

"Can't you reroute the call or something so they can't trace it?"

The van rounded a corner too fast. Jake swayed.

"Mikey, if you don't start driving like a white man I'm gonna let the kid do it."

"Sorry, Seth."

"Go on, Jake."

"I could bounce a signal if I had the software, but they'll be watching. Probably can't get into any of those files anymore."

"Hmm. This is big, I know it. Real big. We need to figure out a way to get a handle on it."

He was quiet for a minute, thinking. Then his father pulled a cell phone from his pocket. He tapped in a number, handed it to Jake.

"Talk to the bitch your mother," he said. "Find out if the guy who was chasing you left a number for you to contact him if you went back to her place."

Jake's mouth was dry, but he nodded.

"And don't say who you're with or where we are. If we can get hold of this spook, we'll just have ourselves a little talk with him. I bet he knows what's going on."

Mikey laughed. It was an ugly sound.

"Hello? Mom? It's me, Jake."

"No, no, I'm fine. Really. Mom, did that guy, the one who I sprayed with the pepper stuff, did he leave a number where I could contact him? He did? Would you give it to me? No, I'm going to come back but I just want to call him and tell him I'm sorry. Please? I'll explain it all when I see you, can I just have the number?"

"Thanks." He looked at his father, then down at the floor. "I love you, too, Mom."

She read off the number and Jake repeated it.

Jake's father wrote the number down. He held out his hand for the phone. "I gotta go now, Mom."

His father shut the phone off. "Bitch," he said.

17

The president of the United States was not a happy man. Nor was his secretary of defense. And neither seemed to remember that Hightower had done everything but jump up and down and spit at them to hurry the connection with the alien ship.

"How could this happen, Larry?" the president asked.

Hightower wanted to deck him. Three steps, jerk him from behind the desk, one short right to the gut to double him up, another punch to the moronic face to straighten him out and lay him flat as a carpet. Oh, but that would feel good. For all the years when one superior or another said or did something stupid and he couldn't respond. Couldn't fight, couldn't run away, just had to stand there and take it. How could it happen? How about, I have a fool for a boss? It was tempting. But no. They'd just throw him out and put in somebody who wouldn't be able to do the job as well. Especially now, with this unknown threat looming.

There came a knock at the door. A Secret Service man came in, leading a military courier with a briefcase chained to his wrist.

"I'm expecting that," Hightower said. He unlocked the case and took the folder from the briefcase. Then he dismissed the courier. When he and the Secret Service man were gone, Hightower scanned the documents inside. Shook his head.

"Jesus, Larry," the president said. "Don't keep us in suspense. What?"

"The outgoing message," he said. "The senders were kind enough to give their names: Karagigian, Davies, Rossini, and Cowart."

The president picked up his phone. "Get me Colburn at the FBI," he said.

Hightower shook his head. Even if they picked up these four clowns, it was probably going to be too late. This cat, he was pretty sure, was out of the bag for good.

"I've already got people in the field," Hightower said. "I'll call them." He pulled his cell phone out.

Steve Hayes caught a commercial jet back to Washington. What was he going to do—hang around the local precinct in New Jersey and wait for the cops to catch Jake Holcroft?

On the flight, he put in a call to the FBI in Oregon and found out that Jake's father had been released on bail—five hundred thousand dollars, put up by his militia group—and that the surveillance team had promptly lost him. He didn't think Jake would go back there, but he told the feebs to keep an eye out for the boy. He should have done that sooner.

Washington was enjoying one of those late fall days when the last dying gasp of summer held the city in a muggy grip. People who'd never been there didn't realize that the country's capital was essentially a southern town and that the weather sometimes got downright tropical, even in the fall.

Hayes caught a cab and went home. He dropped his bags on the floor and went to take a long, hot shower.

When he got out, feeling cleaner and a whole lot better, the message button on his cell phone was blinking. He tapped in the code.

"Hi. This is Jake Holcroft. I—I need to talk to you. To reach a place—to reach a place where I don't have to go to jail! I'll call back in an hour."

Hayes blinked at the phone. Damn! He sounded scared, but the kid had called the number he'd left with the boy's mother. Maybe this wouldn't be such a disaster after all. He called telephone monitoring, but a trace said the call was bounced from three or four substations, the last one of which was a station in South America. Scared or not, the kid was clever enough to hide his point of origin.

Well. He had time for a beer. He'd do that, then wait for the boy to call back. Maybe he could salvage his career after all. But something about the kid's voice was weird. He tapped in his code and replayed the message. Frowned. Something was weird, but he couldn't figure out what it was.

Jack punched the disconnect into the computer his father had provided and the call to Major Hayes ended. He was pretty sure they couldn't trace the call to here, wherever "here" was. He thought he was in New York City but it had been late when they pulled in, he'd been asleep, and he'd been inside since. The house was pretty big, the curtains pulled shut, and there were four men and a woman who looked a lot like the kind of people his father usually hung with: hard, lean, short-haired, always watching. The computer was a top-of-the-line Mac clone, hundred and fifty MHz with an accelerator that pushed that up maybe fifteen percent. Sixty-four megs of RAM, two-gig hard drive, fast modem, and a twenty-inch Radius color monitor. Talking bucks here. You could move mountains with such a machine.

"All right," his father said. "Now, when you get the guy, find out where he is. Tell him you'll meet him there, no matter where it is."

The driver of the van, Mikey, said, "Kid is pretty sharp with that thing."

"Yeah," Seth said. "Here's the drill. If Hayes is in the city, we'll be paying him a visit as soon as we can drive to wherever it is. If he's out of town, we'll rent a plane and fly there. We snatch him, take him to the closest safehouse, and open him like a can of beans. We'll find out what the hell is going on. We aren't going to be caught flatfooted on this."

It was kind of interesting that Seth's father seemed to be in charge. Back home, he'd been the arms instructor but only a master sergeant. Here, he was acting like a general, or a colonel, at least.

"You want something to eat?" his father asked.

"Yes, sir. That would be good."

"Take him to the kitchen, get Marlene to fix him a sandwich," Seth said.

As Jake headed for the kitchen, he hoped Major Hayes was sharp enough to get the warning in the telephone message.

"So what now?" the president asked.

"The field agents have a location on one of those names at Harvard," Larry said. "They'll pick him up. Before we send our message to the alien ship, we need to make sure this guy and his friends didn't say anything we missed. We don't want to spook him."

Laurie watched Larry hold his temper in check. Oh, he was pissed, she could feel him smoldering from here, though he seemed to have it pretty well hidden from the other two men in the Oval Office.

"How is it," the secretary of defense said, "that some yahoo at a university was able to figure out the alien's coded transmission before the military's best cryptographers using the hottest computers in the country managed it?"

Larry shook his head. "We'll ask him."

"Ask him, hell, we should *hire* him," the president said. "Starting to make me wonder if the old saying about 'military intelligence' being an oxymoron isn't true after all."

Larry clenched, even though he didn't seem to react much. Her boss didn't know it, but he was standing on dangerous ground. Wouldn't that sound good on the evening newsbreak? *Chairman of the Joint Chiefs punches out president of the United States. Details at eleven.*

Don't do it it, Larry . . .

He managed to keep it from erupting. "For the record, Mr. President and Mr. Secretary, we had this message translated *before* this college twerp initiated his first transmission. Had we been allowed to respond, we would have gotten there first."

"Not by much," the secretary said.

"In this case, an inch is as good as a mile, sir."

"All right, let's not go pointing fingers, gentlemen," the president said. "Done is done. Let's see if we can salvage the situation, shall we?"

Stewart and Jess lagged behind the others after they finished breakfast and returned to the lab. Karagigian and Jerry were thirty feet away and talking animatedly to each other.

This was all still very much amazing to Stewart, but even more so to Jess. She didn't have the science background and he was trying to explain to her what it was going to mean.

Ahead of them, the professor and his nephew opened the door to the lab.

Four men in dark suits boiled out like disturbed wasps.

They had guns. They pointed the guns at Karagigian and Jerry.

"Jesus!" Stewart said. "Come on!"

He grabbed Jess by the arm and turned.

Behind them in the hall, four more men with guns stood blocking their exit. All of the men wore dead-serious expressions.

"Game over, folks," one of the men said. "Let's keep our hands out where we can see them and everybody moves real slow, okay?"

That was for damn sure, Stewart thought. He nodded.

Man. They were in trouble now.

Hightower took the call on his cell phone. "Yes?"

"We've got them, sir," a voice said. "Three men and a woman, at Harvard. They're SETI people and a radio astronomer."

Hightower nodded. "Figures. Bring them to D.C. HQ interrogation." He thumbed the phone off and looked at the president. "Our people have the four who stole our thunder with the alien. They are on the way here."

The president nodded. "Keep me posted."

In his limo, Hightower wished for the days when he was slogging in the rice fields. At least you knew who your enemy was—everybody other than your own unit—and the politics was far removed. You slogged, you cooked anybody who waved a weapon in your direction, you kept your head down and changed your socks frequently. A lot easier than dealing with an idiot commander in chief and a peacenik secretary of defense. And civilians who stuck their unregulated noses where they damn sure did *not* belong.

He sighed. Well. He had taken the job knowing what it entailed. If you get to be the top dog, you have to watch your rear constantly, there was always somebody out there who would nibble your butt if they could get their teeth into it. And it was your fault if you let them get too close.

Those four civilians would be here in a couple of hours and he'd have dossiers on them to read well before they arrived. This was an interrogation he was going to handle personally. Damned fools didn't know what they were messing in, and he was going to set them straight in a hurry.

Always somebody trying to sneak in close enough for that butt-bite.

Damn.

18

Dr. Karagigian said, "Excuse me, but are we under arrest?"

"Not exactly," the federal agent nearest him said. He was tall, a good six-ten or -eleven. Must have been a basketball player in college, Stewart guessed. A center or a forward, maybe. Not somebody you'd miss in a crowd. Stewart thought that might be a disadvantage in a federal agent, but apparently it wasn't.

The guns had been put away, but the operatives swarmed like roaches over the equipment in Jerry's lab. Two of the men were obviously well versed in computers; their fingers danced like dervishes as they tapped keyboards and downloaded files into portable hard drives.

"What does that mean?" Karagigian asked.

"We'd like you to come with us and answer a few questions," the basketball player said. "Voluntarily."

"And if we choose not to do so?"

"Then you'll be arrested and charged with treason."

"That is preposterous!"

"Perhaps, Dr. Karagigian, but you know about top-secret material. We'll let the lawyers sort it out later. One way or another, you *will* be coming with us. The choice is, to do it voluntarily as good citizens wishing to help their country, or as traitors in handcuffs. That probably won't look too good on your resume. Potential employers take a rather dim view when you check the little 'Have you ever been arrested?' box on an application and then fill in the 'why' blank as 'treason.' "

The professor tried again. "I'd like to call my attorney."

"In due time, sir. Right now, we've got a plane to catch."

"Plane?" Jerry put in. "To where?"

"You'll see when we get there."

"But—my lab!"

"Our people will take very good care of it. Come along, please."

Stewart looked at Jess. "I'm sorry I got you into this," he said.

"It was my choice," Jess said. She reached out and caught his hand, squeezed it hard.

It didn't help much. Stewart had to admit—to himself, at least—that he was more than a little scared. He had visions of himself in a federal prison with a roommate named Billy Bob. Not a pleasant thought.

Sitting at his desk with the door closed and the phones cycled into take-a-message-unless-they-are-threatening-a-shooting-war, Hightower glanced at the face of his politically incorrect watch. He had a couple such timepieces. His favorite was a wind-up Russian pocket watch, eighteen jewels. It had something about World War II engraved on the back, and hammer and sickle in front of a rifle and sword on the metal pop-up cover over the face. Thing was heavy, stainless steel, had an ornate Roman numeral face, very classy looking. You couldn't buy anything like it made in America, and if somebody did decide to produce one in the U.S., it would cost five times as much as the Russian watch—and probably not be made as well.

But today, he wore his Hiroshima wristwatch. It was done like an old aviator's field watch, big, plain, with glow-in-the-dark numbers and hands. Of course, it was a battery-powered quartz and not run off a mainspring, but still, it was interesting. Part of a limited run of less than a thousand, inscribed into the glass was a B-29 Superfortress, the *Enola Gay*. The word "Hiroshima" was imprinted on the watch's blue face. On the back, there was an engraving of Little Boy, the first atomic bomb used in combat, along with statistics: how powerful it was, how many people it had killed outright and with radiation. Today, the Japanese were America's friends, but in August of 1945, they had been killing each other for several years when the *Enola Gay* flew over doomed Hiroshima. His father had been on a troop ship steaming toward Japan when the first bomb fell, and when the second one, Fat Man, dropped from the skies onto Nagasaki, the war was effectively over in the Pacific. VJ Day was less than a week away. Hellish devices, to be sure, but necessary—though it wasn't considered appropriate to speak of such things now.

Just like the people who wanted to get Huck Finn kicked out of the libraries because of the racist language of his times, a lot of folks wanted to sweep the atom bomb under the rug. Stupid. History was sometimes ugly, but it was what it was. That those two atomic devices might have saved a million or so lives—Americans *and* Japanese, those who would certainly have been lost had the Allies invaded the Japanese home islands—kind of got lost in the hand-wringing in today's ultra-liberal press. Those same folks wanted to give money to the great-great-grandchildren of African slaves, in reparation for what had happened four hundred years ago. Hightower had never owned any slaves. Neither had his father or his father's father. And his great-grandfather had lost his leg at Spotsylvania, fighting for the union to free the slaves. For what, so that his great-grandson could pony up part of his taxes as a gift to people who had no more connection to that war than they did to Hannibal and his elephants? Jesus. When did it all end? He halfway expected some feminist to sue all men because Adam got Eve kicked out of the Garden, never mind that the story went it was her idea to eat that forbidden fruit.

Hell, it was Adam's fault because he was so wishy-washy.

Hightower grinned. Well, okay, he took a certain perverse pleasure in wearing the Hiroshima aviator or carrying the Russian watch in a pocket, just because he liked watching those who were politically correct blanch when they saw him wave such things about. But that was a small thing, a tweak of the beard. In his own dealings with subordinates, he made it a point to be scrupulously fair. People who pissed him off should all suffer equally. As his father had taught him, you might not be able to control what you think or what you feel, but you *can* control what you *do*, and that was the important thing. You might personally believe that all the liberals ought to be rounded up and put on a slow boat to China, but if you treated them like everybody else, that was what mattered. Bad thoughts weren't a hanging offense—not yet, anyway.

Hightower looked at the folder on his desk. He had read the material on the four people collected at Harvard. A college professor, a post-doc, a computer student working on his master's, and another one working on her undergrad history degree. Lord. Who'd have guessed that? Had to give them credit, though, because they had figured out Zeerus's code and beaten everybody else to the punch, including the best cryptographers in the service with full access to top-of-the-line computers. He was looking forward to finding out how.

It was too late to put the lid back on this pot. Reports were coming in from all over. The alien's message blanketed the planet, and this was like a dam with thousands of tiny holes in it. You could stop up one leak, a hundred, a thousand, they were small and easily plugged, but there were too many of them. He'd known it was only a matter of time, but he'd hoped they would have more of it.

Well. Done was done. No point in crying about that which you couldn't change. Best to move on. They had sent their own message to the alien ship and were awaiting turnaround on the signal.

He glanced at his watch again. The four college folk would be here soon. He had to figure out what he was going to do with them.

"Major Hayes?"

"Yes. Is this Jake Holcroft?"

"Yessir."

Hayes gripped the phone tighter. Yes! He had decided to play this cool. He had the recorder running and the tap trying to locate the source of the call. "What can I do for you, Jake?"

"You wanted to talk to me."

"Well, actually, a little more than talk. I wanted to see you, too."

"I figured."

"You know you overheard something you weren't supposed to. We have to discuss that."

"Yeah. Trouble rides all parts of that mess, don't it?"

"I'm afraid so, son. You want to tell me where you are?"

"I don't think so. If you tell me where you are, I'll come there."

"My office is—"

"No, sir, not your office. I want to see you alone. At your house."

Hayes smiled. Here, there, it didn't matter where, long as the boy showed up. "I'm in Washington, D.C., Jake. That's a ways from where I saw you."

"I'm not there anymore."

"Can you get here?"

"I can get there. It'll take me a little while. I can be there in four hours. Tell me where."

Hayes glanced at the clock on the wall over the phone. Be pretty late but he didn't want to scare the kid away. "Sure." He gave Jake his address.

"See you." He hung up.

Hayes put the receiver down on its base. He had a sudden flash of fear. How good an idea was it to give the kid his *home* address? Shouldn't he have met him at a restaurant or somewhere?

He's just a kid, what are you worried about?

Well, there was his gun-nut father, for one. Still running around loose.

But he wants to get away from his father. So he comes here. Easy.

Too easy, his little worry voice said inside his head.

Too easy? C'mon. I had to chase the little sucker all over the country, didn't I?

You lost him. You'd never have found him again; this kid is sharp.

But he's just a kid. He's afraid. Worried he's going to jail.

You think so, but it's too easy.

Hayes shook his head. One of his instructors in ROTC had been fond of telling them that if something looked too easy, then it probably was, and the snafu factor was always, repeat, *always* lurking in the bushes waiting for you to relax so it could jump on your ass. Do I make myself clear, ladies and gentlemen?

But—what was to be done? The kid was on his way. Either he'd show up or he wouldn't, and either way, he wouldn't be any worse off than he was now, would he?

Maybe.

Hayes chewed on his lower lip. Maybe. Maybe he'd better replay the kid's message and this conversation and see if there was anything he missed. Might as well, it wasn't like he had anything else to do for the next four hours.

He reached for his phone.

Jake turned and looked up at his father.

"You did good, boy." To the other two men standing behind Jake, Seth said, "Let's go."

"What about me?" Jake asked.

"You stay here. Marlene will take care of you. We'll be back as soon as your friend the major tells us what we want to know."

Jake watched his father and the other men leave.

Oh, man.

Laurie used the stair stepper in her condo's gym—actually her second bedroom. She had been pumping for ten minutes, still had twenty more to go, and had worked up a pretty good sweat. The headband kept the perspiration out of her eyes. One, two, three, four, she had a good rhythm going, her heart rate right in the middle of the target zone for a woman her age, about one-sixty. The electronic box on the upright post of the climber scanned through its functions—steps per minute, elapsed time, number of calories burned. A lot of her friends who worked out on aerobic devices, bikes and climbers and rowers and such, either read or watched the news as they exercised, but she preferred to keep her full attention on the business at hand. According to the experts, you got more out of it if you focused on it completely. It was a kind of meditation, though she usually did more thinking than was considered valid for meditation. Oh, well. At least she wasn't on the phone or the laptop.

Her calves were tight, her thighs already pumped and aching, and thirty minutes was going to be tough tonight. Push, push, push, extend the feet, shove with the toes!

The jog bra chafed under one arm and she adjusted the elastic band so it stopped pinching her. Other than the bra, all she had on was a pair of nylon running shorts. Mostly she wore running shoes when she did this, but sometimes she did it barefoot. Despite the sweat and muscle glow, she felt bloated. It was about time for her monthly visit from Mister Red. That was one part of going through the change she wouldn't mind.

Larry had stirred things up good with this business about the alien. Her boss had almost blown an artery, but things had quieted down, at least for now.

The calm before the storm, she suspected. If Larry was right, this was all going to be big-time public in a matter of weeks, if not days, and when that happened, it was *really* going to stir things up. Laurie had been checking out the spin docs in the administration subtly, to see how they'd handle something this weird, and the feeling she got was not a good one. Some kinds of news just didn't get managed very well, and she had an idea this would be in that camp.

Step, step, step, push, push, push, extend that foot!

So here she was, on a stairway to nowhere, wondering how the approaching spaceman was going to affect her boss's chances for reelection. It was fall, so the thing would get here next spring sometime, and the campaign would be in full swing. Somehow, they had to turn that to their advantage.

Her private phone rang. That would be Larry.

Good. She'd never make her half hour tonight. She let the step she had her weight on settle to the bottom, and moved to the phone.

"Hello."

"Want to see what he looks like?" Larry said.

"Who?"

"You know. The visitor from another planet with powers and abilities far beyond those of mortal men."

"You have a *picture* of him?"

"Yep. We intercepted his latest message to the college types. You're gonna love this."

"Are you coming over?"

"Can't yet. I've got those four yahoos to talk to first. Why don't you meet me at my place, say in two hours?"

"Sounds like a deal to me," she said. She hung up and padded to the bathroom to take a shower. Wasn't life interesting?

19

Hayes had lost track of the time as he played with the message and conversation with Jake Holcroft. He'd listened to them several times. There were a couple of odd constructions in the boy's sentences, but he couldn't see any significance to them. He thought about them for a while, then finally transcribed them onto a sheet of paper and looked at the words.

"Hi. This is Jake Holcroft. I—I need to talk to you. To reach a place—to reach a place where I don't have to go to jail! I'll call back in an hour."

And the line in their conversation that sounded funny went: "Yeah. Trouble rides all parts of that mess, don't it?"

Was this just some new speak kids were using? Or the little genius's personal oddball construction?

What was it?

He glanced at the clock. Almost time for Jake to show up, if he was really coming here. Well. It would be moot, then, wouldn't it? What difference did it make?

But it bugged him.

To reach a place where I don't have to go to jail. . . .

Trouble rides all parts of that mess. . . .

What was it about those sentences?

Hello?

He saw it. The first four words. The first letters of each—

Jesus!

The doorbell rang.

Zeerus met Akeerum on the roof of the tallest building in Aerie City for their duel. Akeerum was three seasons older, at his peak physically, and leader of the Second Wing, the organization that rivaled and usually overshadowed Zeerus's own group, the Red Perch.

Akeerum flexed thick shoulders and spread his heavy arms wide. "Ah, Zeerus. You issued Challenge. So, come fight with me. Let the Ancestors decide who soars and who plummets." He grinned, clacked his teeth, made his thick muscles dance. His rut musk fouled the air.

Zeerus was young and arrogant, but not stupid. Akeerum would tear him to pieces on the ground. He said, "Can you still glide, Akeerum? Unless you've sprained your wings bending low to kiss the backsides of the Cloud Nest's fat and flightless Cabal?"

"I can sail *you* into the ground, you leaf-eating elbow sucker," Akeerum said.

"We'll see about that."

Zeerus took three running steps and leaped, kept his wings folded so his arc over the low wall on the roof was short and fast-decaying. He fell for three heartbeats, then snapped his extenders out, caught air, and banked left.

Akeerum was just behind him, a hair slower, and his wheel left a bit wide. He was big, but he wasn't going to win any aerobatic contests. Zeerus was betting on that.

Zeerus stalled, folded his wings, dropped like a big rock. And knowing that members of the Cloud Nest, the Red Perch, and the Second Wing were all watching, he tucked and rolled in a quick triple front somersault before flaring his span to the fullest. He sailed right and caught the thermal rising from the heat vent over the power conduit on the shorter building next to his launch site. He sank, but began to circle up in the riser as Akeerum dived past and tried to catch his wingtip with one flailing hand.

Zeerus saw the glitter of metal on Akeerum's claws. So. He wore sharpened lengtheners. That was allowed. They wouldn't be poisoned, not for this kind of contest, but they would shred a wing quick enough. It was four hundred body-lengths to the streets below, and a ruined wing would corkscrew you into an uncontrolled spin as you fell. This moment, you flew in Aerie City; the next moment, you'd fly with the Ancestors.

Zeerus felt a cold stab of fear. Well. He had surprises of his own for the treacherous Second Winger.

Akeerum found the thermal and wheeled right, flapped, and bounced upward half a body-length.

You had to give him that, he was mulking strong. It took a lot of power to beat one's wings and rise in full gravity. No Avitaur could fly like a bird, of course; even the smallest female was too heavy, and none had the breast-to-wing ratio of a bird or even a hakteroptis. Still, there were a few who had used weights and exercises and strengthened their pectorals and extenders so they could work the wings to an advantage while glid-ing. Sometimes enough to add a span or so of thrust at a crucial moment. Zeerus himself had done such training, though he wasn't in Akeerum's class. In his hatchling days, before he had become so much the rising politician, Zeerus had been quite active in the summer games. He had done all right at hand-to-hand spin wrestling, had won several long-glide contests, once finding natural thermals over the Suteibu Mountains in which he had been able to stay aloft soaring for the better part of an after-noon. A glorious day, that. Though his strategy and tactics had been bet-ter in games of the mind than of the body, he had flown with the best . . .

No time to think of such things now. Zeerus folded right, fell side-ways. He had the altitude, and the advantage was his.

He flashed past Akeerum, who dodged and curled away. A good move, but not quite enough. Zeerus slammed his fist into the older Avitaur's ribs, heard bone crack wetly.

Got you!

Hardly a killing blow, but it was the first to land from either fighter.

Zeerus twisted, partially spilled air from his luff, and dropped out of the hard-rising thermal. His rate of descent quickly increased in the cooler air. He glided downward and toward the river, seeking the heat vent above the Menahmenah restaurant where a smaller but more fra-grant updraft rose. He should have plenty of time . . .

Behind him, Akeerum cursed loudly and looped around to follow.

All things considered, they were probably evenly matched. Akeerum was bigger and stronger but Zeerus was quicker. And smarter. On the ground, in a contest of pure power, Zeerus would certainly lose, but in the air, big muscles weren't as useful. As long as he could keep Akeerum from closing and ripping, he would win.

He had a plan. Akeerum was mighty, but Akeerum was not particularly bright.

The restaurant's thermal was farther away than he remembered, but he smelled the cooking odors wafting upward now. Savory odors of local meats, boiled, fried, baked, seared, some of them raw. He could sense the main plume of heat there, just ahead.

He had flown this area the first time three weeks ago, familiarizing himself with currents and structures. He had sailed it four more times before he issued his challenge to Akeerum. An Avitaur in an air duel ought to know as much about the arena as possible. As the Sage said, Only a fool soared into unknown air with the cold blue sea waiting below. He was hardly a follower of the Sage, but every now and then, the advice had certain merit.

He reached the updraft, spread wide his wings and caught as much of it as he could, leaned into a tight upward spiral.

Akeerus came in, tried to gain height by flapping so he could top Zeerus, but was too heavy in the cooler sky. The larger Avitaur sliced into the restaurant's pungent thermal two body-lengths below. But he kept using his wings and he gained a little on Zeerus. He loved to use all that muscle.

Good. It was Akeerum's power that would be his downfall.

When the thermal ebbed and dissipated, gave it up to the cold, Zeerus was higher than his original launch, easily five hundred body-lengths above the ground. And Akeerum was right behind him, still flapping to gain the ascension. If he could get a span or two higher than Zeerus when both left the thermal, Akeerum would have the advantage in a long soar.

An advantage Zeerus wanted his enemy to have.

Now came the tricky part. Zeerus put himself into as shallow a glide as he could, aimed away toward the river and away from the center of the city. His destination was not that far, but he had to reach it at

the proper altitude and angle if his plan was going to work. He needed
to defeat Akeerum, that went without saying, but he also needed to do
so in a most decisive manner. And it was risky. A missed angle, a few
heartbeats off, and he would lose. A loss meant the end of his dreams
of power, and much worse. This was not a duel for touch points, it was
to the death.

He was not ready to die.

"Turn!" Akeerum yelled from behind him. "Turn and fight like a
hero!"

Akeerum was well back, but higher than Zeerus, a good two body-
lengths higher. Good.

"Catch me if you can, *stuong*-dropping!"

"You can't flee forever, leaf eater!"

Akeerum had to be feeling in control, Zeerus figured. He was
higher, stronger, older, and they were in a long glide pattern. All things
being equal, he would be able to sail farther than Zeerus. All things
weren't equal, of course; Akeerum was heavier and would sink faster,
but since he *was* higher, it would probably even out. If they touched
down about the same time, it would end in a ground fight, and
Akeerum had a decided advantage there. He was secure in his physical
power, second to none in the city. He was higher and both Avitaurs
were losing altitude at near the same rate, so it was only a matter of
time.

There. Just ahead and to the left, there was the brick distillery
building and the no-longer-in-use cylindrical metal water tower next to
it. The shadowy space between them was narrow but plenty wide
enough for a pair of Avitaurs flying in line to pass through it easily.

Zeerus was aware of other Avitaurs soaring behind them, of some
perched on structures they passed, watching with powered lenses as
the combatants flew by. There was much interest in this duel. The win-
ner would add to his group leadership of the loser's flock, and thus be
able to lead the new and larger combined force into power, kicking the
corrupt Cloud Nesters out in the process.

Yes. There were watchers aplenty. Waiting to see who would survive.

Without making it obvious, Zeerus spilled a bit of air from his
wings, increased the angle a hair. Slowed. He made a half-hearted flap,

then another, striving to appear tired. He dropped a little faster. Careful now, he had to make it look good. . . .

He could almost hear Akeerum mentally grinning. He *could* hear the bigger Avitaur flapping his own powerful wings, gaining a little more height and speed, moving to a point almost directly above and behind the fleeing Zeerus. He would be jockeying for position. Trying to line up for the feet-first power drop, the classic Air Leap, an upward sweep of the wings to drive one's body down, hind claws slashing through the wings and muscle of the helpless victim below, almost no risk at all to the attacker. The mulking coward wouldn't turn and fight? Fine. Step on his back like you would tread on a bug. That was the way of it. No finesse—but certainly it was effective.

Power fliers loved such techniques.

Almost. Almost there . . .

Now Zeerus did flap with real power of his own. Gained a little on Akeerum. Heard Akeerum curse and redouble his efforts. He would not be outmuscled!

Almost, almost . . . Zeerus felt the hint of cold . . .

Now!

Zeerus snapped himself upright as if he were standing in mid-air, stroked hard with his wings, and stalled. Tucked and rolled backward into a ball and fell.

To a seasoned duelist watching, it would seem a grievous error. Akeerum could power-dive and ride Zeerus down like a child's slide, force him into the nearest rooftop or the ground and stomp him. It was a beginner's mistake.

But Akeerum was too busy powering himself forward, using his great strength to ready himself for the Leap, a move to humiliate as well as destroy. Zeerus was running and he was chasing him and he had not expected the coward to just stop! Well. No matter. He banked sharply, spilled air, lost lift but made the turn.

He hadn't expected Zeerus to drop.

Nor had he expected to coast at that precise instant into the icy downdraft that ran down between the water tower and distillery like a cold river.

It was as if a giant slapped Akeerum, batted him down like a kelit bats a moth.

Akeerum screamed.

Such downdrafts were unusual but not unknown. In the days when the old water tower was still in use, the downdraft had been charted and marked with flashing lights. It had been many seasons since the tower had been used for storage, however, and the air next to it had long since been harmless.

But four days ago, massive pumps had been used to divert portions of the river into the great pipes that fed the tower. Those in a position to notice and wonder and speak of this had been bribed or threatened or otherwise silenced. The cold waters of the river now filled the old tank. The Ancestors had built well. There were hardly any leaks. And the downdraft was back.

Akeerum screamed and tumbled, but the scream was of rage and not fear. Even though he wasn't the greatest flier on the planet, he would surely pull out before he hit the ground; one didn't reach adulthood without learning how to handle a simple downdraft.

He would have surely pulled out before he hit the ground—except that somebody had erected a series of poles a few body-lengths down the tower, poles that jutted outward with coils of thorned spring-wire looped loosely between them. All in shadow and painted to look like the dark paving below.

Akeerum hit the wires. Hundreds of metal thorns dug into his flesh as the wire pulled loose from the poles and wrapped itself around the falling Avitaur.

The strongest Avitaur who ever lived would not have been able to break loose in time.

When Akeerum hit the ground, he was wrapped up tighter than a mummified Ancestor. He hit so hard he bounced. Twice.

Zeerus sailed back and forth in lazy figure eights until he reached the ground. He folded his wings and walked to where his dead opponent lay. Smiled down at his former foe.

Winning was good. Winning with style was better.

Zeerus awoke from his dream of past glory, clacked his teeth at the pleasant memory.

Ah, if only his trip to the planet of ape-spawn would go so smoothly.

20

Steve Hayes felt a cold stab of panic. If the warning he'd just figured out in the message was true, that probably wasn't Jake at the door. Who it was and why they were there, he'd worry about that later. Right this second, he needed to prepare to meet a threat.

He had gotten dressed, in anticipation of the kid's arrival, but his gun was in the bedroom on the dresser.

The doorbell rang again.

Gun.

But as he moved toward the bedroom, the oddest thought darted into his mind, like some small animal scurrying across a road in the glare of approaching headlights: He sure as hell didn't want to shoot that thing inside.

His .357 was about as effective a handgun as you could carry. With the ammunition he used, ninety-seven times out of a hundred any single solid hit would take all the fight out of an attacker. Six rounds should put the meanest sucker alive down and out. But in order to get that kind of stopping power, the .357 packed a lot of oomph into each cartridge. And that oomph translated into overpenetration if you missed and a hellaciously big noise even if you didn't miss.

He didn't want to be killing his neighbors. And he didn't want to get kicked out of the military on a disability, either.

Hayes had an uncle who'd been a state trooper somewhere in the Midwest. Illinois, Indiana, like that. One night late, his uncle had been sitting in his cruiser writing an accident report when two armed-robbery felons on the run decided to shoot him and take his car. They opened fire from a few feet away. They were lousy shots, all they did was punch a couple of holes in the cruiser. Uncle Ron returned fire and knocked both felons off their feet with a total of four rounds from his S&W .357 service revolver. Both attackers eventually died.

End of incident.

But it was also the end of his uncle's field career. The blast of the .357 going off inside the car blew out both of Ron's eardrums. Even after several surgeries, he never recovered enough of his hearing to go back on the street. He spent the remainder of his job behind a desk shuffling paper, and retired after twenty years with a partial disability. By the time he was sixty, he was deaf as a dirt clod.

Amazing that Hayes would worry about such a thing with danger knocking on his door, but there it was.

On the top shelf of his bedroom closet was an orange plastic box. Hayes grabbed it, opened it. Inside the box was a .22 pistol. It was an old Erma, a copy of a German Luger. He'd picked it up at a gun show, smoothed the action and polished the feed ramp, then had it nickel-plated for a more or less waterproof kit gun he could take camping or fishing. He figured it would be good for snakes—or shooing off bigger vermin.

He popped the Erma's magazine. It didn't have a lot of stopping power, you'd have to go for a head shot to be sure to put somebody out of the fight, but if he had to shoot, he wouldn't end his career saying "Huh?" And sometimes just waving a gun at somebody was enough to keep it from going any further. A full-sized Luger was a wicked-looking weapon.

The doorbell rang again.

"Hold on a second, I just got out of the shower!" he yelled at the door. He grabbed a handful of loose .22 Mini-Mag ammo from the gun box and shoved them into the ersatz Luger's magazine. Seven, eight—it would hold ten but he was running out of time. He slid the magazine back into the pistol's butt, racked the toggle mechanism, chambered a round, shoved the safety forward and off.

He took a deep breath and went to answer the door.

* * *

Amazing, Hightower thought. The president was right: *Why don't I have people like these working for me?*

Karagigian was a full professor and had some background in government work and a whole list of credits in the field, so his presence here was not so surprising. But this . . . *kid* who got the message, then figured it out? Well, that wasn't on the menu.

Hightower said, "So let me make sure I have this straight. You pulled a copy of the first message off the system after Dr. Karagigian deleted it?"

Steward Davies said, "Yes, sir. It wasn't actually gone. When you delete something, the computer just tells you it is erased and makes that space available for more storage. As long as it hasn't been overwritten yet, you can recover it. Sometimes."

"So why didn't Frick and Frack, the two FBI men who went to see you—and who now have your computer in custody, by the way—find the message on your system?"

He was a good-looking kid, not what you'd think of a computer geek. He smiled. "Because there are programs that overwrite something you don't want found when you delete it. I've got one."

Hightower nodded. He looked at the young woman. "And you just went along for the ride?"

"Why not? Nothing we did was illegal."

"I think your government might argue that point, miss."

"Stewart recorded a message, that was his job. He copied it after Dr. Karagigian told him it was a false signal; that might get him fired, but it isn't illegal. And there's no law that says he can't talk back!"

"After the FBI came to see him?"

"Last I heard, the FBI doesn't make the laws, General Hightower. Or interpret them."

"Aid and comfort to America's enemies is treason, is it not?"

She glared at him. "And is this visitor an enemy? When did you determine that, sir?"

He had to grin at her. Girl had guts. They all did. The kind of people who did the country proud—unless they were in your hair. He sighed. Well. What *was* he going to do with them? Karagigian was cleared to a point not too far below this one, they could muzzle him. And probably they could shut these three kids up, too, if they explained how serious this was and threw a few threats at them. Federal prison was a great bargaining chip. Then again, there was something about these people that he liked and admired. He had a thought.

"So, if you were in my position, what would you do with you?" He waved to encompass them all.

"Throw us in jail," the boy said. "That's the only way you can guarantee we won't tell anybody about all this. And that's what you're after, right?"

"Right." He liked the boy's response. "But there is another way. Congratulations. You just went to work for the government."

"Huh?" Stewart said.

"Son, we'd rather have you for us than against us. You beat my people by a country mile. As of the day you first heard the message from space, you were government researchers. We'll have to *ex post facto* that, get you some GS numbers and a nice salary to go along with it, plus a bunch of secrecy papers to sign."

"You mean we'll get to stay on this? Talk to the alien?"

"Well, you will have to temper your responses, there are other people who will have to be consulted about what you say and when you say it, but essentially, yes."

"I'm in," Stewart said. No hesitation. He looked at his girlfriend. "Jess?"

"If you think it's okay, then okay."

"Dr. Karagigian?"

The professor looked at his nephew, who nodded. He knew which way that wind blew. He looked back at Hightower. "Given our options? We accept."

"Good. I'll have all the necessary arrangements made. You might have to relocate. We'll be setting up a site for this project and we haven't decided just where yet. Probably New York or here in Washington. I believe we can square things with your current employers. Or in your case, Ms. Rossini, your college. Is moving a problem?"

"In for a dime, in for a dollar," Stewart said.

Hightower smiled again. Any time you could turn a potential enemy into an ally, you were better off.

All his problems should be so easy to solve.

* * *

When Steve Hayes looked through the peephole in his door, he saw one man. The guy wore an old army fatigue jacket and green, big-pocket pants, looked to be about forty, with a scraggly beard. By himself? The man glanced to the left and right, and Hayes was sure there were at least a couple of others out there, probably pressed up against the wall out of sight.

Beardo kept his right hand next to his hip and Hayes would bet a year's salary against a quarter that the guy had a piece under that jacket.

No sign of Jake.

He gripped the little .22 tighter. Did he want to shoot it out with two or three armed men?

Not even if he'd had a twelve-gauge pump. Surely not with this little mouse gun. He reassessed his choice of weapons. Maybe a little noise wasn't so bad.

Abruptly, Hayes decided that discretion was the better part of valor. He turned and ran for the fire escape in his bedroom.

The bell rang again, followed by a pounding. He had a good dead-bolt lock on the solid wood door; it would take them some effort to kick it in, even if they had a police battering ram.

He got to the window, peeped to the sides as best he could before opening it. Didn't see anybody on the fire escape or the alley below. He almost opened the window and stepped out, then stopped. Remembered his grandfather's story about alligators in trees. Once, when he was fishing, his grandfather had told him, he'd seen a small alligator drop out of a tree into the river just ahead of his boat. Steve had said, "But alligators can't climb trees!" And the old man smiled and said, "Somebody must have forgot to tell him that."

The pounding on the door came again. Any second now, they would probably try to batter the door open.

Hayes hurried to the bathroom. Quietly slid the small window open, carefully and slowly moved his head out to look at the fire escape above his apartment's window. He was on the third floor of a four-story building.

He didn't see an alligator, but he did see a big man squatting one flight up, a pistol pointed down between his feet. Hayes would have stepped out right in the line of fire.

Damn!

He heard them smashing in the front door to his apartment. Heard wood start to splinter. Must have a ram.

Tactically, this was not a good position. He had to leave. Soon.

Hayes stuck his right arm and head out of the bathroom window. Aimed at the man on the fire escape—lined the sights up on the side of his head—and squeezed the trigger.

Twenty-two or not, it was loud enough to make his ears ring. The acrid smell of gunpowder lapped at him.

The man on the fire escape never knew it was coming. He went boneless and collapsed. Got him right in the temple, Hayes thought. He was probably dead or going to be pretty quick. Hayes would worry about how that made him feel later. He jerked himself back into the apartment, paused long enough to grab his cell phone, then ran to the fire escape and stepped out onto it.

A drop of blood hit his arm, spattered.

He took the steps two at a time.

21

Because she didn't know any better, Marlene let Jake use the computer. He told her he was going to play Myst, and he actually launched the game—but with as much RAM and speed as this thing had, he could toggle between Myst and a bunch of other things without Marlene knowing.

He figured the feds were watching Karagigian's mail these days, and so he punched in the codes he remembered—he never forgot a password or phone number once he learned it—intending to send a message.

But he hadn't done much more than logged on before Marlene wandered back into the room and he had to put Myst back on-screen. She might not be a rocket scientist but she could probably tell a message when she saw one.

"Looks interesting," she said, peering over his shoulder. "Show me how it works."

Well, *piss*! He wasn't going to be able to send mail with her watching. Maybe she'd get bored. Myst was interesting, but there weren't a lot of exploding heads. She was in the militia, she'd probably like that kind of stuff.

"Okay," he said.

* * *

"So," the general said, "how would you protect our friend—or whatever he is—up there from being swamped by other people who'd want to contact him?"

"Change the communication frequency," Jerry said without hesitation. "Ask him to stop transmitting on a band where he's bleeding all over anybody with a transistor radio listening to pop forty and get on a narrow channel nobody is likely to find unless they are specifically looking for it. Ask him to disregard any other transmission if somebody does find him. That would slow down anybody else trying to talk to him. At least until we get the FTL radio built."

The general raised an eyebrow. "Excuse me?"

Stewart said, "Oh, I guess your guys haven't finished translating the last message from Zeerus. He's sent us the plans for a device that transmits and receives a signal faster than light. If we had that, it would be a private line."

"I thought that was impossible."

Dr. Karagigian said, "You know the bumblebee story?"

The general laughed. "I see what you mean."

"Am I missing something?" Stewart said.

Dr. Karagigian put on his lecture face. "Long before your time, Stewart. Some years ago, engineers did a study of bees. Using the knowledge they had at the time, regarding lift, wing surface area, the muscular strength of bees, and aerodynamic theory, they calculated things out precisely and determined that it was quite impossible for bees to fly."

Jess laughed. "That must have gone over big. 'Oops. There goes another one.' "

"Precisely," the professor said. "That an alien is within the boundaries of our planetary system, inside a space vessel in which he presumably rode from a *different* planetary system, makes a lot of our theories about how difficult or impossible such things might be moot. If he can fly faster than light, we can probably take him at his word that he can send messages faster than light, too."

"If it *is* an alien to whom we are talking," the general said. "That remains to be proven beyond a reasonable doubt."

"One way to find out," Stewart said. "Let's build the device. If it works, that would go a long way to convincing most scientists I know."

"And probably most politicians, too," the general said.

* * *

Zeerus smiled at the incoming message. So, it begins. His first connections were already positioning themselves to be his sole contacts on the planet. Good. They indicated they were going to build the communications device, doubtless to make certain they were the only ones talking to him, though they didn't phrase it thus.

Primitive cultures were all alike. Greedy, paranoid, prideful, vain. Also good, because they would be much easier to manipulate. Since this was their first contact with an offworld species other than their own—if you didn't count joyriders who might have stopped by to spy on the primitives for fun a few times—then there would be much made of who got to welcome the visitor. What was the word they used in the most complex of their languages? Clout? The original meanings had to do with patches to protect trees or somesuch. That had somehow been changed so that it also meant striking something with one's fist, but idiomatic usage had apparently transmuted that definition to a kind of intangible power.

Which meant politics. The goals might be different but the process was the same almost everywhere. Power ultimately came from the barrel of a disrupter, but the layers hiding the weapon from view were many and varied. The zelk glove over the durell fist.

The ape-spawn had grasped that early on, though they were far from mastery of it.

Zeerus was a master. He would show them.

He bent to send another message. Assuming they followed the instructions, they should be able to construct the transceiver in a matter of a week or two, none of it was beyond their current level of technology. And for now, he would play along with their request to keep their communications limited.

For now.

22

Business didn't grind to a halt, especially for the chairman of the Joint Chiefs, just because somebody earth-shaking was coming to dinner. There were papers to be signed, reports to be reviewed, orders to be given.

And admirals to be put out to pasture.

Rear Admiral Calvert Ulysses Baxter—"Cub" to friends and enemies alike—was about to retire, and would do so much against his will. Hightower's worry was that Cub would have to be dragged away kicking and screaming. He had the horsepower to move him but he didn't want to use it; he had known the man for more than twenty-five years and he liked and admired him. He was old-style military, damn the torpedoes and full speed ahead. The man loved a fight and never once offered an enemy a view of his backside.

In a shooting war, Cub was the man you wanted barking the orders from the bridge of the ship upon which you sailed into battle. Or the drinking buddy you wanted watching your back if you got into a brawl in a bad port bar in Singapore and the bottles and knives came out. He was a warrior and worth his weight in diamonds when the rockets began to fly. At sixty-eight, he should have already packed his bags—he had served well and honorably for forty-five years. But he didn't want to go; the navy was his life. Unfortunately, there weren't any enemies for him to sink at the moment. Hightower had found a spot for him in the Pentagon doing liaison work with the navy and DOD contractors. Not the most glorious way to end a distinguished career: Cub Baxter had been on warships that had bellowed in anger off the coasts of Korea and Vietnam; had stood fast during the Cuban Blockade; had commanded a task force that unloaded hotware at Saddam in the Middle East—but it was what Hightower could find for him.

But Cub's pugnacious ways had gotten him in trouble more than once when he was asea, and did again while he was pushing paper. The man did not take advice on his personal behavior.

Cub Baxter stood accused of sexual harassment. Which was patently stupid to anyone who knew the man. He might be crude at times, having come up through the ranks, but he was an officer and a gentleman in most matters. At least by the standards Hightower and Cub had grown up with.

Standards no longer in vogue, unfortunately. Hightower shook his head.

Cub looked at him. "Bad, huh, Larry?"

"You know it is."

"Christ, I never laid a hand on her! She's young enough to be my granddaughter! What do you think I am?"

"I think you're one of the best sailors who ever put foot on a United States naval vessel. If it was up to me, I'd put the whole damned mess in a folder and file it where Sam Spade couldn't find it on his best day."

"Last time I looked you were still the chairman of the JCOS."

"Who serves at the pleasure of the commander in chief."

"And you're gonna fire me because I complimented a secretary on her gams?"

"You know better than that. If it was just the once we wouldn't be having this conversation." He tapped the file on his desk. "I've got twenty-odd complaints from five other women over the last year and a half. You've been warned over and over."

"I never touched any of *them*, either. I didn't make a pass at any of 'em. I never use foul language in front of a lady. I am not a dirty old man."

"I didn't say you were. But you and I, we grew up in different times. Attitudes have changed."

"That's for damn sure. You got *guys* wearing makeup and earrings in the service, perverts who run around half naked on tee-vee grabbing their private parts, and dope fiends selling poison on every other corner. You got child pornographers screaming about their right to free speech. Kids beating up teachers, kooks shooting doctors. You think that's better than telling a woman she looks good enough to eat? You think I should stop at one of those shops in the mall and get my nose pierced?"

"No, I don't. You're an old war dog, I don't expect you to change your ways at this late date. But things are how they are, Cub. Even in the service. You know what happened at Tailhook."

"I do and it was a damned shame. I've been to those things and I never saw a woman run the gauntlet who didn't want to. The navy isn't a nursery school; a woman who wants to be in combat needs to be tough enough to walk down a hall full of drunken aviators without coming apart at the seams."

"Maybe so. But here, it's the perception we're dealing with, and my boss—and he's your boss, too—is running for reelection. He doesn't want any stories about the people he has working for him to get in the way of a second term. And the service is high-profile."

"And there's no place for me in it anymore, is that what you're saying? I'm an old fart who's outstayed his welcome?"

Hightower took a deep breath and blew half of it out. "You said it, Cub, not me."

"But you agree." Not a question.

"I'm afraid so."

For what seemed a long time, neither man spoke. Cub seemed to shrink within himself as he looked down the road and saw his career coming to an end. Hightower felt tremendously sorry for him. He was like the old Roman watchdog, was Cub. Ate too much, crapped in the wrong places, seemed more trouble than he was worth—until the burglar came in through a window. That was the problem with combat officers. The guy you need throwing steel is not the one you need shuffling paper clips.

Cub swelled a little, sat up straighter, got a gleam in his eyes. Softy, he said, "And if I want to fight you on it?"

"Then I'd probably get a bloody nose and my butt kicked, because you and I both know you're as tough as boiled seagull. I don't want to shoot it out with you. But in the end, I've got all the big guns. You could hold the strait for a while, go out in a blaze of glory—but at what cost? Even if you won, you know what a Pyrrhic victory is. Would it be worth it? To have half the country think you're a dirty old man who drools on the secretaries?

"Sail away, Cub. Go out with your head up and with your name unstained." He picked up the folder. "Ship out and this goes into a round file, I can manage that much. Take your retirement, open a school for naval cadets, use that forty-footer you got on the bay and teach them about the ways of deep water. Find yourself a girlfriend who likes to sail, and get back to the sea, that's where you belong. This isn't the navy."

Another eon passed. Time dwindled, ran out. Finally, the older man sighed. Nodded. "All right, Larry. You know, I never thought I'd live this long, I figured I'd go down with my ship, it's all been borrowed time for years. I don't guess there'd be any point in making a fuss. I don't really want to stay in a place that doesn't see any use for me. It's not nearly as much fun as it used to be, is it?"

"Admiral, you are not now and never have been a desk sailor. If we get hostilities from anybody we need to reach by sea and you can still walk, I will personally reactivate you and give you any ship you want."

"You would, wouldn't you?"

"Yes, sir."

"Well, I guess that's something."

After Cub was gone, Hightower leaned back in his chair and stared at the ceiling. Cub was right. The world wasn't nearly as much fun as it had been when he was young and full of piss and vinegar. And someday in the not-too-distant future, it could just as easily be him sitting on the other side of that desk being told to pack his gear and cashier out.

Damn. Damn.

Laurie stood in the wings of the press conference room, watching the milling reporters and waiting for the president. Melanie Fawcett stood talking to the new guy from CNN next to the rostrum. The boss was pretty good about giving conferences; he wanted the press on his side. He exposed himself to the corps frequently, at least offered a pretense of openness.

He couldn't micromanage the news, but he could avoid calling on people who pissed him off too bad, and they all knew it out there in media land. He'd usually warm up by pointing at some of his fans for a couple of softball questions like "Who do you like in the Super Bowl?" or "What do you think about the flooding in Idaho?" Then he'd move on to the harder stuff once he'd broken the ice. He was quick and seldom caught flat-footed by a reportorial jab.

This meeting, scheduled for forty-five minutes, ought to be a piece of cake. No big scandals, no new troops killed overseas, no cabinet members caught in a porno theater or anything. The main reason for this one was to crow about the recent economic upturn, to take credit before the opposition party could claim it.

She felt the approach of footsteps, turned, saw the Secret Service contingent flanking the boss fore and aft enter the hall behind her.

She turned back and waved at Melanie, caught her attention. "Showtime, babe," Laurie said.

Melanie nodded, stepped up on the platform, and stood in front of the microphone. Melanie was a pro. She didn't lean over, like some slack-wit actor who ought to know better swallowing the mike while accepting an award: "Ladies and gentlemen, if you'll take your seats, please?"

The sound man played "Hail to the Chief"—the boss liked that—as the president strode onto the stage.

He ran through his prepared speech, not using his notes or a prompter, proving he had a good memory, extolling the virtues of his administration and party in effecting the policies that had caused the economy to continue the climb, that—if you believed him—began the very day he took office. This was old hat, but his delivery was excellent. Even his enemies had to agree that the president was, when he was on, a superb speaker. As charismatic as Reagan, more down-home than Carter, a lot briefer than Clinton.

After his speech, he took questions. A fat woman from a Dallas paper lobbed a pumpkin a blind man could have hit, a real general one about welfare. The boss held up Mom, waved the Flag, passed out metaphoric Apple Pie.

Then the PBS guy asked about funding, another potential home run. The polls were quite clear about that: You didn't screw around with *Mystery!* or *Masterpiece Theatre*, so he couldn't go wrong promising that

PBS wasn't going to get shortchanged again if he could help it. Reporters liked to think of themselves as cultured. That went over well.

Then the boss pointed at the hotshot reporter for MNN, Tyler MacMahon's challenge to his old yachting buddy Ted Turner's CNN.

The reporter's name was Bruce Fosse. "Mr. President, will you comment on the reports of radio contact with an extraterrestrial alien purportedly on a spaceship heading for Earth?"

A few people chuckled, thinking it was a joke, but the hotshot stood there, all serious and deadpan, and a few eyebrows went up. Some muttering began.

"Alien spaceship?"

"What is he talking about?"

"Come on!"

Laurie felt her stomach lurch. She hadn't been expecting this. How would the boss handle it? If he blew it off, pretended it was a joke, most of the reporters here would probably go along—for the moment. But Fosse wouldn't be asking if he didn't already know something. And if the boss shucked and jived his way out of it, it would surely come back to haunt him. But still—

They hadn't had a chance to put the right spin on this yet.

"Our scientists and military are aware of a signal that might ultimately prove to be intelligently produced, Mr. Fosse, if that is what you are referring to. Our universities have maintained SETI and CETI programs for years. Many times radio signals have been recorded that seemed as if they might be artificially produced by someone other than ourselves; unfortunately, none of these has ever panned out. I believe there was one a few years ago that seemed very promising, coming at regular intervals four or five times a week almost always around noon. It turned out to be somebody running a leaky microwave oven downstairs from the observatory."

Most of the reporters laughed. Some of them remembered the story. Laurie wouldn't have, except that it had been in one of Larry's reports on SETI and had made the cheat sheet that summed things up for the boss.

"Next question? Peter?"

Laurie smiled. He had played that fairly well. He'd more or less disarmed it without dismissing it entirely. Some of these reporters were idiots and they'd never see past his reply, but a few of them weren't stupid. Sooner or later, one of these brighter lights would ask themselves—or somebody else—how is it that the president, normally not much of a science buff, would have that particular information right there at his fingertips? Why should he know about it at all, if there wasn't something to it?

It was what happened when people stopped to ask the next question that got you into trouble.

Laurie caught Melanie's attention, gave her a "come here" wave of her head.

Melanie moved into the wings. "What?"

"We need to talk," Laurie said. "That last question is a ticking bomb and you ought to know why before it goes off."

"Jesus. You got a bug-eyed monster from outer space on the way here?" She grinned.

Laurie didn't return the grin.

"Oh, come on. No," Melanie said. "Tell me you're putting me on."

"When you get the mob placated and gone, better meet me for lunch. We'll have to sit down with the boss and a couple of the heavyweights. We have a unique problem to manage."

"Oh, girl, I don't need to hear this."

"Oh, girl, yeah, you better."

With Melanie thoroughly spooked, Laurie turned back to watch her boss work. He was doing fine. Nobody followed up on the alien thing, but by the evening news, somebody undoubtedly would start to ponder it.

Tomorrow might be real interesting.

23

Jake didn't know where they were. A clearing somewhere deep in the woods in New England. When they'd left New York, they'd driven mostly northeast; he could tell because the sky started out clear and he was able to locate Polaris. They got to a place in the middle of the night where they stopped and left the van. Jake didn't remember crossing a border into Canada. Maybe Connecticut or Vermont or Maine—one of those.

One of the men took the van and left, and Jake, his father, and three other men hiked into the woods in the dark. About three miles, Jake guessed. The path was narrow and twisty and a couple of times they stopped and turned off the flashlights at the sound of aircraft, but eventually they made it to the camp. There were five or six other men and two women already there. Greetings were exchanged. Jake and his father got assigned quarters.

It was cold—there had been a few snow flurries last night on the way here—and the campsite was rigged for winter. There were four tents, big military surplus jobs with wooden plank floors, kerosene heaters, and cots enough to sleep six people each. The tents were arranged in a square, and the area in the middle had folding tables with a couple of propane cook stoves and several Coleman gas lanterns.

There was also a fifty-five-gallon oil drum with a big fire going in it, fed by wood the men kept piling up next to it.

It was barely dawn when they got up to eat breakfast. They had bacon, eggs, Bisquick biscuits, and coffee. One of the women—Bertha, they called her—a thin and hard-faced bleached blonde of maybe twenty-eight or so, cooked.

Jake ate in silence. His father and the men who'd come in with them were still pissed off.

Apparently, Major Hayes had understood Jake's message. Enough so when the militia arrived and tried to capture him, he got away. Killed one of the men in the process, too. Shot him in the head. His father and the others had talked about it in the van:

"Son-of-a-bitch is good, you got to give him that," one of the men said. He was a tall red-haired man with a scar on his face.

"He was lucky, that's all," another man said.

"Lucky, hell," Jake's father said. "He fired one small-bore round and drilled Bert right in the head. That's not luck. That's skill."

"I thought most of the feds went to the .40 or 10mm," a swarthy man with a dark three-day beard said. "Military's still using Beretta nines, so what's he doing using a popgun? I never even heard the shot. Not too smart, using that little of a piece. Had to be a pissant .22 or a .25, that tiny little hole in Bert. Got no stopping power."

"Had enough power to stop Bert from breathing ever again," Seth Holcroft said. "Guy who can make head shots in combat doesn't need a big caliber. Difference between a scalpel and a hammer."

"How'd he know to run? That's what I want to know," Swarthy said. "He couldn'ta see nobody through that peephole but Billy. And Bert was up the fire escape, so if he looked out the window, he couldn't see him, neither. How is it a man hears a knock on his door, somebody he thinks he's waiting for, but instead of opening up, he grabs a piece, runs to the fire escape, jumps out, and shoots a guy he can't even see?"

"He didn't shoot him from the fire escape, stupid," Jake's father said. "He leaned out the bathroom window and did it."

"How do you know that?" Swarthy said. If being called "stupid" bothered him, Jake couldn't tell.

"Because Bert took the round in the *side* of his head. If he was doing what he had been trained to do, he would have had his back to the wall with his piece aimed straight down between his feet. See if you can follow me here: The only way he could have gotten hit in the *right* temple would have been from his *right* side. The bathroom is the only place the guy could have made the shot—unless maybe he's the incredible goddamned Spider Man."

"Uh, yeah, I guess."

"And whatever spooked him, he's good. I missed him outside the bitch's place because I was shooting with my bad hand, and now this. We underestimated him. That won't happen again." He ground his teeth together.

Jake said, "I'm sorry."

"Not your fault," his father said. "You did your job. Bert is the one who screwed up."

"I guess ol' Bert paid the price," Red said.

"I guess he did," Jake's father said.

So now, here they were, out in the woods somewhere. Maybe they would try to get the major again. Maybe not. Maybe they'd figure he'd really be on his guard now. And for sure, they would figure the major wouldn't trust Jake anymore.

Not real likely he was gonna get a chance to play with a computer out here, and unless they had a laptop with a wireless modem, he wouldn't be warning anybody.

So, now what?

How was he going to get away from his father?

And if he did, where was he going to go? His father knew where Jake's mother was, he couldn't go back there, his old man might kill her. He needed to warn his mother somehow. Plus he had to stay away from guys like this major who had killed one of the militia. They wanted to put him in jail.

Boy. He was really deep in it now.

Laurie awoke to the smell of fresh coffee brewing and the quiet rustle of the newspaper. She glanced at her bedside clock. Almost seven. Next to her in the bed, Larry read the morning's *Washington Post*.

"Mmm. Morning," she said.

"Morning. You want me to get you some coffee?"

"I can get it."

"Let me. You go do your bathroom things and I'll bring you a cup."

She chuckled. " 'Bathroom things'? Just what is it you think I do in there?"

"I don't have a clue," he said. "I'm just a man."

She got up and went into the bathroom. When she got back, he was sitting up, pillows propped behind him, and had a mug of coffee for her. She slid under the covers and sat next to him.

"Sleep okay?"

"You kidding? Nothing like having the chairman of the Joint Chiefs boink your brains out to put you into a trance. I slept like a rock."

"Good. Glad to be of service."

"We didn't get to talk much last night," she said. She sipped the coffee—it was strong enough to stand a spoon up in it—bent, kissed him on the shoulder. "How was your day yesterday?"

"The usual. Things to do, places to be." He paused for a moment. "I retired Cub."

"Good," she said.

"Why 'good'?"

"Because he was a lecherous old goat who should have left years ago. I heard about the harassment suits."

He shook his head. Sipped his coffee.

She caught his mood. He wasn't happy about this. She frowned. "Where there's smoke there's fire. What's the problem? You fired him, didn't you?"

"Doesn't mean I had to like it."

"Come on. You think it was okay for him to be harassing the women who worked with him? The days of keeping them barefoot and pregnant and slapping them around if they didn't behave are gone— and they should be."

He sipped at his coffee again. "I'm not arguing that. But Cub didn't lay a finger on any of those women, didn't require that they sleep with him to keep their jobs, didn't even ask one of them out for dinner or drinks."

"Right. He just told dirty jokes and embarrassed them by commenting on their tits and asses. He made them feel uncomfortable and insecure. There are unspoken pressures when your boss does such crap."

Larry shook his head.

"What?" She was irritated.

"Somebody tells you you've got great-looking legs, that makes you feel uncomfortable and insecure?"

"Depending on the circumstances, yes. In my bedroom with somebody I chose to be with, that's fine. In my office with a man old enough to be my father, no."

"So if I dropped by the White House and said it, you wouldn't like it?"

"You know what I mean. I'm not beholden to you for my job."

"Cub would never have made any of those women do anything to keep theirs. He didn't mean any harm. That's just how he grew up. He spent forty years in the service, that's what he knew how to do. He was a little crude around women, that's all."

"I can't believe you're defending his actions."

"Listen, I *fired* the man. I told him he could leave and keep his honor or we would drag him through the mud before we kicked his butt out. And why? Because he was 'insensitive.' Because some secretaries got their noses bent out of shape over something he *said*, not something he would have ever *done*.

"His government hired him originally because he was a man, because he'd stand up straight and point his gun where they told him and pull the trigger when they told him to shoot. He did it for longer than any of those women have been alive, did it by the numbers and without question. Gave the military his whole life. Now the rules have changed. Now you have to be careful you don't raise your eyebrow crooked because it might *upset* somebody. Heaven forbid somebody might feel *uncomfortable*.

"I'm sorry, but I don't think sensitivity is something you value highly in a war dog. When I see a tank coming at me, I don't want the guy on my left sitting down to have himself a good cry because the armor is so beautiful with the sun shining on it and all."

She blinked, surprised. "We're not in a war," she said.

"Oh, yeah, we are. There aren't any guns going off in the Pentagon, but it's there just the same. It's everywhere. It's yesterday against today. Yesterday always loses. Sooner or later, you, me, everybody we know, we'll be staring stupidly at some kid young enough to be our son shaking his head as he pushes us gently out the door. And we won't understand why the values we grew up with aren't valid anymore when he does it. Or maybe *she* does it. That won't much matter."

She stared at him. This really bothered him. She'd never heard him open up like this.

"Excuse me," he said. "I feel like a dinosaur. I look at Cub and think, 'There but for the grace go I.' "

"You're not like him," she said.

"More like him than you know."

"I'm sorry," she said. "He was your friend. I shouldn't have said what I said."

He shrugged. Stared into his coffee. "That's the way of it. Always has been. I guess I always knew it in theory. Problem is, the older I get, the more I have to look it right in the face. It's hell getting old, though I guess it beats the other option."

He managed a thin smile.

By the time Hayes got back to his apartment, the NSA plainclothes boys were there and going over the place in a flurry of efficiency.

"We need to call the D.C. cops in on this?"

"I don't believe so, Major," the team leader said. He was a short and wide-shouldered man, built like a weightlifter, probably about thirty but almost completely bald. "One of the boys will fix your door. Your perpetrators took the, ah, *package* from the fire escape with them, apparently. We got enough blood to run a few tests if we need to, but that would be kinda beside the point. None of your neighbors saw or heard anything they'll admit to. I think we have a nonincident here, insofar as the D.C. authorities are concerned."

Nonincident.

Several men had broken into his apartment with what certainly hadn't been good intentions concerning him. He had shot one of them dead. The boy he'd been chasing was still at large. Nonincident. Yeah.

"We're about done here, Major. Soon as our smith gets your door repaired, we'll be gone."

Hayes nodded absently.

His cell phone rang.

"Yes?"

"Major Hayes? Dunsmuir on daywatch. We secure, sir?"

"Go ahead, Sergeant."

"We got somebody trying to sneak into that professor's mailbox you had us watching."

"Yes? And . . . ?"

"Well, sir, it was opened, the program, but then the sneaker logged off. Hasn't shown up again."

Hayes considered it. Probably didn't mean anything. "Thank you, Sergeant."

"And sir? You're probably going to want to talk to the colonel."

"Why's that?"

"I wouldn't want to say for sure, sir, but between you and me, I believe your orders might be about to be altered."

"Thanks, Sergeant."

The connection ceased. He stared at his phone, then at the man working on his door.

Hayes frowned. The FBI would grind away, looking for Jake and his father and the idiot militia. Of course. It was their job and they were better equipped than he was—though it had gotten very personal when the guns came out. He didn't want to get pulled off this, but the military did not *ask*, it ordered. Better go and see what it was about to do with him this time.

24

t didn't make the front page of the papers but the story was there.

Laurie sat in her office, reading the *Post*, wherein a would-be comedian ran with the piece in a short and gossipy editorial:

THE RETURN OF ET?

It was like something from a Steven Spielberg movie at the president's press conference yesterday. Television reporter Bruce Fosse, MacMahon News Network, asked a question about contact with extraterrestrials and was given a serious—if somewhat glib—answer.

Fosse's query about alien contact was deftly fielded by the president. The Search for Extraterrestrial Intelligence (SETI) apparently continues in these days of grant cutbacks and downsized expectations in the governmental scientific community. Is such research just another waste—albeit a drop in the budget bucket—of taxpayers' money? Would those dollars be better spent elsewhere?

Or could *The X-Files'* Mulder and Scully be right?

Is the answer really out there?

* * *

Nobody else seemed to have picked up on it, at least not in the print media, and if Fosse did anything with the story, it wasn't on her tape of MNN's coverage. Maybe Fosse didn't have as much as she thought. Or maybe he was holding on to it until he got enough for a real blockbuster.

Her intercom beeped. "Yes?"

"Laurie? Reverend Jimmy is here."

Laurie folded the newspaper. "Send him in."

James Baumgardner Long—Reverend Jimmy to most—was a minister of the faith and executive director of the American Alliance of Baptists, a relatively new and moderate group whose doctrine lay midway between the strict fundamentalists and the looser drinking-and-dancing Baptists. They dunked instead of sprinkled, but you wouldn't hear Reverend Jimmy throwing a lot of hellfire at his congregation; more likely, he'd be telling them to get out and get politically active. His was an airwave ministry—he had radio and cable television shows that reached millions every week. Which is how he and the boss had met and become allies. Laurie suspected her boss's faith was closer to agnosticism than anything else, but he'd never admit that publicly. Having the endorsement of a man who could deliver that many votes was useful. Plus the Rev could put together, at the drop of a hat, a sign-waving demonstration that would fill a big park or block a bunch of streets. All those mothers with their fresh-faced little children waving signs with her boss's name on them sure looked good on the evening news. The boss attended services in Jimmy's church in D.C. and tended to share more than he should with the man.

"Hello, Laurie," Reverend Jimmy said. He was nearing fifty, tall, stout, with a TV preacher's hair: long, shot with enough gray to make him look distinguished, immaculately styled. He had a big grin and a lot of smile lines around his eyes. He wore a white shirt, a blue double-breasted suit, and hand-made Italian leather shoes—his only vice, he liked to say, and the Lord forgave him the shoes because he had given him terrible corns and bad circulation in his feet to balance them out.

"How are you doing, Reverend Jimmy? Have a seat."

He settled into the overstuffed chair across from her desk.

"Something to drink?"

"No, ma'am, I don't believe so."

"So, what can I do you for?"

"Well, Laurie, it's this alien thing. You know the president talked to me about it?"

"Right."

"I've been discussing the matter with some of my board members and we see the possibility of a few problems down the line."

She nodded, said, "Uh huh," to keep the flow going.

"See, the thing is, there's not much specifically in the Bible that talks about such things. Oh, there's Jacob's Ladder to Heaven and the prophet Ezekiel and his vision of the Lord's chariot—the lightnings and the wheels within wheels and all—that covers UFOs and such, but bona fide space creatures talking on the radio, coming here? That's something else. We're going to have to develop our own policy on them."

"You don't figure our visitor is likely to be a Christian?"

"No, ma'am. It might be a bit much to expect him to be a good Baptist. We could live with a Methodist or even a Presbyterian, but somehow I would be real surprised if he was one of those."

"Could be a Jesuit."

"Hoo, Laurie, don't even think such a thing. Bad enough we have human Catholics, we'd really be in trouble with one from Mars." He smiled to show it was a joke.

"And your problem as you see it is . . . ?"

"Exactly how we regard Mr. Ziroose. Certainly he is one of God's children, no matter where he's from. There is some debate about whether he's got a soul, but we're of the opinion that since he can talk to us, probably he does. Our basic feeling here is that he's kind of like the natives in New Guinea or in Africa before the white man got there. We figure his people are unenlightened because they haven't yet had a chance to hear the Word of God."

She smiled. Nobody quite as arrogant as a true believer. "Not that I want to tell you how to do your business or anything, but pretty much every time the missionaries have gone forth before, they've done so from a position of technological superiority. If the natives gave them a real hard time, the natives eventually got their butts kicked for their trouble when the battleship from back home steamed into the harbor and started blasting. This heathen is coming here in a *spaceship*, Jimmy. He's not exactly on the same level with a head-hunting cannibal in Borneo."

"The principle is the same."

"Maybe not. Maybe Zeerus already *has* a religion. Maybe his religion is run by a god who won't tolerate any others, and if you wave Jehovah in his face, maybe Zeerus will get pissed off and start throwing atomic lightning bolts at your church. We don't know what kind of weaponry he might have. We have to be real careful how we proceed here."

The Reverend Jimmy smiled and she could almost hear his thoughts. When you went forth with the Word, you had to risk a few slings and arrows. Besides, Jehovah could take any of the false gods out there hands down. Jimmy couldn't believe otherwise.

She knew he wasn't going to back off in the face of mere supposition. She said, "So what exactly is it you want to do here?"

"We'd like to have the opportunity to talk to this fellow."

"Talk to him? For what? To lead him onto the proper path?"

"Yes, ma'am. We'd be subtle, of course, we'd feel him out, take it slow and easy. We're not fools, Laurie, it wouldn't be like a born-again handing him a pamphlet on a street corner or clonking him over the head with the devil or anything."

Good Lord, she thought. *That's just what we need. Somebody trying to convert an incoming alien into a Christian. If this got out, not only would the press have a field day, every other major religion would scream loud enough for Zeerus to hear them through the vacuum umpty-dump million miles away. You let the Baptists talk to him? Why not us?*

"Why are you telling me?"

"Well, I thought I would run it up your flagpole before I took it to your boss. You could sort of, ah, preview it for the president, get a feel for which way the wind blows. And of course, your support would be greatly appreciated."

Laurie repressed a sigh. Here was a tricky one. She was willing to bet she'd be getting a call from Father Leon Heroumin in the near future, to hear his pitch for the Catholic positioning. And probably after that, a rabbi, an ayatollah, and some Buddhists and Hindus, too. The line forms to the right, folks. . . .

Here was a big fat can of holy worms.

"Let me mull this over for a while, would you, Jimmy? This is a delicate matter and I wouldn't want to do anything precipitous."

"Of course, Laurie. No rush. We've got months before this fellow gets here, right?"

"Right."

After he was gone, she looked at her schedule. She had a busy day lined up and she had the feeling that it might get busier than it appeared before it was done.

Steve Hayes stood in Barker's office. The colonel sat behind his desk. He looked like a man with a happy secret.

"At ease, Major."

Hayes relaxed a hair.

Barker looked at the file folder on his desk. "This turned into quite a mess, didn't it? You managed to track the quarry down but then lost him, then you got your apartment shot up by some screwball militia. Didn't exactly hit a home run here, did you?"

"No, sir."

"Fortunately for you, this exercise has been rendered moot."

"Why is that, sir?"

Barker's voice turned acid. "I'm sure the chairman of the Joint Chiefs was planning to invite me to dinner to chat about that in great detail, Major. Why, I expect he'll call any second now. 'Why' is not your worry. Suffice it to say that General Hightower is no longer interested in pursuing this matter. And because of your performance, you are being reassigned to a post less arduous than catching an eleven-year-old boy."

"Sir?"

"The sergeant will have your orders, Major. Since it seems you need more practice doing field assignments, we have found one that will allow you to stretch your legs—and your abilities."

Hayes's belly twisted as if he had stepped into an elevator shaft and plummeted now in freefall. This sounded bad.

"Dismissed, Major. Have a nice day."

Hayes went to see the sarge with feet turned to blocks of concrete. Well. Maybe it wouldn't be as bad as he expected.

He was right.

It was worse.

Major Steve Hayes, it seemed, was going on a tour of military listening posts. Six in Canada, four in Alaska, one in Greenland, one to an ice-bound ship north of the Arctic Circle. His tour was for the purpose of "evaluating existing operating procedures and determining salient methods for improving the efficiency of aforementioned operating procedures."

Each stop would require a two-week evaluation period.

He did the math. Twenty-two weeks. Five and half months.

Oh, *man!*

This was Barker's doing. Hayes had never fallen all over himself to kiss the paper-pusher's butt. Barker liked being a desk jockey, probably hadn't spent any time in the field since basic training. And he took personal offense at Hayes's desire to shuck his seat-of-the-pants career. The son of a bitch.

Well. He was certainly going into the field now. Winter was coming and the fields into which he was being shoved were apt to be under six feet of snow by the time he got there. And a ship locked into the ice. Head much farther north at any of these postings and guess what? Pretty soon, you'd be heading south.

Oh, man. Oh *shit!*

After his magnificent defeat of Akeerum, Zeerus effectively held Aerie City in thrall. He controlled not only the Red Perch and Second Wing, but much of the decadent Cloud Nest. You could have drowned out the sound of a thunderstorm with that of beating wings as every Avitaur who knew which way the wind blew flocked to Zeerus's cause.

It was a mixed blessing, becoming the de facto ruler of the city. The task of consolidating his power, of readying an assault on world-wide leadership, took much time and energy. No longer did Zeerus have time to spend a lazy afternoon drinking with old friends and hatching devious schemes. No longer did he have idle hours to waste playing in the city's thermals. Real power was not how fast or high you could soar; real power lay in controlling the fastest and highest fliers.

They were the best of times. He was young, strong, smart, ambitious, and no one could stand in his way. When it came time for Primaster to choose a new governor to replace the suddenly deceased Pleera, there was really no other choice. No other candidate dared offer himself.

Yes. Those were the glory days, the days before the fall.

Zeerus shook his head. Here he was in a half trance, behaving like a relic, an old one who would rather live in the past than in the present. Not a good idea. The glory days were wonderful, but they'd been followed by some that were much less stellar. He would never be that young again, nor, he hoped, would he be that stupid. He had a chance to get back into the game with these humans, and while victory was far from certain, at least there was a chance.

A chance was all he ever wanted. And if he should lose again? Well, at least it would happen in blood and thunder—and the heavens would blaze with the light of many funeral pyres before he was done.

He nodded to himself. Yes. Look around the here and now, look to the future, that was the way. It was fine to glance over your shoulder now and then, to allow the past to wrap its nostalgic wing around you, but too much time spent that way was dangerous. You might blunder into something while blinded by your history.

25

What amazed Stewart first was how much equipment had been made available. There were minis in parallel, mainframes, and monster access to the really big boys, the super-Crays. There was radio gear hooked into giant dishes and routed through half a dozen military satellites. There were translation programs, compression programs, libraries, video, audio, and more storage space than you could fill up in a thousand years. It was better than owning your own Incredible Universe store.

Man. It paid to have the chairman of the Joint Chiefs on your side.

Stewart looked around the inside of the huge lab from the leather chair in front of his console. Shoot, this *chair* probably cost as much as the SETI setup back at school.

Then again, he had beaten all this. He had gotten to Zeerus first. Try to stop it as he might—and he wasn't trying too hard—big flashes of pride kept shining through. Just went to show that the best piece of hardware with the slickest software up and running was still a human. Even brute forcing something like chess, the world champion could still outplay the sharpest computer. No working AIs yet.

Even so, he was out of his league. He knew his trick had a big chunk of luck embedded in it, he couldn't take all the credit. There were guys here who knew a hell of a lot more than he did. He was soaking it up like a dry sponge tossed into the ocean. He'd never get it all, but not for lack of trying.

Karagigian and his nephew were on the other side of the complex, playing with the radio stuff. Jess was down the hall working on the program for the FTL radio Zeerus had sent.

He looked back at his screen. Who would have ever thought it? One minute, he was working on a computer game and listening for extremely hypothetical messages from space; the next minute, he'd started down a *very* strange road . . .

"This way, sir," the air force captain sent to collect Hightower said.

He followed the man down the guarded corridor, through a set of armored doors requiring ID cards and a visual inspection by two more armed military police officers.

Hightower proffered his tag. It had been made with his picture only a few minutes ago; the plastic laminate was still warm.

The man behind the desk slid the ID into a scanner, watched a computer screen in front of him. The second guard kept his hand on his pistol while the ID was checked. "Proceed, sirs," the one at the computer said. "Please stay on the blue line. Moving to another color will cause an alarm."

"Tight security," Hightower said after he and the captain moved past the guards.

"Yes, sir. I couldn't get their own mothers past those two if they didn't have proper ID."

They arrived at an unmarked door. The captain slid his ID tag through the reader, tapped in a code. The red diode on the reader went green and the door's lock clicked. The captain pushed the door open but stood aside to let Hightower pass. "General Carter is inside, sir."

Hightower stepped into the office. The door closed behind him.

It was a small cubicle, no secretary, a basic work space: desk, computer, phones, couple of chairs. General Terry Mitchell Carter, USAF, sat behind the desk tapping at a keyboard. He looked up. "Hey, Larry. Sit down, be with you in a sec."

Hightower smiled and sat. Mitch Carter wasn't much on ceremony. He'd been a pilot in 'Nam; he and Hightower had met in an officer's club in Saigon. Late in '71, Carter's jet had been shot down. He'd parachuted into Laos way the hell and gone into enemy territory and hiked out on his own. He'd walked sixty miles through the most god-awful jungle and swamp and had to shoot a few enemies on his way home. It had taken him four days from the time his plane was shot down until he stepped into a marine outpost carrying a bunch of bananas slung over one shoulder. He said the only reason he came back was to see if they were dumb enough to give him another expensive plane after he had one shot out from under him. They were. By the time he'd rotated out, Mitch Carter had flown thirty-six more missions and collected a chestful of medals and ribbons.

"Got it," Mitch said. He looked away from the computer at Hightower. "So, you've come to see our leftover bin full of Star Wars toys, huh?"

"It was slow at the office."

"I bet. What's up, Larry?"

Hightower thought about it. He didn't have to tell Mitch anything, the man knew how the game was played when it came to need-to-know. But a commander who sent troops out into the field to look for vague targets usually got less than optimum results: Somebody's out there, see, and we want you to find him and neutralize him. Thing is, we can't tell you where he is or what he looks like, you'll have to figure that out on your own.

"I hate that smile," Mitch said. "What?"

"Let me ask you something first. How good are these Special Projects Operating Targeting Systems? If I asked you to pick a fly off the wall, could you do it?"

Mitch leaned back in his chair. "Depends on how big the fly is and how far away the wall is. We've got three of the secret SPOTS kinda-sorta semioperational."

"Why don't you give me the cheap tour?"

"Okay. First, there is the antimissile laser sat, code name Zatoichi—after a blind guy in a samurai movie, I think. Puts out a hard enough beam to scramble a missile's guidance system, effectively blinding it. We can target an ICBM coming over the pole with a ninety to ninety-five percent kill rate, so my guys tell me. Of course, that threat is supposedly gone, right? We haven't spent a lot of time upgrading that one lately.

"Then there is Ball Breaker. This is for incoming asteroids. These are clustered nuclear lances, clean atomics, designed to try to deflect or bust up a big rock heading our way. The theory here is that even if we can't knock it far enough off course, it would be better to get hit with a bunch of little pieces than one giant one. Untested at present, though the computer models tell us it will work."

Hightower chuckled. "Computer models predict global warming but the weathermen can't tell us if it is going to rain a week from next Tuesday."

"My crystal ball is in the shop. What can I say?"

Both men smiled. They were well aware of the old military maxim about no battle plan surviving first contact with the enemy. Theory was not practice.

"Finally," Mitch continued, "there is Peregrine. This utilizes a small, high-tech smart missile piggybacked on a booster so it has escape velocity capability. In theory, if you were looking to hit a fly, this would do it. It's only got conventional explosive capability, not nuclear, but it's supposed to be able to take out a satellite or space shuttle–size vehicle out to orbital distances of about forty thousand kilometers."

Hightower nodded. "In theory."

"Well, we don't get a lot of funding to test the suckers these days, now do we?"

"How much do you need to have all three of these up and running in six months?"

That got his attention. "Whoa. Hold on. What are we talking about here?"

Hightower smiled and told him. When he was done, he had Mitch Carter shaking his head in amazement, quite an accomplishment in itself.

"Jesus H. Christ. I can't believe it."

"I'll send you copies of the conversations. This is real enough."

"You mean surreal enough. Lord."

"We're hoping that it doesn't come to shooting," Hightower said. "But we need the capability if this alien comes in with guns smoking."

"Yeah, I can see that. We know anything about the ship?"

"Nope. Too far away to see, even with Hubble. It might be the size of a VW, might be bigger and better armed than a battleship. We won't know until he gets a lot closer. But if he arrives casting stones, we damn sure want to be able to cast some back. What I want is for these three SPOT systems to be up and running when Mr. Spaceman arrives. It might be that nothing we can come up with will even scratch his paint job, but I will certainly feel stupid if he says, 'I come in peace,' then produces a smoking crater where Omaha used to be—and here we are with our thumbs up our butts."

"I hear that. But six months?"

"Get it built, Mitch. I'll pay for it."

"I'll see what I can do."

"The future of the planet might rest on your shoulders."

"Thanks a whole hell of a lot, General."

"I know you can do it. Either that or I have to put my sister-in-law in charge."

One of Jake's chores was to collect firewood. Given that the snow was about six inches deep, that made it harder. But they needed a pretty good bit of wood to keep the fire in the oil drum going. Once it got roaring, the drum put out a lot of heat. They had propane heaters in the tents, but they had to haul in the fuel for those; the firewood was all over the ground.

Jake's father had shown him what to collect. Anything that was dead and dry, the green stuff didn't burn well and it put out a lot of smoke. Even a bunch of tiny little branches would work, it didn't have to be logs, it just took more of them.

Once he had enough wood piled up next to the barrel to keep it going for a while, Jake got to do his other job: melting snow in a big folding plastic washtub for drinking and bathing water. This was a little tricky, since he had to put the washtub close enough to the oil drum's heat to turn the snow liquid but not so close that he would melt the plastic. Once he had the water, he had to scoop it out with a big ladle and pour it into fold-up plastic water bottles, each of which held five gallons. He could barely move those when they were full, but he didn't have to. They had to stay close to the fire so they wouldn't freeze solid every night. A couple of nights, after the last snow, the temperature had dropped down to about zero, and even with the fire barrel being tended all night, some of the water got pretty slushy.

To drink the melted snow, you had to suck it up through a carbon straw, basically a big plastic tube that filtered the liquid. Or boil it for twenty minutes, which left it tasting pretty flat. Some of the guys used water purification tablets instead, but that was even worse, it made the stuff taste like chlorine or iodine or something.

Bathing was easier. You heated a pan of water over the cook stove, took it into your tent, and sponged off. In a hurry, before it got cold. Even with the propane heater going full blast in the tent, taking a sponge bath was a chilly business. Jake always got covered with goose-bumps.

Other than those two things, he didn't have anything he had to do. Men came and went, a couple of women showed up and stayed for a couple of nights, moving from tent to tent. Jake's father made him sleep in one of the empty tents by himself one night while he entertained a woman visitor. Jake had a pretty good idea what *that* had been all about.

It wasn't that bad. Boring, but it wasn't like anybody was slapping him around or anything. He had helped try to catch that major, it wasn't his fault they couldn't, so they more or less considered him one of the militia. More or less.

His father was usually too busy to do much PT, though he did make Jake get up and hike through the woods a few times wearing a pack full of rocks.

Other than that, Jake was pretty much on his own. Sometimes people would talk to him, not much. As long as he did his chores and kept out of everybody's way, they let him be.

He hadn't figured out a way to get away yet, though he was working on it. He knew he'd never make it out on foot, even if there wasn't snow to show his tracks. They were a lot faster hiking than he was and they'd run him down before he got anywhere close to civilization. There were two little motorcycles, three-wheelers with fat tires, like a Honda or Yamaha or something, that came and went. Plus after the last little storm, somebody had come in on a snowmobile. Jake thought he could figure out how to operate either the trikes or the snow machine, given a chance, but that wasn't likely. As paranoid as these guys were, the little vehicles were always locked when somebody wasn't actually riding them. They didn't chain them to trees or anything, but he'd need some kind of ignition key, and slipping his hand into somebody's pocket while they were asleep didn't seem like a very good idea.

One of the guys who rode one of the trikes a lot was fairly young, maybe twenty or so. Pete, his name was, and he was tall and skinny as a toothpick and had bad teeth. He wore a watch cap all the time because he kept his head shaved bald. He wasn't real talkative unless you could get him on a subject he liked. What he apparently liked was girls—though he used a word that rhymed with "hunts" whenever he talked about them. Another subject he liked was guns. And boosting cars was apparently something he was an expert at, too.

After Jake had been there for a few weeks, he got Pete talking about stealing cars. Jake was feeding the fire with branches, which were getting harder to find within half a mile of the camp.

"So, what do you do if you don't have a key?" he asked.

Pete sniggered and took deep draws on a Kool cigarette. "Sheeit, that ain't nothing. You pop the door lock with a slim jim, crack the wheel lock with a crowbar, hot-wire the sucker."

"Really? So like, if you took the trike out for a ride in the woods and you lost your keys, you could just do that?"

Pete laughed louder, turned it into a smoker's hacking cough. "All that little scooter's got on it is a wheel lock. You can pick that with a paper clip."

"Come on," Jake said.

"You don't believe me? Come look."

Pete led Jake over to the trike parked next to the stores tent. He reached into his jacket pocket, pulled out a little rolled-up leather pouch, unrolled it. Inside were a dozen little strips of metal with various serrated and curved ends, the other ends stuck into little wooden dowels. Pete selected one of these and held it up. "See? Looks just like a paper clip with the end bent a hair." He then pulled a little piece of metal shaped like a somewhat-straightened letter Z out of the leather pouch. "This is a torsion tool. All that crap you see in movies where some dumbo sticks a pick into the lock and jiggles it open, that's bull-shit. You have to put tension on the lock with a torsion tool, like this." He stuck the tool into the keyhole and twisted a little. "*Then* you rake the pins with the pick. If you do it right, a piece of turd like this will take about—ah, there it is. Easy as pie."

Jake watched the lock's bolt turn. He blinked at Pete. "Wow. That's great! You're really good at this, aren't you?"

Pete smiled around the cigarette stuck in his mouth. "Yeah, kid, actually I am pretty good. And check this out, you can lock it back the same way."

Jake watched very carefully.

He was pretty sure he could come by a couple of paper clips with-out too much trouble. Of course, starting a motor in the middle of the night in camp even if he did manage to get the lock undone wouldn't be too smart, but he'd work on that. It wasn't as if he had a whole lot else to occupy his mind.

26

aurie ran into Melanie Fawcett on her way back from lunch. Actually, she heard Melanie's bray of a laugh echoing down the White House hallway before she saw her.

"What is so funny?"

Melanie shook her head. "Read this." She handed Laurie a piece of lined notebook paper. On it, written in an artful, feminine hand—did men ever put little circles over the letter *i*?—was a letter to the alien.

Dear Mr. Spaceman,

I heard you was coming to Earth to visit and I heard you was gorjus so I thought hey if you need a date why not me? I am 5′3″ tall, I have blue eyes and blond hair, weigh 128 pounds (with my shoes on!!!) and my measurements are 37-25-36. I am eighteen and could show you a good time.

Sincerely yours XXXX,
Bridget Folsum (my friends call me Bibi)

At the bottom was a phone number and return address.

"Good Lord," Laurie said.

"There's more. Look at what's clipped to the back."

Laurie looked. Stapled to the letter was a color Polaroid picture of a young woman in a suggestive pose. Save for a pair of electrically bright, fluorescent orange bikini bottoms, the woman was naked as she smiled into the camera lens.

"Spare me."

"We've got a couple of others," Melanie said. "And all things being equal, I expect the gay contingent to put their bids in pretty soon, too."

"Pul-leeze."

"No, seriously. Any time we get any sexy heads of state coming over to visit, we get letters like that one. Girls, guys, and some whose gender is, ah . . . *indeterminate* write in and offer to, ah, take care of the visitor's . . . needs. The boss gets a handful every month—you know, 'Next time you're in Cleveland, drop by and let's party.'"

"Jesus. What a world."

"Ain't it, though." Melanie took the letter back, shook her head. "But you know what this really means?"

Laurie nodded. "Yeah. Word is getting out."

"My sources say MNN is going to play it up big during sweeps week."

"Crap. What do they have?"

"I dunno for sure. I hear they've got a British astronomer who's coming over for an interview."

Laurie shook her head. "Damn, damn. I wonder if we can short-circuit it?"

"National security?"

"Yeah."

Melanie shrugged. "It won't do us any good. The network'll just send their reporter to an affiliate in Canada or Mexico. We can't stop them from blabbing it all over European TV, either. Once it gets out, the media here will scream if we try to shut them down. I'm afraid this milk is spilled all over the kitchen floor, Laurie. We need to get a good mop."

"Yeah. Better get your spin docs working overtime."

"Already got 'em chained to their word processors down in the basement."

"You told the boss yet?"

"Hah! Not me. He likes to shoot the messenger. I'll leave that to you; you're a lot more bulletproof than I am."

"Thanks ever so much."

"Better you than me. I have talked with the new writer and he's working on background stuff. Soon as we get the slant, he's ready to roll on a speech for the boss. It's going to have to be soon. We need to steal MNN's thunder before that storm gets on the air."

"Yeah. Keep me apprised of any new developments, okay?"

"Roger that, sister."

After Melanie went her way, Laurie headed for her office. It was about to be bad day at Black Rock here—she wasn't looking forward to dropping *this* into the boss's punchbowl.

It was worse than Hayes had feared. Here he was on Numbnuts Island, Canada, the second of his stops, close enough to spit into the Arctic Ocean. The temperature was sixty below zero with a stiff breeze that dropped the windchill factor almost another forty degrees. To show him just how cold it was, a couple of the air force boys, egged on by the Canadian liaison troops, had staged a small demonstration. They boiled some water, took a cup of it outside, and tossed it high into the air.

By the time it hit the ground, the boiling water was little chunks of ice.

Winter didn't start officially for another couple of weeks.

Oh, *man!*

The night he arrived, he got the tour from one of the enlisted men, a dour shrimp from South Dakota who didn't think the weather was all that bad, compared to home. Inside with the heaters roaring, it *wasn't* so bad. The building had double walls and doors and triple-paned glass in the small windows, heavy curtains over those. But outside, even with electric socks, heavy boots, long underwear, two pairs of pants, two shirts, a sweater, a fur-lined hooded parka, wool glove liners, and ski mittens, Hayes could still feel the cold. It clawed at him like a thing alive, found the tiniest cracks in his insulated armor and swirled in, trying to freeze him into part of the local scenery. He wouldn't be playing outside much. And anybody with claustrophobia would quickly go crazy here. There were sixteen men cramped into a space the size of his apartment. Last night when he'd gotten here, he was bunked in with a lieutenant who snored like a steam engine and a master sergeant who had, it seemed, a fondness for beans, cabbage, and boiled eggs, the end result of which was enough gas in the air to blow the building apart if somebody lit a match.

Even so, it wouldn't have been so bad if he'd had something to *do*. But aside from asking a few questions they could have faxed in, his job was to sit and twiddle his thumbs. It was punishment, pure and simple. Like being made to write a hundred lines in school, or to divide out a fifty-digit number longhand—and be sure to show all your work, Mr. Hayes.

And for all he knew, this would be the high spot of his tour.

Five months of this and they'd have to ship him home in a box. Man.

Well. At least they had a pool table here. The last place, somewhere in Nova Scotia, hadn't even had a satellite TV. What the men did for fun was eat a lot of fried food then sit around listening to their arteries get hard. The smell of a well-used chemical toilet was already something he'd never be able to forget.

There had to be a way to get out of this. Had to.

Well, one thing for sure, he would have plenty of time to try and figure that out.

Zeerus was well versed in the psychology of a number of races. Avitaurs, of course, and most of the other major species rescued from Earth by the Majae: Terragores, Quicklings, Lutras, and the lot. He prided himself on such knowledge, it had been most useful in his dealings with others. He hadn't had much contact with ape-spawn— Primaster had a few on his staff and in his personal service—and since he didn't have a lot else to do at the moment, he reviewed what he knew. It was fairly basic, but then, apes were fairly simple themselves.

Evolved apes were driven by three desires: food, shelter, and sex. Give a male ape a piece of fruit and a cave and he would immediately set out looking for a female. Once he had these three things, an ape then tended to become paranoid in protecting them. A tropical species, they needed protective clothing in any but the most mild of climes. Probably the distinguishing characteristic of the ape-spawn was curiosity. Put a rock in an ape's cave and it wouldn't be long before he came over to pick it up and touch, sniff, and taste it, heft it, look to see what might be under it. He would consider what uses the rock might be put to as a tool. Then, likely as not, he would take up the rock and bash his neighbor's head in with it—to make sure that neighbor didn't steal his fruit, cave, or female.

Apes and weapons went together like Avitaurs and sky.

A sealed container an ape couldn't get into would drive him mad, he would never stop trying. They *were* great puzzle-solvers. Where an Avitaur would quickly realize that pursuit of a problem was a waste of time and resources, an ape would dog it until he dropped. Apes worried about the ultimate value of pi, about the largest prime number, about things that could never have any practical use for anybody not born immortal.

Zeerus smiled. If he'd had more time when he'd sent the humans the plans for the FTL communication device, he would have just told them such a thing *existed*. If they believed him, they would have pounded away at it until they solved it on their own. If he thought there was a way to get somewhere, an ape would try every possible avenue and if all of them were dead ends, he would strike off into the jungle on his own and beat a new path.

There were some advantages to such single-mindedness. Serendipity sometimes gave ape-spawn tricks and toys they would not have found had they not been blundering around in obscurity. And this drive tended to give them an advantage in the short term. They stumbled over many basic scientific principles a more methodical and leisurely society would not happen upon until much later. Thus apes tended to be extremely deep in some areas of knowledge, if somewhat narrow. On the other hand, apes wasted huge amounts of their lives worrying about things they couldn't know—or couldn't change if they *did* know. Where is the end of cause-and-effect? Where did the universe come from? Is there a deity responsible for the creation of all things? What will happen when entropy claims the galaxies? To what purpose was life spawned?

As if knowing the answers to such esoterica could make any difference in their day-to-day lives. Or as if they could do anything about it if they knew.

As a result of this insatiable curiosity, of the need to know all things about all things, ape societies invented some most interesting mythologies. When they could not readily find an answer for something that impinged on their curious brains, apes tended to make up clever fairy stories to explain things—at least until a better solution manifested itself. A lightning storm could not be a simple natural phenomenon, it had to be the intentional work of some larger, invisible being with great powers. Death as a simple termination was unacceptable, so religions explaining what happened after death proliferated. When an Avitaur spoke of the Ancestors and leaving life to fly with them, of crossing the Bridge to the Other Side, he was being metaphorical, perhaps even poetic, nothing more.

Dead was dead.

When humans and other ape-spawn spoke of their gods, they actually *believed* they were going to join them after their lives ended. Literally.

Amazing.

Zeerus leaned back, rubbed at his snout. Well. This was a short reflection. He knew all he needed to know to lead the humans where he wished them to go. They were curious, gullible, and inclined to believe a tale, were it spun cleverly enough. As long as he had sufficiently detailed and reasonable-seeming answers for their questions, he would have no trouble with them. Of course, their paranoia had to be taken into account, but he knew how to play upon that. He need merely shift their natural suspicion away from himself and onto Primaster and the Majae. To align himself with humans against a larger threat. Apes also loved conspiracies as another means to explain the unexplainable.

True, there would be some work involved, and yes, he would have to glide with a certain amount of care to avoid mistakes, but he was an Avitaur. His kind had ruled the skies on the homeworld long before the human's first distant ancestors scurried around in the underbrush sucking eggs and eating insects. There wasn't an Avitaur born with half a normal allotment of wits who couldn't think circles around the brightest ape-spawn on Earth. And certainly none of them could stand in Zeerus's shadow.

Larry came out of the bathroom naked, toweling his hair. Laurie smiled at him from the bed. "Did I ever tell you you look pretty good for an old man?" she said.

"Wish I felt as good as you think I look."

"Bad day at work?"

He tossed the towel back into the bathroom, shrugged at her. "No more than usual. I sometimes wonder why I don't just chuck it all and retire. Life would be a lot easier."

"But a lot duller."

"Something to be said for dull," he said.

"Uh huh, sure."

He flopped onto the bed next to her. "So, you want to get married?"

She smiled. He asked her a couple of times a week. One of these days she might surprise him with her answer. But not tonight. She said what she usually said: "Not yet."

It was a response he expected. "Let me know when. How was your day?"

"So-so. You know the alien thing is leaking out?" She told him about the letter from the eighteen-year-old offering her services to the approaching visitor.

"She might be surprised if Zeerus turned out to be a bug-eyed slimy monster with tentacles."

"Maybe that would make it more exciting," she said. "Add a couple of tattoos and a nose ring and he'd fit right in, slimy tentacles and all. You remember an old TV show, *Beauty and the Beast*?"

"Can't say I do."

She said, "The beast was a hairy catlike thing, looked like a cross between a man and a lion. Story is, women used to write in by the hundreds offering to have his kittens."

"How delightful. You saw the pictures. No tentacles and he's humanoid, but is that something you'd want to go to bed with?"

She reached over and ruffled his damp hair. "No, but I have strange tastes."

"Funny, you don't taste strange," he said, grinning.

"I expect to see an *Oprah* or *Geraldo* show any time now asking the burning question about what transvestites who love their brothers' wives' sisters think about space aliens coming to visit."

"Tape that one for me," he said. "Come here."

She went, laughing.

27

t was one in the morning and at least a foot and a half of snow lay on the ground where it hadn't been tromped down, higher than that in drifts. The temperature outside was maybe ten degrees above zero, and even with the heaters going full blast inside the tents, they weren't what you would call warm. There was part of a moon and the sky was as clear as glass, the stars sparkling bright. You could even see the Milky Way.

Maybe not the best time or place to learn how to pick locks, but that's what Jake was doing.

Fortunately, the little trike was parked on the way to the latrine, so if he heard anything, that's where Jake planned to scoot in a big hurry.

Earlier in the day—well, yesterday, now—a branch of the militia had struck a great blow for freedom. Four armed men had robbed an armored car carrying money to a federal reserve bank. According to his father, this was justified any number of ways. Not the least of these reasons being to repay those who had put up bail for political prisoners such as he himself had recently been. Jake didn't understand how being arrested for shooting at an FBI agent made you a political prisoner, but he kept his mouth shut about that.

In any event, the rest of the camp had been pleased to hear about it. After supper and the evening political and tactical meetings were done, some bottles full of liquor came out. By the time the bottles were empty, everybody in the camp except Jake was mostly drunk, even the guy who was supposed to be on watch. At the moment, that guy was dozed out next to the oil drum, asleep sitting up.

Jake wasn't ever going to get a better time to practice.

He was also lucky in that the trike was under an evergreen tree with branches held low enough with piled snow to give him a little cover.

Jake squatted next to the trike with the picks he had improvised from two big safety pins. It sure wasn't as easy as Pete had made it look. He had used a pair of pliers and wire cutters, got the pins bent as best he could remember. He shaped one as a torsion tool and got it twisted in the lock okay, but he had raked the other pin over the inside of the lock a bunch of times and it had stayed locked.

His breath made fog in the frigid air. His fingers were getting colder and stiffer. If he had been at home, he could have logged on to the Net and found out something about locks and how they worked. Shoot, he could have found out everything there was to know about locks, who invented them, everything.

His hand slipped and he banged his knuckle on the frigid metal of the trike's handlebar post. Ow!

Come on, think, Jake. You can do this if that dufus Pete can!

Pretend you've got a key and you want to open this thing. How would you do it?

Okay, I'd put the key into the slot—

Wait a minute. Right side up or upside down? Which way would the little notches on the key go?

Aha.

Then what?

Then I'd turn the lock—

Which way?

Hmm. Good point.

Jake pulled the pick out of the lock and looked at the slot. It was dark and he couldn't see much, even with the moonlight reflecting off all the snow, but now that he looked at it, he was pretty sure the key went in upside down and turned to the right, that would be . . . clockwise. He had the torsion tool twisting in the right direction, but if the little notches on the key went in upside down, then the part they unlocked would be on the inside *top* of the notch, not the bottom where he had been raking with the pick.

Well, *duh*! No wonder.

He pulled the pick out, turned it over, and stuck it all the way in as far as it would go, then dragged it back quick like Pete had done.

The lock turned just as easy as if he had used a key.

Wow!

He hadn't expected that at all. Blap, just like that!

His joy was suddenly tempered by the sound of boots crunching through a thick crust of ice over snow.

Uh oh. He wouldn't have time to lock it back. He'd have to hope whoever took the trike out next time would think somebody had left it unlocked.

Jake stepped out onto the path and hurried to the latrine. He circled around it and headed back the way he'd come.

The man approaching was the guy supposed to be on watch. He was walking very carefully, as if he was worried about falling.

Jake nodded at him, said, "Hey."

The guard mumbled something Jake didn't catch and plodded off to the latrine.

Jake, who was really getting cold now, hurried back to his tent.

Inside, the little heater made it feel pretty good compared to outside, even though you could still see your breath in the dry air. His father was asleep, mouth open, snoring lightly. Jake zipped the door flap shut, slipped off his shoes, and crawled into his sleeping bag still wearing his clothes.

He had done it. He had picked the lock on the trike, so that much was doable. The hard part was going to be cranking the motor up and leaving without anybody hearing it. Plus finding his way out of this place. But Pete was always interested in showing off, and he'd told Jake he knew how to use a compass and all. Maybe he could get Pete to show him. His father's compass was right there in his backpack, along with a bunch of other survival stuff. The old man had a firestarter stick, you could just scrape some of the metal off with a knife and it would light up and burn. Plus he had a first-aid kit, fish hooks, an emergency blanket made out of some silvery stuff and all folded up to about the size of a handkerchief, water purification tablets, and like that. When he got ready to bug out, Jake could swipe that stuff.

He didn't know how long they were going to stay here but nobody had said anything about leaving. Sooner or later, he'd get his chance.

When it came, he'd be ready.

Laurie dropped by Larry's after work. When she went to his house, he cooked for her. They were in the kitchen; he had changed into sweats with a big white chef's apron over them.

"How does stir-fry sound?" he asked.

"Oh, kinda like, *crackle, crackle, shhhh, psst!*"

"You missed your calling, you know," he said, smiling at her. "You should have been a comedienne."

She liked making him smile. "That's me, a triple-threat girl. Sing, dance, tell jokes."

He removed an eight-quart pot and an eleven-inch shallow skillet from brass ceiling hooks mounted over the butcher block table next to the stove. Larry liked to cook, had learned to do it as a boy and kept up with it as he traveled around the world in his job. He'd picked up the pot and skillet in France, along with several other cooking vessels. They were stainless steel, coated on the exterior with copper, had long cast-iron handles. These two alone probably set him back five hundred bucks, the whole set must have cost a couple of thousand.

He set the pot and skillet on top of the stove, a black Thermador gas unit with heavy iron grates over the burners. He stepped over to the pantry and removed a two-gallon jug of drinking water, poured half of it into the pot, turned the fire on under it. There was a little *pop!* as the piezoelectric spark lit the gas. Then he went to the fridge and came out with several plastic bags full of vegetables, a Styrofoam tray of peeled shrimp, and a packet of Chinese noodles. He put those down, gathered some Mongolian fire oil, ginger root, and soy sauce. He hummed something by Vivaldi as he assembled his ingredients.

"I love to watch a man cook," she said. "It's so rare."

"Excuse me, but aren't most of the great chefs men?"

"Fat men," she said. "Look at Paul whatshisname on TV."

"That's a non sequitur."

"So? You want to make something of it?"

He smiled again.

"I'm going to go change," she said.

"Stay the way you are."

"My clothes," she said. "Not my triple-threat personality."

"I am relieved. Go."

When she got back, in sweats of her own, he had already cut the vegetables into angled slices. The pepper oil sizzled in the skillet. Larry scraped thin shavings of ginger root into the hot oil.

"New knife?"

He held it up. It looked like a regular slicing knife, long and right-triangular, but the blade itself was white. "It's Japanese. Ceramic. Supposed to stay sharp forever."

The smell of frying ginger reached her. He dumped the shrimp into the skillet.

"Forever is a long time. See, I told you what it sounds like."

"A woman of great wit and wisdom."

"And don't forget gorgeous."

"How could I ever?"

She walked to the fridge, got a bottle of white wine that had been opened, pulled the cork, and poured herself a small glass. She went back to the breakfast nook and perched on one of the four stools. She was perfectly content to watch him cook, but she said, "Anything I can do to help?"

"Nope."

He used a big bamboo spatula to stir the shrimp and vegetables around in the skillet. He'd added carrots, purple cabbage, broccoli, sugar peas, and mung bean sprouts, in that order. The noodles were cooking merrily away in the pot and he poured a cup of cold water into them to stop the boiling.

She watched as he drained the noodles in a colander, mixed them with the stir-fry, and added liberal sprinklings of soy sauce and white pepper. It smelled wonderful. She said so.

"You about ready?" he asked.

"Feed me, Seymour."

He looked puzzled.

"*Little Shop of Horrors*," she said. "It's about a giant plant that eats people. That's what he says when he's hungry."

He smiled and nodded. "How appropriate."

Larry set the table with plates and chopsticks, transferred the stir-fry and noodles to a big wooden bowl, and put it next to the plates.

As she loaded her plate with the delectable cuisine, he went and fetched himself a glass of wine, returned, and sat next to her.

"Mmm. It's wonderful."

"Thank you, ma'am."

They ate quietly for a few moments. Then she said, "So tell me, how do you feel about this alien thing?"

"I'm getting as ready as I can," he began. "I lit a fire under the Star Wars gang, we're working on the FTL radio device, I've got a busload of psychiatrists and psychologists and xenologists—whatever the hell *they* are—lined up."

"Hold up there, *kemosabe*, I didn't ask what you were *doing*, I asked you how you *felt*."

He blinked at her, chewed his mouthful of noodles, then sighed. "'Feel' about it? What exactly do you mean?"

She shook her head. Men. Ask them how they felt about their fathers and they'd start quoting baseball statistics.

"I'm not asking you to let your inner child come out and play here, Larry. Just how this whole deal about the alien is working on your psyche personally. I know this is a big thing with you."

He ate some more, washed it down with sips of the wine. "Yeah, I suppose it is. You know I've always been a science fiction fan. And I've always believed the universe was too big for just this planet to have achieved life, even intelligent life. But that was before I was in charge of the country's defense. I guess I've got mixed emotions about it. I don't think anybody yet realizes what a truly big thing this is. We are not alone. There are other worlds, other . . . people. It opens up things in a way, makes things possible that weren't possible before. I think meeting a representative of another intelligent species is the most significant thing to ever happen to humankind. Not just because of the possibilities of technology or trade or whatever but because it makes the universe so much . . . *bigger!* That we aren't alone, the only freak occurrence of life anywhere, it—it boggles the mind."

She smiled.

"What are you laughing at?"

"You. If you could see your face. You look just like a little boy with a new toy."

He shook his head and gave her a wry grin in return. "Yeah. The problem is, I have to determine if this visitor is good or bad. I want very much for him to be good, but if he's not, then it's my job to control him. And that might include blowing him to smithereens."

"That would be disappointing for you," she said.

"Sure. And maybe a lot worse than just disappointing. Suppose our friend Zeerus comes in throwing death rays and we smoke him right out of the sky—assuming we can. Then what? We've killed our contact with the only other intelligent life we've ever seen. That's pretty awful to think about, but what if he sends a message to his people with his dying breath and they decide to send an armada to punish us for our actions? They might be able to turn the whole planet into a burned-out cinder as easily as you and I stomp flat an anthill."

She finished chewing the bite of shrimp in her mouth. Swallowed and noticed that her throat seemed dry. She drank a big sip of wine but it didn't seem to wash away the feeling. "Oh," she said.

"Yeah. So that's how I feel about it. Anything else you want to know?"

Before she could answer, the doorbell rang.

Larry frowned, glanced at his watch.

"You expecting company?" she said.

"Nobody who wouldn't call first. And nobody who should be able to get past the doorman."

He stood, walked to the front door. Laurie leaned over so she could watch him. He looked through the peephole. Said, "Shit." He ambled back over to where she sat.

"What?"

"It's that reporter from MNN, the one who is always asking your boss nasty questions."

"Bruce Fosse?"

"That's the one."

"What is he doing here?"

"Damned if I know. I probably ought to ask him."

"I'll go into the bedroom."

Laurie did just that. But she left the door open a crack so she could hear when Larry opened the door to the reporter.

"General Hightower," the man said.

"What can I do for you, son?"

"Could I have a word with Laurie Sherman?" the reporter said.

Laurie felt her stomach churn. Uh oh. Nobody was supposed to know she was here. Fosse didn't ask if she was, he just flat out asked to talk to her.

This was bad.

Real bad.

28

Stewart and Jess were eating dinner in the Burger King around the corner from where they caught the bus to work.

Jess was not happy.

Stewart took a bite out of his double-cheese Whopper and a sip from his Coke. Around the mouthful, he said, "I don't understand what you're so upset about."

"You and I and the professor and his nephew have been shanghaied, practically kidnapped and dragged to Washington, without any kind of due process, and you don't see what I'm upset about?"

"We're on the inside of what is maybe the most incredible thing to happen since man discovered fire. The U is giving us leave without penalty. We're getting paid a whole hell of a lot more than I was making at the SETI shack or you were making at the library."

"That's not the point!" She set her drink down hard enough for some of it to slosh out and puddle on the table.

Stewart thought about telling her she should have left the plastic lid on and used the straw, but decided that maybe this wasn't the best time to be commenting on her fast-food manners. "Okay, so I'm stupid. What is the point?"

"We didn't have any choice."

"Yeah, we did," he said. "We could have gone to some federal pokey and counted rivets in the ceiling until they decided to let us out—instead of being part of this."

"That's what I mean! I went along because that didn't really appeal to me, and yeah the work is interesting, but this kind of thing is a blatant abuse of power."

Stewart chewed on a couple of fries. "I don't disagree with you."

"Then why aren't you more upset about it? It isn't right."

The fries seemed awfully cold and greasy in that moment. His stomach was twisted into a chilly knot and his appetite was pretty much gone. He dropped the half-eaten potatoes onto his tray. "Would it do me any good to be upset? There's right and there's reality."

She glared at him. "Excuse me?"

"Look, the summer I was sixteen, I stayed with my cousin in Boston and worked as a lifeguard at a country club where his folks were members. My uncle is a doctor, and this was a fairly exclusive place. Exclusive in that unless you were white, Anglo-Saxon, Protestant, and upper-middle class or rich, you couldn't get past the membership committee. But if you were a member, you could bring a guest to swim at the pool. So some girl who wanted to pull her old man's chain brought a black guy to the pool one day. The manager let them in, no problem, but before the black guy could get into his suit and into the water, we had a sudden accident. One of the spare chlorine bottles sprang a leak. So the manager shut the pool down, sent all the swimmers home. I was at the pump house when it happened, learning from the senior guard how to do backwashing. There wasn't any leak."

Jess blinked at him. "They shut it down just to keep a black guy from swimming in the pool?"

"Exactly. This wasn't Mississippi or Louisiana, this was a suburb of Boston. The pool manager had his orders. He called the club president, who had a word with the girl's father. She didn't try to bring another black guest in. Later on in the summer the manager and I got to talking. He told me the committee that ran the place didn't want any niggers polluting their water."

"That's awful."

"Yes, it is. Awful, illegal, immoral, whatever. But they did it. This wasn't 1920, it was *five years* ago. And probably they are still doing some variation of it. If not there, then at some other ritzy club. Those old hatreds go away real slow. And it's no wonder most black people were happy to see O.J. skate, whether they thought he was guilty or not. They've been getting screwed for a long time."

"So, what are you trying to say here, Stew?"

"That stuff like this happens. It's not the way things *ought* to be but it's the way things *are*."

She bristled. "So we're just supposed to let it slide? Shrug it off, say, 'Oh, well, that's how things are,' and stick our heads in the sand?"

He felt uncomfortable, even miserable; he didn't know why he had started down this road. He wished he had kept his mouth shut. Too late now. He said, "No, I'm not saying that. I'm saying we have to pick our battles. It's a whole lot better to sneak around behind a machine gun blasting at you than to charge headfirst into a spray of bullets. Think about it. What could I have done at the pool? I was sixteen, it was a done deal. If I had complained, raised hell about it, what do you think would have happened? I didn't have any power, I'd have gotten fired, the policy would have stayed the same, nobody would be the loser but me."

"So you kept your mouth shut and played it safe," she said. "You didn't do anything. You kept working there."

Oh, boy. You could freeze nitrogen on her tone.

He shook his head. "Oh, I did something. I wrote a letter to the local paper. I signed it, but asked them to not print my name or anything. I figured the paper had more clout than I did. I tried to do the right thing."

"What happened?"

"Nothing. They didn't print it. Didn't investigate it, as far as I could tell. But two weeks later, we had a round of layoffs. Too many guards, they said, they had to let a few of us go. Three of us got the ax. But a week later, two guards were rehired. I wasn't one of them.

"That fall, I found out from my cousin that the publisher of the paper was a member of the club. The editor gave my letter to him and he passed it on to the committee, name and all. Wasn't going to do me any good to apply for a job there next summer, and I shouldn't bother asking for a recommendation, either."

"No good deed goes unpunished."

She stared at him. "So that's it? We just sit back and allow ourselves to be part of a conspiracy. We help the government hide all this
from the people?"

"Jesus, Jess, this is the United States military we're talking about
here! If we stand up and spit in their eye, they can put us in a hole so
deep it'll take a month for the sunshine to reach us!"

She stood, abruptly. "So that's how it is. I see." She turned and
started away.

"Where are you going?"

"To get some fresh air. It's getting stuffy in here."

He stared after her as she stomped out of the Burger King. He felt
sick. God, he hated to argue, especially with Jess. She wasn't stupid—
why couldn't she see? Standing on a principle was all fine and good
unless it raised you up to where the monsters could see you. If a car ran
a red light and plowed into you, yeah, you were in the right, but you
could be dead right. Who the hell did that serve?

The president of the United States sighed and leaned back in his
chair behind the desk in the Oval Office. "Busy day," he said.

His chief of staff nodded. "Yes, sir," Laurie said. "But you'll get a
two-hour break at four."

"Oh, boy. Okay, anything else?"

Laurie thought about it. Decided to bring it up. "Well. There's one
small thing. Reverend Jimmy."

"What about him?"

How best to broach this?

He looked at her, eyebrows raised.

Straight ahead, she decided. "He wants to talk to the alien."

"Talk to him? What do you mean?"

"Near as I can tell, he wants to take a shot at turning Zeerus into a
good Baptist."

The boss laughed. "You're serious?"

"Afraid so."

He shook his head. "Lord. What do you think?"

"I think it would set a bad precedent. You let Jimmy talk to him,
you'll have an avalanche of other religious leaders pounding on your

door demanding the same. We don't know anything about the space-man's culture or religion. This could be a nasty can of worms. He might take offense at somebody trying to convert him. Or what if he liked what Buddha had to say but hated Jesus? I don't think we want to start down that path."

"Jimmy has been a good supporter, as well as being a friend. How do we go about this without pissing him off?"

"I've been thinking about it. Have him write a letter. Same for the Catholics, the Moslems, whoever. Tell each of them we'll encode the message and ship it up to the visitor as soon as it is feasible."

"Meaning it won't be feasible any time soon?"

"Yes, sir. Or we could offer a general overview of Earth's religious beliefs and put the letters into that as sort of an addendum. Sort of a 'Here's what we believe' kind of thing."

He nodded. "Yes. That would work. He's going to be a few months coming, we can offer him background for his visit. That ought to include religious and political systems."

"Going to ask for his vote in the next election?"

He smiled. "Nothing so blatant, Laurie. But I am the leader of the only superpower on the planet. I'd think he'd be inclined to take a cer-tain amount of notice of that."

"Of course," she said.

"Okay. I'll tell Jimmy our policy forbids direct contact with the space guy except for official military stuff, at least until he understands the socioeconomic and political situation better down here."

"Good thought, sir."

She grinned inwardly, but kept her face neutral. This had been easy enough.

"Hey, Major," the top kick yelled from the rec room. "You ought to come in here and see this."

At the base in Greenland, Hayes had his own room—if you could call the six-foot by eight-foot coffin a room. The cot took up most of it, with just enough space at one end for a small chest and a lot of wall hooks, upon the latter of which most of his clothes were hung. He lay on the bed reading an old John D. McDonald novel about the boat bum–cum–salvage expert Travis McGee. Now there was a guy who had a good idea. Take your retirement in installments while you were still young enough to enjoy it. Plus all those good-looking women.

"What is that I should come and see, Sergeant?"

"The news, sir. The dish is working and we're getting the MNN feed. Looks like the Martians are coming to Earth."

Hayes folded over the corner of the page he was reading and dropped the book onto the cot. Stood carefully to avoid hitting the wall and edged past the cot toward the door.

In the rec room—a space that was all of twelve feet by twelve, and whose rec capabilities consisted of a television set and a rickety card table with a chess set on it—the entire station's compliment sat on folding chairs watching the tube. All four of them: a second lieutenant who must have pissed somebody off royally to deserve this, the sergeant, and two enlisted men. The room stank of stale sweat and mold.

"Check it out, sir," the top kick said. He was probably forty-five and about to retire, and old enough to be the father of the lieutenant or the enlisted men.

Hayes pulled up a metal chair and sat.

"This . . . is MNN," a deep voice like that of Darth Vader said.

The talking head behind the desk, a young man with dark, wavy hair, flashed his bleached teeth at the camera. "Welcome back. I'm Barry Peters, it's fifteen minutes past the hour, and you're watching MNN's News Wrap.

"Are we about to be visited by an alien from outer space? According to scientists at Comb's Observatory in northern England, that's a distinct possibility. Reporter Bruce Fosse has the story."

The news reader vanished, replaced by the image of two men standing in front of what looked like an old Atlas booster rocket. Probably a museum somewhere.

"Yes, Barry, I'm here with Professor Harold Ellis-Parker, a radio-astronomer with the Comb's Observatory's Search for Extraterrestrial Intelligence, or SETI, program. Professor Ellis-Parker, can you tell us why you think we're about to have company from another world?"

The professor, a white-haired man of sixty-five or so, dressed in gray tweeds probably forty years old and somewhat worn at the elbows, said, "Indeed, Mr. Fosse. We have received signals produced by some intelligent entity. Our observations indicate that the source of these signals is, according to Doppler shift, coming from within our solar system and moving in this direction."

The image of the two men was replaced by an animation of a satellite sailing through space, passing Jupiter. The professor's voice-over continued.

"While we have been unable to translate the encoded message yet, it is highly unlikely such a transmission could have been produced by any natural phenomenon."

The camera cut from the animation back to the reporter and professor.

"Tell me, Professor, have you received confirmation of this signal from other sources?"

"We have. Our colleagues in Russia have intercepted the signal, as have the new Toowoomba Radio Telescopic Array in Australia."

The reporter said, "And have SETI observation stations in the United States reported such signals?"

"No, and that is decidedly odd, given the number of stations in your country. I would have thought it impossible for them to have missed it."

"Thank you, Professor." He turned to face the camera. "We've been speaking with radio-astronomer Professor Parker-Ellis of Great Britain's Comb's Observatory. United States officials have declined to comment on this story, but later in the news we'll be talking via satellite link to Dr. Lloyd Sturt in Australia. Back to you, Barry."

The image blinked and the announcer was back. He smiled. "So we have company coming, eh? Guess we'd better dust off the good china.

"In other news, teachers in Chicago met to consider a strike earlier today. . . ."

Hayes blinked and tuned out the announcer. So, there was something to all this alien stuff after all. He wished like hell he was back in Washington, where he could put a finger on this pulse and find out what the truth was. Being cooped up in a windowless room there was a whole lot better than being here. At least it was warmer.

But what, he wondered, did it really mean? Was it true that an alien was coming here?

29

Hightower had told Cub Baxter he could take his time retiring, end of the year, later if he needed it, but the man wasn't going to stay where he wasn't wanted. When Hightower saw the admiral walking down the hall with a cardboard box full of office stuff, he felt a needle of grief sting him.

"Cub."

"General."

"Jesus, Cub, I—"

The older man waved him quiet. "No need to say it, Larry. I might be a senile old salt but I know you weren't given any choice. No hard feelings."

"Thanks."

"Listen, not that it means anything, but you might want to stir up your snoops, have them put a few more ears to the ground. I heard a rumor from an old boy I know that the underground militias around the country are gathering themselves for something big. What with the little dipshit war in Europe and the bug-eyed monsters coming to Earth, you probably don't need another irritant. I know it's the National Guard's bidness, domestic troubles, but—"

"How'd you hear about the alien?" Hightower broke in.

"Well, I'd like to be able to say I've got my finger on the nation's pulse, but the truth is, I saw it on the morning news."

Hightower nodded. Not unexpected. "Thanks. I'll look into the militia thing."

"See you around, Larry. You ever want to get away from this crap and sail to Bimini, give me a call. I got room on my boat for you."

"Appreciate it," Hightower said.

After Cub was gone, Hightower went to his office. To Gray, he said, "I need tapes of the morning news. ABC, NBC, CBS, CNN, MNN, CableNet, and PBS if they ran a story on the alien. I need them yesterday. And you might as well get me the big newspapers, too."

"Sir."

He worked for an hour, filling out forms, making calls, doing the business for which he was paid. Gray came in with a stack of videotapes and three newspapers, put them on his desk.

Hightower plugged a tape into his machine and watched the big screen inset into the wall flower into life. The tape had been cued to the story he wanted:

"—may well be one of the most important stories of the century, CBS News has learned that radio signals from outer space have been detected and confirmed by observatories in at least three different countries: England, Russia, and New South Wales, Australia—"

Another tape.

"—ABC News attempted to contact U.S. scientists at the SETI station in Puerto Rico but we have been unable to do so—"

And other recorded newscasts carried the same messages.

"—NBC News has discovered . . ."

"—stay tuned to CNN for more details . . ."

"—first to break the story, MNN will continue to bring you the latest as we uncover it . . ."

Hightower sighed and used the remote to shut the VCR off. Well. Here we go. One more brick on a truck whose axles were bent and groaning. Bad enough that stupid reporter had tailed Laurie to his place. Even though he'd denied it and sent the man away without seeing her, he was worried about how that would impact on all this. If the president got spooked into one of his this-could-be-bad-for-my-reelection moods, both Hightower and Laurie could be looking for work real soon. Hightower had been quick enough to follow the reporter to the street without being spotted and he hadn't seen a cameraman waiting, so there probably weren't any pictures of Laurie entering his place. The reporter might know she'd been there but he didn't have any proof. If he went on the air with the story, they could give the public butter-wouldn't-melt looks and deny everything. Tell the president it was a rumor started by his political enemies and stand fast.

If the reporter didn't have any proof. If he *did* . . .

Certainly they would have to be more circumspect. Most people wouldn't give a rat's ass that two unmarried people found pleasure in each other's company, even to the point of sleeping together, but the president of the United States was big on the Caesar's Wife Theory that his people must be above reproach. Hightower was working on some backup scenarios but he hadn't had time to get them in place yet. Best he do so ASAP.

He reached for the phone to call Laurie. This was business, and that was allowed.

"Hi," Laurie said. "You've seen the media stuff?"

"Yes," Larry said. "What is the president going to do?"

"We've got him scheduled to speak at six this evening. We've worked on the speech so much we're all sick of it, but it covers us. I'll fax a copy to you."

"What is the gist?"

"We've known about the signal for some time, kept quiet for national security reasons until we could ascertain more about it. Yes, there is an alien coming, yes, we are in contact with him, his intentions are peaceful, it's a wonderful historical event, the meeting of two worlds, blah, blah."

"You don't think it's a little early for full disclosure?"

"We aren't giving full disclosure, just the basic facts and the text of the first message. Face it, you have a college student who broke the code and talked to Zeerus. The message was recorded all over the place. Sooner or later, one of the other receivers will crack it. Yeah, the alien is only talking to us now, and when we get the radio thingamajig working, that'll be better, but we don't want anybody stealing our thunder here."

"I see."

"Not my decision but I agree with it."

There came a quiet pause. She said, "About that . . . other thing. Any thoughts?"

"A few," he said. "Don't worry about it. I think we're clear but if not, I'm working on a safety net."

"Why do I hear 'I hope' in your voice?"

"Don't worry about it, I'll have it covered. Besides, he can't afford to fire us now, there's too much going on."

"You don't know him like I do. He's paranoid as hell about this. He knows too many ex-congressmen and senators who were brought low by what seemed like niggling stuff. Mention Bob Packwood and the boss goes pale."

"I understand."

"We, ah, won't be able to get together for a while," she said. She hated saying it.

"I understand."

"I've got to go, I've got a million things to get into place."

"Of course."

After they disconnected, Laurie felt as if her insides had been scooped out, leaving her hollow. The job was important, the job was who she was, and it had never gotten in the way of her personal life before, not really. Mostly because she didn't really *have* a personal life outside the job. But this, this was a pain in the butt. How long could she leave Larry hanging? Maybe he would get bored and go find somebody else?

He'd better not. She'd whack him with one of his expensive frying pans if he did that.

She grinned at the image of her chasing the military's ranking general around in his kitchen, flailing away at him with a big pan.

The grin faded. She'd seen him last night, but already she missed him.

Damn.

Zeerus stood in a cold and dank alleyway, deep shadows slicing the walls and floor into darkness. He faced a blank wall, the end of the alley, some kind of rounded stone glued into an impassable barrier. He heard a shuffle of feet behind him, heard something small and metal nudged or tipped over to clink quietly. The smell of rancid food from a large container to his left enveloped him. His breath made fog in the icy air. He turned.

Four of them faded in from the shadows, humans, large males. They carried weapons: a wooden club, a length of thick chain, a knife, a hatchet. The men smiled their ape smiles and came toward him, twirling or doing fancy tricks with their weapons. They had some expertise with these killing tools.

Good.

Four was the most dangerous number. Fewer and you could escape, more and they tended to get in their own way.

The four spread out, blocked the alley. His back was to the wall, there was no place to go. He might be able to jump high enough to catch that metal ladder running up the side of the building. A good leap, a hard flap of wings, he could probably make it, it was less than twice his own height from the filthy alley floor.

But—no. Zeerus would not run from ape-spawn.

The largest of the humans, a pale one with the wooden club, flashed his teeth and waved the others back. "He's mine," he said in his too-warm mammalian voice.

Zeerus clacked his teeth in anticipation. The men took notice of his dentition.

"Watch out for those fangs!" one of them said.

The big pale one said, "He won't have them long!" He smacked the club into his empty hand. Then whipped the stick back over one shoulder and leaped, chopped the club down to smash Zeerus's skull.

The Avitaur twisted, pivoted on the balls of his feet, swung a backhand with the fingers knotted into a hard fist. Caught the human behind the neck. Heard bone snap wetly, saw the club fall from suddenly slack fingers.

Two more of the apes lunged, a dark one with the chain and a hairless one with the chopping blade.

Zeerus snapped his wings out and flapped once, hard. The wind blew dust up into the attackers' faces. They uttered expletives and wiped at their eyes.

Zeerus slid in, turned sideways, thrust his right foot out and twisted it in the classic move. The dark ape's belly was soft; Zeerus's claws tore into it and ripped greasy loops of entrails free.

No time to savor the strike! Zeerus leaped, tucked himself into a tight ball, flipped forward over the third attacker, and came down almost on top of the last one, the one with the knife. The human stabbed at him, but Zeerus was faster. He caught the outthrust hand, twisted it, broke bones, tore ligaments, caught the falling knife, and returned it pointfirst to its owner, a short poke into his left eye.

The blade's point exited from the rear of the ape's skull.

Zeerus turned to face the final attacker left standing. The human was frightened—as well he should be. He waved the hatchet back and forth, tried to create a space as he backed up.

Zeerus smiled. You won't get far, little friend. He stepped forward.

The computer's voice said, "Time."

Blast!

Zeerus said, "End simulation."

Around him, the alley shimmered and vanished, the bodies of the would-be assassins dissolved into translucent mist, then air. After a moment, the much smaller confines of the ship replaced the holographic image.

Zeerus removed the sensory clamp from his head and set it back into its slot. Surely he would have gotten the fourth one, no doubt of it, but his allotted time had expired. Ah, well. He would move faster next time. Next time, he would not wait for them, but rather he would initiate the attack himself.

He had caused the computer to use recordings of television transmissions from Earth for the simulation, allowing it to choose images from its library. It was a poor program as such things went, there was no real danger of injury as there could be in more advanced simulacra, but it was all he had.

There were several other programs available to him, most of them not designed for Avitaurs, but he had been able to modify some of them.

A pity he didn't have an Avitaurian Mating Cliff among the selections.

Well, one had to make do. He had no plans to duplicate the slaughter in actuality once he reached Earth, that would be foolish given his longer term goals; still, one never knew how each drop of rain would fall. Perhaps he might find himself in a situation where he could demonstrate the superiority of Avitaur to ape in a physical manner.

One could always hope.

30

Jake tromped through the snow, gathering firewood. He was probably a quarter of a mile away from the camp. He had collected most of the dead wood closer than that a long time ago. Every once in a while some new branches broke off under the weight of the snow piled on them, but not too many were dead enough to burn without smoking. And a smoky fire was a big no-no. The one time he'd thrown some really green stuff on and it started to pour up thick white clouds of smoke, Seth had backhanded him hard enough to knock him down.

You can spot smoke for miles, Jake found out.

It wasn't easy moving around in the woods. He wore snowshoes and a pair of boots his father had brought him. The boots were a couple of sizes too big, so he had on three pairs of socks. No fresh snow had fallen for several days, but neither had it warmed up enough to melt the old stuff completely. During the day with the sun shining, the ground would some-times get pretty slushy, but it refroze every night. If you got off the paths that had been tromped down around the camp, it sounded like you were walking on fresh Fritos—*kaa-runch!*—every time you put your foot down. Even with the snowshoes, it was slow going. You had to kind of shuffle your feet and when it was warm enough for the top layer to turn liquid, that was a big nasty mess, your boots and pants got soaked with icy water. No way he was going to be walking out of here as long as it was like this.

After a couple more late-night practice runs, Jake was pretty sure he could pick the trike's lock in a minute or less. He'd gotten Pete to take him for a ride a couple of times and he was also pretty sure he could drive the thing. It wasn't that hard. The motor started with a push of a button, there was the gas thingee that had to be turned on, the throttle and shift, he could handle those. There was even a headlight, so if he stayed on a trail, he should be able to see in the dark well enough to keep from smashing into a tree or something.

Stealing the trike, driving it, they weren't the problems. Getting away without having everybody in the camp right on his tail, *that* was the problem. No way in the daytime, too many people could sprint fast enough to grab his ass and drag him off the trike. It would have to be at night, and late enough so there was only the one guard on. But at two in the morning, the only sound for miles was the heaters running, and they weren't nearly loud enough to drown out the *vroom!* of a motorcycle's engine cranking up. You could hear an owl hoot a mile away in the silent woods, a motor would sound like an erupting volcano. No way.

He could fix the other bike so it wouldn't run. A canteen of water in the gas tank would do that, according to Pete. So if he could get far enough away from camp before somebody noticed he was gone, it would be hard for anybody to catch up with him. Some of these guys were in good shape, they could run ten or fifteen miles at a good pace with a heavy pack, but on the trike, he should be able to go as fast as them, and if he had a couple of miles on them when they started, they'd never make up his lead. Plus he could get off the path if he had to and nobody was going to run on a foot and a half of old crunchy snow.

Thing was, how to get that lead?

They had radios, they could call somebody, but Jake didn't think there was anybody waiting at the trailheads. Plus, he didn't plan on going back the way they'd come in. There were three other trails leading out, he knew that much, one to the east, two heading north. One of the trails went pretty much all the way to Canada.

There was a lot you could pick up if you kept quiet and listened.

He had his burlap sack almost full of branches. It was getting colder and it would be dark soon. Time to head back. He shouldered the sack and began trudging toward the camp.

Of course, even if he *did* manage to get the trike away from camp, managed to stay on the trail and get away without being caught, there was another question.

What then?

He couldn't go home. He couldn't go to his mom's; his old man would look there first. He could maybe get a message to his mom to move, that Seth knew where she was, but that still left him nowhere. Once she got somewhere else, under a new name or something, he could join her, but what to do until then?

On the one hand, maybe it was better just to stay here. Go along with whatever his old man and the rest of the militia nuts wanted. If he didn't get killed, probably the army or whoever would believe that he didn't have a choice when they grabbed him.

But maybe not, because of the computer thing. They already wanted him and probably wouldn't trust him. But maybe he could explain that.

If he didn't get killed. Which was a good possibility.

The militia had some really weird ideas, a whole bunch of which involved attacking and shooting various targets, some of which could and probably would shoot back. Police stations, National Guard armories, banks, like that. They sat around listening to the right-wing radio at night when the signal was strong, and according to people like that big old fat guy who made fun of everybody, the revolution was about to start. His old man and the others believed that they were ready, they *wanted* it.

Plus all this stuff about the alien had been on the news. The president—known as That Stupid Dickhead and other worse names around here—had made a big speech, saying it was true.

Boy, had that opened a big flood of stuff. Every time the news came on, there was something about how some group in China had killed themselves, or how some church had said it was the beginning of Armageddon, or how the stock market had shot up off the scale.

It was starting to get dark as Jake came within sight of the camp. The lamps were on, the barrel fire going strong.

A deer stepped into the path in front of him, a doe. It stopped and regarded Jake, then dashed off into the woods.

"You better run," Jake said. "Anybody in the camp sees you but me, you'll probably get blasted by a machine gun."

What he needed, Jake decided, was some kind of distraction. Something that would keep everybody's attention long enough for him to get away without being noticed.

But what?

Laurie's direct-line office phone was constantly busy and she dreaded picking it up. She had her secretary screen all the other lines and that kept most of the loons from bending her ear, but it was amazing how many people managed to get her direct line's unlisted number.

"Laurie Sherman."

"Miz Sherman, this is Dan Lotz of CBS. We'd like to set up an on-the-air interview with you for *Alien Watch* tomorrow night—"

"*Alien Watch*?" Laurie interrupted.

"Yes, it's our new late-night program, following Letterman. It'll be running Monday through Friday—"

"What, is this like *Nightline*?"

"Well, something like it. *Nightline* was originally set up during the Iranian hostage crisis to keep the American public abreast of that situation, and since there is obviously a parallel here—"

"What are you going to talk about, Dan?" she interrupted for the third time. "Once you've said 'The alien is coming,' what then? 'The alien is still coming'? We aren't giving out verbatim transcripts of our conversations, for reasons of national security. What is there to say?"

"Miz Sherman, this is one of the greatest events in human history. Our viewers have a need—no, they have a *right*—to know everything about it as it happens."

"I'm afraid they won't be able to get it from me, Dan. I'm strictly limited in what I can say."

"Come on the show anyway. We're trying to get Dr. Benjamin Osgood and Father Thomas O'Rourke on the same broadcast."

" 'Trying' to get them?"

"They are ninety percent confirmed."

She smiled into the phone. CBS was bootstrapping. If they got one, maybe they could get one of the others, and if they had two of them, the third might consider it worthwhile.

"Sorry, Dan. Another time." She hung up.

"Laurie?" her secretary said over the intercom.

"Yes?"

"The guy from William Morris is on line three again. He's upped his offer. He's up to ten million. Says he'll match anything CAA or ICM puts on the table."

Laurie shook her head. "Jesus, don't these guys listen? We aren't in a position to negotiate the right to Zeerus's life story no matter how much he offers! Not a movie, not a book, not an animated television series!"

"It's the sixth time he's called today."

"Fine. Tell him we're considering it. We'll get back to him next Tuesday."

Her private line rang again. "Laurie Sherman."

"Are we having fun yet?" It was Melanie Fawcett.

"Oh, girl, you wouldn't believe how much fun I've been having."

"I think I might. I just got a call from the Boy Scouts of America. They want to know when the alien will be available for pictures. The Girl Scouts beat them by three days with their request. Did you see Leno's monologue last night?"

"Are you kidding? I was in a coma by ten-thirty."

"The alien is the best thing to happen to stand-up comics since O.J. and Bob Packwood. He did five jokes about it. And there is a new Web page on the Internet. Know how a urine sample and the alien are alike in Rome? Both are specimens."

"Boo."

"How about this one? Three aliens go into a bar—"

"Boo, hiss."

"Sorry. I don't make 'em up, I just pass them on."

"I can't believe all this," Laurie said.

"Tip of the iceberg, babe. We've had to put six new operators on fifty lines to handle the calls. Gun stores are selling weapons and ammunition faster than the manufacturers can make them. People are building bomb shelters. A group calling itself the Church of the Immaculate Alien registered in southern California. They're claiming a membership of a hundred thousand already. They are building a landing pad in what used to be a cow pasture in Glendale."

"Jesus."

"He's gonna have to move over, honey. We got the 'specimen' now and he's hotter than the sixth fleet on shore leave. Oops. Gotta run. The BBC is calling from London. Sayonara."

Laurie looked at the blinking lights on her phone. She hadn't seen Larry, save for one time in the hall as he left the boss's office, for what seemed like forever. She was spending more time on the stair stepper and glider than she ever had and it wasn't enough to burn off her frustrations. What she wanted to do was get up, go for a nice ride in the country with the man she was missing, then spend the night in some bed and breakfast, and skip the breakfast, please. What she did not want to do was sit in this stuffy office answering the stupid phones with the cold and crisp winter's day outside calling to her.

Too bad.

She picked up her private line again. "Laurie Sherman."

"Ms. Sherman? Boyd Starling here, Creative Artists Agency. Have you had a chance to consider our offer . . . ?"

Stewart opened the restricted file, using the password he'd swiped from the sloppiest of the military programmers on his floor. All it had taken was a little capture program plugged into the man's workstation while he was in the can. The guy never bothered to log off and rearm his security when he went to the john, he just left his system up. Since there wasn't anybody around but other programmers, he figured he was safe and probably he was mostly right. Any big rascal on his station would be noticed. But his virus alert wasn't tripped because the program was harmless. The capture wouldn't work until the next time the station was initialized, and all it did then was record keystrokes until it reached its 4K limit and upload the resulting file into the interoffice mail buffer. Then the capture deleted itself. It wouldn't steal enough RAM to be noticed while it was running and once it was gone, it was gone, no harm, no foul.

Except that Stewart then had access to anything the other programmer could get into, and since that guy's clearance was higher than his, that was a bunch.

Stewart was working on the dictionary. They figured he already knew enough about it that they couldn't hide anything, but he was pretty sure they were probably hiding something else.

They were.

Lots of stuff.

Man.

31

Hightower sat on his leather recliner in his living room, dressed in his bathrobe, watching a videotape that had been delivered by courier from the White House an hour earlier. On the tape was one Rosa Florita Gomez, aka Rosita G, the latest addition to the daytime talk show wars, according to the coverage card included with the tape. She was, the bio went on to say, a twenty-six-year-old Latina salsa singer turned television hostess.

Hightower looked at the girl onscreen. She was pretty, had thick, blue-black hair worn down almost to the small of her back, and sported enough bright red lipstick to color a matador's cape. She apparently favored T-shirts without a bra and skintight leather pants over six-inch heels. The T-shirt was pale blue, matching the pants. The hooker heels matched the lipstick. Her nipples were prominent.

Oh, boy.

The critical consensus, according to the card, was that Rosita's wit and wisdom could be listed entirely on a sheet of notebook paper—with room left over for a decent book report. However, her program, *Rosita G*, currently drew a bigger audience than either Oprah or Sally.

Since he didn't watch daytime television except for the news, this factoid didn't particularly impress Hightower, though he assumed it was meant to.

The explanatory card and tape of this spectacle were courtesy of Laurie, who was almost a month out of his bed. One of the longest months of his life.

The subject of this taped extravaganza was aliens from outer space.

Hightower watched as the athletic young woman paced back and forth, facing four people seated in chairs side by side on a stage.

"So Meester Carmody"—she pronounced the man's name "Kar-ah-mah-dee"—"tell us how con dis alien con to de Estados Unidos? How con he din' wan' to land in May-he-co or Puerrrto Rrrrico or Coo-ba?" She smiled, and her teeth were so even and bright they had to be bleached or capped.

The accent was so thick you could smother a plate of tamales with it, with plenty left over for chips and dip. God.

His private phone rang. "Hello."

"You get a chance to look at that tape I sent over?" Laurie.

"Watching it now. Nice pants."

"Don't let the sluta picante act fool you," Laurie said. "Little Rosa there grew up in the San Fernando Valley, went to UCLA, and got her degree in music and communications. Held a B-plus average all four years."

"You're kidding."

"Under another name. After she left school, she became Rosita G, headed south of the border, and started singing in Mexico City night-clubs. Hit it big a year ago, top-selling records, came back to do this show. She's nobody's fool."

"So why am I watching this accomplished chameleon? Did I mention how much I miss you?"

There was a pause as that sank in. "I miss you, too." Then back to business: "Because one of those people onstage, the second from the left, I believe, is Michael Carmody, the British computer geek who was one of the first outside the U.S. to record Zeerus's original messages."

Hightower glanced at the screen. Carmody was thin, pale, had a wispy mustache and a big Adam's apple. He wore black-framed glasses.

Hightower said, "So? We're past that. It's public knowledge. That stupid late-night keep-watching-the-skies program has been running with the text of that for weeks."

"But he's one of a handful outside this country who might do something with the dictionary. Our man in London tells us he thinks Carmody is about to break the code."

"Again, so what? Your spin doctors are working overtime, aren't they?"

"You haven't gotten that radio thing up and running yet, though."

"A few more days, my people tell me. What are—oh, I see."

"You're getting slow in your old age."

"Lack of sex," he said.

"You want us to use the FBI or the CIA?"

"No. Let me it handle through MI."

"I really do miss you," she said. "I have to go. I've got a reception at the Italian consulate."

"Bye."

He stared at the screen, brooding. If this geek, as Laurie so kindly called him, could get the dictionary translated, he could call Zeerus in his own language. While they had agreed with the alien that he was to keep his lines closed except to the U.S. contact team, and he'd been doing that so far, a message in his own language might be something that would interest him.

Somebody would have to pay Meester Kar-ah-mah-dee a visit. Maybe Major Hayes. He hadn't heard anything from him lately.

He reached for the phone again.

"Sir, could you tell me what you think about the alien coming to Earth?"

The shot was over the interviewer's shoulder, all you could see was the back of her head, and the man to whom she was talking was young and dressed blue-collar—a leather jacket over a flannel shirt and green cotton work pants. It could have been a big-city street anywhere until the man being interviewed opened his mouth.

"I ain't worried about it, you know what I'm sayin' heah? Ain' gonna botha me none."

The Bronx, no doubt about it. Which probably made it New York.

The camera cut to another interview. This time, the reporter's head and shoulders filled the shot—she was a Kathy or Katie or some such, blond and Barbie-doll pretty, no character lines or features—and she asked the question again.

The woman the second camera cut to was dressed in power rags, a nice Liz Claiborne powder gray charcoal suit, red silk scarf, fifty-buck haircut. She said, "I think it's wonderful. I only hope our patriarchal politicians in Washington don't scare the visitor off."

Another face, a forty-something man with a salt-and-pepper mustache under a spider-veined nose. The director bypassed the question, and the man with the drinker's nose said, "Why don't we talk about it over a drink, honey?"

On her couch, Laurie smiled as she slipped her shoes off and rubbed at the instep of her right foot. Trust a New Yorker to hit on the reporter on the air in front of millions of people.

She wished Larry was here to rub her feet. He could put her to sleep doing that. She hated heels, but they went with the job. Even though they were only three-inchers and well padded, her feet still hurt after standing around at a party for three hours smiling her professional smile as she fielded alien questions. Who was it had written that book about cruel shoes? Steve Martin?

On the television, Barbie turned to smile directly into the camera. "Well, there you have it, Richard. Reactions are certainly mixed here on the streets of Manhattan. One thing for sure, almost everybody has heard about this story. Back to you."

The shot changed to the announcer back in the studio, superimposed in front of the street reporter's image. He said, "Enjoy your drink, Katie." He smiled, revealing some prime orthodontia. The network had hired a new face to anchor the show, some guy from one of the affiliates in Phoenix or Taos or somewhere in the Southwest. He was handsome, deeply tanned, had a little gray at the temples, and looked vaguely Native American. "Well, there you have it. From our studios in New York, this is Richard Margolin. We'll be back for more of *Alien Watch* after these messages. Stay tuned."

Laurie reached for the remote to mute the sound on the commercials but stopped when she saw the first one. It was a CBS network ID and it showed the CBS eye. A tiny animated spaceship flew across the screen in front of the logo and the eye moved in its socket to watch it as the ship zipped offscreen. The voice-over said, "This . . . is CBS. The First Contact network."

Laurie killed the sound. Lord. If this alien bandwagon got any more overloaded, it was going to blow out the tires and drop flatter than a warm glass of year-old ginger ale.

A hot bath, she decided. To soak her feet and wash away some of this hoopla.

The diversion Jake came up with had to do a couple of things. It had to keep everybody's attention long enough for him to swipe the trike and get long gone before anybody realized it, and it couldn't look like an attack.

The militia was always running drills in case they were attacked by anybody. Everybody had an assignment. If somebody came in shooting, there was a battle plan. Jake was supposed to just stay out of the way, to crawl under his bunk and wait until it was over, but everybody who had a gun was supposed to get somewhere and start using it. So it couldn't look like an attack. It had to look like something dangerous but not something coming from outside.

He waited until another night when the militia had something to celebrate. When half the camp was plowed and mostly asleep, he moved.

He'd already swiped the stuff from his old man, the compass and knife and matches and all. He had it in a day pack, along with some cookies, candy bars, sandwiches, and a canteen of water. He slipped out of the tent unseen and unheard by his snoring father. He took several deep breaths of the freezing night air outside the tent, felt the sharpness of it cut into his nose and throat and lungs, then headed toward the supply tent.

The oil drum burned low, the guard tonight was stretched out next to the rusting metal, out cold. He wore a thick parka and was wrapped in a dark green wool army blanket.

Jake headed for the latrine, then circled around to the trike he wanted. It took a couple of minutes to get the lock open. He opened the fuel cock and turned the choke thing on. Then he hurried away, to come up behind the supply tent. He slipped under the back flap and inside.

It was dark, too dark to see, but he knew where everything was, he had marked it all in his head. Next to the rear upright post was a can of what his old man called white gasoline, used for some of the older Coleman lanterns. He picked the two-gallon can up, opened the top, and poured about half of it all over the place. He lifted the rear wall of the tent and moved outside again, left a trail of gas in the snow as he backed away. The stuff burned pretty fast, a lot faster than in the movies, but he didn't want to get too far away. He set the can down, pulled one of the waterproof matches out of the container, held it against the rough checkering. He took another deep breath and let it out. No turning back now, not with the tent soaked with gas. They'd notice that first thing in the morning.

He struck the match, dropped it onto the puddle of gas by his feet.

The match went out.

Crap!

He tried again, and again, the match was extinguished by falling into the liquid.

The third time, he set the match down next to the edge of the gas.

Whuff!

The puddle flamed up and the line of gas leading to the tent lit, faster even than he expected.

Jake hauled butt. He wasn't fifty feet away when the tent went off. He could hear the flames light with a big *whoosh!* and the light of it threw his dancing shadow onto the crunchy snow ahead of him as he ran. He didn't look back but kept pumping, heading for the trike.

Something volatile blew up in the supply tent and there was a boom and a ringing sound, like somebody had hit a big garbage can with a hammer.

Somebody yelled something, Jake couldn't make it out. By now, he was almost at the trike. He hopped on it, hit the starter button.

The engine whined. It was cold and didn't crank up, just went *renh-renh-renh*.

"Shit!" somebody yelled, but it didn't sound close. "Fire! Fire!"

The camp woke up and Jake could see people coming out of their tents. The supply tent was going great guns now, yellow flames roaring up into the night thirty feet high, at least, and enough light to show all the people heading toward it.

The trike's engine caught. Yes!

The engine died.

Damn!

He hit the button again. The engine came to life. Sputtered a little but was running. He didn't have time to let it warm up. He put the trike in gear, gave it some throttle. The trike jumped, the front wheel came off the ground, but dropped back when he eased off the gas. He was moving!

He had mapped out his escape route, he planned to take the northeast trail out of the camp until it branched and connected back to the north trail, then cut back. But there was somebody ahead of him, somebody pulling on a jacket and yelling, so Jake cut to the left and gunned the engine, headed off over the snow and off the path.

The night-crisp snow crunched under the fat tires and the trike sank and slowed, but it kept moving. He gave it more throttle but that only spun the rear wheels, so he eased up and picked up a little speed. He wasn't going very fast, slower than a man could run on dry ground. But this wasn't dry ground and nobody without snowshoes was going to run on the old snow.

"Hey!" somebody yelled. Jake risked a look back over his shoulder and saw a skinny figure standing there watching him. Pete? Could be.

Whatever. The other trike was parked back there but he'd put a whole canteen of water into its gas tank, and even if somebody tried to chase him on it, they ought not to get far. The snow machine would have been worse, but one of the men had taken it back down the south road two days ago and wasn't supposed to be back for another two days, so he had plenty of head start on that.

A tree loomed ahead and Jake cut the trike to his right. He could see the big trees pretty good against the snow and with the tent fire and all, but there were little ones that could mess him up if he hit one. He didn't want to risk using the light yet, not until he was well away from the camp.

Pete—or whoever it was—yelled "Hey!" again, but there weren't any gunshots. There was a big maple tree not far ahead, a couple hundred yards, and once he made that, he could get back on the trail. There was snow on the trail but he could see it was clear of big stobs and stuff, and if he could stay on that, he could go faster.

Behind him, somebody yelled orders. Jake glanced back that way again, saw men throwing buckets of snow on the burning tent. They were pretty busy back there.

Nobody was heading his way.

He looked away from the fire and back in the direction he was heading. He dodged another small tree, hit something under the snow that lifted the trike and him off the seat, rocked the vehicle to one side but not enough to overturn. The wheels settled down into the snow, found solid ground underneath. The trike jumped forward.

He was as scared as he'd ever been but he was also smiling.

He was going to make it.

He was going to get away.

32

For Hayes, it felt as if one of those bored gods who had been meddling with his life finally decided to take pity on him. When he got to his next stop on the ice capade tour, he had new orders waiting for him. He read them, broke into laughter the OOD must have surely thought was insane, turned around, and headed back out to the C-130 that had brought him. He was to report to the Pentagon, to General Hightower himself. He was going home.

Hallelujah!

Once the big cargo plane was in the Arctic air, Hayes did worry a little about why he was being recalled, but not too much. Whatever it was, it had to be better than the ride he'd been on for the last couple of months.

Maybe it was going to be a nice warm desk job. Somehow, the idea of being out in the field wasn't so appealing as it had been before. Maybe the old saying about they also serve who stand and wait was true. Whatever. He was just glad to be coming in from the cold.

Jake's escape turned out to be a lot easier than he'd expected. Oh, sure, he spent a long spooky night in the woods, waiting for somebody to jump out from behind a tree and grab him, but that hadn't happened. He didn't know how fast he had been going, but he had been steadily rolling for several hours, so he must be at least eight or ten miles away. These were pretty big woods. He was cold and very tired when he came to an old logging road just before dawn. He turned and started down it. When the rising sun came up a few minutes later, he knew he was heading east.

He dozed and almost fell off the trike a couple of times, but he came to a railroad track that had a little silver hut next to it, and that woke him up. There was a light signal not too far away from shack, a pole with a black thing on it with red, yellow, and green lights. The green light was on.

He parked the trike in the woods where nobody could see it from the road or the track and went back to the shack. It wasn't very big, probably had some kind of train repair stuff in it, and it was locked. He tried to pick the lock as he had the trike's, but after half an hour, he gave up. But he still had his old man's big survival knife and he managed to get the point into the door frame next to the lock by hammering on the butt with a rock. He threw all his weight against the knife's handle and the lock popped and the door swung open. He looked inside. There were some flashing orange light things and some white-and-red striped wooden posts, plus some railroad spikes and a couple of rails standing up against the wall. A big piece of canvas was folded up and hanging on a hook on the back wall. There was a box with wires in it, some kind of electrical switcher thing, probably had to do with the train signal just down the track. Place was probably eight feet by eight feet and a lot of that was taken up by junk, but there was room enough for him to lie down. He went inside and closed the door. No windows, and it was pretty dark, but there was a bunch of little slots in the door, probably to let the place dry out when it was hot enough, and they let in enough light so he could see after his eyes got adjusted. He put the canvas on the floor—it was heavy and musty-smelling—unpacked his emergency blanket and wrapped it around him, and sat on the canvas pad. It was cold in here but at least it was out of the wind and snow. Maybe he could get a little rest.

He felt himself falling into sleep almost immediately.

Laurie leaned forward and said to her driver, "What's going on?"

"I don't know, Ms. Sherman. The street is blocked."

Since they'd closed Pennsylvania Avenue to public traffic by the White House to keep stray assassins from taking potshots at the building, it was harder to get to work. They had to go in via Madison or Hamilton and the traffic was usually bad, even with ID to get you through. But not this bad.

"We're close enough so I can walk," she said. "Pick me up for the luncheon at noon, would you, Sam?"

"Yes, ma'am."

Laurie grabbed her purse and briefcase and slid out of the car. She started walking toward the White House, but she could see what the problem was pretty quick: There were people milling around, some kind of demonstration. The D.C. cops were good at this kind of thing and they were moving the demonstrators out pretty quick, but traffic was snarled and backed up.

The joys of democracy.

As Laurie got closer, she saw some of the signs the demonstrators waved about: THE END IS NEAR! and REPENT SINNERS! and THE DEVIL IS ON HIS WAY! This last sign had a cartoon demon drawn on it, red skin, horns, and a pitchfork.

Laurie shook her head. She turned to loop around toward the back entrance, saw three cops, two men and a woman, manning a barricade. "What's all this about?" she asked the woman cop.

"Buncha Jesus freaks protesting the guy up in the spaceship. They b'lieve he's 666, come to de-stroy the world."

Laurie smiled and shook her head. "What do they think this is going to do? Make him turn around and go home? They figure he can see them from umpty-dump million miles away?"

"Well, if he was the real Beast, he could," one of the male cops put in. "I think they're just looney tunes, myself."

Laurie shook her head again. She reached for her ID so she could get past the barricade.

"Uh oh," the woman cop said. "Check it out."

The cops' portable radios squawked and a voice said, "Heads up, South! They're coming your way. Chester, Kent, you and Winston get over there and reinforce South! I want a tactical unit over there and I want it now!"

Laurie looked and saw that the crowd had shifted and was heading in their direction.

"Better move along, ma'am. Looks like trouble."

"I work in there," she said. She fumbled with her wallet inside her purse, couldn't get it open.

"Yes, ma'am, but you'd better move just the same."

Laurie saw the crowd surge toward them. The radios came to life with several voices overlapping each other.

"Break out the spray, boys," the woman cop said. The trio pulled canisters from their belts. Mace or pepper spray, Laurie figured.

"Bensen, get your new toy up here."

One of the male cops bent and came up with what looked like a bright yellow shotgun.

The mob boiled closer.

The female cop spoke into her radio. "Command, this is South station. Get some bodies over here *now* or we're gonna get squashed!"

Laurie was in her stubby heels but she turned away from the approaching mass of excited humanity and hurried back the way she'd come. She had a pair of running shoes at the office and sometimes she'd go for walks at lunch if she wasn't busy. She wished she had those shoes now.

She was fifty feet away when the first surge of the demonstrators reached the police barricade. She heard several screams. She glanced over her shoulder.

The cops sprayed the leaders with their canisters and those in front of the mob stumbled or tried to stop but the people behind them kept pushing. The cops fell back, still spraying. The barricade went down. There was a loud boom and she saw the cop aiming the yellow shotgun at the crowd, saw smoke come out of the barrel.

Lord, were the cops shooting the citizens?

People screamed and the crowd broke and began to stream off to the sides, away from the cops.

Another group of D.C. officers moved in the mob from an angle, using clear plastic shields and riot batons to club their way through to where the three cops kept backing slowly away. The yellow shotgun went off again and Laurie saw what looked like a small bag of something heavy bounce off a man's chest as he fell backward, hard. She stared, saw there wasn't any blood on him. Some kind of nonlethal weapon, she realized. Thank God.

Some of the crowd headed her way, panicked. There wasn't any place to go. Laurie was swept up in the fleeing mob. She kicked off her shoes, let them fall, didn't even think about stopping to pick them up. This would not be a good time to fall down. They would trample over whatever was in their way to escape.

She moved, stayed with the majority of the others. Felt a primal fear screaming in her head: *Run! Run!*

A large woman with a sign that said TRUST IN JESUS! did stumble to Laurie's right just then, went to one knee, and a man slammed into the woman from behind. Laurie doubted that Jesus would have approved of the word the man used as he pinwheeled over the woman in a half-flip and landed on his back on the street. She saw somebody step on the downed man's hand, heard his scream. She didn't have time to see what else happened to him, she had to keep running.

As soon as she came to a wide spot, Laurie angled off, got out of the flow. Behind the runners came a dozen police officers flailing their batons.

It was ugly, so ugly.

She saw a cop in a helmet smash an elderly man, hit him solidly on the neck with the long black club. The old man's glasses flew into the air as he crumpled. The cop wore a grim expression. At least he wasn't smiling.

A young woman tried to help the old man up and another cop bounced his baton off her face. Blood sprayed from her nose.

Oh, God, how awful!

Laurie knew that her ID wouldn't help her, these adrenaline-fueled policemen would be too angry to see it. She moved, lost in her surroundings but knowing she had to get away from the street. There was a building entrance. She ran for it. Got inside the door. A dozen people were there in the lobby, staring out.

"What's going on?" somebody asked her.

Laurie shook her head. "I don't know," she said. She looked down at her feet. Her panty hose had shredded on the bottom, one heel was bare. There was a spot of blood on the floor. She lifted her feet, left, then the right. There was a small cut on the bottom of her right foot. Bright red blood dripped from the little wound.

God.

When Jake awoke, he didn't remember where he was. He was cold, though, and what pulled him from his exhausted sleep was a loud air horn, blasting from not far away. He got up, moved to the door, eased it open a crack. He looked at his watch. Past noon. He must have been asleep for five or six hours.

A train was passing, a passenger train, and it was slowing down.

Jake opened the door a little more, leaned out. The signal down the track was red. Must be another train down there somewhere, though he hadn't heard it pass.

All of a sudden, Jake realized something.

A *train*.

He grabbed his pack, shoved the Mylar blanket into it, the knife. Slipped out of the shack and circled around it so it was between him and the train. It was still slowing. He gathered himself. He ran, sprinted. Angled to the track, came up to the side of the train, ran, almost tripped on the ties and gray rocks under them but stayed on his feet. There were four or five cars left behind him. He got next to the space between two cars, then a door with a little step on it. He jumped up, caught the door handle, managed to climb onto the metal step. This was a tall car; the passenger windows were like twenty feet up. Must be a double-decker.

The door was locked. Jake looked through the glass, saw a bunch of baggage piled in bins, an empty space and a door on the other side of the car. Nobody around.

The train started to pick up speed again. Now what? How was he going to get inside? Maybe he could break the glass with the knife?

He sure could not hang on here for long. But the train was rolling faster and faster, had to be going thirty or forty by now. If he was going to jump off, he needed to do it pretty quick, pick a big snowbank or something, or he was going to break his neck—

A man stepped into the empty space, his back to Jake. He lit up a cigarette.

Jake pounded on the window with the side of his fist. "Hey! Hey, mister! Help!"

The man turned around, saw Jake. His eyes went wide. He jumped for the door. Stopped and frowned. Jake saw the problem. The only thing he had to hang on to was the handle. It was a sliding door, no hinges, but if the guy opened it, he was going to get pulled right off the little metal step. Wait—what was—there was a handrail on the side of the car, just a little rod, but if he leaned over a little and caught it . . .

Jake did. The guy slid the door open, reached out, and grabbed Jake's free hand, and jerked him into the car.

"Jesus H. Christ, kid, how the hell did you get out there?"

Jake realized the guy thought he was a passenger on the train. He said, "I'm—I'm sorry! I opened the door, I was sick, I had to throw up and we went around a curve and I fell out. I grabbed on but the door shut! You won't tell my parents, will you?" He pretended to cry.

"Hey, hey, it's okay, everything is all right, don't cry. You're okay. I won't tell your mother."

"Th-thank you, mister! Thank you!"

"How long you been out there?"

"Ju-ju-just a few muh-muh-minutes," he said, sobs filling his voice. He realized that he really *was* crying now, it wasn't faked anymore.

"Thank you, muh-muh-mister!"

"What's your name, kid?"

"Tommy," Jake said.

"Yeah, well, look, Tommy, you go on back to your seat, okay? Kids do stupid stuff, I did some when I was a kid, let's just let it go, okay?"

"Yes, sir."

The man smiled. Jake hurried toward the stairs, saw a sign for the bathrooms, and went into there instead. It wasn't much bigger than a rest room on a jet, but it had a lock on the door. He locked it and sat down on the toilet. Man.

He would stay in here for a while. Then he'd go up into the car. Even if the conductor figured out he wasn't a paying passenger and made him get off the train, by then he'd be a lot farther away from the camp in the woods. Or maybe he could like buy a ticket. It didn't matter where the train was going, but he could figure that out later.

For now, anyway, he was safe.

33

Hightower leaned back in his chair and smiled at Mitch Carter, seated across the desk from him. "One out of three? Is that all?"

"Begging the Lord High General's pardon, but it's only been a few weeks."

"God created Heaven and Earth in six days, Mitch."

"God didn't have to deal with the lowest bidder—or the unions."

Both men chuckled. "So fill me in," Hightower said.

"The blind samurai masseur whatshisname still can't find his ass with both hands. The laser is working but the detection system's computer gets confused if you ask it to walk and chew gum at the same time. We don't know why, it should work just fine but it doesn't. Our chances of getting it fixed and in the air by your target date are not real good."

" 'Not real good.' Which means . . . ?"

"You'd be better off betting money on the Jets getting into the Super Bowl."

"That bad?"

"Not gonna happen without a major miracle."

"Go on."

"If our visitor decides to pull over out by Neptune or Uranus or somewhere to throw a big rock at us, we're in trouble. My tame white coats say they are eighty percent sure that we could pulverize a meteor the size of the *Queen Mary* with existing delivery systems and stock on hand. They are fifty percent sure we could deflect one the size of a real small mountain so it would probably miss us. Anything bigger than that, they are pretty sure we can't do much to stop, slow, or deflect it at all. Might be able to bust it up, but with something as big as, say, downtown Chicago, depending on what it was made out of, it wouldn't help much to break it in half or thirds. The pieces wouldn't burn up in the atmosphere, they would keep on coming, and each would hit with the force of several very large H-bombs. If they all splashed down in the ocean, the tsunami activity from some might cancel some of the others out, though my guys aren't sure. A big rock in the water would swamp coastal cities, maybe spawn a superhurricane; and if it hits land, there is going to be a huge, smoking crater and a blast radius that will flatten buildings for more miles than you want to think about. Plus enough smoke and dust thrown up into the air to make it winter everywhere for a few years, which would maybe kill off most food crops, maybe jump-start a new ice age and starve a majority of humans as a result."

"Wonderful."

"What happened to the dinosaurs, so they say. We got to be top dogs because our ancestors were little ratlike things who stayed warm and didn't need much to eat. The next civilization will probably be descended from beetles. Or roaches."

"You enjoy these doomsday scenarios, don't you, Mitch?"

He ignored that comment and continued: "We're going to try to beef Ball Breaker up. Get multiple-strike capability. In theory, a big enough blast, far enough away and at the right angle, will deflect a monster rock enough so it would miss us. In theory—but not by late springtime. So let's hope the BEM isn't a major league pitcher with a hankering to toss a pumpkin across our plate. We can't hit it back at him if he does."

Hightower grinned. BEM—bug-eyed monster. "So Peregrine is the only one that will fly?"

"Yessir. Our operating system on that will work well enough to nail a pretty small target—if it's close enough. If we know the target's speed and flight path, and they remain constant, we can spike it with one bird out to forty thousand klicks every time. We can hit it most of the time at twice that distance. We can put half a dozen of them up at

once and bracket an incoming vessel so there's no way it can keep coming in this general direction without one of them tagging it. Unless he
can stop his ship on a dime and throw it into reverse, we can thump
him out to high orbit, guaranteed."

"That's what I want to hear. Good work, Mitch. Keep trying on the
others."

"The impossible takes a little longer. What can I say?"

After Mitch left, Hightower buried himself back in reports of that
stupid police action overseas. They were really going to have to shut
this action down. . . .

The com beeped.

"Sir, Major Steve Hayes is here for his 1400 appointment."

Ah. "Send him in."

Hayes marched into the office as though his spine had been fused
solid from the base of his skull to his tailbone. "At ease, Major. Sit."

He sat.

"I understand you've been on a tour of observation bases, Major."

"Yes, sir."

"Enjoyable duty?"

"Bracing, sir."

Hightower grinned. He'd been to a base in Greenland once.
Colder than an ice house dust mop, it had been.

"I have a little chore for you. There's a scientist—a British national
currently visiting our fair land—who needs to be convinced he should
cease work on a certain project. Concerning an attempt to communicate with a . . . visitor of whom you are aware."

"Sir."

"If you can't convince him to give up his efforts, then it would be
very convenient for all concerned if somehow this gentleman were to . . .
lose the tools he needs to complete the project. If you get my meaning?"

"Yes, sir, I believe I understand you."

"If you are wondering why I picked you instead of some hotshot
MI op, it's because you were in on the ground floor and you have some
idea of what we're dealing with. I don't want to open this door any
wider than I have to." That wasn't altogether true, but he didn't want to
get into that. Hayes didn't need to know his real reasons.

"Yes, sir."

"Good. Here's the file. Attend to this soonest."

"Sir."

The young major came to his feet. He was in uniform but indoors and Hightower wasn't big on saluting at work—he'd never get anything done if he had to bend the elbow every time he passed somebody—so he said, "Dismissed, Hayes. I'd like to have your report on my desk within a week if possible."

"Yes, sir."

He executed a snappy about-face and left.

Hightower grinned again. If he had gotten called in to see the chairman of the Joint Chiefs when he'd been a lowly major, he would have had a great deal of difficulty controlling his bladder.

What the young major didn't know was that his maternal uncle and Hightower had known each other well, a long time ago in a war far away, and that Hightower owed that uncle his life. Which was why he was looking out after the boy. Well, not a boy, but certainly young enough to be his son. Despite the nasty report from that fatuous colonel in ops, Hayes seemed sharp enough.

As he turned in his visitor's pass and left the Pentagon, it was all Hayes could do to slow his breathing enough to keep from hyperventilating. Jesus, the old man himself had called him in and laid this on him. If he had to cut the blabbermouthed scientist's throat to shut him up or stop him poking around, he'd do it. No way was he going to screw up an order from the brassiest officer in the United States military, not counting the president. No way, no how.

And the between-the-lines orders had been clear. Only a stupid man would approach this guy—what was his name? Carmody?—and tell him to stop trying to decipher the dictionary code so he could call up Mr. Zeerus the alien for a nice chat. No, what was going to happen was, the message upon which Mr. Carmody was working was going to disappear. Along with any and all copies. Maybe he wasn't the greatest operative since James Bond, but he was better than those klutzes who broke into the Watergate and got Nixon dethroned. He would set it up, execute it, take care of it. And fast. What he did not want was for General Lawrence Hightower to be sitting and drumming his fingers, waiting. In and out, a surgical strike, what-fer-thank-you-sir, that was how it was going to go.

He hoped.

Hayes headed for where he'd parked his car. He would go home, digest all the information about this, then roll. A British national? Maybe a nice trip to England, that would be interesting.

As he drove toward his place, he wished he had somebody to share the sudden excitement of this assignment with. It had been a long time since he'd had a woman staying at his place, and the last one hadn't stuck around long enough for him to feel any sense of longevity with her. Sometimes going home to an empty apartment got to be a drag. No girlfriend, no wife, no kids, no dog, just him and the TV or the latest book. When he'd been younger, that had been more than enough. Shifting from assignment to assignment, having his fun on the fly, partying with women in dozens of cities around the world, yeah, that had been enough ten years past, even five years. But now, he felt a need to run a little slower, speak a little softer, recognize he wasn't getting any younger. The days when he could party all night, then roll into work and do *that* all day, followed by another night without sleep, those days were gone. Sure, the military moved you around, but maybe if he couldn't have a permanent home just yet, he might be able to start a family to take the edge off being on his own for so long.

It was a thought.

It was early the next morning in upstate New York when Jake changed trains. He bought a ticket for Washington, D.C., would have to change trains again along the way. He planned to use the Tommy name he'd given to the guy who'd saved his butt, but the bored ticket guy didn't even ask.

It was kind of amazing what you could get away with if you just looked like you knew what you were doing.

So now he must be at least a couple of hundred miles away from the militia camp and getting farther away every minute. By now they would be looking for him. With any luck at all, they would be heading north. He watched every time somebody came or went from the car. They couldn't know he was on this train, but maybe they would send somebody to check every train they could find. Or maybe they wouldn't even care that much. His old man wouldn't think that Jake would rat on them—hadn't he helped set up the major? But he would be really pissed off that Jake had swiped the trike and run off. Boy, would he.

He wished he'd hidden the trike better, now that he thought about it, but maybe it was far enough off the logging road that they wouldn't spot it. Somebody would find it eventually, but if it wasn't the militia guys, that wouldn't matter. If they *did* find the trike there—his old man and his buddies—they would figure out he'd hopped a train pretty quick; otherwise, why leave his transportation out in the middle of nowhere like that? He should have drained the rest of the gas out, that would have explained it. The trike hadn't had much left, it was on the reserve. Maybe they'd think it stopped running or something. If they found it.

Jake looked out the window. No snow down here, just a lot of bare trees and cold-looking fields, a few roads here and there. He'd never thought about New York having so much country; somehow, he'd thought it would all be city, like Manhattan, but from the speeding train, it looked kind of like Oregon, a whole lot of nothing.

This might be a mistake. Maybe the guy in Washington wouldn't even remember him, it had been a couple of months. Maybe he would just slap him into jail so fast his head would swim. But when he thought about it, Jake couldn't come up with anybody else. Maybe jail wouldn't be so bad. Compared to living in the woods with a bunch of guys who wanted to start a revolution and destroy the country, maybe jail wouldn't be so bad at all.

Maybe, maybe, maybe.

The train car was mostly full, mostly a lot of guys in suits with brief-cases, or with laptops. They were probably on their way to their jobs, and they took the time on the train to work. Jake itched to get his hands on one of those computers. It had been so long since he'd had one.

It seemed as if it had been so long since he'd done anything but be afraid.

He sighed and watched the countryside go by.

34

We here at Channel Seven Action News would like to know what *you* think: If you believe the alien comes in peace as a friend to mankind, dial 555-3145. If you believe he has plans to conquer Earth, dial 555-3146. Your vote is recorded when you hear the electronic tone. We'll let you know the final results of our telepoll on the eleven o'clock report. We began our telepoll during *First Look at Five*: so far, with just over nineteen thousand callers. Fifty-three percent of you said you believe the alien comes in peace, while forty-seven percent said you believe his intentions are warlike. We'd like to remind our viewers that this is not a scientific poll. Bill?"

Laurie was on the stair stepper and she shook her head at the local newscast. God. Nobody out among the general public had a *clue* about what the alien really wanted, and yet opinions were almost evenly divided.

The smiling Bill said, "The stock market was off almost two hundred points at the close of trading today. Investors rushed to unload blue chips. It's been a seesaw all week."

Laurie stared at the screen. Nobody knew how to factor an alien into trading across the board. Guns and ammo were selling like crazy, as were life insurance policies, and mountain cabins. In some cities, bottled water and toilet paper were getting hard to find as the citizenry stocked up.

It wasn't a damned hurricane, it was an alien in a spaceship, still months away! What, did people think he was going to come down and start robbing outhouses, for Christ's sake?

Who knows? her little inner voice said. *Maybe he eats toilet paper? Maybe it's the medium of exchange on his world? I'll give you two Bountys and a Northern Tissue for that car, pal. . . .*

Ridiculous. How stupid could you get?

It was going to play hell with the boss's reelection campaign. Until he had Zeerus in his pocket, the alien was a very big, very loose cannon. He could go off and blow things right out of the water.

They almost had that faster-than-snot radio thing finished. Maybe that would help.

Abruptly, the idea of continuing to climb endless stairs to stay in shape became tiring. Laurie stopped. Her heart pounded and she realized what she wanted more than anything else in the world was to sit down with Larry, have a glass of wine, and talk about all this. Then take a nice hot shower and crawl under the covers with him and *stop* talking about all this.

Damn! Why couldn't she? Just go and do it?

Because if you get caught, you get fired and you are out of the game.

So what? Maybe I should get out of the game. It all seems like so much effort for not much return. So . . . wearing—

Blasphemy! You've spent more than half of your life—all of your adult life—to get here. You are at the top of the food chain, the biggest shark in the unelected sea. You've reached the pinnacle of staff jobs. You've got more clout than governors, congressmen, senators. Have you lost your mind?

Maybe I have.

McDonald's is the perfect place to discuss supersecret government business, Stewart thought. Nobody would suspect, or notice. The harried parents with their flocks of screaming, fussy children were altogether too busy to pay attention to a couple in the back booth hunched over a tray of burgers and fries. The teenagers who sat together in laughing clumps were too interested in seeing and being seen, in being cool and having somebody—anybody—notice. The businessmen with jackets off and ties loosened, alone and reading the paper as they mechanically ate, had other things on their minds. All the crap about the alien, the suddenly spooked economy, the state of the world.

It was the Chinese curse: The times had become interesting. Real interesting.

The phenomenon of McDonald's bothered a lot of people: How could it have become such a monster place, serving billions and billions, more meals every day than the army and navy and marines combined? Stewart had seen a number somewhere, something like seven percent of everybody in the United States ate at the golden arches every day. That was a lot of burgers. It sure wasn't because the food was the best around.

Stewart had thought about that, and he thought he had an answer. Fries in Wisconsin tasted pretty much the same as they did in Miami or San Diego or Dodge City. Or Russia. When you went into Mickey D's, you knew what you were going to get, pretty much every time. Yeah, you could get wine with your burger in France and in England they called the pickle a "gherkin," but the basic foods were going to be almost the same. And it was going to be cheaper and faster than trying to feed yourself or your family at almost any place else.

There was a lot to be said for cheap, fast, and consistent.

Stewart looked down at his Double Quarter Pounder with Cheese, then up at Jess. He was thinking about all this because he was embarrassed. Because she was telling him why she bothered with him.

"—partially, I guess, it's enthusiasm," she said. "Not that you're dumb or ugly or anything, but there are guys who are a lot better-looking or smarter or both—"

"Thanks, Jess. Don't sugarcoat it like that, tell me what you really think."

She ignored him and went on: "Because you seem to enjoy what you're doing almost all the time. People like being around that. I like it."

"Well, if you can't have fun, why bother? Life's too short."

"That's where I think you're wrong, Stew. Some things, you shouldn't have fun with. Some things are too serious to shrug off. Our government—and now us, because we're a part of it—is doing all kinds of illegal stuff. Those files you found, showing some of those covert operations to keep this whole mess quiet, that's not right. You can't let stuff like this slide. You can't let people push you around, just sit back and let things blow over without taking a stand."

"I don't disagree with you," he began. "But—"

"No 'buts' about it! You see it going on and you're not doing anything to stop it. That makes you part of the problem and not part of the solution."

The food on the tray looked suddenly as if it was some kind of foreign thing. As if it were carved from wood, a decoration, serving some purpose he couldn't understand. He couldn't eat it. The idea of picking it up and biting into it was enough to make his stomach hurt. Jess was right. He did tend to go about his introverted way, minding his own business. But she was also expecting way too much. And she sounded awful damned righteous.

He said, "We've gone over this before. What do you want me to do? Am I supposed to grab my sling, run down to the river, pick out a couple of smooth stones, and go try to kill Goliath? No offense, but David had it easy. All Goliath had was a sword and some big muscles. The guys running things today are a lot bigger and better armed. They have 'national security' on their side. The law, remember that? Not to mention we signed papers swearing we'd keep our mouths shut. We don't, and that makes us crooks, doesn't it?"

"There's no need to get sarcastic—"

"Yes, there is! You're talking as if all of the problems in the country, all this double-dealing conspiracy crap, is somehow *my* fault! Like I need to be pounding on the door at the *New York Times* or grabbing the microphone away from Dan Rather on the *CBS Evening News* and blurting all this out. As if I can stop it all by myself!"

"You don't understand," she began.

"Oh, but I do. You want a knight in chrome armor to come charging in on his white horse to bring the nasty, lying government to its knees. You think it can be done—and that I'm the guy to do it? I'm supposed to be like Keanu Reeves, saving all the passengers on the bus from Dennis Hopper's bomb? Man. How do you get there from anywhere? I'm a computer geek, not Arnold Schwarzenegger. This isn't a movie where the star wins because the scriptwriter says he does!"

She leaned back, her eyes going wide. He'd never talked to her like this before.

"You're saying I'm stupid?"

Oh, Christ! Where did that come from? How did women make these kinds of leaps of logic? "I didn't say that!"

"You might as well have said it."

"Listen to me. What I *said* was, I got some more information. What I *said* was, I was going to collect it, pile it up, and then see what I could do with it. That I was going to try to figure out how to use it to do something about the problem." That seemed perfectly reasonable to him. A logical way to proceed.

"Which sounds like a polite way of putting it off to me," she said.

He shook his head. Talking to her sometimes was like talking to a wall. Right at this moment, he felt like he could communicate better with Zeerus than Jess. And it pissed him off. She wanted to blame him for this. He'd never asked to be here. It was this or a federal jail, and how the hell much good could he do anybody from there?

And if she was so smart, why wasn't *she* doing something about it? He didn't see her out on the front lines waving a peace sign at guys with big guns. There was fair for you. Don't do like I do, do like I think *you* should do. Man.

She glared at him, waiting for his answer.

His simmering temper boiled over. "Hey, tell you what—you believe anything you want. I'm done here!" He stood, turned, walked out.

It wasn't until he'd stomped almost four blocks that his breathing slowed and he stopped shaking.

How the hell had he gotten into this mess?

Better—how was he going to get out of it?

To amuse himself, Zeerus crafted a series of responses to questions and comments he expected to hear from the apes, as soon as they were able to use the FTL device they had nearly finished building. As curious as they were, the earthlings would want to know much more of the who, where, what, when, why, and how they had already been throwing at him in their less-than-subtle way. When they had instantaneous communication, they would try to trip him up.

Most of what he would tell them would be true, enough so that slipping the lies in would be swallowed much easier. Who he was, things about his planet, generalities about space travel and galactic civilization.

It wasn't until he got to the "why" of his trip here that the need for any great skill would arise. Here he must be subtle. He would have to create an image of the Majae, of Primaster, that was suitably gray. To paint them as some kind of heinous villains who went around doing evil just for the joy it brought them, well, that would be stupid in the extreme.

No, the trick was to put it forth that his enemies were well intentioned, that they had nothing but the good of their client races in mind. *Their* vision of good.

Which just happened to be, more or less, true. Ape-spawn did not take well to paternal guidance on any scale. Being told what to do and when to do it by another race, no matter how benign, ah, that would not go down well. Especially when he made it quite clear that Earth would soon fall under the sway of the Majae—unless they were willing to allow Zeerus to help them avoid such a fate.

He smiled. Oh, they loved this kind of thing, the apes. They saw conspiracies everywhere. Somebody wanting to steal their food, their cave, their mate. They would believe him, enough of them.

As he drew nearer his destination, there were also some practical matters to which he must attend. Doubtless the authorities, those in charge of the war making, would want to control everything about Zeerus's approach. How close he should come, what orbit he should assume, how the actual meeting between the visitor and the natives should take place. Certainly in their places he would wish to do the same. One did not open one's door to any stray visitor from afar without due consideration and caution. He could well understand how they would wish to control him.

Of course, he could not allow them to do it.

The balance was tricky. He had to appear on the one hand to be friendly; on the other hand, he had to demonstrate a certain strength. He was not going to park in a high orbit and await their pleasure. He fully intended to make planetfall and to do so in a most public place. One loop so they could all see he was there and then straight in, retro-repellors blazing. It was his intent to arrive in some large city, a greenery preserve, perhaps, in direct view of millions and under the watchful electronic eyes that could transmit the event to billions more. It would be carefully orchestrated and very dramatic.

Here I am, apes. Behold!

Doubtless, too, the war makers would issue commands to deny him a landing on the planet. If he failed to respond or ignored these commands, there was a high probability the apes would slip into fear mode and use their primitive weaponry to attempt to stop him. While this stolen ship was hardly a Battle Lance, it did have some basic defense items. According to the computer, the ship had electromagnetic pulse generators capable of disabling virtually anything electronically guided that a young type-one civilization could use against it. Any missiles they fired at him should suddenly go blind, deaf, and stupid. In addition, the ship carried several small, low-wattage laser prongs that could blast conventionally armored terran aircraft from the sky in a matter of a few milliseconds. The interior shields, a dozen sheets of crystallized carboflex pressure stressed between the inner and outer hulls, were designed to stop metallic micrometeors traveling well in excess of planetary escape velocities. They would stop virtually any projectile that somehow miraculously penetrated the external duralloy hull. It was unlikely the apes had any weapons capable of even denting the exterior, short of tactical atomics, and unlikely in the extreme that they would want to use those in the middle of one of their larger cities.

So, they probably couldn't hit him with anything until he was in atmosphere, and even if they did, they probably could not damage his ship.

He would of course hold off on *telling* them he was going to land until the last minute, but when he announced it, he would make it clear he *was* going to do it and that they would essentially be wasting their time and energy attempting to stop him.

Once, as a wingling, he had gotten into a tussle with a larger and stronger Avitaur. Enraged, Zeerus had put all of his power into a kick. His claws had been dulled, according to the conventions of the day that sought to keep hot-tempered winglings alive until they became adults. Even so, the kick had been well executed. He had slammed his opponent square upon the great breathing nerve plexus under his ribs. Zeerus expected to see the larger male go down like a boulder shoved off a cliff. At the very least, he should have fallen back, stunned, winded, vulnerable. Instead, his opponent absorbed the kick as if it were nothing, laughed, then proceeded to thrash an astounded Zeerus into unconsciousness.

When you hit an opponent with your most powerful attack and he laughs at you, well, your fighting confidence just disappears.

He wouldn't shoot back at the apes unless it was absolutely necessary; he hadn't come to make war with them. But when their stone-headed spears and rocks bounced off him without results, it certainly would impress them. It would establish at the outset that he was superior to them in his technology and that had his intentions been aggressive, he could have done them major damage.

I could have hurt you, but I did not. Does that not make me your friend?

Apes generally had little or no respect for the weak but were very careful indeed around those stronger than they. They would be taught to respect Zeerus and with that respect, he would have an advantage he could use.

And certainly would use.

35

When he got to the train station in Washington, Jake went straight to a phone. The big building was too warm and smelled kind of like sweat. No point in putting it off, he figured. Although he had slept on the train quite a bit, he was tired and dirty, he needed a bath, and if he had to go to jail to get rested and clean, he was just about willing.

He dialed the number he remembered. The phone rang.

"Hello?"

"Major Hayes?"

"Yeah." There was a pause. Then, "Jake?"

"Yes, sir. I'm surprised you recognized my voice."

"You saved my life with that 'T-R-A-P' message, I'm not likely to forget that."

"Are you still looking for me?"

"Not officially, no. When we went public with the stuff about Zeerus, you got lost in the shuffle. Nobody cares that you hacked into a mailbox anymore. We're way past that."

Jake felt a great sense of relief, as if he'd just shrugged off a coat made of iron. "Oh, man."

"What can I do for you?"

"I—I escaped from the militia. From my old—from my father. I don't have any place to go."

"Where are you?"

"At—at the train station. Here—in Wuh-Wuh-Washington." To his horror, Jake felt himself about to start crying. *Stop that!*

"Stay there. I'll come and get you. Don't worry. We'll figure something out."

After Jake hung up, he felt a little better. Whatever was going to happen from now on, he wouldn't have to do it all by himself.

He went to the magazine stand and bought the new issue of *MacWorld*. He found an empty seat in the waiting room and started to read the magazine. Some of the new Mac clones were really spiffy.

Hightower opened his door. Laurie stood there. He was surprised, but happily so. "What—?"

She stepped forward, hugged him, kissed him deeply. He shut off his wonder and enjoyed the embrace. They stood there clinched for what seemed like a long time.

Finally she broke the kiss and leaned back, without letting go. "Aren't you going to invite me in? Or do you have other company? Got yourself a new girlfriend already?"

"You speak foolishly, woman."

If their clothes didn't exactly fall away like flower petals, they did manage to get undressed without tripping and breaking something.

Two minutes after he opened his door, they were in his bed.

Time ceased to matter much after that.

Later, when he was tired, sated, and very happy, he said, "Not that I'm complaining, but what brought this on? I thought you'd decided we needed to put this on hold for a while."

She stretched, like a tabby just waking up. Made a squeaky little sound halfway between a grunt and moan of pleasure. "I changed my mind."

"What about the risk of being seen?"

"You saying it wasn't worth it?"

"No, ma'am, not me, un uh, I didn't say that."

They grinned at each other.

She said, "I looked up and realized that there were two things in my life I enjoy doing. You and work. And lately, in that order, too."

"I'm honored."

"Well, you should be. I gotta go to the bathroom."

When she came back, he was sitting up, pillows propped behind his back. He had turned on the television and was watching MNN's news.

The streets of Capetown were a war zone. A jerky amateur video from a hand-held camera showed hundreds of people, mostly men, charging an automobile. It was a police car, and the two officers inside scrambled out. They did so shooting.

The camera operator's voice was thick with amazement and fear.

"Good Lord, look at that! Look at that! They're shooting into the crowd! Look out!"

The shots popped, part of the mob went down, but the others surged over the two cops. The camera shook, then steadied. The mob used flails, clubs, pitchforks, spears on the officers. The cameraman used his zoom, centered on the fight. One cop was white, the other one was black. The mob was colorblind, it attacked both cops equally. Flesh tore, bones broke, blood flowed. Somebody swung a baseball bat. The white cop's head caved in.

"They're killing the police! They're killing them! Oh, no, how awful! Stop! Stop!"

After a few seconds, that the two policemen were dead was a given.

Its rage unsatisfied, the mob attacked the car. They shattered the glass, pounded on the body, and with the hive-mind in full control, tipped the wounded car onto its side. Somebody speared the gas tank, punctured it, and gasoline spewed from the gaping wound. It was like watching an animal being slain.

Some of the rioters smoked cigarettes or pipes. One of the smokers got too close to the car.

The gasoline ignited. There was a *whoosh!* and a spray of flames blasted the mob. Several people were close enough so that their clothes flamed. They screamed, became running torches.

Like the Red Sea under Moses' command, the crowd opened up to allow the burning ones through.

The fire raced up the leaking gas to its source. The car exploded. Bodies flew, screams burst from cooked throats—

"Shit!"

Then the picture spun as the cameraman dived or was thrown to the ground. Five feet away, a black hand and arm, mostly soaked in fresh blood and partially charred, flopped in front of the lens.

Whether the arm was still attached to somebody couldn't be seen.
"South Africa just declared marital law," Hightower said.

Laurie stared at the screen. A talking head came on.

"I know. The boss got a call for help from the PM this morning
saying it was in the works. Seems some of the native populations have
a legend about men from the stars coming to help them throw off
oppression. They think Zeerus is their version of the Messiah, come to
help them take out the white governments. Half of Africa is infected. It
makes the Mau-Mau rebellion in Kenya in the fifties look like a Sunday
school picnic."

Hightower shook his head. "Barbarous."

"I saw the D.C. cops smashing heads two blocks from the White
House," she said. "The man from outer space has struck an ugly chord
in a lot of people. Just him being there has already caused a lot of mis-
ery. Even death." She waved at the television.

"It's not his fault. We did it to ourselves. Our own paranoia, our
own fears. The real brutes live up here." He tapped his temple with one
finger. "They hide in caves whose entrances are closed by only the
thinnest sheets of civilization. A sudden wind or rain washes that cover
away, the reptile brain rushes outside, and it's *The Lord of the Flies* or
'The Monsters Are Due on Maple Street.' "

"That's kind of cynical, isn't it?"

"I'm a professional warrior," he said. "I know how easy it is to
arouse that primitive beast, to free it and set it raging."

"I think a lot of that is testosterone," she said. "A male thing.
Women don't behave that way."

He laughed. "Really? You put a gun or a knife in the hands of a
woman whose children are being threatened with serious injury and
you have the deadliest creature on the planet."

"You know what I mean."

"Yes, I do. Women seldom kill for sport or pleasure but they are
certainly capable of as much violence as men. 'If you're captured by the
Indians, don't let them give you to the women.' We come from killer
stock. Almost all of us are capable of it, it's just that some of us are more
restrained. Even so, we have wiped out more of each other than were
ever eaten by lions or tigers or bears. If Zeerus drops a bomb on Earth,
he'll have to kill half the planet to begin to approach the numbers we've
amassed through wars, inquisitions, wife beating, and stickups."

"Not a pretty picture, is it?" she said.

"No. It isn't. But it's what we have to work with. Maybe in another thousand years we can build thicker doors to keep the monsters in their caves. I hope so."

"You'd be out of a job."

"And happy to see it."

She leaned over and kissed him on the shoulder. "My reluctant warrior. I like that."

"How about this? You like it, too?"

"That little thing? Poo."

"It gets bigger."

"Prove it."

He did.

36

When Hayes saw Jake sitting in the train station, his first impression was, *He's so little!*

Yes, he had seen him before, at his mother's, and he remembered what the boy looked like, but somehow the size hadn't come across before. For somebody who had done all the things he had done. This kid was four-foot-something and maybe eighty pounds.

"Jake."

The boy looked up from the magazine he was reading and smiled. "Hi," he said.

"You have some luggage?"

"Just this." He patted a small day pack.

"Okay. Come on."

"Where are we going?" There was a hint of fear in his voice.

"My place. I figure we can eat some dinner, you can clean up, maybe sack out for a while, then we can talk."

"That sounds real good, Major, sir."

Hayes grinned. "Why don't you just call me Steve. I'm not the militia."

Once they were in the agency car, Jake told him about his adventures since last they'd met. Hayes kept shaking his head, amazed. He said, "So, you think this was in Connecticut? You suppose if we backtracked your trail and sent the FBI and local police, maybe the National Guard in, they could maybe find this campsite?"

He didn't say anything about what might happen if the authorities did find a heavily armed militia group ready to shoot it out with them.

"Yes, sir, they probably could find the camp. Only thing is, once I took off, they would have known the location wouldn't be secure anymore. I'd guess they'd packed it up and started moving before I ever got to the railroad track. By the time I woke up and caught the train, they would have cleared out."

"They really are paranoid, aren't they?"

"Yes, sir. They think there is a war coming. They are ready to fight. They expect a lot of them will die."

Hayes shook his head again.

Back at his apartment, Jake took a shower. None of Hayes's clothes would fit the boy, they'd swallow him up, but one of his ex-girlfriends had left a couple of pairs of jeans and shirts behind. While even these were still a little big, they would work until he could wash the boy's own clothes, or get him some new ones. Hayes put a BYU sweatshirt, a well-worn pair of 501s, and some white cotton socks on the toilet and went to the kitchen to see what he had in the freezer he could thaw. Not much, he usually ate out, but there were some hamburger patties and a bag of crinkle-cut potatoes. He stuck four of the patties into the microwave oven and hit the thaw cycle controls, then put the french fries on an aluminum foil tray and into the oven.

Ten minutes later Jake came into the living room. He'd rolled the pants legs up three or four cuffs, the sweatshirt sleeves likewise. It made him look even younger and more vulnerable. Abruptly Hayes felt a little ashamed of himself. He had hunted this child, thought of him as he might a trophy head.

"Thanks for the clothes," he said. "They must be real old if you used to wear them."

"They belonged to a friend. We'll get yours washed or maybe pick up some new stuff at Kmart or somewhere."

Jake made a face. "Kmart?"

Hayes shrugged and grinned. "I'm not sure if Saks has a branch here."

The burgers were thawed enough to pop into the oven. The potatoes still had a way to go.

"We'll have some supper in a few minutes. You can go take a nap if you want."

"I'm okay. I got some sleep on the train. What happens to me now?"

"What do you want to happen?"

"Well, I'd like to go live with my mom. Thing is, she is going to have to get a new place, since my father knows where she lives. I tried to call her, to tell her where I was and what was happening, but her phone has been turned off. Her roommate's phone."

"I'll see if I can get somebody there to drop by and pass a message on to her," Hayes said.

"That would be good."

"In the meanwhile, you can hang out here if you want. I've got to take a little trip out of town, but you seem to be pretty good at handling yourself on your own."

Jake smiled. "I've been doing okay, haven't I?"

"I'd say so."

"I saw your computer. A Pentium PC. You got any games? Internet access?"

"I think there's an old copy of Wing Commander and Flight Simulator floating around here somewhere. And yes, I have access to the Net, though I don't use it much."

"Okay if I light it up?"

"Sure."

He watched the boy hurry to the computer, switch it on, and wait for the system to load. On the one hand, it was a little odd to have somebody here in his apartment when he'd spent nearly all the time he'd lived here alone. On the other hand, it definitely added something to have another person's energy helping fill up the place.

He had a priority ride on a fast military jet to London leaving in the morning. He could fly there, find the professor's house and lab, and take care of that business, be back here by tomorrow night. It would be kind of nice to have somebody waiting here when he got home. If he'd gotten married when he first thought about it, he might have had a son Jake's age by now. He'd never thought much about being a father, but the idea of it didn't seem so farfetched as once it had.

Interesting.

Jake's hands danced on the keyboard, shifted to the mouse. The computer's screen flashed. This was the boy's element. He was doing what he knew how to do best. Kind of fun just to sit back and watch that kind of childlike energy. It had been a long time since he'd felt that way.

In her office, Laurie sat and stared at the wall. This whole business with Zeerus was getting way out of hand. There were people who had jumped off of bridges to keep from being molested by the space monster. Whole villages' worth of folks who had packed up the kids and dogs and shotguns and driven into the hills to hole up. Some hamburger chain—was it Wendy's? Burger King? she couldn't remember—had a line of alien toys coming out. Interesting, given they didn't have a clue as to what Zeerus looked like.

There were three alien-is-coming! TV movies in production, based, of course, on a *true* story!

A theatrical release had been given the green light at Fox or Universal.

A Broadway musical was being touted—the rumor was that Andrew Lloyd Webber was involved. Probably going to be a cross between *The Phantom of the Opera* and *Miss Saigon*. Maybe a little *Cats* thrown in.

Still months away and the alien was already way past being a little cottage industry, he was big business.

And yet there were thousands, maybe millions of people around the world and even in the United States, who, when asked, claimed to have never heard of Zeerus.

Probably the same people who wanted to sit on a high-profile murder case who swore they'd never heard anything about it. Who would want to be tried by a jury of people who never read the news, watched TV, or talked to their neighbors? They weren't *her* peers.

"Laurie?" came the voice over the intercom.

"Yes?"

"I've got Bruce Fosse on line four."

"How sad for you. I have no desire whatsoever to talk to him."

"He says it's personal."

"Hah! Personally, I'd like to see old Bruce try to fly off the Capitol dome by waving his arms up and down real fast. We don't do lunch together."

"He said you might say something like that. He says to tell you he's got footage of you and your grandfather making out."

Laurie went cold. Chill bumps frosted her skin and she felt her belly twist as if she'd just gone over the first drop on a giant roller coaster.

Oh, no!

"Laurie?"

"Four, you said?"

"Yes."

"I'll take it."

She stared at the phone as if it had suddenly turned into a serpent. If she reached for it, she knew it would sink its fangs into her hand, that the bite would inject her full of deadly poison. But if she didn't answer it, the man on the other end of the phone would kill her anyway. If he wasn't lying.

She took a deep breath. Picked up the phone.

Jake slept late. By the time he woke up, Major Hayes—Steve—was already gone. He'd left a note. He'd gone out and bought a bunch of groceries before he took off, so there was food, soft drinks, a new pair of jeans, a couple of T-shirts, even a pair of sneakers. How'd he have time to get all that?

It was pretty overwhelming. Jake was in a place where he'd been invited, there was a computer he could use, and while it wasn't home, it was a lot better than being chased by the militia and the FBI and every-body. Steve was going to get in touch with his mother. The militia was still out there but probably more worried about him than he was about them.

Things could be a lot worse.

Jake got a Coke from the fridge and popped the tab. He padded barefoot over to the computer and powered it up. He logged on to the server, went online and checked his mail, then wound his way into the newsgroups and ran threads for information about the alien. He'd been out of the loop for a while, he needed to get caught up. He wondered if he could call EZ Mail back in Oregon and have them forward his mail. He might have some font money in his box.

Hey, he was perfectly willing to sit here and wait for Steve Hayes to come home.

Things could be a whole lot worse.

* * *

Stewart lay in his bed, staring at the ceiling, too wired to sleep, too rattled to work, too depressed to get around the problem. Every time he thought about fighting with Jess, his stomach knotted and he felt sick.

The more he thought about it, the worse it got. At first, he had been really pissed off, certain he was right, willing to hold his ground for ten thousand years if that's what it took for her to see it. Hell with this!

Then the cloying tentacles of doubt had undulated into his anger, coils of questions, slimy uncertainties, sucking at his resolve.

How can you be sure, Stewart? Do you know so much that you can be absolutely certain *of your stand? Hmm?*

The problem with being reasonable, with trying to see somebody else's viewpoint, was that you couldn't ever be *certain*, you couldn't be dogmatic, that was religion and not science; and whatever else he was, he was a scientist, even if not a very good one.

What, Stewart old son, if you're wrong?

Once that doubt slithered into your garden, it was almost impossible to get rid of it. It was the one thing you could envy about a fanatic: Fanatics were always so sure.

And after enough time wrapped in the loops of uncertainty, he knew what he had to do.

Steve Hayes occupied the passenger seat of the jet fighter and watched with interest as the pilot maneuvered the craft up to the tanker—a KC-10 he thought he had said—still a mile or six ahead of them. Most of the flight across the Atlantic was going to be well over supersonic speeds, but they'd slowed down some to take on fuel. A jet this small didn't have transatlantic range all by itself, at least not at the speeds they were cranking.

"Everything okay back there, Hoss?" the air force major piloting the F-15E said over the com.

"Five by five, Major."

"Okay, if the passengers will extinguish all smoking materials and return to their seats, the captain has illuminated the fasten seat belt sign while we get our drink."

"You the man."

He grinned into his oxygen mask. It wasn't the most comfortable ride he'd ever had, but it was pretty damn fast. With any luck at all, he'd have his visit with the English professor wrapped up in a few hours and if he could catch another scalded dog like this one, be home before it got good and dark.

There were certain advantages to living here in the future.

Stewart knocked on Jess's door and took a deep breath. Righteous anger could only last so long. Being right—in your own mind, anyway—was cold comfort when you were standing up there on your mountaintop with your arms crossed and your nose in the air, all by yourself. That was a lot lonelier place than he wanted to be in.

Dealing with people was tougher than dealing with video games where you could make the characters do anything you wanted. People were much, much harder.

She opened the door. Before she could say anything, he said, "Okay, look, I'm sorry." He wanted peace, not war, and if what it took was to apologize, he could live with that. Being right was why religious wars were so bloody—nobody was wrong on either side. If you had your Creator's backing, how could you be wrong? And there were an awful lot of people who'd gotten slaughtered despite their belief. Dead right or dead wrong, the key word was "dead." A God capable of building a universe from scratch, if there was such a being, could hardly be bothered to take sides between two warring anthills on one little planet on the edge of one little galaxy out of all the millions and millions of galaxies, could He? He'd have to have better ways to spend His time.

Stewart wasn't ready for this relationship with Jess to be dead. Being right didn't matter here.

"Come in," she said.

Inside the little place she'd gotten, he stared at the junked-up floor. "Listen, I'm going to take everything I've got and go public with it. Even if I get busted from the job and thrown into jail, you're right. I can stand by and do nothing or I can give it a shot. I'm going to go for it."

There. That ought to do it. It was what she wanted, and deep down, once he got past the reactionary anger he'd felt, he believed she was closer to the right path than he was.

Intellectually, anyway.

Okay, sure, it would probably get him creamed, but it was always easy to be brave in the abstract. You could fight the purple slime monster on screen all day long and it didn't matter, you didn't have anything to lose, it was just a game. When you got shoved into the real trenches and the other guy's army came charging across the field, you had to do *some*thing, even if they outnumbered you a thousand to one. Run, hide, or fight.

Jess was right—even if it was a bitter pill and was going to taste real bad going down. And probably poison him, too.

What the hell.

She smiled at him, and that was worth something. Then she said, "I don't think that's such a good idea. You made some interesting points when we talked about all this earlier. I've always been an all-or-nothing person, kind of like John Galt, wanting to stop the motor of the world when I saw injustice. Maybe you should just sit on this a while longer. I mean, who is it going to help if the *New York Times* comes out with a big exposé about all this? People are already scared to death about the alien, it won't help things if they find out their government is lying to them yet again."

Stewart knew his mouth had gaped and he was staring stupidly at her. Jesus! He'd come here, rolled over, given her exactly what she'd asked for and *this* was how she responded? Man, man, he didn't know *any*thing about women at all!

"Uh . . . ?"

She laughed. A happy sound. "Gotcha, didn't I? You didn't expect that, did you?"

He shook his head. "I don't, I mean, uh, what?"

"As long as you understand what I was trying to say, that's what's important."

"Huh?"

"As long as you were arguing with me, I had to make my point. But once you got it, well, see, that was what I wanted."

"Oh, man!"

She laughed again.

Truly, there were some things he did not think he was ever going to understand. If he tried to get his mind around this so it made sense, his head would probably explode.

But then Jess hugged him and he had better things to do than worry about it.

37

arry was off on some supersecret mission somewhere, probably the Star Wars stuff, and Laurie couldn't get him. She didn't want to leave any messages, though it was a little late to worry about that.

That bastard Bruce Fosse!

He had what he said he had. She had seen the tape of her and Larry clinging and soul-kissing in the doorway of Larry's. It wasn't much footage, a minute or so, but enough to recognize both of them when they broke apart and started pulling each other's clothes off before the door closed and blocked the view.

Damn!

Of course she could deny it. The first jury had kicked the cops loose in L.A. even after seeing the Rodney King tape, hadn't they?

Yeah. But it wasn't a jury she had to face, it was her boss, the president of the United States, and he had a bug about such things. Caesar's wife and all.

Fosse had her over a barrel and he'd known it. She sat in her office, recalling the conversation after he'd dropped by with a copy of the video.

They watched the tape in silence. After it was over with, she said, "What do you want, Mr. Fosse? Why don't you just run with this?"

"Call me Bruce, please. I don't want anything in particular, Laurie, certainly not to hurt you. Just a little quid pro quo, is all. You scratch my back, I'll keep yours off the air." He laughed, amused at what he considered his wit.

So it was blackmail.

He hurried to try and make it look like something else. "Look, I'm a good reporter. I get the stories I go after, if anybody can. I'm not asking you to give me anything I wouldn't eventually be able to get on my own."

"But . . . ?"

"I just want to be near the top of your list, that's all. If you're going to give something to the media, it's just as easy for you to dial my number early as late, isn't it? I'm not asking you to give away any top secrets, nothing to compromise your position. Just give me a fair shake, is all."

It sounded so tempting. *Hey, you don't have to put out or anything, no threats against your virtue, just be fair to me.*

How could she argue with that? Of course, being nice at the point of a gun wasn't exactly the same as being nice from the goodness of her heart. It would be easy to go along with what he wanted. Who would it hurt?

She saw the trap, despite the thick layer of silk covering it. The threat would always be there. He was smart enough to realize that if he came on like gangbusters and threatened her outright, she might get her back up and tell him to piss off. He'd get an exclusive story out of it if she did, president's chief of staff caught in a tête-à-tête with the chairman of the Joint Chiefs. It would get big play for a few days—but then something else would come along to knock it out of the spotlight and that would be that. Fosse would become persona non grata with the administration—and her successor, she sure wouldn't be here—for the flak he caused. You don't reward the man who embarrasses you, right or not. It would be a Pyrrhic victory in the long run if MNN kept him on the White House beat. It wouldn't do his career any real harm if he switched to another area, probably, but why risk it if he had her on a string?

"Call me first," sure, that was how it would start. Then it would be "I just need to confirm something I heard, I won't use your name, just a 'high administration source.' " The more she told him, the worse it would get. And the demands would get a little bit more insistent each time until one day she couldn't refuse to tell him anything. She remembered the old Lyndon Johnson quote. If she were a man, it would apply to her: Bruce Fosse would have her pecker in his pocket.

No. She wasn't going down that road. So she got fired. It would be a long fall, but she could go and get a job, write a book, she wouldn't starve.

Of course, it would probably get Larry fired, too, and that was tougher. She needed to talk to him before she drop-kicked Fosse in the family jewels. But she had to get him pretty quick—she couldn't put the reporter off for long. He wanted an answer and better he should get a big exclusive story than none. Who knew but that she could figure out a way to defuse what was on that tape?

Though Laurie couldn't for the life of her figure out how to negate it. That was no colleague hugging a colleague, there were shirts being pulled out of pants, butts being groped, and pure lust fogging the lens.

Damn.

Hightower returned from his visit to Mitch's testing ground, feeling a little better. Peregrine seemed to be working just fine. Better to have it and not need it than to need it and not have it.

His private line rang as he was walking into his place.

"Hello?"

"We've got a problem, Larry. A big problem."

He moved to the fridge, got a beer, poured it, listened to Laurie lay it out for him. He held the glass of beer but didn't drink from it. When she had run down, he heard the faint overtone of panic in her voice: "What are we going to do?"

"What do you want to do?"

"I want to tie a barbell to Fosse and drop him into the Potomac, that's what I want to do, but I don't believe that would help. He probably has copies of the tape stashed everywhere. He disappears and it goes out on the air."

"Come on. You don't think he believes we would try to *kill* him?"

"I don't know what he thinks, but he has to have thought about it. He's threatening a couple of powerful people who know folks who do such things."

"Really, who is that? I know a couple of forgers and some computer hackers, but I don't know any freelance assassins."

"It's not funny, Larry. I'm scared."

"I know. Listen, it's going to be okay. You tell him to shove the tape where the sun don't shine."

"Really?"

"That's what you want to do, isn't it?"

"Yeah, but—"

"Go ahead. What's the worst thing that can happen?"

"We both get fired."

"So what? I can retire with a full ride any time. You're the smartest woman I know, it wouldn't kill either of us. Maybe we'd be better off."

"Given a choice, I'd rather go out on a high note."

"Maybe we can arrange that."

"What are you talking about?"

"I've been working on something. You trust me?"

There was a pause. He considered drinking from the beer. Nope. Not yet. He needed to hear this.

"Yes. I trust you."

Ah. That felt good. "Then tell your reporter friend to get stuffed."

"You're sure?"

"I'm sure."

"Okay. I will." There was a short pause. "Listen, Larry, I—I love you." She hung up without waiting for his reply.

She'd never said that before, not out loud.

He smiled and sipped the beer. It was very good. It might be the best beer he'd ever had. He took another sip.

Yes. Definitely, it was the best beer he'd ever had.

The stealth mission turned out to be a cakewalk. The little cottage in the outskirts of Guildford was a modest affair, had a small fenced yard and a garden. When Hayes knocked on the professor's door, there was no answer. Given that he knew the good doctor was currently en route on a commercial jet from the United States, this was no great surprise, although there could have been a housekeeper or someone watching a pet.

He tried the door. It wasn't even locked. Amazing. Maybe he could get assigned to England? Sure safer than D.C.

Inside, he found the professor's personal computer and powered it up. The files he had come looking for were right there, not even encoded. The backup disks were in a box in the desk drawer. He searched them, took the one he wanted. It seemed a shame, but he had the computer erase all the files and then reformat the hard drive, effectively wiping it clean.

A search of the bungalow showed that the professor was a bachelor and that he didn't have any lockboxes or safes or other disks hidden away in any secret compartments. Hayes was quite thorough. It took a while but he was convinced there weren't any other backups.

Of course, the professor would not have had any reason to feel paranoid about this, so why would there be? If he had a copy at his office and one here and one on his laptop, he would feel pretty secure.

Hayes stepped outside. He smiled and waved at a neighbor as he left. She waved back.

At the professor's office at the local university branch, the visit was pretty much the same. If he had a secretary, she was not about. Hayes waltzed in, found a copy of the file on the office computer. He ran a find-it utility program and looked for additional copies. There weren't any to be had. He deleted the file, made sure it was gone and unrecoverable, then left.

One more stop. The professor was due to arrive on a flight from the States in three hours. When he finished with customs and went to catch a ride, Hayes would be waiting for him. The man was going to lose his grip on his computer when Hayes ran into him, and that laptop was going to hit the ground hard. And when Hayes apologized all over himself and picked the fallen instrument up, Professor Carmody's software was going to have a close encounter of the destructive kind. Hayes had a powerful magnet in his pocket and instructions on how and where to put it so that a computer disk bathed in the magnet's rays was going to cease to be of any use as a storage medium.

Bye-bye translation file.

Maybe Carmody could reconstruct things, but after a few days, according to the information contained in Hayes's orders, it would no longer matter.

He smiled. This spy stuff could get addictive, especially if it was this easy all the time.

38

Late in the day, the call Laurie had been dreading finally came.

"Laurie, would you come to the Oval Office, please?" It was the boss and he didn't sound happy.

It was a long walk. It seemed to take years. It also seemed to take only a few seconds. Time, like everybody who had ever been to the dentist knew, was very flexible.

She paused outside the doorway, took several deep breaths, nodded at the new Secret Service men manning the watch. Here we go. Bye-bye, job.

When she stepped inside, she saw Larry standing with his legs apart and his hands crossed over the small of his back. The president sat behind his desk glaring at Larry.

Her gut lurched. She swallowed bile.

"I've got something to show you," he said. "And I wanted General Hightower to see it at the same time." The president held a remote control for a video player. The screen was down. He touched the play button. He did not ask her to sit.

There they were, Larry and her, in living hormonal color.

Laurie watched her boss peripherally rather than the tape. His jaw muscles flexed and released as he gritted his teeth.

When the tape finished, he shut the player off and swiveled his chair to face Laurie and Larry. "Well? What do you have to say about this?"

Laurie couldn't gather enough moisture to speak. It was noon in the middle of the summer in the Sahara Desert in her mouth.

"Very nice," Larry said. "What is the point, sir?"

"Point? Point! Did you see that?"

"Yes, sir," Larry said. "But I still don't understand. Husbands and wives do such things all the time, don't they?"

That caught the president by surprise. His eyebrows nearly crawled up into his hairline.

To say that Laurie was also surprised would have been a major understatement. She thought her heart stopped for a moment. What on Earth was Larry doing?!

"Husbands and wives?"

"Yes, sir." Larry glanced over at Laurie, then back at the president. "We wanted to tell you earlier, sir, but we both thought you have enough on your plate. We sneaked off to Virginia about a year ago and had a quick civil ceremony. We were hoping to keep it secret until after your reelection, then go for the big church wedding."

"Married? You two? Really? You—you should have said something!"

"We haven't even told our families, have we?" Larry said.

Laurie found her voice from where it lay dessicated under the desert sands. "No. I haven't told a soul."

The president shook his head, waved one hand as if waving to a crowd of admirers. "Well, I'll be damned. Congratulations."

"Sir, if this is going to cause you any political problems, I'll be happy to offer my resignation—" Larry began.

"What? Oh, no. Getting married isn't a problem. Married is good. There's no conflict here."

"We hoped that reporter wouldn't spill it, but—"

"Wait. The man who sent this tape, he knows about you being married?"

"Well, he said he did. I assumed he must have come across it somehow, it's a matter of public record in Virginia. We did use our own names."

"Son of a bitch."

"Sir?"

"Never mind. Look, I couldn't be happier for you. I'm sorry we can't keep the lid on this, we'll have to shortstop this idiot reporter. I don't know what he thinks he's got here, but his butt just got added to my list."

"Not your fault, sir. We should have told you sooner."

"Ah, it doesn't matter. When you get around to the church wedding we'll throw you a bash."

"Thank you, sir."

The president looked at Laurie. "You're not going to quit and have babies, are you?"

She smiled. "No, sir. You don't need to worry about that."

They waited until they were outside on the grounds before they said a word. Larry smiled at Laurie. "Great day, isn't it? Nice and sunny, a little cool—"

"You dickhead! Why didn't you tell me you were going to do this? You have the paperwork to back it up?"

"Sure do. You can bet there will be a federal agent checking it before the day is out. Our boss will want to be sure. A search will find us. We are entered into the computer, there is a photostat of our license, all the proper signatures. Unfortunately, the judge who performed our ceremony passed away from a sudden heart attack about four months ago. But he was almost eighty. He had a long and happy life."

"You dickhead."

"I told you I knew some forgers and computer hackers."

She smiled and shook her head. "I can't believe it."

He stopped walking and looked down at her face. "So the question changes now."

She looked puzzled.

"It's not, 'Will you marry me?' anymore. It's 'Do you want to stay married to me?'"

Her smile was bright enough to rival the sunshine. His heart soared.

"Yes," she said. "And I guess we'd better book that church pretty soon, huh?"

He took a deep breath, let it out. "Yes. I guess we should."

"Meanwhile, why don't you give me a ride home?"

"Your place or mine?"

"Whichever," she said. "They are both ours now, right?"

"Yes, ma'am. Anything you say."

39

"Sorry about your mother," Major Hayes said.

"That's all right," Jake said. "It's not your fault she moved. She wants to get away from my father. I understand that."

"She'll turn up. We'll find her eventually."

"Yeah."

They were walking toward the river. It was sunny and mild, not much foot or auto traffic.

"Meanwhile, you can stay at my place."

"That's a lot of trouble for you."

"Not really. I'm gone most of the time. You can start school, you'll be gone all day, too. It's a big apartment, plenty of room. You can teach me more about the computer. I'll teach you about basketball."

"Cool. You know, you really ought to sell the Pentium and get a fast Mac. Prices on them are low, 'cause of how Mac screwed up businesswise, but the OS is much better."

"We could look into it. What say, you want to stick around until we turn up your mother?"

"Sure."

They both smiled.

* * *

"Good morning, Mrs. Hightower."

"Good morning yourself, Mr. Sherman. Seems fair—I'll take your name, you take mine."

They were in his bed. *Their* bed. She rolled over and hugged him.

"You don't think this will get dull, now that we're legal?"

"A forged marriage license and computer fraud is legal? Foo, that just makes us that much more illicit. Adds a little spice."

"Just what we need," he said.

They both smiled.

Stewart watched her as Jess padded into the bathroom. She was gorgeous, she was naked, as was he under the covers of her bed, and he was amazed at how lucky he was. Jess was wonderful, he had a front-row seat at history, life was pretty good. He might even have time to get back to working on his game.

"Hey!" he yelled after her.

"What?"

"I love you!"

She turned and looked at him. "Me, too, you. Even if you are a little dense."

They both smiled.

Millions of miles away from his destination, Zeerus slept and dreamed. Once again he fought his way up from obscurity, rose to power, was defeated but escaped from the Paxus Majae's justice.

In his sleep, Zeerus smiled.

40

Hightower used every bit of his skill to try to talk the president out of it.

"Sir, we can't begin to sort out all the repercussions of firing on such an . . . emissary."

The president leaned back in his chair and steepled his fingers. A bad sign. "In this country, General, we *invite* foreign ambassadors to visit. If we tell them *not* to come, then they had better, by God Almighty, not try to put a foot into our sovereign territory!"

"With all due respect, sir, this is not your usual foreign ambassador."

"No, that's right. He's much more dangerous. Who knows what might happen if he lands here? He might be carrying some alien disease that would make bubonic plague look like hay fever. He could have some kind of bomb on board that would take out half the country. We can't risk it."

"Sir—"

"It is no longer open for discussion, General. I am the man in the hot seat, it is my call. Warn him off. Tell him we don't want any trouble but he needs to park his ship in orbit and wait until we figure out a way to get him down."

"It'll take months for us to get a shuttle ready to fly, Mr. President. Unless we can get the Russians—"

"No, sir! No Russians! If he wants to land in Red Square, that's their business, but if he wants to put it down in Nowhere, Montana, that's our business. And it is not going to happen."

Hightower shook his head. It was just the two of them and he wished he had some help.

"Sir, we're not sure we can stop him."

"Then you had better bust your buttons trying, General."

"Yes, sir."

General Hightower shook his head. They were inside the hardened bunker under the Virginia hills that served as HQ for Mitch's new and improved Star Wars Weapons Center.

"Crank it up," Hightower told the communications operator.

"Yes, sir."

It didn't take long.

"Greetings," Zeerus said.

"Greetings," Hightower said. "This is General Lawrence Hightower, chairman of the Joint Chiefs of Staff."

"The top military man," Zeerus said. "I am honored."

Top military man but one. Hightower thought. But he had the ball now and he would carry it as best he could. He said, "Our calculations of your approach show that you are still planning to touch down just outside Clover, Montana."

"There are no cities near the site," Zeerus said. "No inhabitants other than wildlife."

"That's not the point. We cannot allow you to land."

"We have discussed this at some length, your scientists and I. My vessel and I pose no threat to your ecosystem; any bacteria or viruses I carry are harmless to your species. My landing site was chosen for its remoteness. There is no reason why I cannot touch down at my planned destination."

"There is a matter of our national security."

"You are a military being and I appreciate your problem, but this is not open to discussion. I mean you no harm—you will have to accept that and be content."

Lord, he was as bad as the president.

"Zeerus, if you attempt to make planetfall within the confines of the United States, Canada, or Mexico, we will be forced to prevent it."

"You must do what you must do," Zeerus said. "But I have been inside this ship for far too long. Make no mistake. I *am* coming down. This conversation is ended."

"Jesus," Mitch said. "Jesus."

Yeah. The alien he wanted to shake hands with was finally here and he was going to have to blast it out of the sky.

Hightower shook his head.

"General Hightower?"

"Right here, Mr. President." Hightower gripped the telephone tightly.

"What did he say?"

"Just what he's been saying, sir. He's coming whether we want him to or not."

"I'm sorry to hear that. You know what you have to do."

"Yes, sir. I know." He broke the connection.

Hightower looked at Mitchell. "Your birds ready to fly?"

"As ready as they'll ever be."

"All right. Let's warm them up."

On his ship, Zeerus allowed himself the luxury of laughter. Oh, but it was going to be interesting. While this vehicle wasn't a combat ship, it certainly boasted technology superior to anything this planet had. And once he got close enough, even if they did have weapons capable of stopping him, they would not be able to use them. In their atmosphere a large nuclear explosion or unleashed singularity would be far too dangerous and they must surely know it.

He was really looking forward to stretching his wings again. Who knew? Maybe even gliding a bit.

Hightower sent one final warning, when the ship was still a hundred thousand kilometers away. "Zeerus, alter your course and assume a parking orbit." He looked around the interior of the command center. Dozens of men and women pretended to be looking anywhere but at him. "Please."

No response from the incoming alien.

Hightower sighed. "All right, Mitch. Shoot him down."

"Yes, sir." To a red-haired NCO sitting behind him in front of an electronic board, General Mitch Carter said, "Fire Peregrines One through Eight to intersect with the target at sixty thousand klicks."

"Yes, sir," the NCO said. He turned to his left. A second NCO, this one mostly bald, sat ten feet away in front of a matching control board. "Turn your arming key, on my mark."

"Copy, arming on your mark."

"Mark."

Both NCOs twisted cylindrical keys inserted into their control birds.

"Confirm status," Red said.

"P-1 through P-8 are armed and launch ready," Baldy replied.

"Status confirmed." Red lifted a cover plate and punched the button under it. "Missiles away, sir. We have eight in the air."

"Put the rest of them up there, Sergeant. Second salvo at forty thousand, third salvo at twenty thousand. Keep the last three birds in reserve."

"Yes, sir."

The NCOs went through the same sequence as before, twice more. "We've got twenty-four missiles in the air," Red said. "Three still cold on the ground."

Hightower looked at his old friend. He felt sick. "That's it."

Mitch glanced at his watch. "Going to take a while to get there, but, yeah, that's it. It's all over but the crying."

Zeerus's sensors detected and analyzed the first eight missiles when they were still half the planet's diameter away. The computer gave him the analysis and he shook his head. Simple rockets with chemical explosives, the most rudimentary guidance systems.

Children's toys.

"Computer, what is the best way to deflect these fireworks, so that they do not threaten the integrity of this ship?"

The computer told him. Ah, yes, he remembered that option. Simple and effective. Might as well begin with that.

"Do it."

The computer utilized a small portion of the power available to it, generated an electromagnetic pulse, and emitted it in a tight beam at the oncoming rockets.

* * *

"Sir," the red-haired NCO said, "P-1 through P-8 are at fifty-six thousand kilometers and on course to intersect with the target at— Jesus!"

Hightower frowned. "What?"

"Sir, the first salvo just . . . veered off course!"

Hightower and Mitch both moved to look at the tracking scope. The blips representing the two dozen missiles streaking toward Zeerus's ship were each tagged with a code.

The first eight Peregrines had just splayed like spastic fingers. They headed everywhere but at the blip representing the alien ship.

"Christ, it looks like the Blue Angels doing a starburst," Mitch said.

"Get the trajectories," Red said.

Baldy said, "Those suckers are gonna wind up on Venus or Mars or somewhere. None of them will get within a thousand klicks of the target."

"Shit!" Red said. "Sorry, sirs."

"I understand the sentiments," Hightower said. "What's he doing to our missiles, Mitch?"

Mitch shook his head. "If I had to guess, I'd say an EMP. They are supposed to be hardened against that but he's scrambled the onboard computer guidance systems with something."

"Can we compensate from here?"

"Not with those eight. They are too far off course, don't have enough fuel to make radical turns."

"What about the others?"

"Maybe. Lock P-9 through P-16 on a glide and shut off the onboard computers," Mitch said.

"Yes, sir," Red said. His hands danced on the control board.

"Will that work?" Hightower said.

"Should. The missiles are on an intersect path, to impact at forty thousand kilometers. If the computers are off, they can't be used to turn the birds. As long as he stays on the same path, we've got him."

Hightower nodded. Mixed emotions flowed in him. He didn't want to destroy Zeerus, but he also didn't want to lose the battle.

They watched the tracking screen.

The dot of Zeerus's ship and the next eight missiles drew nearer each other.

* * *

"Why are those next eight rockets still coming?" Zeerus asked the computer.

It did not know. The generated EMP had no effect.

"Speculate."

The computer did so. The most likely possibility was that the computers controlling the missiles had been deactivated, to forestall an EMP.

"What do you recommend? What is the easiest method?"

The computer told him that evasive action would have a high probability of success.

"Take it."

"He's altering his course, sir," Red said. "He's dropped three, no, four degrees."

"The birds will fly right over his head," Baldy said.

"Can we set them off in close enough proximity to damage him?" Hightower said.

Red said, "No, sir. The angles are diverging real fast at those distances. By the time they draw abreast, it would be like you standing on the steps of the Capitol in Washington and us setting off a firecracker in Baltimore."

"Mitch?"

"Turn the computers back on," Mitch ordered. "Change course before the angle gets too great."

"Yes, sir."

The blips responded, very slowly to Hightower's eyes.

"There they go," Baldy said. "He's hit 'em with something again."

The ground-based computers projected the new course for the eight missiles. None of them would pass close to Zeerus's vessel.

"Damn!"

"Spread the last eight out," Mitch said. "Shotgun pattern. If he plans to land that thing in Montana, there are only so many orbital paths he can take. Get as many of them covered as you can."

"Yes, sir."

"Warm up the last three Peregrines."

"Now what are they doing?" Zeerus asked.

The computer ventured a speculation.

"What are our options?"

The computer gave him a list. Aside from EMP and evasive action, there were several things. The charged-particle meteor deflector was one.

"What would that do?"

The computer told him.

Zeerus grinned. "Yes. I like that."

"Sir, he's at twenty-eight thousand kilometers, on direct collision course with P-21. We've got a recon sat footprinting the path at point of impact."

"Show us," Mitch said.

Red touched controls. A television screen blossomed next to him, and a larger screen lit up on the wall of the control room.

"Images from the recon sat," Mitch said. "That's the bird, from behind. I don't see the alien ship."

The image was fuzzy, looked like a small, dark oval with a glint of light in the middle of it.

"Heat sig," Mitch said, pointing at the glint of light. "Should be soon. Our bird is going out as fast as he's coming in."

"Why hasn't he dodged or hit it with a magnetic pulse?" Hightower said.

"I dunno. Maybe he doesn't see it."

"He sees it," Hightower said.

There came a soundless, brilliant flash onscreen.

"Yes!" Baldly said. "We got him!"

"No," Red said, a second later. "Look. He's not even close."

The alien ship's dot was still on the scope.

"What the hell happened?" Hightower said.

Mitch looked at the two NCOs and the army of technicians and scientists. "He just blew up our bird somehow. From a thousand kilometers away."

"How?"

"I don't have a goddamned clue."

Hightower shook his head. "Anything else close to him?"

"Nothing we can catch him with. Do we want to put the last three rockets up?" Mitch said.

"He's going to be in thick atmosphere soon, isn't he?"

"Yeah. Maybe we should have used vacuum tubes for the computer. We could still intercept him once he hits the atmosphere. ICBMs or fighters."

Hightower shook his head. "What if we could shoot him down and his power source—whatever the hell it is—lets go with the force of a hundred megaton nuke in our atmosphere? What kind of footprint will that leave on our world? And where?"

"I see your point. What are you going to do?"

"What he wants us to do. Let him land."

"Christ, Larry, the president will have a stroke."

"Do we have a choice? We can't knock him down. He's just demonstrated a superior technology, waved off the best we could throw at him like a man shooing flies. If we can't stop him, then maybe we ought not to piss him off any more than we already have."

"I'm glad I don't have your job."

"I'm thinking about giving it up. Meanwhile, I better get my ass to Montana."

A battalion of marines surrounded the site, blocking unauthorized entry. You could not approach closer than five miles on the ground. The FAA had put a hundred-mile buffer around the location and air force helicopter gunships crisscrossed the sky enforcing that zone. There weren't too many local people to get upset about it, fortunately.

Hightower considered wearing combat gear but had opted instead for a dress uniform. Once the alien stepped onto U.S. soil, he was going to be treated like an ambassador and not a criminal. Even the president was smart enough to know when he'd had his butt kicked. At least the missile snafu had been kept from the media, so that wasn't so bad. Might as well be gracious now that he had no choice.

"There it is," somebody said.

Binoculars came up. Hightower scanned the sky with his own pair, spotted the dot coming in. It didn't take long.

The ship was at least the size of a city bus, maybe bigger, and it didn't make any noise. No rockets blasting fire or smoke, no power hums, nothing. It came down dead quiet, settling as slowly as a tired helium balloon in the dry Montana afternoon. It was eerie.

The ship floated to the ground, touched down. Dirt bulged around the edges and the ship sank maybe a foot into the earth before it stopped. It looked kind of like a cross between the space shuttle and a Romulan ship from *Star Trek*, was a flat gray color except for the bottom section, which was black.

Hightower stood next to half a dozen dignitaries, including the vice president, and was staring right at the ship when the hatch appeared in the side, about six feet above the ground. He didn't see anything slide up or down or sideways, but a rectangular opening was all of a sudden just *there*. A ramp extruded from the bottom of the hatchway, oozed out and to the ground like mercury filling an invisible mould.

He felt his heart quicken.

Nobody moved. Nobody said anything.

The first visitor to Earth from another planet stepped into view on top of the mercury ramp.

Hightower moved first, took long strides, so that he reached the base of the ramp at the same time that Zeerus, looking every bit like a red-skinned humanoid pterodactyl bodybuilder on steroids, got there.

"Welcome to Earth," Hightower said. He extended his hand.

Zeerus flashed needle-sharp teeth in what must be a saurian smile. He took Hightower's hand in his own. It was warm, not at all scaly feeling.

"Thank you," the alien said.

The two shook hands. Hightower grinned.

Son of a bitch.

EPÍLOGUE

Area 51?" Jake said. "Roswell? Hangar 18?"

He was working on the computer, checking his e-mail.

Behind Jake, Hayes laughed. "If we knew that, it wouldn't be a secret location, now, would it?"

Jake said, "Does he really look like that picture on TV?"

"Pretty much. Tall, red, scaled, head like a flying dinosaur, muscles like Schwarzenegger."

"Cool."

"Maybe we can meet him someday."

"That would be outstandingly cool!"

The doorbell rang.

"Get that for me, would you, Jake?"

"Sure."

Jake stood and headed for the door. Hayes smiled. He knew who it was.

The boy opened the door.

"Mom!"

"Baby!"

She rushed in and gathered Jake into her arms. They hugged for a long time before they broke it up.

"How did you find us?"

"Major Hayes found me."

"Oh, wow." For a moment, he looked around. "I've been staying here. Do we, uh, I mean, where are we going to go?"

"For now, you and your mom will stay here," Hayes said. "She, uh, has a job here in Washington, if she wants it."

Jake's mother smiled at Hayes.

"And there's an apartment for rent right down the street that's pretty reasonable. If you and your mom are interested."

Jake grinned. "Cool."

Larry and Laurie sat in Benjamin's, the new restaurant that served the best crabcakes in Washington. Not too many people knew about the place yet, so it was only crowded but not overrun with luncheon diners.

She said, "Primaster, Mr. Sherman?"

"That's what Zeerus calls him, Mrs. Hightower."

"And he's some sort of intergalactic villain? A dictator?"

"Makes Hitler look like an Eagle Scout. Or so Zeerus would have us believe."

She sipped at her white wine. "But you don't. Believe him."

He shook his head. "I can't read him, his gestures, his voice, his whole manner is too alien. He could be telling the absolute truth—or he could be lying through his pointed teeth. You know he eats fifteen pounds of raw beef or pork every day? He would gobble it down alive if we'd let him. But something just doesn't feel right about this.

"He says he will give us the stars," Larry continued. "He is willing to share his technology with us. He says we will need it when this Primaster shows up."

"What are you going to do?"

Larry shrugged. "Same thing we've been doing. Keep him talking. Keep the experts fabricating theories. Have the scientists watch every breath he takes. Wait and see what happens. Worry like hell."

"You could retire."

"I could. So could you."

"What, and leave show business?"

They both smiled.

Jess peeked over Stewart's shoulder at his computer screen. "What is that?"

They were back in his apartment—well, his *new* apartment—just off campus. School was boring after working with the secret stuff, but at least they'd let them back in without penalties. Cost them a semester, that was all.

He said, "It's a little program I, uh, *borrowed* while we were in D.C."

"What does it do?" She kissed his bare shoulder.

"Oh, it lets me keep up with a few things. Gives me access via a side door to some stuff."

"Secret military stuff?"

"Well, yeah."

She kissed his shoulder again. "Ah, you are a pirate, Stewart."

"Yes, ma'am. Say, do you want to get married or something?"

A long heartbeat passed.

"Sure. Why not? Then my folks won't complain about us living together."

They both smiled.

Alone in a very large and very comfortable room, bathed in invisible security beams, his every moment photographed, his every sound recorded, Zeerus considered once again the enormity of his task. It had seemed so much easier in theory than it was in actual practice. That was how it always seemed to go with every major undertaking, was it not? Still, it was going well.

He had allowed them to study his ship, made available to them the computer's stores concerning its technology, if not its history. He wouldn't want them getting the wrong—or rather the right—idea about the Paxus Majae.

Gifting a lowly civilization star drive technology before it was able to achieve it on its own was as big a crime as any Zeerus had committed, but past a certain point, it did not much matter. If Primaster captured him, he was doomed already, there was no point in holding back now. How many more times could they fry his brain?

No. He would arm these humans with what they wanted and he would mold them into what *he* wanted. If he had enough time before Primaster came for him, he would have an army to protect him.

If he had enough time.